HELL AND HIGH WATER

CHRISTIAN UNGE

HELL AND
HIGH WATER

Translated from the Swedish by
George Goulding and Sarah de Senarclens

MACLEHOSE PRESS
QUERCUS · LONDON

First published in the Swedish language as
Går Genom Vatten, Går Genom Eld
by Norstedts Förlag, Stockholm, in 2019
First published in Great Britain in 2021 by MacLehose Press
This paperback edition published in 2022 by

MacLehose Press
An imprint of Quercus Publishing Ltd
Carmelite House
50 Victoria Embankment
London EC4Y 0DZ

An Hachette UK company

A CIP catalogue record for this book is available from the British Library.

ISBN (MMP) 978 1 52940 805 8
ISBN (Ebook) 978 1 52940 804 1

Designed and typeset in Minion by Libanus Press Ltd
Printed and bound in Great Britain by Clays Ltd, Elcograf S.p.A.

Papers used by Quercus Books are from well-managed forests and
other responsible sources.

CHARACTERS

TEKLA BERG
Doctor in the Accident & Emergency department of the Nobel Hospital.
A rising star in her profession, she has a special talent: a photographic
memory, which is both a blessing and a curse for her.

SIMON BERG
Tekla's younger brother.

MONICA CARLSSON
C.E.O. of the Nobel Hospital, she will go to any lengths to make it more
successful than the competing Stockholm hospitals.

GÖRAN COLLINDER
Chief physician of the Nobel Hospital.

GREGOR DABROWSKI
Editor and husband of Monica Carlsson.

HÅKAN DAHL
Chief Inspector of police.

EVA ELMQVIST
Runs the Nobel Hospital's Intensive Care Unit, its flagship department.

ERIK "EJE" ERIKSSON
Self-proclaimed "road captain" in the Red Bears motorcycle club.

FREDRIK FRANCK
Secretary to Monica Carlsson.

JONNA FREDÉN-HANSSON
Nina Umarov's business partner.

JOAKIM ("JOCKE") HENRIKSSON
Husband of Nina Umarov.

JOHAN "THE COUNT" HOLMSTRÖM
Vice-president of the Red Bears motorcycle club.

CHRISTIAN JENSEN
President of the Red Bears motorcycle club.

ANITA KLEIN-BORGSTEDT
Doctor in the Accident & Emergency department of the Nobel Hospital and chair of its trade union branch.

ASTRID LUNDGREN
Sister of Magnus Lundgren.

MAGNUS LUNDGREN
Police officer and S.W.A.T. team member.

PIRKKO MÄKINEN
Nurse in the Intensive Care Unit of the Nobel Hospital.

ÅSA MALMBORG
Stockholm County Council Commissioner for financial affairs.

TARIQ MOUSSAWI
Doctor in the Accident & Emergency department of the Nobel Hospital.

REBECKA NILSÉN
Investigator at the Swedish police's National Operations Department, the N.O.D.

HAMPUS NORDENSKÖLD
Doctor in the Accident & Emergency department of the Nobel Hospital.

BORIS PETROV
Accountant to the Umarov family and Victor Umarov's business partner and ghost translator.

MARCUS SAFADI
Säpo (Swedish Security Police) officer.

RAGNA SIGURDSDOTTIR
Doctor in the Accident & Emergency department of the Nobel Hospital.

TATIANA SOKOLOVA
Organiser and mother hen of the Umarov family's stable of prostitutes.

DARIA UMAROV
Victor Umarov's first wife.

ELENA UMAROV
Victor Umarov's second wife.

KAMILA UMAROV
Younger daughter of Victor Umarov.

NINA UMAROV
Victor Umarov's elder daughter and the owner of a successful real estate agency.

SARDOR UMAROV
Victor Umarov's son and right-hand man.

VICTOR UMAROV
Patriarch of the Umarov family. Uzbek, shaped by the fall of the Soviet Union and the emergence of the new Russia, he is now an influential figure in Stockholm's criminal underworld.

LORIK XHAFAS
Member of the Lions, an Albanian crime gang.

PROLOGUE

Monica Carlsson slowly drew the bowl closer and picked out a liquorice monkey. The salty tang right at the back of her palate distracted her for a moment as the 24-hour news played out soundlessly on the screen in front of her. She let her gaze drift from the dead-straight platinum blonde hair of the news anchor to the column of smoke a kilometre away, on which she had been keeping a watchful eye for the last half hour. Her vast office was pleasantly quiet, except for Fredrik's increasingly agitated telephone voice outside the door.

On the skyline she spotted two new features on the top of northern Europe's biggest prestige building project. The hospital roof had been crowned with two helipads. Two! While the budget for the overdue replacement of the plumbing at her own hospital, the Nobel, had been halved.

For the third time in twenty minutes, Fredrik knocked on the door and looked in.

"Isn't it time now?"

Carlsson pushed her feet into her high-heeled shoes. Straightened the gold pen next to the keyboard.

"Göran's rung for the third time. The situation's chaotic. What shall—"

"What was the name of the doctor who took care of the stabbing down there?" Carlsson interrupted in a calm voice.

Her secretary thrust his hand into his pocket, took out a piece of paper and read: "Tekla Berg. But . . ."

Carlsson turned her attention back to the screen. The clock up in the corner showed 21.43.

She looked out at the city. My God, what was going on? First gang members with drawn weapons in A. & E., and now this. Who on earth would want to be C.E.O. of a hospital?

She considered her alternatives. Let her fingers play with the gold chain around her neck. The new burns unit had cost the taxpayer 120 million kronor, and yet Uppsala was made the national centre. It was like owning a luxury restaurant with a kitchen full of expensive ingredients and a platoon of celebrity chefs standing around with no guests to cook for. She knew what the solution was, she understood who the key person was, she just did not know how to catch their attention. But she had an idea.

She took another liquorice monkey and got to her feet. Her knees were hurting, but she was not going to take any more pain-killers today. Carlsson adjusted the belt of her trousers and buttoned her jacket. Sauntered to the large oval window. Did it look like an enormous, waking eye to someone in the houses on Ringvägen? One which never blinked?

Her mobile showed 21.48. Those five additional minutes would surely have meant at least one new patient for the burns unit.

Carlsson called out:

"Fredrik, you can sound the major incident alert now. And make sure you put that Tekla Berg woman on it."

I

"Unstable knife injury in Room 1," Emil said through the partly open door. "23-year-old male. Five minutes."

Tekla spun around on her stool and met the nurse's tense look.

"Have you tried to get hold of the anaesthetists?"

"They're on their way."

The headache hit her, an ugly little blast striking between the frontal lobes.

Tekla put down the scalpel, peeled off her plastic gloves. She told the patient he could get dressed.

"Have you finished?" the man said in surprise.

"Your anal abscess needs to be debrided again so I'll fix a follow-up appointment for you in Outpatients."

"Can you say that in plain Swedish?"

"The pimple in your rectum's going to have to be squeezed again."

The man avoided Tekla's eyes as he struggled to his feet. His body language told her that his masculinity had taken a knock.

Tekla stepped out and set off at a trot towards the triage rooms. Her sweaty palms stuck to the stethoscope, which she was pulling out of her pocket. Her pulse was rising, she knew what stressed her the most, and it was not the incoming patient with the knife wounds.

She went into Room 1.

Cassandra, an efficient assistant nurse with white, cropped hair and a spider's web tattoo on her temples, turned to face her.

"Apparently he's lost a lot of blood."

Tekla saw that Cassandra was waiting for something and she

knew immediately what it was. She weighed her different options as she put on a plastic apron and fresh gloves.

"O.K., try to get hold of the consultant on call."

"What about Hampus?"

Flash Hampus, who had been doing his best to out-manoeuvre her ever since their first night shift together a year earlier.

"Waste of time."

Anki, a second nurse, pulled up the emergency trolley and opened the medicine refrigerator. Menthol-blue light flooded out and immediately the room felt a little cooler.

"Is there anything I should be getting ready?" she said.

"Some morphine might be a good idea."

Silence. Tekla stretched.

"Ten milligrammes of morphine, please."

The headache made Tekla feel sick. She picked up the tube of Lypsyl lip balm, made sure her back was to the room, unscrewed the top and tipped out a little ball of paper, smaller than a frozen pea, which she popped into her mouth and swallowed with some water. Seconds later it kicked in. She shivered all the way down to the base of her spine. Each time, the taste of bitter almonds was just as nauseating. Tekla put away the Lypsyl tube.

A minute or so later, her chief source of trouble came in through the swing doors. Tariq Moussawi, the consultant, ambled over, almost gliding across the floor. He had thick dark hair streaked with grey. The stubble lay like a jet-black shag rug over his face. He said nothing, just stood there with his hands behind his back, waiting for Tekla to get her visor on. Her plastic apron flapped around her.

"Come on," Moussawi drawled, and gestured for her to spin around. Reluctantly, she did as she was told. Felt the man's warm, moist breath on her neck, smelling faintly of garlic. Suppressed the urge to retch.

Moussawi tied her apron and took a step back.

"What is it?" he asked brusquely.

Tekla avoided his eyes, afraid to reveal how stressful she found the situation.

"Nothing."

"I mean the patient," Moussawi elaborated.

"Oh. A man with knife injuries in haemorrhagic shock."

Moussawi gave a barely perceptible nod.

"I thought I might need some help," she said.

"I don't think so."

Tekla was unsure what the Baghdadi consultant meant by that. Presumably that he was now in charge, that knife wounds were only for experienced surgeons. And preferably men, because women could not take the pressure in A. & E. Perhaps adding something about all the operations he had performed during the war, with nothing but a penknife and head torch.

"Give me a shout when you've reached your limit," he went on.

So he was just going to stand there and gawp, and hope that she would make a mistake so he could tell Göran and the others how useless she was.

"What?"

"You start, and we'll see how it goes."

This was how Moussawi worked. You swam or you sank. Not unusual among senior male doctors. She just had to suck it up. Grit her teeth. Ignore him. Tekla wanted to ask him to leave the room, but she was interrupted by Emil.

"Another alert."

"Another one?"

"A three-year-old with seizures."

A gnawing pain in the pit of her stomach. The only reassuring thing right now was the kind look in Emil's eyes and she clung to that for a second. And tried to put the gorilla beside the E.C.G. machine out of her mind.

"When?"

"Now! We'll take it in number two."

Emil pushed open the sliding doors between the two rooms.

Tekla turned and saw the ambulance roll in, presumably with the small child.

She had no choice, so she turned to Moussawi:

"Can you . . . ?"

He held out his empty hands and shrugged.

"I'm not here."

"O.K. In that case we'll have to get Hampus," she said to Cassandra, making little effort to hide the aggression in her voice. She was not going to waste any time thinking about Moussawi's unorthodox teaching methods. He would step in, but only if it became absolutely necessary.

On shaky legs, Tekla walked into the second emergency room, feeling like a fledgling ejected from its nest that had landed under the nose of a hungry fox.

A paramedic was standing by the trolley, applying three fingers to the tiny child's soft ribcage to carry out chest compressions. An A. & E. nurse was ushering in the panic-stricken parents. A beep came from the oxygen monitor, which was getting a weak signal from the patient's earlobe.

The father, all testosterone and sparse stubble, was shouting:

"Do something! He's dying!"

Tekla could see that the C.P.R. was working and the tube was in the right place. The child's fingers felt cold and lifeless. Mustard-yellow shit was seeping out of his shorts.

"What's his name?" Tekla said calmly.

"Oscar," the mother said, hurrying over. "He . . . he has Gaucher disease type 2, serious neurological damage since birth. Just so you know."

She sobbed out the words between her tears, looking as if she might faint at any moment.

"Sit down," Tekla said, pointing to a chair. A nurse came over to help, but the mother waved her away.

The father pointed straight at Tekla.

"Save him, you!"

The mother pulled down his arm and wrapped herself around him.

Tekla let her eyes travel from the concentrated look on the faces of the ambulance staff, past the bloodshot eyes of the parents to a yellow wall chart in the corner of the room. For four long seconds she could see before her Gupta's *Textbook of Paediatrics*, page 1364, right-hand column.

"Wake up!" the father yelled. "What the hell are you up to, do something!"

Tekla looked away from the wall and ran her hands over the little boy. His whole body was twitching. Carefully, she pulled back his eyelids and saw that the pupils barely reacted to the light.

"How long have you been at it?"

"Twenty-five minutes," came the grim reply from the paramedic behind her back.

A nurse was squatting beside them, trying to insert a second cannula into the boy's wrist.

Anki's voice could be heard from the other room:

"Knife injury incoming!"

Tekla felt the boy's stomach and found the scar from the operation. She turned to the mother.

"The spleen's been removed, right?"

The mother gave a surprised nod. "Why do you ask?"

"And he's been having a lot of seizures recently?"

"For some months. We must have been here twenty times."

A lucid moment seemed to hit the father and he clutched desperately at his wife.

"But you're not to give up." He stared at the doctor's name badge. "Do you hear that . . . Tekla Berg! Or I'll bloody well—"

"Tekla!" Anki called again from the other room. In the ambulance bay, the sound of the sirens bringing in the next patient was dying away.

"I'll be back," Tekla said. An assistant nurse led the parents away. And to the rest of the team:

"Keep the compressions going. And we need one more needle. Pull out all the stops."

Tekla went back to the first room.

The anaesthetist with the Polish name and a lackadaisical look on his wax-like face was known in-house to be a man of few words. Tekla brought him up to date.

"I'll do the airway. You deal with the rest," he said.

Tekla wondered if he was joking, but heard no more. He brought out his tubes and his intubation gear, and filled syringes with white liquids. A nurse in a blue cap worked alongside him, as if they were preparing a routine anaesthesia for surgery. Out of the corner of her eye, Tekla saw that Moussawi was still there, loitering by the aluminium cupboards. He was following her every step.

The doors slid open. She walked up to the ambulance personnel, a man and a woman. The blonde woman reported:

"23-year-old man with a knife injury in his left flank. We got to the scene outside the restaurant only about a minute after it happened. He's lost a lot of blood and is in shock. Blood pressure 80 over 40. Pulse 120. We applied a compression bandage, but it's slipped down with all the bleeding. We've put a large-bore cannula in his right arm."

Tekla thanked them. The emaciated ambulance man handed her a wallet.

She glanced at the driving licence. The name sounded Finnish. Twenty-three years old.

The fair-haired patient on the trolley had a crew cut and tattoos on his upper arms that crept from under his dark T-shirt. He was gasping and grimacing with pain.

"Can you open up wide?" Tekla said.

The man was exhausted, but he slowly opened his mouth, and Tekla could see that his airway was free. Breathing rapid and shallow. Ice-cold fingers. The monitor showed ninety-two per cent oxygen saturation. The anaesthetist applied a mask and increased the oxygen flow. Tekla listened to the lungs. No breath sounds on the left side.

Tekla suddenly had tunnel vision. In her mind, she was being pitched between the two emergency rooms. Tried to focus on the young man in front of her. Was this the result of some settling of scores between gangs? Or a robbery? A crime of passion or a drunken brawl? She saw before her images from the garage down by the river in Östersund, near her home of Edsåsdalen. An eternity ago. Memories revolving around different kinds of substance abuse. Around Simon. Around their father. Another life, yet fragments that would remain forever in her mind.

The patient groaned with pain. His abdomen was tight. Other than a mass of tattoos and some old scars covering a forearm, his skin was intact. She loosened the bandages and saw the wound: a horizontal gash, about two centimetres wide, a perfect hit between the sixth and seventh ribs in the left thorax. The knife had perforated the lung, and the pleural space was now filled with blood, reducing his oxygen saturation. He had probably lost between one and two litres of blood. A delicate situation, he could crash at any moment.

But there was something that did not make sense. The injury was high up in the ribcage, not in the abdomen. So why was his belly so tight? Tekla tried to leaf through Moore's *Trauma*, but was aware she had missed a few lectures in just that course. She also remembered why: her brother's first overdose. She opened her mouth to ask Moussawi for help, but something held her back.

Agitated voices could now be heard from Room 2. Tekla hurried there and sat down next to the mother. The father was pacing up and down, talking animatedly into his mobile.

"What's your name?" Tekla said.

"Sophia."

"Hi, Sophia. Have you discussed resuscitation?"

The mother nodded and looked into Tekla's eyes.

"We've signed something to say we don't want him put on a ventilator. But Janne's . . . he hasn't accepted it. He's always working . . . he's a firefighter, many weekends and nights. And Oscar's been sick for so long . . . we can't take . . ." She shut her eyes and covered her face. Then she gripped Tekla by the shoulder and whispered:

"Don't let him suffer."

A thought flashed through Tekla's mind, about that one second when everything comes to a standstill, when decisions are taken: Paul Tibbets flying *Enola Gay* over Hiroshima, did he hesitate?

"Get me ten milligrammes of Stesolid," Tekla said to the nurse, who gave her a questioning look. "Give him five."

"But . . ."

"I'll do it myself. And fetch some Claforan. We won't bother with cultures, just do the antibiotics quickly."

The nurse brought the syringe and the medicine. Tekla lifted the cap of the little catheter on the back of the boy's hand and injected five milligrammes of Stesolid.

She returned to the patient with the knife injury and said to her emergency team: "We have to roll him onto his side."

Then she saw: another bleeding wound, further down the flank, in his lower back.

"So, two injuries," she said aloud. "One in the thorax and one above his left kidney. We need to get him to surgery."

"Fifty over unmeasurable," the anaesthetist said, holding the oxygen mask to the patient's face. Two men rushed into the room, closely followed by a night nurse who was doing her best to keep them out.

"You two, you are *not* allowed in here . . ."

The men ignored the nurse.

Tekla had time to register that they were wearing leather waistcoats with the same badges. White T-shirts. One of the men was in chocolate-coloured leather trousers, the other in stone-washed jeans. Both were bulky, like old weightlifters whose muscles have turned to fat. Arms and necks covered in tattoos. A shaved head and fluffy goatee on the first, and a bleached crew cut on the second. They took up position at the foot of the trolley. Tekla glimpsed a pistol in the waistband of one of the men.

"Will he make it?" the slightly taller one asked in a strong Finnish accent.

Tekla saw the terrified nurse behind them go to the telephone and pick up the receiver. The shorter man turned to her and shook his head. The nurse put down the receiver and backed away. Stared at the pistol in his hand.

"He's lost a lot of blood and needs to go for surgery."

The larger of the intruders came close to Tekla and put a hand on her shoulder. She could feel his rings against her collarbone and tried to ignore the pistol just within sight.

"We're counting on you –" he looked at her name badge – "... Tekla Berg." Then he stepped back and stood beside his companion.

The father barged his way in from the other emergency room and shouted:

"He's not breathing!"

Tekla turned, picked up a syringe from the anaesthesia trolley. She held it by her side as she walked over to him.

"Oscar is terribly sick, you know that. Gaucher type 2 is incurable. And you've decided that you don't want him to suffer. But this may be blood poisoning, so we're giving him antibiotics. I had to sedate him heavily, but I don't have time to explain any more now."

"He's not bloody well breathing!" The eyes of the firefighter father looked as if they were about to pop out of their sockets, he was so angry.

Tekla leaned towards him.

"And now you need to calm down so we can get on with our job."

She drove the syringe into his muscular thigh and squeezed out all of the liquid.

He shouted in pain, but he had no idea where it was coming from. His hands reached for Tekla's throat, but one of the bikers pushed him away and shoved the drugged father back into the other room. He stumbled and the last Tekla saw was that he had collapsed onto a chair.

Tekla turned to Moussawi, and the scene seemed to freeze. She knew there and then that he had seen it all. She was in deep trouble.

Thursday evening, 6.vi

"Can't get a blood pressure reading," the anaesthetist shouted.

The room swayed around her. Tekla felt sick and registered that sweat was trickling down her spine. She was on the point of leaving the room or telling Moussawi to take over when she heard the voice of Emil, like a circus ringmaster's, coming from the doors:

"Hampus is on his way!"

Tekla took a deep breath, closed her eyes and took herself back to her native Jämtland. To the rowing boat by the small lake. To Simon and her father, waiting for her to pour coffee from a steaming thermos flask. Saffron-yellow autumn colours on the carpet of leaves by the water's edge. Simon telling her to be careful with her piano fingers. Tekla saying: "You're welcome to play the piano yourself, you idiot. I can hold my drumsticks with my feet if I have to." Pappa smiling, a cigarette in the corner of his mouth. "Quiet now, so we get a bite before it's late and Mamma goes to sleep." As if their mother ever bothered to stay up for their sake, Tekla thought.

Bang! Anki slammed the door of the medicine cabinet.

Tekla opened her eyes. Took three quick steps over to the stabbed gang member.

"Get me a drain. Largest you have."

She tilted the bed, foot-end up.

"I'm intubating," she heard the anaesthetist say, somewhere in the background. His voice sounded distant and metallic.

The bikers were following the drama with grim expressions. Keeping a tight hold on their pistols. Tekla heard one of them speaking on his mobile.

Just as she was pulling on her sterile gloves, Hampus Nordensköld came into the room with another nurse. His hair was all over the place.

"What's going on here?"

Tekla had never seen him on such a high.

The shorter of the bikers, with the shaved scalp, held up his arm and stopped Nordensköld from getting to the patient.

"One doctor's enough. She's got the situation under control."

"Excuse me . . ."

Tekla was amused to see the anger bubbling up in Nordensköld's face.

"You can go into the other room," she said. "A boy with Gaucher who has sepsis. Find a place for him in the I.C.U. and get his dad a bunk." Tekla looked over Nordensköld's shoulder and saw the father sitting, propped against the uncomprehending mother's shoulder. "He'll be asleep for at least four hours."

As if Nordensköld had the faintest clue about Gaucher disease, Tekla thought. But like all male doctors, he would rather tell a bare-faced lie than admit his ignorance.

Nordensköld pushed his fingers through his unruly mop of hair and lumbered through to Room 2 in a huff.

"Scalpel," Tekla said, once the wound was clean.

"No pulse," the anaesthesia nurse called out, a note of desperation in her voice.

"Cardiac arrest," the Polish anaesthetist noted, his tone laconic.

Tekla was just about to say "compressions, please" when the taller biker took three steps forward and started C.P.R. In the right rhythm and with the right pressure, perfectly executed.

"Keep going, doctor," he rasped.

She took the scalpel from Cassandra and made an incision along one of his left ribs. She then used her index finger to dig a canal over the rib and in towards the chest cavity. Suddenly, fresh blood came pouring out over the patient's flank and down onto the pale-grey linoleum floor.

"Blood," she said, as if anyone could possibly have missed the deep red fountain spurting from his side.

The doors to the room opened again and the lead nurse came in.

"Some more bikers are here, outside."

The two in the room looked at each other in surprise. Tekla felt as if she were in the middle of an episode of the T.V. series *Sons of Anarchy*.

"You take over," the beefiest of the bikers grunted. Cassandra put down the dressings she was holding and heaved herself up onto the trolley to continue pumping. The shorter man felt behind his back and drew out his pistol. Pointed it in the direction of the doors.

Four other men came in, and the first bikers relaxed. The same gang. They talked animatedly, and Tekla picked up something about Albanians and rats.

She was standing with her finger inside the warm chest cavity and could feel faint pulsations from the heart massage. She was trying to focus, even though sweat was running into her eyes and stinging like vinegar.

"Drain."

The noise level was rising.

She took the thick plastic tube from Anki and pushed it in with a rotating movement. Fresh blood flowed out into a bag, which Anki just had time to connect.

"Is there any O neg on the way?" she called to the lead nurse, who was standing rooted to the spot by one of the walls.

"I've got it here."

"Hook it up under pressure."

Tekla looked over her shoulder. Moussawi was still in the same place. Arms folded. His face wore a different expression from before.

After another minute or so she heard the anaesthetist say to Cassandra:

"Pause for a while."

For a few seconds the room was deathly quiet. The gang members waited.

"Weak pulse," the anaesthetist said.

Tekla closed her eyes for a second. She saw Simon's cheerful toothy grin and his cheeky eyes before her.

The sound of metal on wood and rubber squeaking could now be heard from the entrance to A. & E. The S.W.A.T. team marched in, all three with weapons drawn.

Tekla could just see the policemen throw the bikers onto the floor and handcuff them. She tried to concentrate on sewing the thick drain into place in the patient's ribcage, finally managing to secure it with a few rough stitches. One of the policemen – two metres tall and preposterously broad-shouldered – came up to Tekla and pulled down the lower half of his balaclava. There was a camera attached to the top of his helmet. He stopped by the monitor, which was showing a cardiac rhythm of 120 beats per minute.

"All good, doctor?"

At first Tekla was startled to see the large automatic weapon around his neck, but his sympathetic look calmed her. She tried to smile.

"He'll make it, I think."

"Good work. Any minute now you'll be rid of these jerks and be able to get back to normal."

An assistant nurse came in from the corridor, pushed past the policemen and shouted:

"We're in major incident mode! Söder Tower's exploded."

Tekla dropped the forceps and needleholder onto the sterile blue cloth and saw how the policemen first started talking into their radios and then with each other. The atmosphere at once became charged. She heard the words "explosion" and "fire".

The tall policeman came up to her again.

"There's been a blast in Söder Tower, followed by a blaze. Our team's been called there."

"You won't be leaving us the gang members, I hope?" Tekla said, as she taped a large dressing over the drain. The anaesthetist hooked up another blood bag, the pressure was now a stable 80 over 60.

"The regular police patrol will have to take them to the station on Torkel Knutssonsgata."

"Tekla!" Cassandra shouted from the far side of the chaos. "The incident commander wants to talk to you." She held up a telephone.

Tekla checked with the anaesthetist that the patient was under control, then removed her blood-covered gloves and plastic apron.

"He's stable. We'll swing by X-ray on our way to the I.C.U." In the other room, the little boy was about to be taken to the paediatric intensive care unit by another anaesthesia team.

Tekla took the telephone and introduced herself.

"I've been instructed to tell you that you're to lead our first medical team at the fire," incident commander Leif Törblom said, in what sounded to Tekla like a slurred voice. "We're busy setting up a team of core staff, but we need to get more doctors out to the scene quickly."

Tekla looked around. She had no choice but to do what the incident commander said: put on her rescue jacket and make her way to Söder Tower. She left the emergency room, stopped by a washbasin and quickly swallowed a bomb, which she washed down with luke-warm water. In the ambulance hall she met Johan and Jessica, who had been assigned as nurses to the first response team.

"We're off then," Tekla said. She saw the policeman from the S.W.A.T. team turn and fix his blue eyes on hers before he climbed into a silver-coloured van and disappeared in the direction of the fire. She had a funny feeling about it. Who had "instructed" Törblom that Tekla, and no-one else, was to head up the first response team?

"Is he dead?" Johan said.

"Don't know."

"He must be, no?"

"Can't you just wait!" Tekla snapped. "How am I supposed to take his pulse with all this going on?"

She knew she ought to apologise to Johan for losing her temper, but after all the patients she had taken care of she was beginning to feel that she had had enough. Her fingers were still resting against the throat of the injured man and she let her eyes stray for a few seconds' respite. The flames had already reached halfway up the tower where the building was being renovated. The smoke rose like a black pillar against the sheer pink veil of the evening sky. She would remember every detail; that was her blessing and her curse. Tekla shivered at the cold air brushing the back of her neck, while the heat from the fire vibrated two hundred metres away. There was a smell of burnt plastic and scorched skin. Every now and then the rumble from the fire was drowned out by exploding panes of glass and the sirens of the emergency vehicles.

"Where did you find him?" she said. She gave up trying to find a pulse.

"Outside the switchroom. Under a spiral staircase."

Tekla got to her feet and looked at the firefighter. Only now did she see how sooty and sweaty he was.

"Sit down and take a rest," she said.

The firefighter sank onto a roll of hoses, opened his jacket and wiped his hand over his dirty face. His head fell forwards, as if the vertebrae in his neck had given way. Tekla saw how his whole body began to shake. She knew she should be going up to him and putting a hand on his shoulder, but instead she stayed where she was and stretched her aching back. For the first time in more than two hours she let her shoulders drop a few centimetres.

"Was he the last one you got out?"

He nodded.

Tekla looked over at the inferno. The last of her patients would be the first to die. The body wouldn't be easy to identify. She stuck her hand into one of the pockets of the rescue jacket and brought out a black triage card to mark him as dead, the plastic reflecting the flames.

"How many have you taken care of?" the firefighter said.

Tekla did not even have to think. She could describe each and every one of the casualties: colour of clothes, hair type, facial expression, body temperature. Down to the smallest detail. Everything, except their smell.

"This one makes twelve," she said.

"They should have stayed put. Not run out into the stairwell."

"You'd never have been able to get up to eighty metres with those ladders anyway."

The firefighter shut his eyes, trying to shield himself from the truth.

"How many dead?" he said.

"Only one, so far. But several of the worst injured may not survive."

Tekla stood there, staring at the scorched body. It was a failure, in so many respects. She turned to face the reassuring darkness over by the Bofills Båge apartment building, got out the tube of Lypsyl, shook yet another little ball into her hand and swallowed it quickly. Did not even notice the bitter taste. It would take effect after a minute or so.

Somebody squatted down next to her.

"Hardly looks like a human being," he said. It was Johan.

"More like a charred animal carcass on a smoking battlefield," Tekla muttered, and was about to ask for a bottle of water when she suddenly saw the burnt man's chest move.

She leaned forward, her knees sinking into the soft earth. She put her ear to the place where there should have been a mouth, but where now there were only large, copper-red blisters covered in soot and blood.

"He's breathing!"

She took a torch out of her breast pocket and shone it into the eye that was not covered in burnt flesh.

"He has pinpoint pupils. We need to set up an I.V.!"

Johan went to fetch his emergency equipment bag while Tekla examined the crooks of the arms, but the fire had destroyed every visible blood vessel. Face, torso, arms . . . she estimated that eighty per cent of the surface area of his body had third degree burns. The clothes were gone, even his genitals were unrecognisable. She palpated his head with the tips of her fingers and found a spongy recess at the back.

Johan returned in no time.

"It'll have to be intraosseous," Tekla said. "Here, there's a relatively undamaged patch on one of the knees."

Johan brought out the drill and attached a needle with a yellow top.

"Why didn't I look for a pulse in his groin in the first place . . ."

Tekla took aim at the bone surface of the right shin, close to the knee, grasped the drill and braced herself. She drilled all the way down to the marrow. Not so much as a shiver of pain from the patient.

She looked the man over. Normal build. Normal height. Impossible to guess how old. No hair left. Face basically gone. The whole head a smoking, bloody lump of meat. The body a black carapace of scab. Pictures of Pompeii came to Tekla's mind, how people had been buried alive in whatever position they happened to be in. Many appeared to have been asleep when the volcano erupted. How had it felt to be lying there? What would she herself have wanted? For somebody to save her life . . . like this? Or just give her pain relief, so she could go to sleep and never wake again?

A second later, Tekla emptied a whole ampoule of Naloxone and followed it up with some ordinary saline solution.

"Intubation next," she said.

Just then she heard a deep voice behind her.

"Is he alive?"

She saw a policeman out of the corner of her eye, but turned back to Johan.

"Get out some Ketamine. And two bags of Ringer."

She began reading from memory the left-hand column on page 2127 of the *Textbook of Burns*. Did the sums out loud: "A patient weighing seventy kilogrammes with eighty per cent burns will need twelve litres of fluid over the following ten hours. Difficult if it's intraosseous, but we'll start off like this. Then they'll have to put in central venous lines in A. & E. If we get there in time."

"Has he said anything?" the policeman asked, now standing next to her. He looked as if he had decided early on to compensate for his lack of hair by spending late nights at the gym and growing a neat Captain Haddock beard. There was not so much as a thread out of place on his outfit.

"Does he look as if he could talk?" Tekla said.

"He doesn't speak Swedish?"

"I hope that was a joke."

"Have you seen any tattoos?"

"On the twenty per cent of his body area which is intact, no, I've not seen any tattoos. Now please get out of my way, I've got to intubate."

Tekla resisted a strong impulse to barge the policeman aside.

The burns victim began to move his arm and turned his head in Tekla's direction.

At that, the policeman leaned forward and said in a loud voice:

"Do you hear me? Nod if you can hear me. Witnesses report

seeing a green van with four or five men escape from the scene just before the explosion. You were involved, weren't you? Did they run off and leave you? Where were you meant to meet up? Talk!"

No reaction.

"Did you put a bomb in the basement?" the policeman shouted in English, as if he assumed that the injured man's eardrums had burst. "What did you do outside the . . . what the hell's the English for *elcentralen*? What did you do outside the switchroom?"

The man was now waving his arm about in an involuntary movement and Tekla sensed that his one eye was trying to focus on her. She pushed the policeman away.

"I have to intubate right away if he's to have even the slightest chance of surviving."

"Just one last thing," the policeman said, again leaning over the injured man. "If you've blown up that building and injured those people then I will personally see to it that you and all your relatives from whatever fucking Middle Eastern country you come from get to suffer for all eternity. No prophet will be able to protect you. You can forget all about the virgins in paradise. Do you hear me?!"

Tekla pushed the man away, but he deliberately took his time stepping back.

"What the hell are you talking about?" she shouted at him. "How can you know that this is some kind of terrorist attack? It could just as easily be an accident!"

The other officers had to restrain their leader, who looked as if he wanted to go up and stamp on the injured man with his big boots. He stared at Tekla, a scornful smirk on his face, before slowly moving off. The other policemen, both regular officers and members of the S.W.A.T. team, also took a few steps away, and the light from the flames returned. Tekla put her hand on the injured man's forehead. His leg lay uncovered.

She bent forward, carefully stroking him, and whispered:

"It'll be alright, you'll see. Things'll be fine . . . Now you can sleep."

She took her laryngoscope and was just about to turn her attention to the man's head when he pointed his index finger at her. At Tekla's face. She leaned over to try to catch what he was struggling to say. Heard his short, laboured breaths. Words being pushed out slowly, hesitantly. Then his arm fell again and he lapsed into unconsciousness.

"What did he say?" Johan asked.

"'Swimming,'" Tekla said, and shivered. "It sounded as if he was saying something about swimming."

NOBEL HOSPITAL

6–7.vi, night

Facing backwards in a car had always made Tekla feel sick. The ambulance was swaying to and fro, but she gritted her teeth, took deep breaths and concentrated on the one thing she had to do: keep her burns patient alive. At least until they got to A. & E. On the hill leading up from Ringvägen, she saw an unmarked police car immediately behind them. Its siren was turned off as they approached their destination.

She was carefully pumping an appropriate amount of air into the man's lungs with the help of an Ambu bag. It had not been possible to measure his blood pressure, but she could feel a weak pulse in his groin. She knew he was still alive. Tekla looked at the sticky mess on her plastic glove. Could those almond-white threads, which looked like over-cooked spaghetti, be nerves which had been dissolved by the heat?

The ambulance engine was switched off and she heard Johan open the sliding door.

"How's it going?" he said.

"For me or the patient?"

"I assume that means he's still alive."

Johan scurried towards the rear doors. Tekla envied him his easy-going approach.

"Good driving," she said as she gave a hand with the stretcher. "For once I didn't throw up."

Together they eased the patient out, while Tekla kept the manual ventilation going. Eight more ambulances were waiting in the reception bay, two of them being unloaded.

Tekla spotted the hospital's chief physician coming towards

them. She had never seen him so red in the face. Göran Collinder must have been in a terrific hurry to get over from his apartment in the upmarket district of Östermalm, Tekla thought, because it was the first time she had ever seen him without his dark blue blazer with the gold buttons.

"You're Tekla Berg, right?"

"So it says on my badge."

"And that's the badly burnt man from Söder Tower?"

"One of them."

Tekla now saw that Collinder was accompanied by two men in civilian clothes, possibly policemen. She met the eyes of one of them, but quickly switched her focus to her boss.

"We need to get this man into A. & E.," Tekla said.

"We'll wait here and have a word when you've handed over your patient," Collinder said, looking as if he was waiting to have his order acknowledged, but Tekla only turned and continued in towards the emergency room, where an eager doctor was standing by in a visor and full combat gear.

It pained Tekla to leave the patient. A ventilator and a whole night of having his wounds cleaned awaited him. Torture. Perhaps she should have followed Johan's hint at the scene, that a mercy killing with a good dose of morphine might have been preferable.

Tekla backed towards the medicine refrigerator, where Johan was standing and jotting something onto a screen. He looked up.

"What was that about swimming, by the way?"

Tekla stiffened. "Nothing."

"Go on, tell me."

"I thought he said . . . 'swimming.'"

"When he pointed at you?"

Tekla saw images of the little lake in her mind.

"The odd thing is, I can't swim . . ."

"But why would he talk about swimming?"

"Yes, it's strange," Tekla said, avoiding Johan's questioning look. "Perhaps he was delirious. But he really did seem to be looking at me and asking something. I must have misheard. The only person who knows I can't swim is—"

"Tekla!"

Collinder was by the doors to the E.R., gesticulating. The policemen stood next to him, it was obvious that they were going to stay with the injured man. Now Tekla could see the pandemonium. The hospital was in major incident mode and staff had come streaming in from all over the city to help. More than were needed.

She took off her blood-smeared emergency jacket and hung it outside the ambulance hall, washed and disinfected her hands and splashed cold water over her face. As they began to walk, she was trying to read Collinder's body language. So far, he had not mentioned the earlier drama of the stabbing victim and the child with seizures. Had the staff not yet reported anything untoward to him? Or was it that his thoughts were taken up by the fire?

They passed casualties lying on trolleys outside the already-crowded triage rooms.

"How many have we had in?" she said.

"Five. But only two serious burns cases."

"Why only two?"

"Well, there's your one as well, that makes three."

"But where are all the others? There must be at least ten."

"Uppsala got five and Solna two."

"Uppsala? But we have a brand-new burns unit here at the Nobel."

"We do, but as you've no doubt heard, Uppsala was made the national centre." Collinder tried to smile, but was evidently too stressed to pretend to look cheerful about it. "In any case, the new unit's got plenty to do now. I know someone who's going to be happy."

Tekla left A. & E. and walked past the paediatric clinic, heading towards the central hall. Collinder tried to keep in step with her. She had never before seen so many people in the hospital at this time of night. They met wave after wave of anxious relatives and staff hurrying in from the main entrance.

She turned left.

"Tekla, I want you to be the doctor in charge of that burns victim," Collinder said.

"Doctor in charge?"

"I know it's a bit unusual, but this patient is special."

"You mean, at risk of dying from his injuries."

"That too. I got a call from the head of the emergency response team. If the patient survives, there'll be a police investigation. They say he may have been involved in the fire."

"A victim of it, you mean?"

"Maybe more than that."

They got to the lift hall. Tekla pressed the call button several times.

"Why me? Isn't it usually someone in the I.C.U. who's made doctor in charge?"

"I gather that he responded to Naloxone?"

"What's that got to do with who's doctor in charge?"

"Meaning, we have to regard it as a drug overdose. And the emergency clinic's responsible for all O.D.s which end up in the I.C.U."

The lift doors opened. She stepped in reluctantly, suppressing a wave of nausea as Collinder's aftershave filled the space. She pressed number nine.

"An O.D.? But—"

"You're being made doctor in charge for two reasons," Collinder interrupted her. "Partly because it's an overdose. Partly because there's no known identity and the police want a contact person for whatever happens with the patient."

Collinder checked his watch.

"Don't look at me like that. I'm not the one who decides."

"So who does?"

Tekla saw that Collinder was on the point of saying something, but then he changed his mind.

At last the lift reached its destination. Tekla walked to her office and heard Collinder continue talking behind her.

"The police response team leader says the patient recognised you. Is that true?"

Tekla stopped at her office and unlocked the glass door. It was clear now why Collinder had pursued her all the way there.

"What do you mean?"

"He pointed at you, didn't he? He seemed to recognise you?"

"Give me a break. He just moved his arm when I gave him Naloxone. He was barely conscious. Did you see what he looked like?"

She walked into her office and stopped in front of the window. Felt her heart pounding. Sweat trickled down her spine and her body was shaking. There was only one person, wasn't there, who knew she couldn't swim? But there were plenty of people who couldn't swim.

She needed a bomb. Now.

Collinder came and stood beside her. They could see how, a kilometre away, Söder Tower was still burning. Darkness had settled over the city and the flames now engulfed the building, up to the top floors. There was scaffolding all around the tower.

Collinder was aghast at the sight. "My God!"

"Hadn't you seen it before?" Tekla asked him.

"What was it like being there?"

"Unreal."

Her thoughts circled around all the people she had tried to help at Söder Tower. Was there anything she could have done differently?

"Shelob's salvation," Collinder whispered.

"Who?"

"Nothing."

They stood for a few seconds, staring at the blaze. Sweat was trickling down the inside of Tekla's thighs, yet she felt cold.

"I really do need to change now."

She made to unbutton her trousers.

"Here?"

"I wasn't planning to go home on the Tunnelbana looking like a butcher."

"You know that we change in the cellar. You have your changing rooms—"

"Listen, you," Tekla interrupted, beginning to pull off her

trousers. "I'm *extremely* tired now."

"O.K.," Collinder apologised, turning away. "But you agree to be doctor in charge?"

"Do I have any choice?"

"Not that I can see."

"In that case you have your answer."

"The police will come in every day during rounds. And they'll be expecting a status update."

"Every day?"

"At eleven sharp."

Tekla sighed. "Get the job done faster with the same resources."

"What was that?"

"Nothing."

Tekla took a deep breath and with a sticky hand reached for the Lypsyl in her pocket. Collinder's mobile rang.

"Yes . . . yes . . . she's here with me . . ."

He held out the telephone.

"It's for you."

"Who?" Tekla said, waving the phone away.

"Monica. Just take it."

Tekla hardly had time to work out which Monica he meant before she had the mobile in her hand and was answering.

"Tekla?" a sharp, bright voice said.

"Yes."

"I've been hearing a lot about you during the course of the evening."

"You have?"

"I'd like to talk to you. Tomorrow morning. You're on duty, aren't you? You're due in the I.C.U. at eleven."

"Yes. But how did you know—"

"I'll call," the hospital C.E.O. said and hung up.

Tekla handed back the telephone.

Now she understood.

Shelob.

II

Victor Umarov woke up with a morning erection. It filled him with joy. For a few seconds he fingered his cock, feeling to see if it would stay stiff. He reassured himself that this was not just another shitty dream.

Umarov rolled over and dragged himself closer to Elena. She was still sleeping, blissfully unaware of the wonderful morning gift he had for her. He slipped his hand under her arm, carefully drew away the silk camisole, took her large breast in his hand and began to caress the broad nipple at the same time as he pressed his erection against her magnificent arse.

They would fuck like nobody's business. Hard and sweaty it was going to be, like they hadn't done for many months. Then he would have a case of champagne sent over to his doctor in Östermalm. Champagne, not Russian vodka, which the Swedes were incapable of drinking anyway. Eyeball to eyeball. Just like when he bought the Russian State electricity monopoly at the beginning of the '90s. A firm handshake and a drink. In those days, of course, vodka.

He was thinking so much about how he was going to thank his doctor that he nearly lost his focus. Started to pump so hard he could feel his glutes strain.

Elena had slid her knickers to one side. This could go very fast. She was as wet as the oysters at the Royal Castle Hotel in Bulgaria. Just so long as he didn't come too soon.

But then he noticed that something had changed. His cock no longer felt so hard. He tensed his buttocks, tried to press the blood forward into his shaft, fill it with power. But it was as if someone had pulled the plug out. He imagined one of those enormous, inflatable, plastic figures outside car showrooms in the U.S.A. that collapse when the fan is turned off.

It had lasted less than a minute, and it was as soft and limp as it had been for the whole of the past year.

He turned over and kicked his feet out onto the shaggy wall-to-wall carpet. Stood up, took the pistol out of the drawer in the bedside table, pressed in a magazine and fired off two quick shots. A two-by-one metre mirror shattered into a thousand pieces.

The door flew open and Kamila appeared. She was wearing her dark red flannel pyjamas, her large head of black hair was dishevelled and her teenage expression more angry than surprised. Sardor also came rushing up the stairs, a pistol in his hand.

"Nothing to worry about, it's all cool," Umarov said, avoiding the shards of glass as he walked towards his two children. He put his arms around Kamila and pressed her to him. "Just a little mirror that's bitten the dust."

"A little mirror? You're completely insane," Kamila said.

"But not so insane that I can't get my little princess whatever her sweet heart desires."

"Oh my Gooood," Kamila groaned, stomping back off to her room. "You're so lame, Pappa . . ."

Sardor waited.

"You can tidy up later," Umarov said. "Let her sleep."

"Ha, ha, very funny," Elena could be heard saying under the bedcover.

Umarov left the bedroom and shut the door. He was hungry and desperate for a cup of coffee. Would deal with that incompetent idiot of a doctor later. At the same time, he felt a knot in his stomach: he had to rein in his impulsive behaviour. Put the violence behind him, because he hated losing his self-control. It made him feel a failure.

"I didn't know you still had that old toy pistol," Sardor said.

"Just for self-defence. A bit of nostalgia." He stuck the old Makarov into his dressing gown.

Sardor gave a weary shrug.

"We've got a problem, Victor. There was a row at a hospital last night and—"

"Why," Umarov interrupted, "why can't you call me Pappa, like Nina and Kamila? Or Far. Or Farsan. Whatever. It's as if you didn't know me." He patted his big belly and tweaked Sardor's cheek. "Your own Uzbek flesh and blood . . ."

"One of the Red Bears guys was stabbed at a pub in Söder," Sardor said, turning away and putting his pistol back in the shoulder holster. The grey T-shirt had dark sweat rings under the arms. "One thing led to another. He was taken to A. & E. at the Nobel. The rumour is someone from the Northern Networks cut him down."

Elena sighed loudly as she walked by. "Do you always have to talk shop?"

"I'll be down in five minutes, darling," Umarov said as he waited for Elena to disappear down the stairs.

Umarov pulled his son close, hugged him tightly and tried to keep hold of him. Patted him on the head, just as he had more than thirty years earlier in London. Sardor had been three when Nina started school. Even then, they had very different temperaments. Sardor was a troubled sleeper, often calling out for his parents at night. Nina made friends immediately and was conscientious. By the time he was twelve, Sardor was already going off the rails. But Umarov's memories from those days were sporadic, he knew he had been away a lot, always on the move. His journeys back and forth between the crumbling Soviet empire and western Europe, between Moscow, Kiev, Riga and Hamburg, he and Boris juggling their different contacts in government, the security services and the emerging criminal world in Russia to build up their transport business. The London base had come as their company grew, an attempt at respectability and solidity, at putting some distance between themselves and the chaos of a new country struggling to find its way out of communist times. And then the fatal decision in the early '90s to return to Moscow and try to participate in the privatisation frenzy there. It had all had its price. Images from the time those plain-clothes F.S.B. agents marched into his office a few years later and told him to follow them remained etched on his mind. That is when he realised he had not given his son the upbringing he needed. And that it was too late to do anything about it.

Sardor pushed his father away.

"The Northern Networks?"

"According to Eje, but it's not for sure," Sardor said.

"Didn't Jensen himself call?"

"What difference does that make?"

"When did you last see him? He's as fat as Yeltsin was towards the end."

"Who?"

"Don't you know who Boris Yeltsin is? My poor confused little—"

"Can we just decide what we're going to do?"

Sardor wiped the sweat from his forehead and ran his hand over his short, thick hair.

"Which gang from the Northern Networks?" Umarov said. "The Lions? The K-Men? Jakan Crew? No Way Out, or whatever they call themselves?"

"How am I supposed to know what gang it is? It's just rumours. But I'll take care of it."

"Tell me what Eje said."

"One of the young prospects, Jarmo, was stabbed in the chest. Badly hurt. They don't know if he'll survive."

"But what was it about? Girls? Drugs?"

"Don't ask me," Sardor said wearily. "We agreed that you'd stay away from the detail, didn't we? The less you know—"

"But Jensen's angry?" Umarov went on.

"He's fucking spitting. Knowing him, he'll want to arm every teenager in central Skärholmen with an AK-5. Is that enough for you? You focus on your translations now."

Umarov drew his fingers through his grey-streaked hair, fingering a tangle that had formed overnight. Made a mental note to do something about his hair before the party next weekend.

"Have the Northern Networks been done out of some cash lately?"

"Not impossible."

"Maybe we should find out, reach out to them and lend them a little bit. Why not start a bank?"

Sardor looked over at the glass splinters on the carpet.

"You know what a broken mirror means, don't you?"

"Mirrors can be mended," Umarov answered. "A gang war can do permanent damage to business."

Umarov stared out of the window facing the pool. Elena was shuffling over to the sofa group with a glass of juice and a cup of coffee. The three mastiffs were playing with their toy bears along the wall.

"Fuck!" he exclaimed.

Sardor jumped. "Take it easy, we'll sort this, like I said. We've got it under—"

"The pool looks like shit."

Confused, Sardor shook his head.

Umarov's voice was calm again. "Do you understand how hard I've worked to get control over the heroin in this city?"

"You've sure as hell got more grey hair than you did when we moved here."

"All you see here –" Umarov made a sweeping gesture – "is the result of something I started many years ago in a crappy Russian prison cell."

"And there was I thinking you were a translator of Russian literature. Isn't that what your tax return says? In any case, wasn't it the K.G.B. or F.S.K. or whoever that gave you the job?"

Umarov sighed. "They'd never have released me after just six months and sent me to Stockholm if they hadn't known I'd make a good job of it. How many days of your life have you spent locked up in a three by three metre space? Precisely. And don't forget I've done it twice. When I was new to the business and didn't really know what I was doing, in the early '80s. Prison taught me a lot then, put me in touch with the right people, showed me how to look after myself. But when they got me again all those years later, I decided –" Umarov turned and grasped the hair at the back of Sardor's head – "that I would either build an empire for my family, one that would last and protect them, or I might just as well stick a pistol in my mouth and pull the trigger."

Sardor looked at his father with a mixture of fondness and awe. Umarov smiled indulgently at his son. Let go of him and scratched at an angry-looking patch of eczema above his elbow.

"The Northern Networks, you said?"

"Yes, but—"

"The Tullinge store's full, right?"

Sardor jumped.

"What do you mean?"

"Why so stressed?" Umarov said. "A simple question, my son. Do we have enough weapons, in case this escalates?"

"What do you mean, escalates?"

"Meaning rise, increase, grow."

"I know what escalate means," Sardor snapped.

Umarov put his hand on Sardor's cheek and smiled.

"One never knows with you. So we have weapons to go around?"

"Of course. We moved everything from Haninge to Tullinge after the crackdown at the end of April. But—"

"Good. Even though I'm hoping our business will go to the grave with me and that Nina will lead the family into a new, law-abiding future, you can't imagine how good it feels to have you in charge of things on the streets. Total control over the drugs, the women, the weapons, the cash flow . . ."

Sardor looked uncomfortable.

Umarov took a deep breath, felt that he was beginning to wake up properly. Even the pool could wait today. It had taken a long time to build their fragile relationship with the motorbike gang in

Skärholmen. But the Northern Networks seemed to be strong and on the rise. A full-scale confrontation would be too costly. The men in suits at the F.S.B. centre in Moscow would not be happy if Umarov lost control of the northern link into Scandinavia. He leaned heavily on Sardor's shoulder as he pondered.

"We'll tackle that knife drama with diplomacy."

"I don't think that's what Jensen's hoping to hear right now," Sardor said.

"Which is exactly why you need to persuade him that it's the thing to do."

"Me?"

"Yes."

"But—"

"I'm not coming along. Sooner or later you have to accept that I'll be quitting as *vor.*"

Umarov did not like the Russian term for mafia boss but, in the circumstances, using his title gave him a good feeling.

Sardor was about to say something, but Umarov stopped him.

"Problems are there to be solved. The only question is how. And all the violence has to come to an end. You have to show that you can negotiate as calmly and effectively as a career diplomat. Right, I'm about to piss myself now."

Sardor looked embarrassed.

Umarov limped towards the bathroom.

"Show a little diplomatic finesse. Absolutely no unnecessary war between Jensen and the Northern Networks. Full stop. Keep your temper under control. And another thing, Sardor."

"Yes?"

"Make your Pappa happy."

Sardor turned and left. He was in a hurry to get to Kungsholmen and his yoga class. On the stairs he Googled the word "escalate".

RED BEARS MOTORCYCLE CLUB, SKÄRHOLMEN

Friday, 7.vi

Apart from a pink breakdown truck, all you could see in the street was the wreckage of a Mazda. The high barbed-wire fence surrounding the building was a common feature of the industrial zone, which had lately become known as the car-torching district of the southern suburbs. The business owners had clubbed together and hired a security company to patrol the area. Not that Sardor thought for one second that the Red Bears motorcycle club contributed to the monthly fee.

A heavy gate was pushed to one side by a man with a torso the size of a wine refrigerator.

Sardor pointed to where the man's biker waistcoat was gaping open.

"You probably shouldn't be advertising that thing so openly."

The man pulled a little awkwardly at his leather vest, but made no real effort to cover up his Mini Uzi.

"We're at war."

Sardor sighed. He was already feeling annoyed.

"Not sure how you'll fight it from jail, if they get you for illegal possession of a weapon."

Sardor started walking towards the clubhouse. Ten or so motorcycles were lined up neatly outside, each one with a longer front fork than the next. The chrome detail glittered in the early summer sunshine.

The place looked like any other set of offices in the area: a bunker-grey plaster facade, badly maintained double-glazed windows, white frames. The next muscle mountain was keeping watch by the door to the two-storey building. He had "Road Captain" on his leather vest.

"Everything under control, Eje?"

"Jensen's been in better moods," the Red Bears' Erik "Eje" Eriksson said, as he made a show of frisking Sardor.

Sardor followed a dark corridor into a big room. A long bar counter ran along one of the walls. There was a chunky, brown leather sofa in one corner. A random collection of bottles in various shades of green stood on a low glass table. On the wall there hung a large black, yellow and red flag, with an image of a man wearing a Mexican hat, a pistol in one hand, a sword in the other. There was a billiard table in the middle of the room, and a dining table with about twenty chairs in another corner.

Christian Jensen was there, smoking a cigarette. He sucked in the smoke as if for the last time, and he had an electric guitar without a lead lying across his knees. Two men were sitting on the other side of the table. One had long, neatly combed hair and a leather vest with an exploded skull on it. Sardor nodded at Totte Lidegren. The other man, Penti Harju, was a little older and had ash-grey hair parted at the side and a walrus moustache. There was one more man, somewhat thinner with a shaved head and black goatee – probably dyed because he looked to be in his sixties – sitting at the short end, drumming his fingers on the tabletop. It was Johan "The Count" Holmström.

Sardor had heard why he was called that: when he was younger, Holmström had worshipped a Norwegian heavy metal band, one of whose members had been known as The Count. He was inside now, serving time for murder.

As Sardor walked through the room, he wondered if there was a blueprint for how biker hang-outs were supposed to look. Had they all been watching the same T.V. series?

He went up to Jensen and shook him by the hand. The president remained sitting, presumably because he would have had a heart attack if he had tried to raise his 120-kilo heap of a body from his seat. His legs were as spindly as a goat's and he puffed and panted when he spoke. His long, wispy red beard lay on his chest like a bib.

"I see we have an important visitor," Jensen said.

Smirks spread across the faces of the other men.

Sardor's pulse rose. He tried to look Jensen in the eye, but it was almost impossible to see them beneath all the folds of fat. A glance around the table told him that the dress code was black or white T-shirt, leather vest and dark trousers. A surprising number were wearing trainers. The only one with proper boots and silver toes and heels was Jensen himself. Sardor guessed that the president would be wearing a sheriff's badge if he could. But they had to obey the rules of the main biker gang, their mother chapter.

Silence had fallen over the room. The man at the head of the table was still drumming away with his wiry fingers. His waistcoat proclaimed "Vice-President". There was something smug about his sunken face, Sardor thought. Maybe all that glue sniffing had given The Count senile dementia?

Jensen stroked his electric guitar as if it were a cat.

"Have you lost weight?" Sardor eventually asked, as he pulled up a chair and took a seat between Jensen and The Count. "Suits you."

"And you've got thinner too," Jensen wheezed. "Which means there's not much more to you than skin and bones. Soon you'll be the same weight as your anorexic sister. How is Nina, by the way?"

"All good."

"You're here without the boss, I see."

"He sent me to—"

"Big shoes to fill," Jensen said.

Sardor tried to smile and calmly laid his hand on the table. He pushed aside a sawn-off shotgun.

"I'm relieved you can still talk. I was worried for a while that you'd drowned in your own fat. Rumour has it—"

"So there are rumours about me?" Jensen leaned towards Sardor, in an unconvincing attempt to seem interested. "Or wait . . . can you hear that?"

Sardor played along, putting on a show of concern.

"Your tinnitus again?"

"Out there, it sounds like . . . cannons and drums. Isn't it the sound of war?"

"In my ears it's as quiet as church on a Monday morning," Sardor said. "And you know what? It's going to go on being just as quiet." Sardor patted an AK-5 that was lying on the table. "And that's why these babies are going to stay right here on the table and gather dust."

Jensen suddenly burst out in gurgling laughter. Signalled that he wanted something that he could pour into a glass. A figure in a leather vest with no patch hurried over to the bar and came straight back with two glasses and a bottle of vodka. Jensen poured.

"Time for a toast."

Sardor accepted the small glass from another young biker, a prospect he had seen a few times before at the Årsta store.

"Here's to our wonderful cooperation." Jensen knocked back his glass and challenged Sardor to do the same. He drank. "To the Uzbek–Finnish Friendship Society in the Southern Suburbs."

"But you're not a Finn, are you, Christian? Surely you're more of a fan of sticky pastries?" Sardor said with an amused expression. He knew that Jensen was Danish. Five years earlier he had left the Black Angels in Denmark after an internal struggle which, rumour had it, was about whether those Black Angels would start trafficking drugs or not. Jensen moved to Sweden and Helsingborg, and then made his way to Stockholm and Skärholmen, where he founded the Red Bears. Now they had become a support club, but they still had a lot to prove to their main biker gang.

"And since the whole of Eastern Europe is pretty well represented in your lot, I wouldn't say that you're particularly Finnish, are you?"

Suddenly Jensen looked as if he had grown tired of this charade. Perhaps he could feel a tightening of the steel wire that had been inserted to hold his ribcage together after his by-pass.

"Victor can't stop us from taking our rightful revenge. The kid's only nineteen."

"We know that Jarmo is Penti's nephew and we're sorry he was stabbed."

Penti, the man with the walrus moustache, nodded appreciatively.

"O.K.," Jensen said. "Jarmo was attacked, almost killed, by some snotty kid who wanted a piece of our territory. If we don't hit back, every gang in town is going to think they can do whatever the fuck they want, without consequences."

"But we've no idea what actually happened," Sardor went on. "Maybe Jarmo was just being a little prick, maybe he was trying to hit on the wrong chick in the Kvarnen bar."

Penti reached for his pistol, but Jensen gave a dismissive wave with a chubby hand.

Sardor lowered his voice.

"Victor doesn't want you to escalate this. We'll find the son of a bitch who did it. Give me Eje and the two of us will take care of it."

The Count continued to drum his fingers.

Sardor noticed that Jensen reacted when Umarov's name was mentioned. He was, after all, *vor*, someone you don't wind up. Everyone knew perfectly well that the F.S.B. were capable of sending over a couple of their men before any biker gang or the Northern Networks even had time to reload.

"So you know who the culprit is?" Jensen said, regaining his composure. "That makes things easier, of course. Just give us the name and we won't have to wipe out all the Lions and K-Men in town. It'll save a whole load of ammunition."

"Give us a few days. Your kid's under sedation after all. Make a point of being the perfect nearest and dearest at the hospital. Bring chocolates for the staff and other stuff they like."

Jensen's face had now taken on a purple-blue tone.

"You Russians just don't get it. If you attack one of us, we hit back. It's what's known as a law of nature."

Some of the heavies in the room chuckled. They seemed to think that was acceptable now.

In less than a second, Sardor had pulled out his double-edged knife and driven it through the vice-president's hand, between the second and third metacarpals. The pain skewered The Count's brain and his deafening scream silenced Jensen's laughter.

The gang members had snatched up their weapons and were pointing them at Sardor. At the same time, Sardor had bent down to draw his Glock from the inside of his boot. He now pressed the muzzle against Jensen's fat temple.

Jensen instantly raised one hand and the scene froze.

"I see our would-be Rambo's come to life. His famous temper just got the better of him."

Sardor was breathing deeply, trying to get his pulse down. He held the pistol rock steady.

"Let's go through this one more time. Regards from Victor, he wants you to know that we'll take care of it."

A forced smile from Jensen.

"Of course. We can live with that, like civilised people. Tell Victor. And Eje goes with you."

The Count was snorting hard through his nose, trying to suppress the pain.

Sardor wrenched out the knife. Tucked his pistol away.

Everybody lowered their weapons as one.

"But if you haven't delivered up a name or a head on a platter within one week, we'll open the gates to hell," Jensen said.

"And for future reference," Sardor said, "never call an Uzbek a Russian."

INTENSIVE CARE UNIT, NOBEL HOSPITAL
Friday, 7.vi

The burns unit was right at the back of the I.C.U. and easy to find. Each of the three specialist rooms was as large as a classroom. The environment was so sterile that one could have performed an operation in there. Tekla put on her protective clothing, walked through the airlock and was met by a strange sight: a middle-aged woman bent over the injured patient was raising her reading glasses, as if she were in a museum, examining an unusual species of insect. A nurse stood beside her, winding a fresh bandage around one of the patient's arms. Tekla went over to them.

"How's it going?"

"He was tachycardic this morning and the duty doctor took it as a sign that he was in pain. We've upped the Propofol."

The woman, who was leaning over the patient, looked up and held out her hand.

"Rebecka Nilsén, Inspector of police from N.O.D."

"N.O.D.?"

Nilsén smiled and inclined her head slightly. "The National Operations Department. The police nationwide division, to put it simply. People bring us in on what may be . . . slightly bigger crimes."

"Bigger . . . ?"

"But who are you?" Nilsén said.

"Tekla Berg, I'm a doctor in A. & E. and—"

"Ah, you're our contact person," the woman said, smiling warmly as she removed her spectacles and left them to dangle on her chest at the end of a thin, fluorescent-yellow string. Her salt-and-pepper hair had been tightly combed and gathered in a short ponytail. Tekla noted the dark cadmium-purple lipstick. In short: a stylish woman of fifty plus. "Isn't that right?"

"My boss asked me to keep you updated."

"It's so nice only to have to keep track of one mobile number. So, when can we expect to question our John Doe, then?"

"John . . . ?"

"I know, I'm *crazy* about American movies," Nilsén said with an easy smile. "'Seven', have you seen it? John Doe, the man with no known identity. We're trying to get the forensic specialists from Solna over here, but they're up to their arses in work, if you'll pardon the expression. Or rather, it's a matter of priorities. Everything in life has to do with prioritisation."

Tekla felt a bit awkward when the policewoman winked at her, as if she were a little schoolgirl who would get a reward provided she did as she was told.

Nilsén was apparently not the sort of woman to wait for an answer.

"Your colleagues – or competitors? – on the Solna side are, after all, a little closer to Forensics on the Karolinska campus. Why does everything always have to be about politics . . . ? So, what do you think?"

"About what?"

Nilsén suddenly had an idea. "Wait. Is it O.K. if I record our conversation? Just so I don't forget anything. Not a formal interview, in other words."

"Of course," Tekla said, watching as the colourful police inspector fumbled with her mobile.

"Right! When can we talk to him?"

"I'm not the person to ask."

The nurse cut in: "You can ask Eva."

At that moment, Eva Elmqvist walked in, the intensive care physician in charge of the burns unit. Tekla had seen her in action in a number of acute cases and had been very impressed.

"What are you going to ask me about?"

"When do you think we'll be able to speak to our patient here?" Nilsén said.

Elmqvist laughed out loud as she put on her protective clothing.

"Come back in the autumn. And you should be wearing a face mask. He's very vulnerable to infection."

Both Tekla and Nilsén put on masks.

"What do you mean?" Nilsén said.

"I'm serious," Elmqvist said, taking over the bandaging from the nurse. "Does it look to you as if he's going to be contactable any time soon?" Then she turned to Tekla. "You're from the emergency clinic, aren't you?"

"Tekla Berg."

"Göran called."

Tekla could not help noticing: only "Göran".

"I can well imagine."

Eva turned to the police inspector.

"We'll be in touch. Or rather, Tekla will be in touch, when he comes to. Won't you, Tekla?"

"Absolutely."

Tekla wondered if this was how children of divorced parents felt when their parents discussed dates and times over their heads.

"Purely out of curiosity," Elmqvist said, "not that it's any of my business, but what do you think he's done?"

Nilsén paused before answering.

"We're taking a broad view of this. Our first assumption is that he was someone living in the building, who was down in the laundry or the storerooms and couldn't make it up in time when the fire broke out. As I'm sure you've read or heard, the new electrical cabling in the building caught fire and burned incredibly quickly. All around the basement and then up the core of the building. Including the bike store and the rubbish room. There are many leads in this, and one that we'll be following up is, of course, the shoddy construction materials angle, but that'll be a later investigation."

"Shoddy construction materials?" Tekla said.

"That's what it looks like. Dodgy insulation on the wires and cables. But the main focus is on who this man is and what he was doing in the building. And if he had anything to do with the explosion."

"Which came first, the explosion or the fire?" Elmqvist said.

It was clear from Nilsén's expression that she was intrigued by the doctor, who seemed to be about the same age. "We don't know."

"But he was found outside an equipment room?" Tekla said.

"A switchroom," Nilsén corrected her, unbuttoning her dark blue windcheater, which looked as if it had been bought in an exclusive vintage shop. "Why?"

"Was it locked?"

"The firefighters had to saw open the door to the cellar. What are you thinking?"

Tekla shook her head. "Nothing in particular."

Nilsén looked at her, intrigued.

"I was thinking that he could be a down-and-out or a drug addict," Tekla said.

"Or?"

"Or . . . he could be a lot of things."

"Did you test him for drugs?"

Tekla went through the lab list in her head as she looked at Elmqvist. She had not seen any toxicology tests.

"He had life-threatening burns," Elmqvist said, "and we were focusing on getting him rehydrated and other steps critical to keeping him alive."

"But aren't drug tests pretty standard?" Nilsén said.

"We'll check," Tekla said, butting in.

Elmqvist looked annoyed.

"As you may know," Nilsén said, "because it's been in the media since this morning, we're looking for a green van which was seen leaving the scene. Five men . . . or four, who drove away after the explosion."

"And this could be a sixth member of the same gang?" Tekla said.

"For example."

"So you're saying he could have been placing a bomb in the cellar or something like that?"

Nilsén smiled. "Well, let's not get carried away. We want to talk to him if . . . when he regains consciousness. We'll have to see what the forensics on the scene come up with. The fire service is still busy extinguishing the fire, so they won't be given access until later today."

"You think he's a terrorist, in other words?" Elmqvist exclaimed. She looked almost elated. As if the full force of global terrorism had at long last struck in Stockholm.

"Let me put it like this," Nilsén answered, "N.O.D. doesn't get involved in routine police operations."

"And is it usual for you to question a doctor on your own?" Elmqvist said, looking intently at her.

Nilsén smiled, wide-eyed. "You seem well informed. You've obviously had close contact with the legal world. But yes, we're a bit short on womanpower, and a number of our team are busy carrying out interviews."

"Is this an interview?" Tekla said.

"No."

An assistant nurse came in with a blue basin and began to remove the bandages from the patient's lower legs.

Tekla could smell smoke mixed with disinfectant. Nilsén came a few steps closer and, almost in a whisper, said:

"I spoke to the officer in charge at the fire. Is it true that you . . ." She rephrased what she was about to say. "Did you recognise the patient? From before the time you came across him at the scene, I mean."

Tekla pictured him before her, raising his hand towards her face.

"Why do you ask?"

"His reaction on the spot."

"I gave him an opioid antidote, Naloxone, because of the pinpoint pupils. Then he began to move."

"He briefly came to, in other words?"

"That's how I interpreted it."

"So you did, after all, suspect drug use? Even though you forgot to test for it in A. & E.?"

"For goodness' sake, give it a rest," Elmqvist sighed in irritation.

"He could have woken up for other reasons," Tekla went on. "It's by no means certain that he had been taking opioids."

"But when he came round . . . you didn't recognise him, did you?"

Tekla shook her head but avoided Nilsén's look. The assistant nurse had now removed the bandages from the legs and was carefully wiping away small pieces of charred skin with a sponge. Tekla saw the foot and felt a shock run right up her spinal column and into the back of her head.

Nilsén was looking at her mobile and raised her voice.

"I've got to head off. I guess we'll see each other at eleven tomorrow . . . or perhaps you don't work Saturdays?"

"I'm on duty," was Tekla's curt reply.

"Splendid. One more hard-working member of the community with no real life outside her job. Sounds familiar."

Tekla could not even summon up a feisty look. Her thoughts were elsewhere. Her body suddenly felt welded to the spot.

Nilsén gave Tekla her mobile number, "in case you think of something", and left the room.

Tekla remained standing there, checking the monitor. The patient's pulse was rapid. Good oxygen saturation, thanks to the ventilator taking over from his lungs.

Elmqvist laid down the bandaged arm.

"Poor guy."

"I'll say," Tekla agreed, her mouth dry.

"You seem to be staring a lot at that foot," Elmqvist said, clearly curious. "Is there something special about it?"

"What? No. No." Tekla took a hasty step back. "What about his skull? I thought I felt an indentation there."

"I didn't want to encourage their conspiracy theories," Elmqvist said, "but you're right, he has a fracture in the back of his head. With minor bleeding which doesn't need treating. I've just been talking to the neurosurgeon. We'll hold off and take another X-ray tomorrow morning. No, that's not his biggest worry." She drew the back of her hand gently across his chest. "Within forty-eight hours he'll have sepsis and pulmonary oedema. Then it'll be like sitting in a small rowing boat in a full-blown storm in the middle of the Atlantic. As for fluids, it's going to be a very difficult balancing act."

"How extensive do you reckon the burns are?"

"Eighty-five per cent."

That was close to Tekla's assessment at the scene.

"If he's around thirty years old, then he's got eighty-five plus thirty, in other words a 115 per cent risk of dying."

Elmqvist smiled. "Based on the old way of counting. But you're right: to put it bluntly, his prognosis is crap. The surgeons will have to get to it early if he's to have any chance."

Tekla tried to gather her thoughts. The foot. What was it about the patient's foot that made her whole body react?

Friday, 7.vi

"Be brief and to the point, no digressions," Collinder had said to Tekla before the meeting with Monica Carlsson.

Or else what, she thought as she picked up her mobile. She called the C.E.O.'s secretary, Fredrik Franck, and asked for directions to her office. She left the chaotic morning meeting, where they heard reports on the various burns victims, and eventually found the right lift. No patients had died during the night. A miracle, bearing in mind the extensive injuries suffered by the last patient, the one she was in charge of.

Going up in the lift she thought about the stabbing victim and the little boy with Gaucher disease. The only thing she had had time to read that morning was that they were both alive. The gang member had been operated on and his spleen removed, and he was now in the I.C.U. for further blood transfusions. The boy had sepsis and renal failure. It was not at all clear whether he would make it through the day.

The lift stopped with a jolt and the doors slid open. A long corridor led away towards the short side of the building, the one facing the city centre. She passed about ten empty, glass-fronted cubicles and was met by a thin man with cornflower blue spectacles, thinning hair and a navy-blue collared shirt, still with its shop creases.

"Tekla Berg, I presume? I'm Fredrik Franck. Great that you could get away. She's expecting you."

She.

The room was sober in style with white walls and a black leather sofa on the far side.

63

"Shall I go in?"

"Wait a moment."

The secretary pointed to an invisible spot on the grey-blue wall-to-wall carpet. Tekla came to a halt. Franck knocked on the door.

A muffled "Yes!" could be heard.

The secretary made a sweeping gesture towards the door.

"She'll see you now."

Tekla opened the door and walked in.

The first thing that struck her was the light. She tried to orientate herself, but it was difficult. The room stuck out from the building and had floor to ceiling windows on three sides. The morning sun streamed in and gave one the feeling of being in an airplane which had just climbed through the cloud cover.

A powerfully built woman was standing looking out of the north-facing window. She was wearing a dark purple suit and white shirt. High heels. A massive ring on one hand, visible all the way from where Tekla was standing.

"Our very own hero."

Tekla saw only the back of the short dark hair. She started when the door banged shut behind her.

"I came as soon as I could, but I had to brief the A. & E. doctors first."

The C.E.O. turned and met Tekla's look.

"Rumour has it that you were fully in control at the scene of the fire."

The woman walked over to her large desk and reached for a glass bowl with something black in it.

Tekla grasped the back of one of the two chairs facing the table. There was obviously not going to be any shaking of hands.

"It's hard to get a grip on such a chaotic situation." Tekla felt a little sick. "Do you mind if I sit down?"

"And also that you showed great calm and competence in the way you managed events in A. & E. last night. Two difficult cases at the same time. Not to mention the police barging in. It's not often that we are confronted with weapons in there."

Carlsson picked something out of the bowl and popped it into her mouth, then turned back to the window again.

Tekla took a chance and sat down. The light in the room was overwhelming. Then another association struck her: an open boat on a sun-drenched sea. She could see smoke still rising from Söder Tower a few hundred metres away.

"Have you worked over there?" Carlsson said.

"I haven't been since we fetched the last of the injured—"

"The showpiece," Carlson interrupted. "A sinking Titanic. If the consultancy scandals or the bungled construction work don't turn out to have been the actual iceberg, something else will come up soon, I guarantee it."

Her eyes were now fixed on something further away on the horizon.

"Oh, I see. No, I've only worked in—"

"Umeå. A residency in internal medicine from 2010 to 2015, followed by a sub-specialisation in emergency medicine. Before that, medicine and general medical training at Uppsala 2003 to 2010, and, in parallel with all of that, postgraduate studies at Uppsala 2003 to 2008. Dissertation in neuroscience. Why neuroscience?"

"Just turned out that way," Tekla lied, trying to work out what was going on. She saw no papers on Carlsson's desk.

"You were apparently the youngest woman since Hilma Strålin to defend your doctoral thesis."

"That's more than I knew."

"And then a bit of work on the side in psychiatry."

"Addiction care," Tekla corrected her.

Carlsson sat down in her chair immediately opposite Tekla and reached for the glass bowl.

"Have one. Good for people with low blood pressure like you. You tend to get dizzy, I see."

Tekla helped herself, putting one of the sugary-salt liquorice sweets into her mouth. She felt her jaw contract.

"Sometimes."

Tekla tried to wipe her sweaty hands on her trousers without being noticed. She saw a snow-white streak in Carlsson's otherwise jet-black hair. It reminded her of a badger. The C.E.O. was wearing heavy eye make-up that set off her green eyes and she had a thick amber necklace.

"Have you noticed that the number of drug overdoses has increased during the last week?"

"Not really, but—"

"Something has happened which I don't yet understand. And there are more on the way."

Tekla thought about the burns victim. Had he O.D.'d on some form of opioid after all?

"Honestly, I can't for the life of me understand why one would want to take drugs," Carlsson said.

"It may not always be a case of wanting," Tekla said.

Carlsson looked fascinated as she met Tekla's eyes.

"I prefer a decent glass of white myself. A Domaine Leflaive Montrachet Grand Cru, for example. What do you say?"

"I don't know much about wines."

"No, otherwise you'd have known that a bottle of Leflaive would set you back fifty thousand kronor."

"Per bottle?"

Carlsson smiled.

"What are you trying to run away from?" Carlsson said.

"I'm sorry?"

"One's either chasing after something one desires or running from something one's afraid of. You've managed to do more in fifteen years than most doctors achieve in a lifetime. So my suspicion is that you're trying to *escape* from something. Correct?"

Carlsson took another liquorice monkey and pinched it between her front teeth. She looked over at the north-facing window again.

Tekla breathed a sigh of relief as Carlsson took her eyes off her. She considered what to say. Death was always just around the corner. All her life, Tekla had woken up in the mornings and leaped out of bed, afraid of missing out on something fun. And fear of death had hung over her like a sword of Damocles. So yes indeed, she had been rushing, running fast, doing many things in parallel, afraid that life would suddenly come to an end.

Carlsson let the question go. "You heard that those idle sods at N.S.K. couldn't accept more than two patients yesterday?"

"As far as I could tell—"

"Two! At a burns unit which cost the taxpayers more than 300 million kronor. What a shambles. Insane. If this had happened in Britain or the U.S.A., heads would have rolled on the other side of the Solna Bridge a year ago. But not in this socialist empire of ours. Feeble bloody politicians, don't want to get their well-manicured fingernails dirty."

Tekla couldn't help staring at Carlsson's perfectly groomed, dark-red nails; they looked as if they could claw out the eyes of any animal you might care to name.

"You published an impressive number of articles during your time in Umeå. Do you like to keep lots of plates spinning at the same time?"

"I don't dislike it."

Carlsson smiled, clasped her hands in front of her and looked curiously at Tekla.

"Type A, in other words. But without the sport. I see you don't have time for that."

"I use the stairs when I can," Tekla said.

"But you forget to eat. Have another one."

Carlsson pushed the bowl forward. She reached out a finger, touched the keyboard and looked at the screen beside her.

"But you don't have that much contact with . . . Clemence Rågsjö these days, do you?"

Tekla froze.

"We haven't been in touch for a while."

"So I gather. It would seem that your old research supervisor had certain views on the research you were doing."

Carlsson took her eyes off the screen. She got up and limped a little as she walked back to the panorama window.

"Tekla, the fact is that those of us who have that little extra something, who want to get to places beyond the reach of others, we sometimes have to push the boundaries. You and I see opportunities where others see obstacles. We see clear paths where others see impassable swamps." The C.E.O. stared at Tekla. "Am I right, Tekla, that you find it hard to talk to anyone about your need to achieve your ambitions?"

Tekla was not sure if she was expected to answer. She thought the best way of dealing with this bizarre situation was to look as non-committal as possible.

"Certain people, like Göran, feel content and comfortable with what they have. They're like –" Carlsson stroked the lapel of her jacket – "curling stones which glide smoothly forward without the slightest friction. To go somewhere else, to change direction, is against their nature." She turned and tapped on the window. "*That* place over there is not something to be proud of. It's the very definition of a failure. And people like you and I don't want to fail, we don't accept failure."

Tekla was finding it hard to hide her confusion.

"What do you think about chance?" Carlsson said.

"Chance?"

"Chance."

"Not sure I think all that much about it."

"Good. Neither did my father. He was a pastor and said that it's either God or science that can explain the world. Nothing in between. He hated chance."

Tekla was about to mention games of dice, but thought better of it.

Carlsson came back to her desk and leaned very close to Tekla.

She seemed to be contemplating some weighty decisions. Then she suddenly clapped her hands together.

Tekla flinched.

"You know why we became doctors, don't you?"

Tekla looked up and wondered what sort of doctor Carlsson might be. A pathologist perhaps? For her part, the answer was clear: to save lives. As many as possible. And without discrimination.

"Because we're heroes. And heroes can keep secrets like nobody else. Comes with the job description, one might say."

Tekla sat dead still. In the circumstances, she would not have been surprised to see Carlsson unfold a cape and fly up into the sky with a large S painted on her back.

Carlsson walked round the table and sat down in her chair again.

"What do you say to having coffee together one of these days? Just you and me."

"We . . . could maybe do that."

"I have a favourite place, but I can't tell you where it is. If I did, I'd have to kill you." She looked up. "Just kidding."

Carlsson looked down at her computer screen again.

"The Nobel Hospital will win back its reputation. I'm going to see to that."

Tekla listened. Once again, she had no idea how to answer.

"You can leave the door open when you go."

Tekla stood up. She would have liked to walk out backwards, so as to keep an eye on the situation, but then she would probably have tripped over her own feet.

In the lift on the way down she wondered whose hero she actually was, and whether she had, indeed, obeyed Collinder's instruction to stick to the point.

69

Saturday morning, 8.vi

In an attempt to turn his thoughts to something else, Magnus Lundgren focused his mind on Sixten Andersson's square face, with its age spots. He jumped down into the boat and began to tidy up. It would be nice to be out on the water again soon, he was sure it would calm his nerves. He needed to talk to Håkan Dahl, even if his old mate scoffed at his misgivings.

Andersson was a retired fisherman from Trosa, whose fishing cottage Lundgren had been borrowing for more than ten years. As a thank you, Lundgren would leave a five-hundred-kronor note and a bottle of brandy next to the coffee kettle in the mini-kitchen. He also got to use Andersson's motorboat, which had a cabin large enough for two, in exchange for filling it up with two-stroke fuel and leaving it chained to the ramshackle jetty. For his part, Andersson told Lundgren about the secret fishing spots, the ones which only the old guard in the area knew about. And shallow inlets, always south-facing, where it was most likely that the water temperature would have risen by a few tenths of a degree and got the sea trout going. Lundgren used to check with a thermometer; seven degrees was perfect. He had found a few choice places where there was a prevailing south-east wind. Andersson would bang on at him every time he came to fetch the key: "It has to be a *steady* wind."

Lundgren would drive out on a Friday evening, stopping very briefly at Andersson's apartment in the centre of Trosa, and then go on to the cottage before it got dark. He would bring along a loaf of bread, some sausage and beer, fill the stove with firewood and light a cigarette. Then he carefully sharpened his fish hooks by the light of the candle, checked the weather forecast and made a plan for the following day. He would usually go to bed fully dressed, set the alarm, and sleep better than he did the rest of the year. In the morning he hurried out before sunrise, taking his three favourite fishing rods, among them a wonderful nine-foot Berkley. That and his Shimano reel, mounted with eighteen-millimetre braided line, would guarantee a direct connection between fisherman and fish. The right feeling. On bright days, he would also bring along his Polaroid sunglasses, so that he could see the fish chasing after the lure. Not for nothing did his sister Astrid call him a fishing fanatic.

Today was a Saturday at the beginning of June, not the ideal season. But this time was not so much about the fish as the company. Lundgren looked at his watch. Annoyingly, Dahl was late, he had said that he needed to fix something before the party that evening.

Lundgren put out the cushions in the stern and was coiling two hawsers together when he saw Dahl walking along the jetty towards him, his kit bag over his shoulder and two rods in his hand. Tight, brown leather jacket, blue jeans, heavy leather boots and, as always, a navy polo shirt.

Lundgren immediately felt his pulse increase slightly.

"Is that old tub still afloat?" Dahl said, tossing his kit to Lundgren.

"It's good enough. We can't all afford a Buster XXL."

Dahl loosened the bow rope and shouted:

"That didn't cost me a single krona."

"I can imagine," Lundgren muttered to himself as he put his friend's fishing gear in the bow.

Dahl jumped down into the boat and took out his mobile.

"Christ, this is going to be nice. I'm disconnecting right now. There." He switched his telephone off. "Even a boss is entitled to take time off. Let's go."

"Aye, aye, Cap'n," Lundgren said, untying at the stern. He started up the motor and gave an extra tug at the canvas cabin of the boat, to secure it. Then he took a cold Lapin Kulta from the cooler bag and waved it in front of Dahl, who accepted it gratefully.

"I expect there's a lot going on at the moment," Lundgren said.

"I'll say," Dahl answered, taking a mouthful. "After the Söder Tower business, everyone's on their toes."

"I was thinking about this evening too."

"Yes, but that's under control. I skipped all the activities. Bungy jumping and so on."

"Cool that you wanted to tag along today."

"Hell, who'd miss a chance to hang out with their best friend?" Dahl replied as he looked across the water. "Happens way too seldom."

Lundgren reversed out from the jetty and steered the boat away from the inlet. The sun was climbing above the horizon and there was a light breeze blowing in from the south. Pretty good conditions, Lundgren thought, as he opened the throttle. After all the years, he could read Dahl like a book. He looked relaxed. The hand drawn through slicked-back dark hair and the legs casually crossed up on the seat suggested assurance and harmony. Lundgren could not understand how a man with so much going on was able to unwind. It was impressive. Lundgren could hardly manage to keep the three rooms in his apartment tidy, do his work and take himself off to the gym on a regular basis.

"Everything alright?" Dahl yelled over the din of the engine.

"All good, thanks," Lundgren answered, holding up his can of beer in a toast. He was trying to decide when the time would be right for a chat, but felt they should start fishing first.

"Why don't we have a game one of these days?" Dahl shouted. "It's been a while."

"Absolutely," Lundgren answered. "I can book a court this week. Are you doing any jogging?"

"You *are* allowed to say I've got fat." Dahl smiled, patting the beginnings of a beer belly. "Five more years to the Big Five O. It's O.K. to have put on a pound or two by now, isn't it? Lucky for you that you get so much exercise at work."

"Have you started to plan for your party?"

"I thought I'd leave that to you."

"Sure," Lundgren said, the irony in Dahl's remark not lost on him. He had never given a party, never invited Dahl to anything other than take-aways, and only ever saw his sister Astrid, Dahl and a handful of other people. Dahl on the other hand had Stockholm's largest social network and loved both going to and organising big parties. Besides that, he was a good cook, especially when it came to meat and barbecues.

"What's it going to be?" Dahl asked with a smile. "Roast beef and potato salad? Plus a few cherry tomatoes?"

"And some cans of beer," Lundgren said. "But I think I'll leave the entertainment to you."

"Thought you'd say that," Dahl said, looking superior. "You ought to come along this evening. While we're on the subject of entertainment . . ."

After twenty minutes at full speed, Lundgren slowed down and turned in by a rocky outcrop. At this time of year, there was a chance of finding trout among the reeds along this stretch of the coast. When they had slid into the cove, he stopped the boat and put the engine into neutral, leaving them to drift. He looked at Dahl, who was happily swigging his beer. The big pouch of snus he had taken was breaking up and leaving black streaks between his teeth. They took their time assembling their fishing equipment.

Lundgren drank a few mouthfuls of Lapin Kulta and thought about the time when they were living in Dahl's mother's old four-room apartment in the Drakensberg area. Removal boxes lining the sitting room walls remained unopened during the three years they were there. A balcony one could hardly get onto because of all the empty beer cans. The steady stream of girls. That was during their first year at police college and much had happened since then, especially in Dahl's life. Lundgren had slaved away for a while on the administrative side and then taken the big step of joining the S.W.A.T. team, where he was now one of the senior and most experienced members. Dahl had given up asking him what would be his "next move". Was there even going to be one? Meanwhile, Dahl had been making ever greater strides in his career.

"How's Angelica?" Lundgren said.

"No idea," Dahl answered as he tied on a lure.

"But she's happy in Malmö?"

"I don't get what she sees in that I.T. guy."

"As if you cared."

"True," Dahl said with a smile.

The boat was lying almost motionless, sheltered as it was from the sea. Lundgren felt the sun warm his face and took off his down vest.

"And the kids?"

"Thought I'd bring Mattias along for a short trip to Alaska this summer. He's studying in Lund now, but should be able to take some time off." Dahl tried a first cast. "Some real fishing."

"Wow. Sounds expensive. And Sara?"

"Nothing doing. Can't get her out of the teenage morass. Since I don't have Facebook or any other social media app, I don't exist in her world."

"You could try ringing her."

"She ignores my calls. Just texts if she wants me to Swish her some money. And you?"

"You mean holiday plans or . . ."

Lundgren stood up at the other end of the boat and cast.

"Actually, I wanted to hear if you'd recovered from your latest crash-and-burn," Dahl smirked.

Lundgren adjusted the drag on his reel.

"We had a call-out on Thursday evening. Armed bikers at the Nobel Hospital because a member of their gang was in A. & E. after being stabbed."

Dahl gave his friend a surprised look.

"What's that got to do with your love life?"

"The doctor who looked after the injured guy—"

"Ah!" Dahl burst out. "Now you're talking."

"Dead good-looking," Lundgren said.

"There you go. Did you take her number?"

Lundgren rubbed the stubble on his face. "Sadly not. Don't even know her name."

"O.K. Well, you'll probably get another chance. Age?"

"Like, thirty. Maybe thirty-five."

"Perfect. Tall, short?"

"Quite tall and thin. Short, dark hair parted at the side."

"Sounds a bit boyish. Kind of your type, right?"

"And she wouldn't even register on your radar," Lundgren said. He could see the doctor's eyes before him in A. & E. "There was something Sami about her. Something with her eyes . . ."

"You need sex, that much seems pretty clear," Dahl said seriously. "Were you involved in the fire too?"

"Yes. It was terrible."

"I'm glad I've climbed the greasy pole and don't get called out on routine ops any longer."

"Congratulations on the new job, by the way."

"Thanks," Dahl said. "Superintendent has a ring to it that Inspector doesn't, I think."

They fished on in silence. Opened another beer each. Lundgren realised that he could not wait any longer. He swallowed a few more big mouthfuls, then said:

"Tell me, what happened in the end with that money from Haninge?"

Dahl tucked in another pouch of snus and made a long cast towards the reeds.

"Why do you ask?"

"Just wondering," Lundgren said, feeling how the palms of his hands began to tingle as they broke out in sweat.

"Don't worry about that," Dahl said quietly. "It's all cool. Totally cool."

"But the investigator I gave the bag to—"

75

"It's cool," Dahl interrupted. "Did you hear me? You can drop it."

"It's just that—"

"*I* haven't said a word about Solvalla, have I?" Dahl cut in with a steely look, putting his rod down in the boat.

"Because you promised me you'd never mention it again," Lundgren said, avoiding Dahl's eyes.

"Then surely you understand that it's not something I want to *have* to raise," Dahl said. He leaned against the skipper's seat.

"Well, in that case, don't," Lundgren said.

"I feel I really don't have a choice, now you've started banging on about Haninge," Dahl said in a hard tone.

"I thought we had a deal?" Lundgren said. "I know I really messed up at Solvalla, but that was ten years ago and I've stopped gambling."

"And I magicked away that debt collector, didn't I?"

Lundgren nodded; he would have preferred never to hear about that episode again. He said:

"And that's precisely why I felt bound to help when you asked me to, out in Haninge."

Dahl crumpled up the beer can and dropped it in the bottom of the boat.

"Any chance of another one?"

Lundgren bent down and took out two more from the box.

"That means we're square, then?"

"We're even," Dahl said. "Solvalla–Haninge, check, check."

They stood and looked in different directions for some long, silent minutes.

"Sorry," Lundgren said and turned to Dahl. "I've just become a bit paranoid now that Central Investigations have got going. All units are being scrutinised. Are you sure you removed me from the raid?"

Dahl suddenly spread his arms and laughed.

"Don't I always deliver on a promise?"

"Yes, but—"

"Well then. You can rely on me. Your name is not in the report. You were shown as off sick when the raid happened."

"For sure?"

"For sure. Just relax now and enjoy the fishing."

Dahl stood with his legs wide apart, braced against some wavelets which were rolling in against the boat.

"Are you not joining us this evening, then? It's going to be wild."

"I can imagine," Lundgren said. "But it's your gang."

"You know Petter too."

"But not from schooldays. In any case, stag parties aren't my thing. Too much testosterone."

Dahl gave a laugh. "Says the two-metre tall, hundred-kilo action copper."

"One ninety-eight," Lundgren said. "But, sad to say, I passed the one hundred mark some months ago." He looked up at the sky. Seagulls had begun to circle the motorboat and some clouds had drawn in from the south. He would have liked to hear more about the money, but knew he would never get anywhere with Dahl. He kept his secrets well. Always had.

"Heard anything more about the van that disappeared?" Lundgren said.

"From Söder Tower?"

Lundgren nodded and got out another beer. He looked away at the horizon, as if to try and see if the smoke column was still hanging in the sky.

"Not a peep," Dahl said. "But what a blaze."

"It's a miracle nobody died."

Lundgren's thoughts drifted away and ended up with the good-looking doctor from A. & E. last Thursday. He was hoping that he'd get to see her again, while knowing full well that it would probably never happen.

"What are you thinking about?" Dahl said.

"The fire."

"You're lying."

"I am?" Lundgren said.

"You've never been able to lie. You're way too decent for that."

"Good job that there are some who've not made it their speciality."

"What?"

"You heard."

"What the fuck do you mean?" Dahl said.

"Nothing."

"Go on, say it," Dahl spat.

"Forget it."

"Dead right. Forget it."

"O.K. Chill," Lundgren said and left it at that. He thought about all the times he had seen Dahl lose his temper when drunk. All his inappropriate remarks. All the stupid moves, especially against women in pubs. It was actually weird that they were still friends. He had never confronted Dahl after any of the idiotic things he'd done, he had just let it all go. It made him feel spineless.

Lundgren took out another beer from the freezer bag and threw it to Dahl.

"Here. Cool yourself down a bit and we'll see who gets the first bite."

"Shall we bet five hundred?" Dahl teased him.

"I don't gamble."

"Really?"

"Anymore."

"That's right," Dahl said with a sneer. "The devil's given up alcohol in old age."

GULLMARSPLAN, STOCKHOLM
Saturday morning, 8.vi

Tekla was woken by a car hooting outside. She went to close the balcony door and, at the same time, realised she was frozen. She had to stand in the hot shower for a long time before she stopped shaking. The apartment was not as soundproof as it might be, but apart from that she liked her home of a little over a year. She had bought it for three and a half million, the exact amount the bank had been prepared to let her borrow. Her search engine had been set to map view, she had checked to see how close to the hospital she could come and still get a two-room flat. She ended up in Gullmarsplan, an area she had never heard of, or had any connection with. But she was happy there.

She went into the kitchen. The key to the cupboard above the microwave was at the bottom of the packet of rooibos tea. She opened it, took out the old ice cream box, which was behind some wine bottles, flipped the lid open and confirmed what she already knew: only ten little balls left. She took one, tore apart the soft toilet paper and poured the white powder into a glass of cold coffee from the day before, stirred with a spoon and drank it in one. Her breakfast cocktail: a double kick, amphetamine and caffeine, those siblings who go so well together.

The flood of random images at last began to fall into place, each in its own pigeonhole. Tekla had started to take amphetamines in order to be able to study and work in parallel. She needed money, partly to pay for her mother's private dementia care home, partly to support Simon's wayward life. She studied medicine during the day and had a job in psychiatric care in the evenings and at night.

She upped the dosages to be able to cope. Reckoned it was self-medication rather than abuse. When she needed to wind down, she would take sleeping tablets, sometimes even benzodiazepines. But it was mainly her photographic memory that benefited from the amphetamines. At an early age, she had noticed how the mental images from her days would spin around when she was trying to get to sleep. She was kept awake by them. As a teenager, she tried hash and alcohol but it only made the sleeping problems worse. Soporifics gave her a hangover the next morning and other psycho-active drugs just brought with them side effects. It was not until she read an article about an Indian memory master who had had similar difficulties and who had used cocaine to sleep that she tried taking amphetamines when she went to bed. She noticed at once that the mental images became calmer. They began to find their proper slots in her brain. Like a stormy sky full of whirling leaflets which suddenly descend and settle into small, clearly marked boxes. With that came peace of mind and, with the help of sleeping pills, a good night's rest.

Tekla lay on the sofa and ran through the events of the previous day. For a moment her thoughts dwelled on the patient with the burns injuries in the I.C.U. To the right: the bare wall, a window giving onto the rest of the department, closed Venetian blinds. She knew exactly how many slats there were. The man's weight displayed in bright orange digital numbers: seventy kilos. In her mind's eye she saw every detail on the metal frame, the thick mattress with the hourly vibrating function that prevented bedsores. Diagonally up to the left: the monitor. Pulse 104. Saturation 92.

Tekla rubbed her temples. Her memory was functioning perfectly, like a camera incessantly taking photographs.

But the foot. Why could she not see the burnt man's foot?

Tekla went into the hallway, put on her coat and a pair of Converse trainers. She pulled the apartment door shut without double-locking it. It was six in the morning. Tekla usually walked to the hospital through Skanstull, turning left on Ringvägen and reaching the Nobel after a brisk twenty-minute march. But today she instead turned right after the bridge, passing the seedy beer dives on Ringvägen and cutting across Lilla Blecktornsparken to Katarina Bangata. She slowed down, feeling sweaty, and took off the thin H&M coat, which was almost falling apart at the seams. She needed some new clothes. Tekla regretted not having put on socks, her feet felt sticky in the red Converses. She wished that she had put on a skirt, or lighter trousers, rather than the washed-out jeans which she always seemed to end up wearing, regardless of the season. But there was really no point in throwing on anything but one's most comfortable clothes just to walk to and from the hospital, with no chance of meeting anyone who would care or even notice.

She let out her short hair, put the hairband in her pocket and took a can of Coca-Cola from her shoulder bag. Drank half of it, disposed of the rest. Here, only a hundred metres down from Ringvägen's morning traffic, it was quiet. There was not much to see or explore in this corner of Södermalm. No hip bars like the ones on Skånegatan, the epicentre for all the I.P.A. haunts.

On the first floor, just above the words ". . . Restaurant & Bar", the blind was pulled down. Just as it had been the other times she had passed the building in the last few weeks. The apartment where Simon lived, for which she had been paying all these years. A heavy outlay, which she had financed with the help of many extra shifts and by swallowing countless bombs. She keyed in the code, ran up to the first floor and rang the doorbell. It still said *Simon Berg* on the handwritten piece of paper just above the letterbox. No-one opened. She waited for five minutes, rang his mobile but there was no answer. Nor was there a ringtone to be heard inside the apartment. She was beginning to think that it was pointless. He had probably been evicted. Or he was staying with some friend and smoking dope from morning till night.

She went out into the street again and got to the hospital an hour before the morning briefing.

Tekla came to a sudden halt outside the hospital entrance: the burns victim's foot had acquired a shape and, with that, her pulse increased. She had to pass by the I.C.U. before she started work.

All was quiet there. The night team were in the process of handing over to the day staff. Tekla tracked down the nurse responsible for Burns Room 1.

"I just wanted to check something I forgot yesterday."

The nurse, Pirkko, seemed uninterested.

"Go ahead. The assistant nurse is in there."

"Thanks," Tekla said as she went into Room 1. The assistant nurse was reading a book with a brightly coloured cover.

"Hi," she said in surprise.

"Tekla Berg. I'm the doctor in charge. Just wanted to see how he's doing. Pirkko out there said it was O.K."

The nurse waited for her to continue.

Tekla clarified:

"You can go on reading."

"O.K.," the nurse said, subsiding back into her love story.

Tekla tried to focus on her breathing. She pretended to sway a little and grasped hold of the bed.

The nurse looked up.

"Are you O.K.?"

"Ahh . . . just a bit of hypoglycaemia. Didn't have time for breakfast."

The young woman put her book down on the windowsill.

"Shall I get you some juice?"

"Thanks. That would be good."

The nurse hesitated for a second.

"It'll only take a minute. Ring the bell if there's anything."

When the nurse had gone, Tekla looked at the patient in his bed. The sheet covered his body, apart from his face and the bandaged arms. She carefully drew away the fabric at the foot of the bed, uncovering what she had come to see.

Half of the right foot was relatively undamaged and she could see the big toe sticking up. The joint was noticeably crooked. Tekla had only seen one like it before, on the person she had grown up with. She had played with him on the beach, buried him in sand until only the toe was visible. And the happy face, of course. The toothy grin, the straggly, dark hair. The dimples which often appeared when he was in a good mood.

Tekla allowed her exhausted body to collapse on the bed. It was in breach of all the rules of hygiene, but right now the laws of gravity had the upper hand.

She poked carefully at the big toe. Heard the assistant nurse out in the airlock.

Tekla jumped to her feet and straightened the sheet. Now she really was about to faint, so she began pumping her feet.

The assistant nurse came in with a glass of juice and a rye bread and cheese sandwich.

"Here you are."

"Thanks a ton," Tekla managed to say. She stared at the patient's head. Wrapped up and impossible to identify.

One shoulder was bare. It was muscular. That wasn't right, was it? He had never been particularly strong.

She drank the juice, put the sandwich down on the bedside table and left the room. In the lift on the way down she tried to compose herself. Sat down on an empty bench outside the hospital entrance, next to the fountain. It was a beautiful early summer morning. Glorious, in fact.

That toe, it was identical . . . Tekla felt the nausea hit her like a fist in the midriff. She suddenly vomited on the ground in front of her. The sour taste of juice and puke.

Could it really be Simon?

Could it really be her own brother who was lying there in the I.C.U., with eighty-five per cent burns?

Monica Carlsson was sitting with her feet up on the footstool, resting her sore back in her easy chair. She was holding a large cup of black coffee and had the *Svenska Dagbladet* weekend magazine on her lap. She could hear Gregor's footsteps going into the bathroom and realised that her delightful morning interlude would soon be over. Carlsson pressed two codeine tablets out of their strip and swallowed the pills with the coffee. She continued reading about a new method for treating varicose veins. Akademiklinikens latest efforts with her thighs had not been impressive. She had called the chief physician at home and given him an ultimatum: either he paid back the cost of the treatment and gave her a gift voucher for thirty thousand kronor, or she would call her old school friend Torbjörn Hedenius, a Stockholm county councillor, and ask him to revoke the clinic's licence. "He owes me a favour," she told him matter-of-factly. The money was in her account that same afternoon and three days later she had a matte gold envelope with a handwritten address lying on the hall carpet.

Gregor Dabrowski sank into the sofa and put his coffee cup on the glass table.

"You know that's made of glass?" Carlsson said without raising her eyes.

"Sleep badly?"

Dabrowski picked up *Dagens Industri*'s weekend supplement.

"That's so typical," Carlsson said.

"There's nothing new about your sleeping badly, is there, darling? Maybe you should quit your late-night drinking."

Carlsson hauled herself to her feet and limped to the open kitchen area with its long, one-piece L-shaped kitchen counter. The company which delivered it had had to use a crane to manoeuvre it in from the balcony. The pavement on Skeppsbron had been blocked for half a day to get the monstrosity in.

She began cutting the grapefruit and turned on the juice machine.

"Typical patriarchal behaviour."

"What?"

"Just because I ask you to be careful with our furniture, you claim that I suffer from insomnia. Too bad for you that you can't blame it on my period any longer."

Dabrowski turned the pages of the pale pink newspaper.

"Don't you think you're being a bit touchy?"

"There you go again."

"What?"

"Referring to feelings and biological clocks instead of being rational and sticking to the facts."

Carlsson poured the juice into two large glasses and filled them with crushed ice from the refrigerator door. She walked over to her husband, a senior editor at Sweden's largest book publisher, and held out the glass.

"Here you are . . . *darling*."

Dabrowski took the juice.

"There's no need to be sarcastic."

"That's true. You're way too affected by your feelings, always have been. That's why you were never made C.E.O."

Dabrowski put down the newspaper.

"I meant, you shouldn't use terms of endearment unless you mean them," he said.

"Says the man who's bought ten roses for his wife every Friday these last five years. I wonder which particular guilty conscience they're intended to ease."

Tenderly, Dabrowski took his wife's arm and patted the sofa cushion next to him with his other hand.

"Come here and give an old man a hug instead of being grumpy. What's happened this week that's made my sugar pie sourer than this hideous juice?"

Carlsson smiled and shook her head.

"If only you knew."

"Tell me."

Carlsson went back to her favourite chair.

"Why don't you start up on your own?" she asked.

"Too late."

"You've just grown bitter. You're still the best editor in town. More Nobel Prize winners to your credit than anyone else."

"It's not enough."

Carlsson pulled at her gold chain.

"Anyway, I wonder who's the bitter one around here?" Dabrowski said.

"What are you insinuating?"

"Darling. I know how badly you wanted the top job at the N.S.K."

"And?"

"You didn't get it."

"Nope. I didn't get it," Carlsson said.

She got up and went over to the refrigerator. Poured a glass of white wine which she immediately drained.

"A bit early for that," Dabrowski's soft voice said.

"Why don't you get a grip on your own life instead?" she snapped.

"You're avoiding the question. Why are you being so contrary today?"

Dabrowski finished his juice.

"I've been waiting for the right moment," Carlsson said and sat down on the sofa.

"For what?"

"To open fire."

"Isn't it a bit early for the hunting season?"

"I'd say the timing's perfect."

Carlsson picked up some Yahtzee dice and rolled them from hand to hand. She looked at her husband's big nose. His distinctive high forehead. The thin lips which were often pursed, particularly when he was reading some new, Hungarian author. Every now and then, when he was pondering something, he would pause, stare out of the window and take off his glasses. Then he would put them back on and continue reading.

Carlsson let the dice bounce across the glass tabletop. A straight. She picked up her mobile and called Fredrik Franck, who answered after the first ring, in spite of the early hour.

"Good morning."

"It's time to deploy Kallax."

"Now? It's Saturday."

"Text me when it's done."

"But—"

Carlsson cut off the call and carried on flicking through the magazine until she found an article on how to cook a perfect prime rib on low heat in a clay pot.

Tekla could still taste vomit in her mouth, but the nausea had gone. She wondered what could best distract her from that foot in the I.C.U. Her thoughts turned to the boy with Gaucher disease. There had been no time yesterday to find out what had become of him, so she decided to go to the paediatric I.C.U.

"Where is the three-year-old boy from Thursday evening? The one who was admitted to A. & E. with seizures."

An assistant nurse who recognised Tekla showed her the way.

"Have you met his family?" Tekla said. "His father was very agitated."

"Fathers can be a real handful," the nurse agreed, deadpan.

"Especially policemen and firefighters. They probably see a load of shit out on the streets."

"Like us."

"Shit?"

The nurse smiled. "That too. But we can wipe that off."

Tekla smiled. "True."

"I think you know the way now," the nurse said and left.

Tekla wriggled out of her coat and hung her bag next to some face masks in the airlock outside the room. She went in, sat on a chair and lowered the side bars on the large bed. Oscar was lying asleep with a tube in his windpipe. The sound from the ventilator was pleasantly soporific. Tekla took a few deep breaths and felt the tiredness hit her. She grasped the boy's hand. It felt warmer than in A. & E. the other night. She looked at his peaceful face and let her own eyelids sink in time to the hissing of the ventilator.

Suddenly Tekla heard a girl's voice behind her.

"Who are you?"

She turned and saw a straight-backed, thin creature with long, flaxen hair standing immobile hardly twenty centimetres from her. She had not heard the door open.

"Hi."

No answer. Just big, staring, bright blue eyes.

"I'm the doctor who took care of Oscar when he was brought to A. & E."

"You don't look like a doctor."

Tekla smiled. Felt totally numb.

"Because I'm not dressed in white?"

The girl nodded silently.

"I haven't started work yet."

"So why are you here if you haven't started?"

The girl was wearing a red denim jacket over a white T-shirt with some glittering text on it that Tekla could not read. Loose black pirate pants. Her eyes had gone from scared to a little more confident.

"Are you Oscar's sister?" Tekla asked.

She nodded.

"What's your name?"

"Iris."

"Hi, Iris. My name's Tekla."

Iris put her head to one side and clumsily folded her arms. She looked as if she were imitating a grown-up.

"What a funny name."

"You asked why I'm here," Tekla said. "It's because I wanted to see how Oscar is feeling."

Iris looked nervously at Oscar, who was lying very still in his bed. It was the first time she had taken her eyes off Tekla.

"He's quite sick," Tekla continued. "But right now he's sleeping. They're giving him a lot of medicines to make him better."

The girl seemed to be pondering something. Her arms fell to her sides. She waited. Then she rubbed one of her eyes.

"Can I sit on your lap?"

Tekla was taken aback. Her body stiffened. She wanted to find an excuse, say that she had to leave, but there was something about the girl that she could not resist.

"Of course."

Iris approached Tekla cautiously and sat on her knee. She laid a little hand on Tekla's, which in turn was holding Oscar's.

"He's sweating," Iris whispered.

"Maybe he's dreaming about deserts."

Tekla wanted to put her arm around the girl and give her a big hug, but restrained herself.

Iris turned slowly to Tekla and looked her in the eyes.

"Do you think so?"

"I think he's comfortable and enjoying a good sleep. Look how nicely someone's made his bed. Wouldn't you like to lie in a great big bed like that?"

"No."

"And that tube in his mouth. Maybe they're giving him Coca-Cola? Litres and litres of it."

"I like Fanta."

"When you're ill, you can choose what you want."

"My Pappa says that soft drinks aren't good for me."

"And what does Mamma say?"

"She's frightened of Pappa."

Tekla gave a start.

"I see. Frightened? But here in hospital it's the patient who decides. Does Oscar like Coca-Cola?"

"Yes."

"Then he can drink as much as he wants."

Iris burrowed in between Tekla's arms and pressed her little head against her breastbone. Tekla was aware of a faint buttery smell from the girl's hair. She wondered if she should follow up on the bit about the mother being afraid of the father, but did not want to spoil the cosy moment. Tekla had chosen not to have any children because she was afraid that she would pass on her mother's gene. The defective gene which could cause Huntington's disease, the terrible dementia disorder. The gene which Tekla did not know if she was carrying. For which she had never dared to have herself tested. But which raised every kind of barrier to any relationship and the prospect of having children of her own.

"Do you have any brothers and sisters?" Iris said.

"A brother."

"Do you look after him?"

Tekla swallowed heavily. "I try to. But he's . . ."

"Is he sick too?"

"In a way, yes."

Tekla allowed herself to put one arm around Iris.

They sat quietly for ten minutes, sunk in their own worlds, and then a nurse came in and broke the spell. Iris did not move and pressed her hand even harder against Tekla's. It was as if she had been transported into a happy state which she absolutely did not want to surrender. Tekla stood up carefully and drew her sweaty hand out from between those of brother and sister.

She noticed that Iris was unwilling, but she helped her to sit by herself on the chair.

"Don't tell the parents I was here," Tekla said to the nurse.

"Don't?" she answered in surprise.

"No, and no-one else either."

"Fine, no problem."

Tekla left the room. She could see the girl's blue eyes before her all the way to the morning briefing.

GRÖNVIKSVÄGEN, BROMMA
Saturday, 8.vi

Umarov looked down at the pool from his bedroom window. It aroused many feelings. Mostly of hopelessness and anger. But he was not going to give up. The two years in prison at the beginning of the '80s had turned out to be a blessing for Umarov. He had been given his two-year jail sentence while a minor hoodlum on the make, trying to scratch a living in Moscow as part of the Uzbekh diaspora there, found guilty of attempted blackmail and threats against government employees. The system that put him away, and the people within it, were as corrupt, violent and lawless as he himself. While in prison, he lived a life of black and white, with a clear structure. He won respect and access to new social circles because he knew how to fight. But it never went to his head. He just made sure to project enough of a macho image to be discharged from jail with accreditation in criminal circles, and to pick up fresh skills and valuable contacts.

The connections he made as a result of his arrest, trial and incarceration formed the basis for his new transport business. He and Boris were part of the new commercial links between East and West. Some of their dealings were above board, others less so. Many of their activities needed the help or connivance, in various ways, of the security services, themselves working hard to adapt to the new reality. And that did not come cheap, there were always backs to be scratched, quids having to be repaid with quos. After his return to Russia in the early '90s and his and Boris' success in fronting the acquisition of the State's privatised electricity monopoly, true to form, Umarov was not always as careful as he might be about discharging his obligations.

That was the pretext for the F.S.B. to arrest him again – almost twenty years after his first trial – and sentence him to death after a farce of a trial. Then, following six months in prison, a "last chance", as the bald F.S.B. agent put it. Three conditions. First, he had to give up his entire fortune, all the assets he had built up within transportation and electricity generation; second, he was to move his family to Stockholm and take control of the heroin market in the Nordic area with the benefit of the shipments coming from Afghanistan via Eastern Europe, the "northern route", making regular payments to the F.S.B.'s fourth division, its economic security section; third, the death sentence was only suspended. If he failed to satisfy their demands, they would "send somebody", as the agent drily added before pushing the contract across the table for Umarov to sign. Up until now, Umarov had done as he was told, and the briefings with the F.S.B. representative at various Irish pubs across town were rather jolly affairs. The Russians seemed confident that Umarov was doing his job as *vor* in Stockholm.

Umarov ran his index finger across the piles of freshly laundered shirts. Black or white? Easiest would have been to alternate every day. Or black in daytime and white at night? Black for everyday use, white on special occasions? But he had never been one for routine. Organised? When it was necessary. Given his dyslexia, it was an irony that Umarov acquired the official job description of translator of Russian literature. His old friend Boris helped him with the odd translation, for the sake of appearances; Boris was also the family's accountant.

Umarov buttoned his shirt, gave himself two squirts of Old Spice, pulled on his trousers and the black Ecco shoes. Nina used to make fun of his shoes, but he did not care. Functionality had always been his style.

Umarov took the spiral staircase down to the living room. He pressed the button to raise the wooden blinds covering the thirty-metre wall of floor-to-ceiling windows. Like a space film in which the craft awakens and slowly lets in light from the rising sun, the different parts of the huge living room were now gradually being bathed in light. The opening ceremony took about twenty seconds; the machinery was a decade old, but, like a trusty T62 Russian tank, it worked. Seeing Lake Mälaren come to life fifty metres below him was Umarov's favourite moment of the day.

"Morfar, do you want to play with us?"

He turned, had been so wrapped up in his own world that he had not heard the twins, his granddaughters, sneak up behind him. In a moment of panic, he thought he might be standing there naked, but no, he was wearing trousers and shoes. He relaxed.

"My little darlings."

He squatted down and hugged Nina's children, Emily and Kate. They were in identical white flannel pyjamas with a pink bear pattern, and they smelled of raspberries.

"Show Morfar your sweets."

The twins looked at each other wide-eyed and shook their heads so that their dark curls swung to and fro.

"Uh-uh, we haven't got any sweets."

Umarov pretended to be surprised.

"Uh-uh. So those aren't raspberry jellies you have in your hands behind your backs?"

The twins giggled, tried to keep their mouths closed.

"Don't tell Mamma."

Umarov put his index finger to his lips.

"I promise. I'll be as silent as that Egyptian mummy I told you about yesterday after supper. Do you remember?"

They nodded seriously, remembering the dramatic yarn about the pyramids at Luxor.

"It's time for breakfast now. Who wants some hot chocolate?"

"Yaayyy!" the twins squealed in unison.

Their mother Nina was in the kitchen, preparing breakfast. Umarov kissed his princess on the forehead.

"Did you sleep well, Pappa?"

"Like a bear in winter."

94

"I'm glad you managed to rouse yourself from your hibernation," Nina said with a broad smile. She was already made up: red lipstick on her full lips, discreet mascara and a bronze eye-shadow which made her dark hair, combed tightly back with a side parting, look jet black.

"It isn't every Saturday morning that one has the whole family sleeping over." Umarov looked around the enormous kitchen. "Where's Joakim?"

"He left early," Nina answered as she arranged some small, thick, pancake-like shapes on a plate. "Tennis with a buddy."

"You know Coco can do that," Umarov said as he pointed at the frying pan.

"Not as good as my crumpets." Nina smiled. "Do you remember how our nanny in London used to make them? They're best with honey. Sit down, Pappa, and I'll make you coffee. It's not often I get a chance to look after you. You need it, you look worn out."

"Thanks a lot!" Umarov said with a laugh.

Umarov enjoyed seeing his eldest child in such a good mood. Freshly showered and wide awake. Yet there was something about her that worried him. Was it to do with her relationship? Umarov supposed she was glad to be at home for once. He had always had a feeling that Jocke did not show her the appreciation she deserved.

He took a seat in the dining room, which faced the back of the house. The sliding doors were open and a cool June breeze swept across the stone floor.

Sardor came in and leaned on the back of a chair. He was wearing a leather jacket. A large mug of coffee in one hand, book in the other.

"Hi."

"Hey, Brorsan," Nina said. "Unusual to see you with a book."

Sardor looked uncomfortable.

Umarov got up and contemplated the bronze-brown water of the pool through the kitchen window.

"The colour reminds me of our courtyard in Tashkent in autumn.

Mud, woodchips and rusty buckets. Everything I've wanted to get away from."

"Come on, Pappa," Nina said, her hand on Umarov's shoulder. "It's surely not as bad as that?"

"Yesterday I ran a pool shock with chlorine, the second time this week. But no results so far. The service guy has also been to take a look at the filter system. He told me, 'It's running like my old Audi from 2001.'" Umarov snorted. "I don't want an old Audi. The pool has to be looking nice for next weekend, for Elena's garden party. I'm not giving up. In the end, Kamila and the twins will get their perfect pool."

"They're quite happy as it is," Nina said.

"Have you seen them swimming in the past week?"

"It's still too cold," Nina said, in an effort to humour him, while she gave her daughters Nutella sandwiches and heated up the hot chocolate in the microwave. She was ready for the day's showings, dressed in dark blue business suit and black blouse. A red silk scarf around her neck.

Umarov poured coffee from the silver pot, put it in the middle of the enormous glass table, sat down next to Kate and patted her curls. He turned to Sardor.

"How did it go with Jensen and the leather-trouser mob in Skärholmen yesterday?"

"They didn't exactly roll out the barrel."

Nina unbuttoned her jacket and settled down to the family breakfast.

"I chatted to Jensen," Sardor said. "He did seem to get the point in the end. We have a week to find whoever stuck a knife in Jarmo."

Umarov reached for a leather case and his lighter. He knocked out a cigarette. A gas flame shot from the silver lighter, which he moved back and forth at a distance from the cigarette. Then he held it in front of his mouth and took a drag on it, the way he usually did. Although there was no smoke, he could feel the warm tobacco down his windpipe. He closed his eyes and put the cigarette on the table.

"And then you created your usual scene?" Umarov took another non-puff.

Sardor fingered his book. "They provoked me."

"So *you* were the one who turned violent?" Umarov said. "I seem to remember asking you to be diplomatic."

"Do you always have to go looking for someone to blame?" Sardor said.

"When two people get into a fight, inevitably, there's *one* who's at fault."

Nina got up. "I have to go to the office. Jonna's in New York over the weekend and I've got to tie up a deal."

Umarov realised what was wrong. Nina was avoiding his eyes. And her behaviour was unnatural, her body language strained.

"Is it that island?" Sardor asked his sister.

"Kaggholmen, yes. Why?"

"A whole island. Sounds expensive."

"It's on offer for 33 million. A Dutchman's buying. Anything wrong?"

Sardor got up, ignoring his sister.

"I need to deal with Tatiana," he said. "She doesn't have the situation with the girls under control."

Umarov smiled at Emily and Kate, whose mouths were covered in Nutella.

"I've told her I can get someone to handle the Colombian chicks. But she refuses."

"I appreciate your concern for your employees," Umarov said.

"Employees?" Sardor asked. "Tatiana's more than an employee, isn't she? She's been with us since we came here."

Nina glanced at her brother, then at Umarov. She wiped the Nutella off the twins' faces.

"I can help if necessary," she said.

"I don't want you dragged into this," Umarov said, shaking his head. "You know that."

"All I'm saying is—"

"No!" Umarov roared, slamming his hand down onto the glass table.

The twins jumped.

Umarov took a few testy air puffs and then stubbed out the unsmoked cigarette.

"How many times do I have to explain that there's a whole Chinese wall between what Sardor does and what you do, Nina?"

Silence in the kitchen.

"I'm *vor* in Stockholm, translator and low-key businessman who lives off the return on old capital. O.K.? Nobody touches me. Not the gangs. Not the bikers. Not the police. Christ, I even have a harmonious relationship with the tax authority. And you, Nina, are a female mirror-image of me. You're not even supposed to get a parking ticket. Understood?"

"Yes, Pappa," Nina said.

"You must never, ever touch anything illegal."

"There's no need to go on about it."

"Come here," Umarov said. "Look at me. Is there something wrong?"

"Why should there be anything wrong?" Nina asked, anxiously.

"You'll tell me if there's something on your mind, won't you?"

"For sure."

Sardor put his cup down.

"Do your thing and we'll all be happy," he said to his sister.

"Don't worry, no-one's going to take your slice of the pie," Nina said with a smirk. "You can relax."

"I'm not dead yet," Umarov said, sounding weary. He was feeling heavy and worn down, and this depressed him. This was precisely what he had wanted to avoid: two children bickering over their inheritance. How could he have made such a mess of their upbringing? Why had only Nina managed to stay away from crime? He should have been tougher with Sardor and made him continue with his studies. "In any case, it's all settled. You can stop squabbling."

"I've not seen any papers," Sardor said.

"Cut it out," Umarov bellowed.

A belly laugh from Nina. "As if Sardor could read any papers!"

Sardor began walking to the door.

"You need more sleep," Nina shouted after him. "I can get my doctor to prescribe some sleeping pills. Something to dampen all that testosterone at night."

Without turning, Sardor said:

"Someone's got to do the dirty work."

ÖSTERMALMS SALUHALL
Saturday, 8.vi

Nina parked her black Cadillac Escalade outside the entrance to Östermalmshallen food hall. She remembered Jocke's surprise when she bought it. She'd said it was for the safety of the children. But, actually, she had liked the shape and the big seats. And how quiet it was. But yes, it was sometimes difficult to find a parking space.

She walked into the food hall and over to Melander's fish store, which was as busy as ever. Her mobile rang: Jonna.

"Why aren't you answering?"

"I know perfectly well that you've called like fourteen times. But there's no need to get worked up," Nina said, helping herself to a queue number. She nodded her recognition to the owner, who put a glass of fizz in front of her. She sipped the ice-cold Cava and picked up a piece of cheese. Manchego. It reminded her of the time when she and Joakim had gone down to Oviedo on the Spanish coast and drunk gallons of *cidera* until they could not bear so much as to smell a bottle of cider. Life before the children.

"For God's sake, Nina. Don't tell me that a major disaster has escaped your notice?"

Nina was struggling to find somewhere quiet to take the call. She was amazed that the ladies she had to push past had not yet put away their long fur coats. It would soon be mid-summer. Talk about "ushering in spring in a sweat". Why did the fashionable ladies of Östermalm have such a passion for furry animal fashion? She preferred black leather.

"I was just going to buy some shrimps for the family and try to put aggressive brothers out of my mind for a few hours."

"What's Sardor done?"

"Well, I'm certainly not going to let him ruin my Saturday evening."

"Have you had a row?"

"Have we ever done anything else?"

"You ought to talk it over."

Nina smiled to herself.

"Sardor's not really the kind of guy you talk things over with. He's not in touch with his inner self."

"But maybe you could try."

"Can we please for once stop trying to analyse my family? It feels like we've got more important things to deal with."

Nina drained her Cava and caught the owner's eye, resting her finger on the glass to get a refill. The only ones drinking were she and a man with a bulbous nose a bit further away. The ladies next to her were clutching their handbags to their bosoms and would not let their guard down until they had got home a few blocks away and poured the first sherry of the day.

"Are you enjoying the heartbeat of the big city?" Nina said. "Personally I'd rather die than live in New York. Even though this place can sometimes feel a bit claustrophobic, because everybody knows everybody. You can't really call Stockholm a cosmopolitan city. Not to mention all that Venice of the North stuff."

"Can you just focus a little?" Jonna said.

"You sound like Pappa. If there's one thing I'm good at, it's focusing."

Nina thought about Umarov and what he had indeed taught them: to pull out all the stops when it really mattered. He could come across as boisterous, extravagant even, and lacking in concentration, but countless times Nina had seen his associates try to manipulate Umarov by fiddling with the numbers because they thought he would not notice. It always ended badly for them.

"Nina, what are you talking about?"

"The art of chilling out when circumstances allow it."

Nina had always envied her father his ability to put work to one side. He would busy himself with his pool or join a neighbour in grappling with some incomprehensible building project for months on end. Not to mention his obsession with his grandchildren's activities.

"Would that save our skins now? To bury our heads in the sand?" Jonna said.

"I'm not sacrificing my me time."

Nina's eyes met those of the bulbous nose, and she recognised him. The managing director of a finance company, recently divorced.

"Everything comes out in the end. If anyone should worry, it's you."

"We need more information," Nina said.

"How can you behave as if nothing has happened?"

"I already told you. Shouting and panicking won't make matters better."

"And you haven't got hold of him yet?" Jonna asked.

It was Nina's turn to order. She put down her glass.

"Wait a second," she said to Jonna. "Two kilos of fresh shrimps."

Then she carried on: "I've called several times, but I only get the answerphone."

"Could he have taken off?"

"Might be even worse."

"What do you mean, worse?"

"There's a man in intensive care at the Nobel Hospital," Nina said. "Badly burnt and unidentifiable."

"And you think that might be him?"

"We can't rule it out. I'll take care of this though. But first I need a little break, just this evening."

Nina produced her platinum card and got a white plastic bag in exchange. She walked out to her S.U.V. and saw a traffic warden busy fixing a yellow ticket to the windscreen.

"I'll try to relax," Jonna sighed.

"You're not making much of a job of it."

Nina smiled at the traffic warden and ripped up the parking ticket. Then she called Jocke and told him she was on her way home to Karlaplan. The traffic light on Karlavägen was red. She turned down the music and stared at an elderly man taking his dachshund for a walk. She wondered how she would be able to stop the looming catastrophe. Maybe it was time to make an appointment with the dentist.

Saturday, 8.vi, 11 a.m.

Eva Elmqvist put her hand into her frizzy hair and scratched at her scalp.

"As I expected, he developed pulmonary oedema during the night."

Tekla had to make an effort to take in what Elmqvist was saying about the patient. She dreaded to think how she would react if she were to see the toe again. The wiring in her brain had obviously gone wrong and made her think of Simon. It was absurd.

"Just as you thought," Tekla said.

They were standing outside the staff pantry, each holding a plastic mug of coffee.

"And he's in septic shock," Elmqvist continued. "Needs a high dose of vasopressor. But he's still urinating, which is good."

"Are you going to operate?" Tekla said.

"You seem to know a hell of a lot about dealing with burns victims."

"I can stop asking, if you like."

"Not at all. The plastic surgeons had two goes at him before the oedema set in. They've started prepping for a skin graft, but they want to remove more dead tissue first. And now we have problems with his airway. He needs a tracheotomy, but the ear, nose and throat surgeons aren't playing ball. No surprise there. I hope we'll get one during the course of the day. That's all on the medical front. You'll handle the exchange with the police, then?"

"Do we know anything more about who he is?" Tekla said.

"The police are working on that, but I gather it may take some time. They're trying to get hold of X-ray records from some dental surgeries in Söder, there's no national register and no way of knowing where to look, actually."

"Bureaucratic Sweden."

Elmqvist shook her head.

"It probably wouldn't be quicker in any other country."

"Unless you could afford to throw a lot of private money at it."

"And we don't want that, thank you very much."

Elmqvist left without saying goodbye.

Tekla headed for Room 1. Once inside, she noted another change: the smell of infected skin. Like the meat counter at the Co-op on a hot day.

Nilsén was discussing something with the nurse in charge. She brightened up when she saw Tekla.

"Aha! Our informant."

Tekla looked surprised.

Nilsén smiled. "Tell me."

"The doctor in the I.C.U. just said that they're having problems with his fluid balance. The situation is delicate."

Nilsén picked up her mobile, pressed Record and put it on a table next to the bed.

"I've noticed that you always hedge your bets."

"How do you mean?"

"Problem. Delicate situation. Why do we never get any clear figures, like 'There's an eighty-five per cent risk he'll die in the next two days'?"

"I can lie to you if that'll make you feel any better," Tekla said.

"You don't need to. I can't stop myself from analysing things. People and events."

Tekla stole a look at the monitors. The patient was more tachycardic today.

"But will he make it?"

"That's by no means certain."

"And when can that . . . tube in his throat be removed? Or could you maybe lighten the sedation somewhat so we can try and talk to him?"

Tekla smiled.

"That sort of thing only happens in the movies. I'm sure you understand."

"And I who love films," Nilsén said with a dreamy look in her eyes.

"He's in worse shape than yesterday," Tekla said.

Nilsén looked with distaste at the ventilator, at the same time as Tekla approached the bed and brushed against the sheet, which had slipped aside. She saw the foot and gave a start. Her chest tightened and she had difficulty breathing. But the feeling quickly passed.

"We really do need to talk to him," Nilsén said to herself, as if she were trying to come up with some clever way of waking the patient that the doctors had not thought of.

Tekla noticed that Nilsén was wearing a new shade of lipstick today, more of a raspberry pink. Her hair was combed back smoothly. Today she was wearing a thin, loose-fitting dress in a dark green material with matching belt and bare shoulders. High-heeled white sandals. She looked as if she were going to the opening of an exhibition at Liljevalchs art gallery.

"Why's it so important for you to speak to him?"

"You're bound by medical secrecy, aren't you?" Nilsén said.

Tekla nodded.

Nilsén fixed her eyes on Tekla and seemed to make a spontaneous decision.

"The forensics have found traces of saltpeter, sulphur and ammonium sulphide in the garage. In other words, bomb-making material."

"Bombs?" Tekla exclaimed.

"We suspect that the men who left the scene in a van had been in the garage and we can't rule out that our dear patient here in this bed belonged to the same group."

A storm of thoughts flew through Tekla's mind.

"You mean that they were actually trying to blow up the tower?"

"It's *one* of our lines of inquiry. We're drawing no hasty conclusions."

Tekla nodded and went on:

"But he responded to Naloxone. Doesn't a junkie who was asleep in the cellar sound more likely? There are quite a few of them in the city's cellars and garages, are there not?"

"So you did test for drugs after all?"

Tekla sighed. "Unfortunately not."

"How long afterwards can one do it?"

"Several days, but the problem is that he was given morphine and many other drugs as soon as he got to A. & E. It's very difficult to know what's what."

"O.K. But we mustn't rule anything out. Even bomb makers and terrorists take drugs. My group is following up every conceivable lead."

"Are there many of you in the investigating team?"

Nilsén's serious expression softened unexpectedly.

"There are enough. It won't take us long to crack this little nut," she said, and Tekla imagined hearing the sound of a walnut being split open in front of the Christmas tree at the Nilsén family home.

"And what about his identity?" Tekla said.

"Why do you ask?"

"Just curious."

"Curious – I know the feeling. We're working on it."

Nilsén left the burns room.

The nurse was busy resolving a problem with the central line on the patient's throat. Affecting indifference, Tekla took a quick look at the foot.

"Do you mind if I examine him a bit while you do that?"

"Please go ahead. I'm just trying to flush out this line, which isn't working properly."

Tekla put on plastic clothes and gloves. She pretended to listen to the heart and lungs, but she was focused on trying to find undamaged parts of the body, at which she could have a closer look. One shoulder and the area down towards the side of the breast cage were relatively uninjured. She ran her index finger along the hollow in the upper edge of the collarbone. Hadn't Simon broken it when he was small? Fallen off his bicycle? The burns victim's collarbone had not been broken. She had a clear memory of Simon sitting with his legs crossed on the beach by the little lake. Small blue bathing shorts with a white drawstring tied in a bow at the front. He was building a sandcastle with a moat around it. She compared what she remembered of that part of his body, the size of the palm of her hand, with the patient before her. They looked the same. But would one expect any great variation between the collarbones of two slim young men? She moved on towards the left hand: the little finger was red but not burned. She flexed the joint, while recalling an image from the time when she and Simon had been to a party in Umeå with some of his friends. They took turns trying on a wedding ring which one of them had just bought. It was far too big for Tekla, but Simon grinned triumphantly and declared that "the ring fits me better, so I'm the one who's getting married". What her mind was showing her now, though, was the ring finger. Not the little finger.

"How's it going?" the nurse said.

Tekla was yanked away from her memories. An enquiring look met hers.

"The question is, will he make it?" she asked.

"Not according to the surgeon who was here this morning. What did he say again? Something like 'Why waste operating time on someone who's going to die anyway?'"

Tekla tried to regain control of the situation. She needed her Lypsyl to get those thoughts sorted into their right slots. Why could she not let go of the crazy idea that it was her brother lying there before her? Was it anything to do with that promise she made to her father on his deathbed? Or the other thing he had said about their mother's illness? Which Simon was never told about. She examined her mental image of the collarbone from another angle. Saw every shadow on his skin. Briefly savoured her incredible gift. Which had also, it is true, caused her no end of difficulty over the years: bullying, exclusion, introversion, isolation. Then again: it had saved her so much time during her studies.

"I've just got to fetch some more Chlorhexidine," the nurse said. "Will you be here for a while longer?"

"O.K.," Tekla said, and watched the nurse walk out through the airlock.

She bent over the injured man's face and tried to see something of his eyes, but the eyelids were still swollen. There was a smell of hand sanitiser and burnt hair. She saw images before her of the time when they scraped sweat and skin from their bodies in the sauna by the lake and threw it onto the heater. But she could not make out the odours.

"Oh yuck, what a stench," Simon had shouted.

"I like the smell," Tekla had said and flicked more water onto the stones.

Tekla held the burns victim's hand and whispered:

"Simon, is it you? Just give me a small sign. Squeeze my hand if you can hear me."

But all she felt was her own aching back as she leaned forward. The only sound she heard was the insistent pumping of the ventilator.

"Please, at least move a finger. Simon, is that you in there? Can I help you? All I need is a tiny little sign that it's you. Like when you imitated the slurping sound I made at the dining table, do you remember? You hated it and said it sounded as if I was inside your ear and walking through mud. I still slurp just as much. It's been so long since we last saw each other, but I promise I'll make enough revolting noises to give you a fit when you come to again. Simon, can you try slurping a little?"

It did not help that she raised her voice. The man in the bed did not move a muscle.

She laid her other hand on the patient's bandaged forehead.

"You know I can't swim. Pappa never had time to teach me. Was that what you meant? Who's done this to you? Nod, move your head a little if you can hear my voice. I do so very much want to help you. Never mind what you've done, nobody should have to suffer like this. I know you're a walking disaster. Sorry, but you've always been, and always will be. But I love you for who you are. Can you remember what Pappa said? That no-one can be held responsible for the parents they end up with. He knew very well what a rotten father he was. Absolutely for sure. But at least he knew it. I'm not sure Morsan ever really realised quite what a bad mother she was. Simon, please move your head."

She shifted her position. Waited for some reaction from the man in front of her, but it never came. She looked at the monitor and saw that the pulse had increased a little. Was that just a coincidence, or was it his only way of communicating with her?

"If you die, I'll die too. I don't believe in God, so I can't ask him or her for help. All I can do is ask you to survive. Because if you don't, then I have no idea how I will—"

"All good?"

The nurse was back.

Tekla pretended to be taking the man's pulse from his wrist. It must have looked rather awkward.

"Fine, thanks. Me, I mean . . . but if you mean . . . him . . . the patient . . ."

She let the burns victim's hand fall so it thumped against the side rails of the bed, avoided the nurse's puzzled look and left the room, feeling anything but calm.

The refrigerator was filled to bursting with beer. Dahl took a cold one, opened it, drained half the bottle and burped out loud. His shirt was still soaked with sweat from the fencing, which had been the last activity of the day.

Oskar came into the room and propped his large belly against the table protruding between the high windows, which looked out on Kommendörsgatan.

"Nice place, right?" Oskar said.

"For sure," Dahl replied, although he was not particularly impressed.

Oskar poured himself a gin and tonic and chewed on a lemon wedge.

"Crazy. How much do you think he actually makes?"

"No idea," Dahl said. "But I heard he sold his latest game for about ten million."

Oskar laughed.

"And then some, I suspect. Insane that it should have turned out to be just Petter."

Dahl remembered a tall, lanky fellow who shone at chemistry and physics but always came in last on "The Killer", their three-kilometre loop in the forest. Since then, his and Petter's lives had gone in different directions.

The stag party had apparently begun at Rasmus' home with a kidnapping and a hood over his head. As agreed, Sanna had left the door open and made sure that they got to bed really late the night before. Then the action moved to Mattias' pub in Sollentuna and a first-class champagne breakfast. After that, bungy jumping in Nacka Strand and lunch in town at the Dubliner. Dahl had joined them there after his fishing expedition with Lundgren. There was a quiz with a faded pop star over lunch. Rasmus managed the music trivia questions splendidly. But his eyes kept dropping rather obviously to her neckline. Lucky that she was good at small talk. Lunch was followed by a manicure at a salon on Sveavägen, fencing and swilling beer among hundreds of sunbathing summer students in Observatorielunden, and then they had ended up in Petter's enormous apartment. Until then, it had had all the classic stag party ingredients. But now Dahl was to take over and raise the bar.

They went into the living room. Rasmus was there in his Superman outfit, beer in hand, deep in conversation with Petter. Dahl felt a sting of envy when he saw them with their heads together, shutting out everybody else from their profound conversation, just as they used to in their student days, while the other guys were talking about sport, girls and how not to flunk their studies, Rasmus and Petter's discussions had always been more highbrow. At the time, most of them did not have any idea what path they would follow in life, but, looking back, they had all done well, Petter evidently the best of all.

He sat down on the long white leather sofa and drummed out the beat of Beyoncé's "7/11" on his thigh. Petter's Spotify playlist, of course. The beer was flowing. Whisky was brought out. Pizzas on the table. Music pumping. Dahl wondered what the neighbours would say, but Petter was bound already to have bought them off with tickets to some concert. In addition to the computer games, Petter also had some projects going in the music industry. Dahl had no idea what they were about. Petter was primarily Rasmus' friend, one step removed from Dahl's world. In their twenties, they all used to hang out together; if you called one, then you called them all. Parties, events, trips. They did things as a group. When they reached the thirty mark and some of them were breaking up from long-term relationships and others decided to keep going and the children began to arrive, it became clear who the real friends were. Dahl was not actually close to anybody. Their meetings became less frequent. He and Angelica were the first to have children, they bought a terraced house in Farsta and life soon became a treadmill. And it worked out fine, up until a second child came along. But he had no cause to complain. He was still in good shape, liked his job, enjoyed hunting and fishing with Lundgren. Besides which, his career had gone steadily upwards.

He looked at his watch. It would soon be time. He sent off a question to the number he had been given. Then he got up and knocked his mobile against the beer bottle.

"Listen up, guys, there's going to be a little surprise soon." He turned to Rasmus. "Rasmus. You're the best. I hope your marriage lasts a whole year before Sanna realises what a loser you are."

He raised his glass of champagne.

"Skål to Rasmus!"

"Skål to Rasmus!" they chanted in unison.

Dahl noticed how the tension in the room was mounting. They could tell that what he had laid on was something special. And it was obvious that there was a struggle going on between him and Petter over who was the better fixer. Petter had done well for himself, Dahl had to concede that. There was a gilded grand piano standing in the corner of the living room, he drove a Ferrari and regularly spent weekends in the South of France or in London. But he had no family. Dahl's relationship with his children might well be dreadful, but . . .

There was a ping from his mobile.

We are here.

He did not understand why they were writing in English, but he went out into the hallway.

"Close your eyes," he shouted over his shoulder.

Two lightly clad girls brushed past him with great self-assurance and took their place in the middle of the living room. Wolf whistles and shouts of "*hurra*" from the assembled company. He walked in behind them and said:

"Let me introduce Anna and Petra!"

The girls did not look as if they were called Anna and Petra. Valentina and Olga, more likely. Dahl found them reasonably good-looking, especially Petra. Slim but with quite big breasts. Dahl thought she looked like Angelina Jolie, with full lips and a kinder face. A soft, slightly shy expression. She was younger than Anna, who was more like a typical hooker: short fur jacket, tiny skirt and a little too much make-up.

Petter changed the music to "I Keep Forgettin" by Michael McDonald and had Rasmus, or Superman, sit on a chair in the middle of the floor. His hands tied behind his back. The others were lined up on the leather sofa, like children about to watch a magician. Dahl saw that their eyes were ablaze, but at the same time they avoided looking at each other. Everything they had done so far that day, they could go home and tell their women about. From now on, it was going to be: "Then we ate, and had a sauna and headed off to Café Opera. It was nice, but I was a bit tired." The tacit understanding.

The Anna girl took charge and began to strip. She was wearing black underwear with hold-ups. She danced provocatively in time to the music, grinding her rear end against Rasmus. He did his best to look unaffected as he nodded at the guys on the sofa, who were grinning and raising their beers. Petter was the only one on his feet. Every now and then he looked in Dahl's direction. The pleasing thing was that the balance of power had shifted slightly. The boys seemed satisfied. And they all knew who had arranged for the girls to come.

Dahl helped himself to a large glass of whisky from a silver tray which Felix brought around. Just like some head waiter. He looked at the other girl, pretty Petra who was dancing by herself behind Rasmus' chair. She was wearing a cut-off denim skirt and black tank top with a gold pattern. She had let down her brown hair and her gorgeous lips were pouting, but she was not looking at the men. Seemed to be in a world of her own. Probably high. Dahl was well aware how these girls lived. They were part of an ugly industry involving human trafficking, drugs and violence. Even so, right now all he could see was their slim, young bodies. He thought of Angelica, who had always been a little overweight.

He drained his glass. Shuddered. Started on a new, cold beer. Felt the intoxication kick in just as the girls began to caress and kiss each other above Rasmus' head. Christer, Mattias and the others clapped and wolf-whistled.

After a ten-minute show the girls were left wearing only thongs. They flexed their lithe bodies into various fuck-poses. Everyone in the room was frenetically drinking beer.

Petter went up to Anna and whispered something in her ear. She began to loosen Rasmus' rope, took him by the hand and led him towards the bedrooms at the far end of the apartment. Petter showed them the way. Dahl saw what Petter was trying to do. He wanted to regain the upper hand, but, after this, Dahl would be the uncrowned king of the gang.

The music pumped on, Petra put on a shirt which Felix lent her and asked Mattias for some champagne. The boys took it in turns to chat to her as she sat there on a piano stool. Although they all tried to look natural, they were aware that this was a once-in-a-lifetime experience. Dahl was on his seventh beer but felt surprisingly energetic. Sharp and alert. Pumped up with adrenaline. He was exchanging small talk with Oskar about some football match, but kept stealing looks in Petra's direction. Could not stop staring at her beautiful face. She really shone, looked so glamorous with her champagne, her legs crossed, and the golden grand piano completing the picture. Oskar walked towards the kitchen to replenish the bar and the man talking to Petra went to the toilet. Dahl moved in.

"Hi."

"Hi," Petra said, her foreign accent obvious. She was even prettier close up. Perfect teeth, sparkling in a shy smile. How old might she be? Not less than eighteen, he was certain about that. Twenty-two?

"You danced really well."

"You think so? Thanks!"

It felt right. Her tone was kind and she sounded honest. They kept chatting. She told him about her family outside St Petersburg, that her mother was sick and needed care. That she only planned to stay in Sweden for a year or so to earn enough money for her mother's medical care. That she wanted to be a professional dancer. Maybe go on to study psychology.

Anna and Rasmus came back. The boys clapped and Rasmus knocked back a whisky and soda. Petter looked nauseatingly pleased with himself. Dahl met Petra's eyes and felt the anger flare up again.

She stared into his eyes. He could smell her perfume. She let her hand drop to his jeans, stroked his erection. His whole body was about to explode.

She took his hand and headed to the hallway with him.

They went into Petter's large bedroom and within a minute they were naked. Dahl lay on his back and Petra sucked his cock. Oh my God, how she could suck. Suddenly Petra brought out a condom and began to roll it onto Dahl's cock.

"Let's do it without?"

"No way," she said with a smile and kept rolling down the condom. He sat up.

"Cut it out. I'm completely clean."

She hushed him and kept going.

Dahl lost his temper. He was not going to let her spoil this moment for him because of some bloody principle. He was the one taking the risk after all, fucking a whore without a condom. And he was prepared to take it. He!

"Look, if you don't want to, let's leave it," she finally said.

He could see Petter's self-satisfied smile before him, and felt the rage boil up again.

"We're going to do it, and we're going to do it right now," Dahl snapped and hit Petra in the face.

She looked back at him in terror and was climbing off the bed when Dahl hauled her back and pressed her throat down onto the sheet. She fought back but he weighed almost twice as much as she did. She stood no chance.

He grasped her hands in a practised grip and prised her legs apart with his knees. Petra screamed, but Dahl pushed her face into the large down pillow. The music was pounding loudly outside.

He masturbated his dangling cock back to stiffness and drove it in up to the hilt. Deep. Warm. He came after twenty seconds. Shivered. Quickly began to feel cold. Let his sweaty body fall over hers.

She lay still. Totally limp.

"Sorry," he managed to say. "I'll pay you extra."

It was around one in the morning when Sardor found a space outside Evil Eye Tattoo at Magnus Ladulåsgatan 25. As he parked, he spotted Tatiana's trademark frizzy head of hair outside the front door. She was smoking agitatedly.

He locked the car and went up to her.

"How bad is it?"

Tatiana snorted and flicked the cigarette stub onto the road.

"Fucking terrible. She's devastated."

"Does she have to go to hospital?"

"Not for anything physical."

"Then why are you so upset?" Sardor said.

"What do you mean upset?"

"You look stressed."

"What the hell do you expect?" Tatiana shot back. "That I don't give a shit about my girls when they're raped?" She keyed in the code and walked into the house. They took the lift to the fourth floor.

Sardor looked at Tatiana. She was nervously fingering her gold necklace.

"What are you gawping at? If you're not happy, I can call Nina."

"You always know just what to say, don't you?" Sardor said.

The lift stopped. Tatiana unlocked the door to a six-room apartment with a large kitchen. Four bedrooms which the girls shared in pairs. For the moment, only Svetlana and Olga were at home. And Kaisa, of course. All three were sitting on stools in the kitchen, drinking tea out of large mugs.

"What happened?" Sardor said. He inspected the strangulation marks on Kaisa's neck. Deep purple bruises which went all the way around her throat.

"A Swedish bloke. Middle-aged. Big. Completely O.K. to begin with. But he didn't want to use a condom."

"And then?"

"He suddenly whacked me," Kaisa said. "I was totally unprepared. And he was strong. Grabbed my hands so I couldn't get away. He obviously knew how to do it."

"Do what?"

"Lock my hands behind my back."

"It was him, the cop," Tatiana said, shaking her head. Her apricot-coloured hair was standing on end. Despite their rule about not smoking indoors, she took out another cigarette and turned to the girls.

"Only me, and only today. Forget you saw this." Then to Sardor: "You'll have to deal with this. We can't take it to the police."

She lowered her voice and put her hand on his.

"And sorry for saying that thing earlier. I didn't mean that Nina is better at—"

"No worries," Sardor interrupted. He was tired. He liked all the girls, in different ways. Kaisa had only been in Tatiana's stable for about six months, but you could tell that they all liked her. She was sweet, unspoiled. Sardor did not think that she was doing a lot of drugs. Certainly nothing heavy.

"That fucking creep's going to pay for this. I promise you." Tatiana turned to Olga. "Have you checked down below? Is she hurt?"

"No," Kaisa said. "It was O.K. He came quickly."

She began to cry. Her make-up was now long since removed, but it had left a blueish smudge on her face.

"Come on," Svetlana said. "Let's go to bed."

Sardor and Tatiana watched the girls disappear down the corridor. Sardor poured himself a glass of water.

"When did it happen?"

"Around ten o'clock," Tatiana said.

"He rang me several times during the evening," Sardor said. "I just ignored him." He laughed to himself. "I'll take care of it."

"I don't care if you know him," Tatiana said. "You mustn't let him get away with this."

Sardor was thinking. "This is great," he said.

"How the fuck can it be great?" Tatiana said angrily.

Sardor explained. "We can use this. We're going to pay Håkan a little visit."

STORA ESSINGEN, STOCKHOLM
Sunday, 9.vi, dawn

The large split-level house was at the bottom of the hill, discreetly hidden behind luxuriant vegetation, facing the water. An onshore wind was blowing and the sheets on the sailing boats at the moorings a little way off were snapping loudly. The apartment blocks of Gröndal rose on the other side of the sound and Sardor had also admired the view from below the house. He had been there for a barbecue the previous summer. He knew that a big, new Buster boat was tied up alongside the jetty.

They parked by the gates. There was nobody around, no barking dogs. Just a dull roar from the traffic on Essingeleden.

Sardor saw Dahl's Range Rover on the drive and wondered if he was alone or if one of his children was there. Because he did have a family, didn't he?

He stopped, turned his back to the wind and brought out a small bag from his jacket pocket. Stuck his little finger into the white powder. Brought it to one nostril and sniffed.

"Want some?"

"No need."

Eje Eriksson hugged the baseball bat and waited. Looked around. He pulled the blue hoodie over his shaven head. Only the goatee stuck out.

Sardor opened the gate and walked towards the back of the darkened house. A large terrace at the front looked out over the water.

"You cover the front in case he tries to run off. I'll ring the doorbell."

"And the family?" Eje said.

"Don't know if he has any."

"And we'll deal with him here?"

Sardor nodded.

"But this is just to teach him a lesson." Sardor looked around one last time.

"If you say so . . ."

Eje went around to the front of the house. Sardor walked up to the door and felt the handle. It was open. Maybe Dahl had been too drunk to lock when he got home.

Sardor opened the door and marched in.

He saw the kitchen straight ahead and the enormous living room sprawled on the right. Large windows and sliding glass doors, the Gröndal street lights across the water. To the left was a corridor with closed doors.

All of a sudden, a woman in black knickers and an oversized shirt emerged from one of the rooms. When she saw Sardor, she started to scream. He realised that he was holding a pistol and moved it out of sight. She was followed by a large man wearing only boxer shorts.

"Quiet," Dahl said and told the woman not to worry. "Go back to bed."

"But—"

"I know him," Dahl said. "Just go and lie down."

The woman reluctantly went back into the room and closed the door behind her.

"How did you get in? Did I not lock?" Dahl walked towards Sardor. When he saw the pistol, he stopped.

"Anyway, what the hell are you doing here?"

Sardor put the gun away in his shoulder holster. He could smell the alcohol on Dahl's breath as he walked past him into the kitchen to pour himself a glass of water.

"I'm sure you know," Sardor said and fell in behind him.

Dahl jumped. "My God, you guys scare people."

He had spotted a giant holding a baseball bat on the balcony outside the kitchen. Sardor let Eje in.

"Hey, what the fuck . . . ?" Dahl said, suddenly sober.

"You've put your foot in it," Sardor said quietly. "You raped one of the girls."

"Come off it," Dahl said. "She—"

"I've seen her. Strangle marks on her throat." Sardor held up his mobile with a photograph of Kaisa. "Not nice. Not nice at all."

"She went along with it."

"Listen, I don't give a shit that you're a cop. We've got things on each other, both of us, but this time you've gone too far. Big time."

Dahl walked past Eje into the living room. The parquet flooring felt sticky under his feet as he went and sat down on the sofa next to the soapstone fireplace. He drank some water.

"Who's the chick?"

"A girl," Dahl answered.

"Hot. Maybe a bit on the young side."

Dahl ignored the comment. She was Isabelle Åkerlund, a 31-year-old police trainee whom Dahl had been seeing for a few months.

"I can pay. I'll pay and you keep your mouths shut. Simple. Just as long as you push off so I can get some sleep."

Sardor saw the pleading look in Dahl's eyes. The grovelling disgusted him. But at least, for once, the roles were reversed.

"You didn't give Kaisa the same chance, did you?"

Dahl took a deep breath but did not answer. Sardor beckoned Eje.

"So what now? Are you going to beat me up or something? Look –" Dahl put down his glass – "I'm sorry. Don't know what came over me. Everything went blank. I'd drunk way too much."

Sardor saw Kaisa's throat before him, felt the hatred pulse through him. Loathing for these cowardly bloody punters who mistreated the girls. Not that they were his girls. There was no question of proprietorship here, just unadulterated fury.

"I didn't mean it to happen. Really not. I was so—"

"Pissed and horny," Sardor interrupted.

"One hundred," Dahl said.

"A hundred thousand?"

"Yes."

Sardor smiled. He enjoyed seeing Dahl on the back foot.

"Forget about it. There's something else you can help us with."

"O.K.," Dahl said, looking relieved.

"We'll talk about that later. But I can't let Tatiana down. She's seriously pissed off."

Dahl shook his head. "So what are we going to do?"

"I have to be able to show some blood."

Dahl got to his feet and walked up to Sardor.

"Two punches on the left side?"

Sardor nodded at Dahl.

"Three."

"No rings," Dahl said.

Sardor nodded again.

While Eje did the dirty work, Sardor looked out through the panorama windows. The first light of morning broke the darkness and the birds began to sing in a new day on Stora Essingen. He was looking forward to a yoga session in the afternoon.

"Have you got any decent whisky?" he said.

Dahl groaned and wiped blood from his split lip.

"Sure. Single malt. Will that do?"

Dahl got back up and stumbled over to the drinks trolley.

"Perfect," Sardor said and took out his mobile. "We can drink while we're taking the photographs."

Tekla changed into some washed-out, dark blue tracksuit bottoms, her most comfortable bra and the pullover her mother had knitted, which she just managed to finish before she began slipping into the fog. She then pulled on the windcheater she had bought in Umeå while she still nurtured a vague hope of becoming an outdoor type, and trainers. She held her mobile in a firm grip. Not that she worried about some dirty old man jumping on her, she was more like one of those emaciated gazelles on the savannah which the lions turn up their noses at, but she needed to be accessible just in case Simon called. He was a night creature, always had been. A few hours after her visit to the I.C.U., it once again felt odd to think that Simon might be the burns victim. It must be her tired brain which was making the wrong connections, seeing and hearing things that did not make sense. She needed more amphetamine.

The door behind her slammed. Loud music was pouring out of the brick building on the other side of the street, she saw people at the open windows, smoking. Tekla crossed the road, let a taxi pass, carried on until she was on the cobblestones that covered the whole square. She closed her eyes, felt the uneven surface under her rubber soles, thought that this could be a place somewhere in southern Europe, a warm evening with cheerful laughter from a trattoria. At long last, a bit of summer and warmth had found its way to this remote spot on the map of Europe.

She opened her eyes again. The flower shop was shut. The kebab joint was open, but there were no clients. A few characters appeared to be ambling aimlessly around the edges of the square. Maybe people with troubled minds who were unable to find any rest in their lonely, cramped apartments. Or junkies on the prowl for the night's first fix.

A strong smell of freshly baked Danish pastries hit her as she entered the 7-Eleven. A young man in a baseball cap greeted her from the cold section, where he was putting out bottles of sports drink. Tekla returned his hello and pulled her hood over her head without really knowing why. Silly and irrational. She knew nobody in the area, had only lived in her apartment for a year. But when she went out at night it was as if she wanted to turn into someone else, most of all she would have liked to be driven around in a car with tinted windows and a chauffeur, pointing and saying "go there, we haven't looked for Simon there". She bought a coffee and a packet of chewing gum. On the way out, she held the door open for an old man with a Zimmer frame. The coffee was hot and scalded her mouth. She waited a little and looked towards the centre of town. The sky above her was dark, but, over to the left, the last rose-coloured rays of the sun were trying to hold on to the day. When the coffee had cooled a little, she knocked it back, feeling the warmth of it inside her, and went across the road, down to the water's edge.

Her headache was pounding at her temples like a rock crusher. Images crowded in her head, jostling for her attention. The blazing skyscraper. The tortured faces of the casualties. And what the hell had really happened in A. & E. on Thursday evening? The knife victim and the three-year-old at the same time. How could she have made a decision like that? And what would the consequences be? She was glad it was the weekend and that Collinder might not yet have discovered anything. All hell would break loose on Monday morning.

The marina was lifeless and still. A few boats remained on land, waiting to be put out into the cold, black water in the inlet. Her only connection with boats was the dinghy in the little lake at Edsåsdalen, which they used to go fishing. Tekla saw her father's calloused hands row steadily out to the middle of the still lake. As if all the fish were lying there at its deepest point, waiting to be caught.

The contented look on Pappa's face when he baited the hooks and saw her and Simon's eager anticipation. Simon's winsome smile when he said "ladies first", at which she took the rod from him and cast. He had never shown any jealousy. Not even when she was given a moped, several years later, and it was the one thing in the world he wanted more than anything else. "Your big sister can look after herself," was their father's reasoning. Of course she lent it to Simon when no-one was looking. He valued and repaid her trust to the full, polishing the paintwork with his old Iron Maiden T-shirt every time he went out for a ride. "Good as new." He kept on grinning his vulpine grin.

A cold breeze was blowing in off the water. The effect of the coffee had all but worn off, and she could not stop thinking about Simon. After a long walk at Hellasgården, nearly three months ago, and the row they had then, they had spoken only a few times on the telephone, and not seen each other since. It was the longest they had ever been apart. She was aware how badly she felt, somehow crippled.

She stopped by the vertical cliff at the bottom of the long slope, knowing that she was too early and he always late. For a few minutes, she savoured the scene. There, from the darkness of the forest, she could gaze undisturbed across the water.

The mighty shape of the Nobel Hospital rose on the other shore. So full of history, suffering and knowledge. Most of the windows were dark; she wondered what was going on behind the ones which were lit up. An operation to mend a ruptured aorta? Perhaps someone wrestling with an urgent caesarian which was about to go terribly wrong? Was somebody running past one of those windows in A. & E., needle in hand, ready to drain the tamponade that was killing the man with the heart attack?

However hard she tried, she could not put the image of the burns victim's foot out of her mind. Could it be Simon? She tried to laugh the idea off as absurd, but instead felt a lump in her throat. She would have to wait to see what the D.N.A. tests revealed. Because otherwise, imagine if she were wrong – then she would have exposed her brother as a drug addict. And maybe he was, but he did not take heroin, so far as she knew, which it seemed the burns victim had done. There was no reason to hurry, the police were pushing the investigation as fast as they could. And in the unlikely event that it was him, then what was the connection to that van? Could Simon have had anything to do with a bomb? She broke into a genuine smile. She could picture their father laughing at Simon when he complained about the recoil on the elk rifle. They were practising shooting at bottles filled with sand. Only a month to go until the elk hunt. Simon did not want to shoot anymore. Tekla took over the rifle. Simon was accurate with his air pistol, but he preferred Lego.

She had to assume that the intubated patient was not Simon. The oddity of the foot was a coincidence. A trick which her dysfunctional brain was playing on her. She really ought to focus on finding him and then give him a piece of her mind. The only thing she knew was that she would do anything for her brother. Wherever he was. Whatever his condition. Whatever it took.

She looked at her mobile. Ten long minutes left.

The bridge was just visible through the trees. The cars up there in the air were a distant, formless roar. In the background, beyond the bridge: apartment blocks elbowing aside the forest.

She sat down on one of the logs of the outdoor gym. Someone had discarded a tin of snus, which she did not feel like picking up, and yet it bothered her.

"Hi."

Tekla looked up. Had not heard him coming.

"Where were you?"

"Jumpy?"

He sat on a log next to hers, legs crossed, his bright yellow trainers shining in the half light. They looked new.

"Makes you want to work out."

He shrugged off his rucksack, its orange straps flapping.

"Not particularly," she said, her voice flat. Her heartbeat dropped steadily. She just wanted to get away from there as quickly as possible.

But he always liked a bit of a chat to begin with, and she had long ago accepted the rules of the game. If she talked to him for a few minutes, pretended to be interested in his update on some girl, or grief with a supplier or some customer, he was satisfied and disappeared. When she had, on occasion, showed signs of impatience, he acted like a five-year-old and wanted to drag things out.

"How do you manage to keep fit if you don't exercise?"

"Good genes," Tekla said.

"Are your parents sporty?"

She smiled and thought about her mother's thin upper arms, a pouch of skin and fat that drooped as she knitted.

"That would be an exaggeration."

"But you have done sports, right?" he insisted, interest in his voice.

Tekla thought about her friend Anna-Stina's brave attempts to drag her along to the group work-outs at Umeå. How she had joined in, perhaps three times, lying on the floor of a gym that stank of sweat, doing sit-ups, push-ups and burpees. All it did was hurt her body and it gave her no joy, no kick. Her limbs didn't seem to respond properly when they were loaded, the movement was disjointed and jerky. Anna-Stina's disappointment when Tekla said she wasn't coming along the next time.

"I don't as a matter of principle."

He studied her from top to toe in surprise.

"Unbelievable."

She saw him check out her small bust, give her body a greedy look, the way men sometimes do in a bar when they think they are paying a compliment by admiring someone in a really bestial way. She wanted to be looked at discreetly, from the side, as if she were forbidden fruit. Not like a slab of meat someone wants to throw on the grill.

"I expect I'm meant to be saying thank you now."

He put his rucksack down on the bare earth and took out a cigarette.

"Want one?"

"No thanks."

"You don't smoke, do you?"

Tekla shook her head.

"I guess it's only Polish builders who smoke on the job these days." He drew in a long puff. "Were you on duty at the fire?"

"Yes."

"How was it?"

She regretted her answer at once.

"It was . . . a big fire."

"Were there many injured?"

"You know there were. And I can't tell you anything. Confidentiality."

"That's so bloody crass."

He looked disappointed. Probably did not know what the word meant.

It struck her that she knew nothing whatsoever about him. Did he have a proper job as well as this? Family? Had he given her his real name? Presumably not. But she did have his mobile number. No doubt a separate "work telephone". She was curious. He seemed nice, despite the jargon and his fixation with talking about girls all the time, all the allusions to sex. Luckily, he seemed to have other customers to meet that evening. It was, after all, Saturday. He played around with his mobile, texted.

Finally he flicked the cigarette butt onto the footpath.

"How much do you want?"

"Forty."

He paused, held his rucksack in one hand.

"Wow, I'm assuming you're not selling on? You know it's strictly for you?"

"It's only for my own consumption."

"But last week you took twenty-five."

"I've got a lot on at work at the moment."

"Anything you want to tell me about?"

She tried to smile.

"We can talk any time. I'm way good at keeping secrets. Promise. And I'm cool if you want more. It's good for business, nothing less. But better to have a client in the long term. You know that—"

"I just need some more bombs at the moment."

"Bombs?" He smiled. "You know we say we *bomb* when we take a little ball, right? But we don't usually talk about *bombs*."

"Whatever," Tekla said, she just wanted him to go away.

"You're really funny, doctor."

"Yeah, right."

Tekla wished she had not told him she worked as a doctor. She had always been too trusting, something that Simon often pointed out.

He picked up a shopping tote from the alcohol monopoly store, Systembolaget, and from that got out a freezer bag filled with small paper balls. He put Tekla's supply into a separate freezer pouch.

"Here."

"Thanks."

She had already worked out how much she owed him, and handed over the notes. He put them in his jacket pocket.

"Aren't you going to count?"

He gave her a condescending smile.

Tekla was conscious of the fact that he was expensive. But he was also the only one she knew who prepared the little balls for his customers himself. The mere thought of sitting at home with some scales, a tiny spoon and some toilet paper made her paranoid. She would probably get the volumes wrong, end up with more or less than 0.2 grammes. And she could afford it. So far.

She got up and he grasped her hand. His was sweaty and warm.

"Take it easy, yeah?"

"Are you my dad or something?" she said and pulled her hand away.

He spread his arms.

"Just give me a call. The customer is king."

He disappeared off the way he usually came, over towards Liljeholmen, where she supposed most of his clients were. Or Hornstull. She had never seen him by Gullmarsplan.

She closed her eyes and soaked up the silence.

After a minute or so she turned and saw that he really had gone. Alone at last. She grabbed the plastic bag and got out a little ball. Tossed it into her mouth, then realised she did not have any water. Shit. Nothing to wash it down with. Her mouth was bone dry and there was no chance that she would be able to swallow. But neither could she wait till she got home. The headache was pounding. Her body cried out in pain.

Tekla looked around desperately, hoping for a discarded water bottle.

Nothing.

Her only option was the water down in Årstaviken.

She slithered down the slope. Balanced on a smooth stone and bent down, scooping up water with her hand. Swallowed the paper ball, which had begun to break up.

She closed her eyes. It should only take a minute or two for the effect to set in. She could taste stagnant water and toilet paper. Tekla got out a piece of chewing gum. Immediately felt better. She was shivering and realised that she would be freezing before she got home.

ACCIDENT & EMERGENCY, NOBEL HOSPITAL
Sunday morning, 9.vi

Although she had emptied a bag full of chocolate wafers and grapes and drunk half a litre of Fanta from the Ica store on Gullmarsplan, Tekla was already hungry, and by eleven o'clock had to make straight for the staff pantry. She asked an assistant nurse, who was heating food in the microwave, if it was O.K. to take a sandwich from the patients' refrigerator.

"Yes, go ahead, my dear. Everyone does it. Courtesy of the County Council, you know."

"Thanks."

She poured herself a large glass of milk and felt some of her strength return. She still had to do half the day shift and was already exhausted. No matter how fast she worked, new patients were forever being added to the list. The only advantage of working weekends was that neither Collinder nor anyone else from management was in the building.

"What's that stench?" Tekla said.

"That's what everyone's asking."

Her visit to A. & E. the previous day had really affected her. Normally she did not find it so hard to concentrate. She texted Simon for the tenth time that day. No answer. She remembered how he had disliked technology when he was a child. Always preferred board games to the Ataris his friends fiddled away at. He probably hated everything about the digital age. If she only knew where he was living, she would leave him an affectionate hand-written note.

Tekla noticed the assistant nurse looking at her, so she raised her eyebrows and gave her a questioning look.

133

"I just wanted to say that there are many of us who think you did absolutely the right thing the other evening. You were fantastic. Don't let anyone give you any grief. They wouldn't if you were a man."

"You mean the knife drama in A. & E.?"

"And that little kid at the same time. And then straight off to the fire. You're awesome, Tekla. Don't forget that."

The assistant nurse – Tekla saw that she was called Viola – came closer and said in a confidential tone:

"You're the only one who understood that it was a status—".

"Status epilepticus."

"—and blood poisoning. You took a chance with all those meds and saved the kid's life."

"Not sure everyone sees it that way."

Tekla knew there was a risk that Oscar had sustained brain damage. So for what sort of life had she saved him? Had she given him, and his family, another six months of a medical nightmare? She thought about what his sister Iris had said.

"Of course they do."

Viola put her hand to Tekla's cheek. It was unclear who should have been stroking whose cheek, but the gesture seemed to come naturally to Viola.

"Do you have someone you can talk to at home, dear?"

Tekla reacted as if she had had an electric shock, her face twitched and Viola drew her hand away.

"I manage."

"I'm sure you do. But occasionally it's nice to have someone to share one's existence with," Viola said, and left. All of a sudden, Tekla longed to be at home in Edsåsdalen. She drank some more milk and pressed the button for "Coffee Extra Strong". The bright green machine hummed and coughed out a black sludge. In Italy it would not be called coffee. But Simon loved it, he always made his coffee "as strong as Farsan's witches' brew in the cellar". But what bothered her more than anything else just then was the sour stench pervading A. & E. Didn't it smell of old garbage?

The burns patient from Söder Tower had been operated on again during the night, more dead skin had been removed, and they were beginning to prepare for a cadaver skin graft. The knifing victim who had come in on Thursday night was now in post-op. He had lost his spleen and been given a total of eleven bags of blood, but had pulled through. Incredible, given the circumstances. Tekla suspected that his ribcage must be very painful after the heart compressions his friend had performed on him. She smiled. She also realised that she was going around trying to interpret the looks on the faces of the staff. She was probably reading too much into them, but it seemed to her that some colleagues were more taciturn than usual. In her imagination she saw two different buttons: a green one in favour of euthanasia, and a red one against. And herself on a soapbox giving an impassioned speech about this complex issue and how it was not something you could paint in black and white. Or red and green.

"The waiting room's pretty full," a nurse called to her from the nurses' station. "Where's the other doctor?"

"I don't know."

That other one, unfortunately, was Hampus Nordensköld. She had not seen much of him. He was no doubt very competent, otherwise he would not have been appointed a consultant at the Nobel Hospital's Accident & Emergency department, but he had done precious little to share the benefits of his expert knowledge.

"Tekla?"

"Yes?"

Cassandra, the nurse with the spider tattoo, hailed her.

"Could you do me a favour and take a look in Room 8? Saturation is down to eighty-eight, even though she's had four litres of oxygen.

Room 8. Like rat number eight in the cage to the left. Is the idea to dehumanise and create a distance, so that one can cope with all the shit? Is it because the anthill has become too big for people to be able to relate to it?

Tekla went in to see an Iraqi-born woman with cardiac insufficiency. She seemed to be quite unaware of her condition, of the fact

135

that it is an illness with a higher mortality rate than all the cancers put together. After that, Tekla had nine other patients waiting for her. In addition, there were sixteen patients in A. & E. who had not been attended to. Nordensköld was nowhere to be seen and Tekla considered asking the nurses to track him down, but she supposed he must be busy with something important. Her headache had started to take on another colour. From pumpkin orange to brownish-black.

Half an hour later, as Tekla was sitting with a patient with a suspected blood clot in his leg, Viola put her head round the door and held out a telephone.

"It's for you, Tekla."

Tekla held up her plastic gloves and indicated to Viola that she was busy with an ultrasound.

"Can it wait?"

Viola shook her head and covered the mouthpiece of the telephone as she whispered:

"It's the C.E.O. She sounds pretty determined."

Nina closed the glass door and pushed a bronze-coloured Nespresso capsule into the coffee machine. She saw Jeanette approaching with an open laptop in her hand, but Nina waved her firmly away. Showing clear signs of irritation, Jeanette turned on her heels outside the door and walked back to reception. Nina sat down in the leather armchair, kicked off her shoes and put her feet up on the footstool. She looked out over the water. Rested her eyes on the tower on Kastellholmen island. The sky was cornflower blue.

She took out her mobile.

"It's him," she said when Jonna answered.

The heavy Manhattan morning rush-hour traffic could be heard in the background.

"You're joking!"

Nina drained the hot espresso. She looked around once more, making sure that Jeanette had not crept back in again.

"No, unfortunately not."

"So what happens now?"

"We have to . . ."

Nina got to her feet. A disturbing thought went through her mind: what would *really* happen if Pappa found out about everything? The answer was simple: he must never be allowed to know. It was unthinkable. An unqualified disaster. Not to mention the mischief Sardor might make of this whole mess.

"The only thing they know is that Oleg was there. They've been to the hospital and checked . . . It's him."

"Shall I come home?" Jonna said.

"Why?"

"I can't . . ." Jonna groaned into the receiver.

"Do you really think now is the time to start moaning?" Nina went over to the counter and pushed in a new capsule. The machine hummed. "Are you or aren't you my partner? And by the way, I sold Kaggholmen today. I got it up to thirty-five."

"Well done you, but—"

"No buts," Nina cut her off. "Grip."

"But what are we going to do?" Jonna asked.

Nina took the double espresso and stood in front of the mural. She stared at the oil paint, the thick brush strokes. She remembered the time Umarov had taken her and Sardor to the Tate in London. Her father explaining to them where art was really to be found. "The only museum one needs to visit is the Hermitage in St Petersburg. This is a Wendy house in comparison." Sardor spent most of his time trying to annoy his older sister, but Nina took it all in. Her interest had been aroused in earnest when she stood in front of a painting by Malevich. "How impressive, a black square," Sardor had sniped, walking on. Nina remained standing there for a long time, fascinated by the simple beauty. Once she and Joakim could afford it, they had started buying all the art they had been able to get their hands on. But the many house and apartment deals had drained their finances, leaving them with no funds for the moment to indulge this passion. That was what the Söder Tower deal was meant to change.

"He mustn't be allowed to speak, that's all."

"But surely he's seriously injured?" Jonna said. "Is he even going to regain consciousness? What'll happen if he survives? He knows everything."

"He *won't* talk," Nina said, controlled irritation in her voice. She drank her coffee. "Don't I usually sort things out?"

She heard at once how she sounded like Umarov.

"I hate to admit it, but yes you do," Jonna said. "Although I'm not sure I always want to know how."

Another thing Nina had learned from Umarov: discretion. Never disclose too much. Keep sensitive stuff to yourself. Only let on to close confidants, and even then only if absolutely necessary. There was one fundamental secret which she had to bear all by herself, however. Umarov must never find out that, when he was released from prison in Moscow and allowed to start his new life in Stockholm, the F.S.B. had imposed a fourth condition, on Nina alone. She remembered how the bald man had come up to her at the university café. He said he was from the Centre. Later she found out that was the nickname of the F.S.B. headquarters. They would let Umarov go and send him to Sweden, but Nina had to keep a close eye on him. And report regularly to a contact person. What could she have said? That she wasn't prepared to do it? That her father's death sentence should be carried out? She had been left with no choice.

She met the F.S.B. representative every six months, at the dental practice on Humlegården.

"Just don't rock the boat. I'll take care of this," Nina said. "I stand to lose as much as you if anything gets out."

"How do you mean?"

"You don't want to know."

Nina saw Jeanette come back and this time she let her in, having put Jonna on hold.

"Yes?" Nina asked.

"Two things. Don't forget the Fortifications Agency. Your guests are coming on Monday."

"And thing number two?"

"Your father called. He says he can't get through on your mobile."

"I'm in a meeting, tell him."

"Will do. And I'll say your phone's switched off," the capable Jeanette suggested, and left the room without waiting for confirmation.

"Are you still there?"

"I'm already up to my neck in this," Jonna said.

"But the less you know, the better."

"I don't want you keeping me in the dark."

Nina sat down at the desk. The screen lit up when she nudged the mouse.

"O.K., suit yourself. I've got contacts."

"Some Russian guy?"

"I'm not telling you any more than that."

"And if he doesn't fix this? There must be guards there."

"They know how to get in."

"They?"

"As I said. Trust me."

"So long as it doesn't blow up in our faces."

Nina laughed.

"It won't. Make the most of your stay in the big city and have some fun on your last day. See you tomorrow."

Nina hung up on her colleague and searched for the number of the dental clinic. She had to move fast now, before the window of opportunity closed.

"Tekla. How are you?" Carlsson said.

Tekla was still tense and trying to shed the feeling that something unpleasant was about to happen. Being summoned to see the hospital C.E.O., on a Sunday, got Tekla imagining that more details had surfaced concerning the young child and that she was now going to get the sack. When she saw how relaxed Carlsson looked, as she leaned against the desk with her hand in the bowl of liquorice, she thought it less likely that the hour of reckoning had come.

"I'm fine, thanks."

"It's good of you to come."

The new tone of voice surprised Tekla. Equally, she could not help wondering what would have happened if she had *not* dropped everything and run straight to the top floor.

"Are things going O.K. down there in the bowels of the earth?"

Tekla suppressed a snide remark about Flash Hampus and other work-shy doctors.

"We've got a lot of patients today."

"And loads of beds to accommodate all those poor wrecks."

Tekla did her best to return the C.E.O.'s ironic smile.

"Right?"

Carlsson hung her red jacket over the back of her chair. She was wearing a shirt with padded shoulders, a style which had not been seen since the end of the '90s. Carlsson picked up a copy of *Connoisseur* magazine and flicked through it idly.

"I heard there's a bad smell. Not here though."

Tekla took a deep breath. Carlsson was right. It really was the only place in the hospital where she had not noticed that stale smell.

Carlsson put the magazine down.

"*Is* he actually a terrorist?"

There it was. The reason why she had been summoned. Of course there was an agenda. From their first meeting, Tekla had realised that one wasn't summoned to see the hospital C.E.O. on a whim.

"Believe you me, no-one ever tells *me* anything."

Carlsson came uncomfortably close to Tekla, who could smell a whiff of alcohol. Or was it a cloying scent? Tekla looked along the gold chain and saw what was weighing it down on her chest: a chunky golden dice.

"It's as if I'm at the tip of a pyramid," Carlsson said pensively. "I'm totally reliant on the two stones that hold me up. Sometimes I can feel a contact with the four stones underneath them. But that's as far as it goes."

Tekla could picture it. She thought of Simon and his fascination with large constructions. How he was constantly building: Lego towers, pyramids of pine cones, sandcastles.

"Whereas you are surrounded by a whole army of stones down there. A circle of stability. And you can choose which ones you want to lean on. I can't."

Carlsson picked out a liquorice monkey and began to chew.

"Do you know who my two stones are?"

"No."

"I hardly even do myself."

It struck Tekla that she had forgotten to take off her plastic apron. Should she start tearing at it here and now?

"I see you have a lot to do down there."

"An awful lot."

Tekla took off the apron.

"Many of them wrecks."

"I don't know if—"

"I like to call a spade a spade. They're wrecks and we're their salvation. Our job is to bring on board the ones who can survive the journey to dry land."

"There are several who are very sick."

"But not all of them can survive."

"That depends on the condi—"

"This society is in a putrid condition," Carlsson said firmly. "And we have to do what we can to cut away the dead flesh. What was it like growing up in Edsåsdalen?"

It felt as if someone had grabbed Tekla by the throat from behind and was squeezing, so that she struggled to breathe and her voice failed her.

"Maybe a bit quiet at times."

"I can understand that. Not so much sunshine either, I imagine."

Tekla saw Simon playing on the beach. The lake became very warm in the middle of summer and they used to paddle around until late into the night. During the days, their father would sit and read the newspaper, every now and then looking up at the children as they played in the canoe by the water's edge. Tekla used to bury Simon in the sand, with only his head poking out.

"Summer was perhaps a little short."

"But you had a feeling of control, didn't you?"

Was it really that, Tekla wondered. The only time she could really relax was with Pappa and Simon, when it was just them in the forest or on a mountainside. Far from their mother's sharp tongue or Simon's friends, away from their father's sticky bottles in the larder.

"You don't need to answer," Carlsson said, lowering her voice. Tekla felt the warmth from the C.E.O.'s body. She tried not to blink.

"I know you're your own woman. Just make sure you keep it that way. Don't let anyone bully you."

Carlsson's summary of the work situation was pretty accurate. Yet Tekla could not help feeling that she was actually referring to something else.

"Keep your eyes and ears open."

"I will."

Out of nowhere the C.E.O. said:

"The best intensive care unit in the county. Highest levels of patient satisfaction. Shortest waiting times in A. & E. And cutting-edge research which has those puffed-up professors on the other side of the Solna Bridge drooling."

"Doesn't exactly sound like the Nobel Hospital," Tekla said, adding: "any longer."

Carlsson fixed her eyes on Tekla.

"Precisely."

Tekla sensed that there was more to come.

"But that's how it's going to be."

"Sounds expensive."

"That's the very reason I'm so glad we have you here."

"Because?"

Carlsson picked up her reading spectacles and went over to her computer.

Tekla assumed that this was when she was meant to take herself off soundlessly. She waited for a few seconds in case there was more to come, but Carlsson was engrossed in something on the screen. As she left the room, Tekla wondered how Carlsson imagined that she was going to make all this happen. And why? What was her motivation? She found herself again with the memories of the summer with Simon on the beach. And then she saw what it was that her mind had been trying to alert her to: Simon's ears. The large birthmark on the upper edge of the right ear.

As Tekla walked into the department, she had to pause to catch her breath. She dried the sweat from her forehead and began to move towards the burns unit. On the way, she bumped into Pirkko, the nurse who had taken care of the burns patient earlier.

"Don't you usually come in around eleven?" Pirkko said.

"Yep. But I remembered something else I have to check."

The patient's right ear was not burned. Tekla's brain had registered that, but not flagged it before. At last she would find out whether it was Simon lying there on the bed.

Pirkko was carrying a pile of yellow blankets and walked alongside Tekla.

"We've been baking, how about some coffee and a bun?"

"No thanks."

Tekla wiped some more sweat off her brow.

"Maybe something to drink at least?"

"It's O.K. I'm not staying long."

Tekla felt a tingling sensation in the palms of her hands.

Pirkko turned off towards Room 2 and said:

"Let me know if you need anything."

Tekla went into the airlock and started to put on her plastic clothes. The gloves were sticking because of the sweat, but in the end she was ready and pushed open the door to the room.

At first her brain did not take in what her eyes were seeing: somebody holding a cushion over the patient's face.

Tekla walked rapidly to the bed.

"What the hell's going on here?"

The man stopped what he was doing, but he did not look around.

She knew at once how dangerous the situation was: she was alone in the room, no nurse or assistant nurse there. And someone was trying to kill the patient.

The man, who was wearing a black windcheater with a hood, let go of the pillow, swung around, grabbed the overbed table, and sent it flying at Tekla as he began to make for the window.

Tekla backed away to avoid the table, but tripped on her plastic coat. On some subconscious level, she had spotted a pair of scissors lying on a chair next to some bandages. She managed to get around the table, grabbed the scissors and ran at the man.

As he pulled open the window and took a first step onto a chair, presumably to jump onto the fire escape, Tekla was able to strike. She came from the side and threw her full weight against him. The scissors stabbed straight into his groin. Tekla lost her grip on them: they had gone in all the way up to the handles.

The man fell to the floor and shouted out in a language Tekla did not recognise.

As she regained her balance, she saw the man pull out the scissors and scramble to his feet. He staggered to the door.

Tekla screamed as loudly as she could. She hesitated for a second. Should she stay and see what had happened to the patient, or follow the man?

She turned to the ventilator, reconnected the tube and heard the machine give a first breath. Then she rushed off after the man.

There was nobody outside the room.

"Someone's tried to kill the burns victim in Room 1! Call the guards!" she yelled, watching the man limp around the corner.

Pirkko emerged from Room 2.

"The patient in Room 1's been attacked. Take care of him. And ring security and the police."

Then Tekla began to run after the assailant.

He made his way over towards the lift lobby and opened the

door to the stairwell. Tekla took out her mobile and sped after him. Her first thought was to ring 112, but Pirkko would be sure to do that. She reached the door leading to the stairs, hesitated for a micro-second, then opened it.

She could hear footsteps some floors down and set off in pursuit. There was no sound of any slamming doors so she kept going all the way down to the basement.

On the lowest level, she saw splashes of blood on the floor. She opened the door to one of the service tunnels and was hit by a stale smell.

But there was no-one to be seen.

A long corridor ran to the right: he would not have had time to go the full length of it. There was a bend at the beginning of the service tunnel on the left. Tekla ran in that direction.

She stopped before the corner and listened. It was dead quiet. Could he be standing on the far side with a pistol?

She took a chance and stepped around.

There was blood on the painted yellow cement floor, outside a large door. No signs to indicate what was behind it.

Tekla tried to control her breathing and clutched her mobile. She looked around. There was nothing there she could use to defend herself.

She saw two people dressed in white come walking towards her further down the corridor, seemingly oblivious to the drama.

She opened the door to find yet another corridor leading to one of the short sides of the hospital. At the far end, a hundred or more metres away, she saw the man hobbling along.

Tekla gave a yell and began to run after him.

He did not turn.

The exit, she thought. He knows there is an exit to the staff car park.

"Stop!"

The man did not look round.

Suddenly, there was a ring on Tekla's mobile. She felt the pressure on her chest as she gasped for breath, and realised she would not be able to catch up with the man.

She stopped and turned around. The service tunnel was empty.

The ringing continued. Tekla answered.

"It's Cassandra in the I.C.U. Where are you?"

"I . . ." Tekla tried to catch her breath.

"Hampus wants you to come to the I.C.U."

"Is it urgent?"

"No cardiac arrest, but I think you're needed."

"I'll be there in five."

As she hung up there was a beep from her mobile. She held up the screen and read: I NEED HELP!

Tekla stared at the sender. It was Simon's number.

The ancient Greek sculptures were not the main reason why Umarov was drawn to the Victoria and Albert museum. It was more prosaic, more a question of logistics: they were living in South Kensington, Daria loved to shop at Harrods and the children's school was in Prince's Gardens. The V. & A. lay at the centre of this triangle and had a café which she liked, an attractive inner courtyard in which Nina and Sardor used to play when they were small. Above all, Umarov wanted to move about as little as possible in this city that he used to call "the most bewildering place I know". Until he and Daria decided to become expatriate Soviets, he had not travelled much in the West.

He flopped onto the bench under the 1856 polychrome stained glass windows and stared up into the vaulted ceiling. It was magnificent and vaguely reminiscent of the Perlov Tea House in Moscow, just a little less ostentatious. He straightened his tie, which was too tight around his neck, and wiped sweat from his forehead.

"I've got to have something to drink," Daria exclaimed, dumping four large carrier bags on the floor.

"What would you like?"

"Some sort of fresh juice." Daria pulled off her fur coat and let it fall onto a chair.

Umarov got up to buy an apple juice for his shopaholic wife. It was not going to be easy. He went out into the hall and looked around. It was full of coffee-drinking Londoners, but Boris was nowhere to be seen. He did however spot Kristina Lind from Jönköping coming towards him, with Nina and Sardor on either side. They were in their school uniforms and Sardor was towing his rucksack along the ground, as if dragging an animal carcass that he had found by the roadside.

"Do you want anything? I'm buying an apple juice for Mamushka."

"A Coke," Sardor said. "Water," Nina replied.

"And you?"

The freckled au pair smiled. "I'm fine, thanks." She seldom wanted anything, perhaps afraid of appearing greedy. She also seemed to be religious, and drank no alcohol.

Umarov went over to the café and bought his family their drinks and some pastries. The children tucked in while Daria poured out her juice.

"Why are you so stressed?"

"Me?" Umarov said in surprise.

"No-one else is looking around every five seconds. Who are you expecting? And why the grey suit? You look like Yeltsin."

"Thanks for the compliment," Umarov said, again looking over in the direction of the entrance to the hall. He held in his stomach and felt offended at the comparison.

Just then, Umarov saw his friend of twenty-five years walk into the gilt hall. Behind Boris was a man in a dark suit, heavier shoes than any Englishman would wear at this time of year and a coat from some distant decade. The beige colour and broad lapels reeked of Eastern Europe.

"Why don't you go to the Natural History Museum?" Umarov suggested to the children.

"Yes!" Sardor said and immediately jumped to his feet.

Boris came over to the table. "Daria! How have you managed to become even more beautiful than when I saw you last week?"

"Give it a rest," she said, but she smiled at Umarov's best friend and stood to greet him. They kissed each other on the cheek.

"This is Igor Galitsky," Boris said, introducing a man who could not be anything other than a Russian politician who had spent years climbing the greasy poles of the Soviet State apparatus. Galitsky held out his hand and greeted Daria and Umarov in formal tones.

"I'll take the children off," Kristina said as she packed up Nina and Sardor's bits and pieces.

"I'll stay here for a while," Daria said. "Shall we say one hour?"

"Fine," Kristina said, and left with the children.

"Shall we get a breath of air?" Umarov suggested, pointing towards the exit. The three men left the café and went out into the courtyard, where a crowd of people was sitting in the chill, trying to catch the last of the afternoon rays. The sky was pale blue, with the spring sun still providing some warmth along one side of the garden. Boris took a packet of Marlboro from his coat pocket and proffered it. Umarov and Galitsky each took one. Boris held out his gold lighter for them, just one of the many expensive accessories he carried around in his pockets. His job as a corporate lawyer in London during the latter part of the '80s had made him "disgustingly rich", as Umarov liked to say. Boris used to counter with: "You just need to help yourself to a bigger piece of the pie, and then you too will be able to afford to buy your suits on Savile Row."

They smoked their cigarettes and waited for a couple with a pram to pass the bench where they had seated themselves. Some small children were playing by the water, their parents resting on the grass a little way off.

"Boris has spoken warmly of you," Galitsky said as he looked out over the pond. "He says you're a man of integrity."

Umarov knew he would have to choose his words carefully. He was fully conscious that the man beside him worked for Anatoly Chubais. He had probably also met Yeltsin, but that was less significant; Chubais was the brains behind the privatisation wave which was now sweeping the former U.S.S.R., and a man who impressed Umarov.

"I like to have a firm grip on the numbers."

"Victor has built up his transportation business in no time at all," Boris said.

"I know," Galitsky said. "It's people like you we want back home."

"What do you mean?" Umarov had established his transport

company in northern Europe in just a few years, and had been able to use his contacts within the Soviet government during the Gorbachev era and the emerging business class to set himself up there as well.

Galitsky threw his cigarette butt onto the gravel and ground it under his shoe. "Have you met Anatoly Chubais?"

"I haven't had that honour."

"But you know what we're doing? What we've done with the State oil and gas monopoly, for example?"

Umarov knew what Chubais had done with Rosneftgaz the year before. The Soviet Ministry of Fuel and Energy had been privatised in no time at all and the former State enterprises were now falling like ninepins as the oligarchs rolled their bowling balls. He had observed at a distance what was going on inside the old Soviet Union, but he had thought all along that it did not concern him, that he had moved to London for a reason, and intended never to return. Besides which, Daria loved her new life.

"It's hard not to notice."

Galitsky laid a skinny hand on Umarov's knee. It felt awkward, but Umarov would never dare react to it in any way. The bureaucrat, clearly a powerful and influential man, looked straight at Umarov. "You may think there's time enough, that only four months have passed since the fall of the Soviet Union. But you have no idea, things are moving very quickly, and you need to act before it's too late."

Boris could tell that his good friend was not getting the message, so he jumped in:

"This is an opportunity, Victor! Are you in or not?"

"In on what? What are we talking about?"

"The electricity monopoly," Galitsky said. "The world's fourth largest energy producer after the U.S.A., Japan and China. Six hundred and eighty thousand employees. That's what Chubais is aiming for, but it'll take time. There are a number of people who want a slice of the pie."

"And?"

Galitsky turned to Boris. "I thought you said he was smart."

"He's just a bit slow on the uptake sometimes when he's stressed," Boris laughed. "Victor, this is a gift horse, you and I are being invited onto the privatisation train."

Galitsky stood up and held out his hand to Umarov. "Give it some thought," he said. Then he walked off towards the entrance at the far side of the courtyard.

Boris and Umarov remained sitting. They stared at the children playing around them. Boris took out a cigarette and lit it. "You can keep the transportation business going, but I need you back home. We have to act now."

"But what does the Kremlin say?"

"So long as one's open with the K.G.B., they're happy."

Umarov had a thousand questions, his future plans had all been turned upside down. What would Daria say about their moving back home?

He left Boris and went back to the café. Daria was playing with Nina. Kristina had just come back with the children.

"Anyone interested in Indian instead of pizza?" Umarov said, looking at the hungry faces before him.

"I am," Daria said and got up. "Isn't it great to be living in a cosmopolitan city, where you can get anything?"

Umarov felt a knot in his stomach. He knew that he would have to choose between his wife and this opportunity. In the new home-land that was now called Russia and had an alcoholic president with a shock of white hair. Where there were endless potential new business breaks. But right now, he would not let anything get in the way of his Friday evening with the family.

"Well then," he said, planting a kiss on Daria's dark purple lips, "tonight we'll have Indian."

III

HANINGE INDUSTRIAL ZONE
Five weeks earlier

Lundgren was trying to keep his nausea in check and looked out through the tinted windows of the S.W.A.T. team's first minibus.

"Do you have to drive like a lunatic?" he shouted to Matte up front.

Silence in return. He pulled down the balaclava and took some deep breaths.

"How much longer?"

"Two minutes," Stefan answered from the seat next to him. "Put your mask back on."

Lundgren drew up his balaclava again. They were two units, one minibus per unit, each unit comprising two groups of six. They were followed by three patrol cars from whichever police section was running the actual intervention, in other words, regular police officers, who would be seizing the goods, making the arrests and so on. The S.W.A.T. team always went in first. Organised crime meant heavy weapons.

Lundgren tightened the straps on his bullet-proof vest and checked his MP5 one more time.

"Thirty seconds," Matte called out.

Everyone braced for action. The vehicle braked, veered right and accelerated again. After a few more seconds it screeched to a halt. The side doors were opened and they jumped out.

Lundgren was struck by how cold the air was. It must have been close to freezing. Typical late-April weather. Two cars were parked a way off. No motorcycles. No people. The observers, who had carried out the reconnaissance and watched the industrial premises overnight, had reported that only two men had gone in and none had left.

The building stood on a large, open, asphalted piece of ground, about fifty metres from the nearest other structure. The property was fenced off, but the gates were open, which was strange considering that it was Walpurgis Night, the evening before a public holiday, and the sun had just set. By now, the people working there should have left to go and eat candyfloss with their families around a celebratory bonfire. Lundgren held the automatic weapon against his chest, the barrel pointing downwards at an angle. His Sig Sauer was in its holster, the rest of his equipment stowed away too. In front of him, Stefan had taken the lead. Lundgren looked up at the second floor. There were two brightly lit signs with red lettering against a white background: AIR SOURCE HEAT PUMPS and P.F. PRINTING AND COPYING. What he saw corresponded pretty much to the description given by the field officers at the police station earlier that day. They had shown them drawings provided by the building owner. The biker gang's premises were in the basement. But he was the only one who knew where the refrigerator with the cash was.

The first unit advanced swiftly towards the ramp leading down to the garage and smashed in the double doors. There was a series of loud twin blasts. They had decided on a lightning attack with flash-bangs. According to the field officers, there were likely to be weapons on site.

They entered a large room with copying machines and cardboard boxes piled against the walls, but no people. The strip lights were on. It looked neat and tidy.

Lundgren's group fanned out. Each man knew exactly what he had to do. Lundgren turned and spotted the police patrols through the garage doors. They were waiting outside the building until Lundgren and his group had secured the premises. The heat in the room was considerable and Lundgren was sweating.

"Clear!" Lundgren yelled as he continued into a corridor.

They searched methodically through room after room. Constantly covering for each other. They had done this so often that it sometimes felt like being inside one of those Chinese dragons you see in parades. The creature slithered on, searching a kitchen which was empty of people but crammed with pizza cartons, styrofoam boxes and beer cans. Another room was full of banana crates.

Lundgren remembered the floor plan, knew where the room with the refrigerator was meant to be.

The next door was shut. And locked. Stefan broke it open and here they found the first people: four young men of what looked like South American origin.

"Police! On the floor!" somebody shouted. The men held up their hands and fell to their knees. Pockets and waistbands were searched. Lundgren wished that he did not have to wear leather gloves, they made it difficult to feel sharp objects. Everyone was afraid to be jabbed by a needle; luckily that had never happened to him. He pulled at his jacket and undid the top button to give himself more air.

The men were handcuffed, then guarded by a member of the unit until the regular police officers dawdling behind them could take over. Lundgren and four more continued along the corridor. A boiler room with an electrical switchboard. Two rooms with camp beds. Sweet wrappers, plastic bottles and other rubbish strewn across the concrete floor. There was a stench of urine.

"Clear!" Matte called as he kept going.

Lundgren pulled the lower part of his balaclava down a little. His only problem with the equipment was the heat. Even as a child he had been teased because he sweated so much. His head was boiling. He let the MP5 hang on its strap on his chest and took out the Sig Sauer, which was lighter to carry. Pulled his mask up again.

In the next room, they finally found the core of the operation: the lab.

"Police! Down on the floor!"

Five young men at first stood still, and then began to follow orders. The aluminium tables were piled high with scales, baskets full of plastic bags, rubber gloves, spoons, tape, white tins, glass jars and mounds of white powder.

Matte and two others secured the room and began to put handcuffs on the men.

Lundgren continued down the corridor. He made sure two more rooms were safe and advanced towards the stairs at the end of the passage. A last room on the right. That was where he was heading. Lundgren went in.

Two men were sitting at a table. They were drinking beer, and stared in surprise as Lundgren burst in. One of them turned off the blaring music.

"Police," Lundgren said and he was just about to add "Down on the floor!" when he heard Stefan shout, "Clear!" some way off.

Lundgren knew he had come to the right place. His pulse quickened.

"Where's the fridge?"

The sweet smell of hash pervaded the room. The men were red-eyed and appeared to be high. One of them, with dark hair and a skull-shaped earring, eventually pointed to the refrigerator. Lundgren went over and started to pull it out from where it was wedged, under the draining board.

"Clear!" Stefan's voice could be heard again, now closer.

Lundgren dried the sweat from his eyes and put the Sig Sauer on the countertop. Christ, it was hot. He tugged at the refrigerator door. Slowly, it began to give way.

Lundgren heard footsteps approaching in the corridor.

"Quick. In there," he whispered, pointing at a door.

The men went into a storeroom.

"Everything O.K.?" he heard a voice behind him ask.

Lundgren turned. Realised instantly that he had to decide if Stefan had seen or heard anything. He decided to chance it.

"Empty."

"Great. We can push off then. We're done. The patrol with the investigators and the forensics is arriving."

"Got it. I'm just going to use the toilet." He pointed at an adjoining bathroom, the door to which was wide open.

"O.K."

When Stefan had left the room Lundgren went over to the refrigerator and dragged it from underneath the counter. Pulled out the plug and saw, taped to the back, bundles of bank notes. A shitload of money, to quote Håkan.

He felt his pulse accelerate. Got out a paper bag and started to tear off the wads of money. The sweat stung his eyes and he lowered the lower part of the balaclava again to breathe properly.

"Do you need any help?" One of the men had come back out of the storeroom.

"Wait," Lundgren hissed as he continued to fill the paper bag. When he had finished, he went over to the door and opened it a crack. The corridor was empty but voices could be heard twenty or so metres away. He turned and stared at the man. Suddenly he realised that he was not wearing his mask and that he had shown his face. Shit!

He raised his MP5 and pointed it straight at the man's face. His companion, the one with the skull earring, came out, just as Lundgren pulled up his mask.

Lundgren's over-heated mind was whirling. Should he shoot, claim self-defence? But they were unarmed. And there were two of them. One shot in the head each for two young junkies. It just would not fly.

"Chill, dude," the first man said. The other looked terrified. Presumably had no idea what his friend had done wrong.

"Shut your face!" Lundgren blinked hard to be able to see through the sweat. "Fuck!"

"Take it—"

"Give me your I.D.s!"

The man with the skull earring carefully brought out his old, worn, black leather wallet. The other man did the same. "Can you point that somewhere else?" Lundgren lowered the MP5 and stuffed the wallets into his bullet-proof vest.

"So I know who you are . . . if you blab."

Both men stood stock-still and waited.

"Do you hear me?" Lundgren hissed.

"Relax," the man with the earring said. "We'll keep our mouths shut."

"Lie down on the floor."

The men did as they were told and Lundgren handcuffed them. Then he called out into the corridor:

"I've found two more. Over here!"

Three uniformed officers arrived to take care of the last men. Lundgren left the room and took deep breaths. Once the corridor was empty and silent again, he removed his helmet, tore off his balaclava and unbuttoned his jacket. He drew his hand over his sweaty face and closed his eyes for a few seconds.

SÖDERMALM, STOCKHOLM
Monday morning, 10.vi

Tekla stopped in the middle of Skanstull Bridge and caught her breath. There was a taste of blood in her mouth and she felt sick. She looked up and across at the Essinge islands and Västerbron Bridge on the horizon. It was only five in the morning and Stockholm was bathed in a beautiful light. Had she got any rest at all that night? It had felt more like fitful sleep interspersed with Oxazepam tablets, coffee, her bombs and all the images from the chase through the hospital's service tunnels the day before.

The cars on Skanstull Bridge were whizzing by behind her, but she barely noticed the traffic, morning cyclists and Tunnelbana trains a little way off. She got out her Lypsyl tube, unscrewed the cap and shook out two bombs. She swallowed them with mouthfuls of flat Ramlösa mineral water and kept walking in the direction of Skanstull. She increased her pace, took out her mobile and stared at the text message for the hundredth time.

I need help!

It was unlike Simon. What did he mean, help? All he had to do was call. Why didn't he answer when she rang? Was he stoned? Had something serious happened? If it was an emergency, surely he would have called the police or an ambulance. Of course, he had always been wary of policemen. He invariably turned to her when he had done something stupid. Ever since their teens, she had been his guardian angel, his fixer, saviour . . . basically a substitute parent. But for heaven's sake, if he needed help, why not just answer? At least her text messages. She had sent eight follow-up questions and texted him again: Do you need money?

At Skanstull, Tekla crossed Götgatan and walked towards Lilla Blecktornsparken, paused by the Thai kiosk and took some deep breaths. The nausea returned. She was smart enough to realise that she needed to eat. Her stomach was burning and rumbling. All the pills and bombs were making her dizzy. There would be something for her to eat when she got to the hospital. It was Monday morning.

She was not looking forward to seeing Collinder, who would have heard about both the knife drama and the small boy in the emergency room by now. Not to mention the assault in the I.C.U. yesterday. Tekla had been questioned by the police for over an hour when she came back up from the service tunnels.

She took out her mobile again. No answers. She called for the tenth time. The same answerphone recording: "Simon here, leave a message." At least it was his telephone, that much was clear. Tekla had left several messages. "Where are you, Simon? What's happened? Call me back . . ." But something was not right. Why send a text and then not answer?

Just as she was about to put away her mobile, there was a ping. She stared at the screen, holding her breath. It was Simon:

We've got to meet up!

She called straight back but got the answerphone.

"Fuck!" Tekla shouted, so loudly that a young girl exercising her dog in the park quickly turned and walked away from the lunatic with the mobile.

She called twice more, but there was no answer. Instead, she sent a text message: What do you mean, meet up? Where? When? What do you want, Simon? Tell me what's happened. I won't be angry. Promise. But please just answer your phone. Or send a text and explain.

After ten long minutes without an answer she had to take two Oxazepam to stop herself from going to pieces with worry. Goddamn bloody Simon, Tekla thought, and she kept walking until she reached Katarina Bangata 71. She punched in the door code and walked up the stairs. Stopped outside Simon's apartment and called him again.

Put her ear to the door, but heard no ringtone from within. Peered through the letterbox: all was dark and quiet inside.

"Simon!" she yelled, without getting any reply. "Simon, are you there?"

She tried to see if there was any post lying on the doormat, but it was too dark and the angle was wrong. All she could glimpse was the old rag rug from Edsåsdalen on the floor of the hall.

Tekla sent a few more texts, but in the end she gave up. She went out into the street and stood there for a while, gathering her thoughts. She had to try to think rationally.

After the attack in the I.C.U. the previous day, she told the police that she had caught a man trying to suffocate the burns patient, that she had stabbed him in the groin with some scissors and then chased after him. "No, I wasn't hurt." "No, I didn't think about the fact that I was in danger down in the service tunnels." "And no, I repeat, I never saw his face." She even told them about the message from Simon, gave them his number and told them that she had not been in touch with her brother for some time. She left out the drugs, however. They asked her what she thought his message might have meant, but she had not mentioned her concerns about dope or money. Nor did they seem particularly interested in that line of inquiry, their focus was on the incident with the assailant in the I.C.U. And no, she did not know which language he had sworn in. And for the tenth time, no, she had not seen his face. In the end, she had asked to be allowed to go back to A. & E.

She went into the Pressbyrån newsagent in Skanstull and bought a coffee. Wondered what to do. Which of Simon's friends might he possibly be hanging out with? In her mind, she ran through her mobile contacts and concluded that she did not know much about his life in Stockholm over the past year. They had always met alone. She even thought about how she might be able to trace a mobile, but was conscious of the fact that she knew nobody in the police. She herself had no close friends, so to whom could she turn for help?

Barely two hours left until she had to go to work. What if she just failed to show up? Searched for Simon instead? But where would she look? If he really needed help, surely he would answer her messages. Assuming he was the one who had sent them. It all seemed so strange, so *not* Simon. He hardly ever texted, always rang when he wanted something. Or just turned up on her doorstep. And could she now dismiss the bizarre idea that Simon was the burns victim in the I.C.U.?

Tekla was aware that what she needed was a good night's rest. No more bombs or other things which could affect both sleep and mood. She drank some of the coffee and took out the Lypsyl again. Shook a bomb into her hand, swallowed and began to walk in the direction of the Nobel Hospital. Her mobile rang and she looked at it: unknown number.

"Tekla."

"Monica here. Would you like to come up and see me before the morning meeting?"

Monica Carlsson . . . Tekla nearly dropped the mobile.

"Of course," she said at last.

"Come when you can. I'm here."

Tekla looked at her watch. Six-twenty, Monday morning.

"Come in," Carlsson said.

Tekla had taken the time to change. After the events of the last days, she was prepared for the worst.

"Do you want some coffee?" Carlsson said, getting up from her chair. She was wearing tight silver slacks, a mint-green blouse and the same gold chain as before.

"No thanks."

Carlsson seemed surprisingly wide awake, given the early hour.

"More drug overdoses have come in over the weekend."

"Yes?" Tekla said.

"I've had calls from a number of senior consultants. Same thing for all hospitals."

Tekla wondered if it was just overdoses that Carlsson had on her mind this Monday morning.

"You look exhausted," Carlsson went on.

"That's one way of putting it," Tekla said as she sat down. Carlsson stayed by the table and picked up a piece of paper.

"Some morning reading from Göran. He rang and disturbed me yesterday, in the middle of pre-dinner drinks. About the goings-on in A. & E. on Thursday."

Tekla braced herself. This was it.

Carlsson put on a pair of reading spectacles with a thin gold frame. "He writes: 'After an emergency call involving two patients with life-threatening conditions, she waited twenty-five minutes before calling the other duty doctor.'"

Tekla saw little Oscar before her in one room and the knifed gang member in the other.

"I asked for help. I think the first on-call was——"

"Hampus."

"Hampus Nordensköld was down as first on-call and——"

"Göran writes that Hampus was in the unit, busy dealing with a severe case of pneumonia."

Or having sex with a nurse in the clothes storeroom, Tekla thought. She could not make out whether Carlsson was angry or furious. Where was this heading?

"I gather that it was a while before he arrived," Carlsson said, looking up from the printed copy of the email.

"I have no idea how long."

She knew perfectly well. It had taken Nordensköld precisely twenty-seven minutes to get himself over to the emergency room. She saw the hands on the clock both when the patient arrived and when Nordensköld came in. An eternity. And not acceptable.

"But in the end he did turn up, whatever had been keeping him," Carlsson said. "And took over the emergency with the Gaucher disease boy."

"Yes," Tekla said, swallowing drily.

Carlsson looked down at the email again. "'After she had already administered a lethal dose of Stesolid', according to Göran. I've seen the prescription, I assume that's correct," Carlsson said. "The nurse in Emergency Room 2 said that they protested against the high dose but you said: 'Just get it ready, I'll give it myself'."

Carlsson put down the report and cast a searching look at Tekla, who wiped some sweat from her forehead.

"I administered the Stesolid myself," Tekla said. She was struggling to get the words out. Her tongue was sticking to the dry roof of her mouth.

"But that's active euthanasia," Carlsson said, fascination in her eyes.

She picked up a piece of chewing gum from the table and held it out to Tekla, who declined.

Tekla imagined Carlsson choking on the chewing gum in her windpipe and her face turning bright blue. How she then threw herself over the C.E.O. and tried to perform a Heimlich manoeuvre on her while screaming for help. Nobody came. Carlsson fell to the floor. Stone dead.

Tekla took a deep breath.

"But he survived. It was sepsis. And a status epilepticus."

"You were taking a very big risk with such massive doses of Stesolid. Just admit it."

Tekla closed her eyes. Saw the text before her. Then looked Carlsson right in the eyes.

"I will use treatment for the benefit of the sick according to my ability and judgment and I will seek to avoid anything which causes harm or pain."

"The Hippocratic oath," Carlsson said, walking around the table. She sat down in her chair. Tekla was confused. The C.E.O. looked so calm.

"Parts of it," Tekla said. "I knew that the boy was suffering from Gaucher type 2. An incurable illness, besides which his pupils were almost non-reactive after twenty-five minutes of C.P.R. He could have been brain dead. The parents had also signed a form to say they didn't want him put on a ventilator. But he wasn't dead."

"He may, however, be brain-damaged now for the rest of his miserable little life."

Tekla fixed her eyes on Carlsson. "You and Göran can do what you like with me, but I will *always* try to save lives. At any price. That's why I became a doctor."

Carlsson smiled and nodded.

"The father seems to have gone into a state of shock and fallen asleep in the emergency room."

Tekla thought about the full ampoule of Propofol which she had injected into his thigh.

"I had a guy with knife injuries in the other room."

"I know. Some unfortunate gang member."

"Who it was going to be easy for me to save."

"Do you mean that, if you'd had more time for the child, you wouldn't have given Stesolid?"

"I did my best under the circumstances," Tekla said, feeling more certain than ever that she had done the right thing, even though her hands were shaking and sweat was running down her spine. She did not care if it cost her her job, she would stand by her decision. "I chose to focus on the stabbing victim, because I knew I'd given the child what he needed: antibiotics."

She was genuinely trying to be self-critical. But she kept reaching the conclusion that she had indeed done the right thing. She saw his little ribcage rise as the air was pumped in, but a long time had gone by. His brain had been without oxygen for some critical minutes. She could have handled the father with a little more tact, but her priority right then was to save lives. Two lives: the young gang member's, and the little boy's.

Carlsson chewed away slowly and looked again at Collinder's piece of paper.

Tekla lowered her voice. "And I would do the same thing again if the situation repeated itself."

Carlsson put the paper down and looked Tekla in the eye.

"Super good."

"What?" a confused Tekla said.

"Spot on. Brilliant." Carlsson laughed. "You're fantastic. I couldn't have done better myself."

"But . . ." Tekla looked at the piece of paper on the table.

"Göran can shove this wherever he wants. I certainly intend to tell him that he's got a world-class emergency doctor in his clinic. Someone who dares to go above and beyond and live up to the Hippocratic oath in full."

Carlsson crumpled up the paper and threw it into her waste-paper basket.

Tekla's first thought was that the C.E.O. was pulling her leg, but then she saw that Carlsson's face was very serious.

"He's getting all worked up about nothing. I just don't understand how he can sometimes get things so wrong."

Tekla was one big question mark, trying to keep up.

"You can forget everything that happened in the emergency room on Thursday. Göran's complaints aren't going any further. But tell me what happened yesterday," Carlsson said, sounding concerned. "How are you feeling?"

"Ummm . . . I'm O.K."

Tekla was still in a daze.

"Not totally O.K., it seems to me. You don't look as though you got much sleep last night. But it was lucky that nothing happened to the burns patient."

"Yes, that was . . . lucky."

"Fantastic timing that you surprised him. Do you have any idea who it was?"

"No. If I knew that—"

"You would have told the police. I realise. I just thought your memory might have cleared a bit overnight."

Tekla caught Carlsson's knowing smile.

"And then you chased after him down into the service tunnels. Brave."

"I wasn't really thinking."

"No, you were on autopilot," Carlsson said and nodded. "Sometimes that's useful. I was actually sitting and eating *moules frites* at Musslan by Vasaparken. Have you been?"

"I haven't."

"They go amazingly well with a good Belgian beer, maybe a Tripel Karmeliet. We should go one day. And I want you to promise to tell me if you need anything."

"Need?"

"Yes, if you need to speak to someone. You can come up and see me whenever you want."

Tekla felt as if she had just climbed off the Insane ride at Gröna Lund amusement park and someone was asking her if she wanted to play chess and have a cup of tea.

"O.K. I'll let you know if I need to talk."

Tekla left Carlsson's room in a state of bewilderment. She checked her mobile, but it was as dark as her headache. No signal from Simon. If they could only establish the identity of that man in the I.C.U., she could let go of all her crazy thoughts. She pondered what Carlsson had said about the increased number of drug overdoses in town and wondered what Simon was up to. Whether he had perhaps started taking heavier drugs without her knowing about it.

Tekla went down to the emergency room and saw Moussawi's large silhouette come ambling along. She straightened up, raised her head a few centimetres. She had to carry herself better.

"I think we should start with a minute's silence for the victims of the fire," Collinder began. "We didn't have time for it on Friday." Anita Klein-Borgstedt was the last to sneak in and sit down in the conference room, which had filled up with doctors and medical students. There was the occasional awkward look, as if they had just been asked to take off their clothes for a group hug. Tekla was aware that there were more eyes on her than usual. The rumours about the attack in the I.C.U. had spread. She sent another message to Simon.

Hello there? Can you please answer?! What did your message mean? Call me!

"Thank you," Collinder said, breaking the uncomfortable silence. The moment of remembrance was over. Life in A. & E. moved on. Could she breathe more easily now? Collinder had not said anything to Tekla.

"I think everyone knows that we had an incident in the I.C.U. yesterday evening, which Tekla Berg was caught up in. We're all grateful for the fact that it ended . . . well . . . for both Tekla and the patient. The police are of course involved and investigating the matter. So, I think we can leave that for now."

Collinder had fired off his summary without once turning towards her.

"And how did the rest of you survive the weekend?" Collinder said.

Survive the weekend. That was how he saw their mission: they were at war, the flood of patients was the enemy and Hampus Nordensköld and Tekla Berg were the cannon fodder – two doctors who could be held accountable for all the shit that had happened during the last few days.

Nordensköld looked as if he had managed to make it to the on-call room that night. His dark brown hair was damp and, as always, neatly parted and combed. Tekla was trying to work out whether or not Collinder was going to tear a strip off her. Had Carlsson already had time to talk to him?

"Perfectly O.K.," Nordensköld said. "I admitted quite a few patients. The most exciting thing was probably on Saturday. An overdose, total goner."

"A bit more detail, please," Klein-Borgstedt's clear voice could be heard from the corner of the table. She was like a theatre director sitting in the front row of the stalls. Every line from the junior doctors could be improved on. Ragna Sigurdsdottir, who knew Klein-Borgstedt from their time in Solna, had once said that her large mansion in Djursholm was like "a posh version of the Natural History Museum". Even her three children were exemplary: an engineering physicist with a large house in Tullinge and four children at Adolf Fredrik's Music School, a doctor in the more elegant part of Bromma who was about to get a PhD in genetics, and a lawyer at the National Audit Office. "And she hasn't yet decided which law firm to go for," Klein-Borgstedt had said with an exasperated look.

"Well, it was a bog standard heroin O.D. Some down-and-out," Nordensköld drawled. "But he was hard to crank up again."

Nordensköld leaned right back, tilting his chair.

"May I suggest that we stick to our usual terminology, Hampus," Collinder interjected, politely but audibly for everyone's benefit. "And we say 'homeless', not 'down-and-out'."

Tekla stole a look across the table, in Moussawi's direction. As ever, his hands were clasped in front of him and his gaze was fixed just above Klein-Borgstedt's head. It was as if, from where he was sitting, he could read the huge Harrison's medical encyclopedia and a number of the other volumes that filled the four shelves running along one of the walls. Thirty-four portraits hung behind Moussawi, one for each of the chief physicians since Alfred Nobel's hospital was opened by King Oscar II in 1902. In her Icelandic accent and slightly mischievous way, Sigurdsdottir had told her that "Göran had all the portraits re-hung so that his would end up at eye level". Apparently, it had been knee-high before, which had infuriated him. Tekla wondered what a conference room looked like at the N.S.K., in the northern part of the city. They had probably rationalised away all physical books. She imagined abstract works of art on white walls and sliding doors which opened and shut soundlessly. Ecological cleaning products. Hospital clothes with a cool logo, young doctors with gilt stethoscopes around their necks and the latest model sneakers on their feet.

Nordensköld let the chair fall back with a thud.

"A 39-year-old man who was found in Björns Trädgård. He was unconscious, maybe Glasgow Coma Scale 4, with small pupils. Judging by his clothes, there was no doubt he was a down . . . homeless."

Nordensköld glanced across at Collinder.

"Eventually we discovered a wallet with an identity card in his inside pocket. When he got to A. & E. he was unconscious, I intubated and took samples and ran a C.T. scan of his head. Nothing there. He's in the I.C.U. and hasn't come round."

Nothing there. So his head was empty, then, Tekla wondered, but she kept her question to herself. Everyone in the room was waiting for the story to continue. No-one had missed the little detail that Nordensköld himself had intubated the patient. He had done one year of his specialist training as an emergency doctor and really had no business intubating anyone by himself. But, like many young male doctors, he suffered from hubris. Tekla could not help being impressed by his audacity.

She looked around the flaking old table and wondered if anyone there would dare to analyse what Nordensköld had done. Fifteen doctors. Another twenty or so junior doctors and medical students were standing along the yellowing walls. The ones sitting around the table were the permanent body of doctors. The elite force. All the others in the room would kill for a place at the table.

"It doesn't sound like a normal heroin overdose," was Klein-Borgstedt's dry summary. "I presume you gave an antidote?" Tekla loved it when Klein-Borgstedt took the floor. Her comments were delivered in a low voice, almost in passing; she was brisk and always to the point.

"Absolutely," Nordensköld answered, sounding annoyed. "I repeated the Naloxone which he had already been given in the ambulance."

"But he's still in the I.C.U.?" Klein-Borgstedt said.

"Yes. Why do you ask?"

The pitch of Nordensköld's voice was no longer quite so sharp. It was as if a soft-boiled egg had suddenly found its way down his throat.

Moussawi tapped on the table with his fingertips and cleared his throat.

"O.K., Anita. We're just going to have to give it a little more thought." Moussawi pointed his large, hairy index finger at Nordensköld and then at his own broad chest.

"If we hadn't closed down all our research, the standard here wouldn't be quite so disastrously low," Klein-Borgstedt muttered. Everybody heard what she said.

"Please, Anita," Collinder said. "Not now, thank you."

Tekla reflected on how different their personalities were. Moussawi, who looked like one of Saddam Hussein's generals, accustomed to handing out orders to his soldiers. Nordensköld, who should probably have stayed on some beach in Australia and spent his life surfing. Sigurdsdottir, better suited to an Icelandic soap opera. Klein-Borgstedt with her string of pearls, from the elegant district of Östermalm, who had washed up in the southern part of the city because . . . well, for reasons that were unknown to Tekla.

She was following the drama around the table. By "we", Moussawi meant himself and his favourite, Hampus Nordensköld. Moussawi would never discuss a difficult case with Tekla or Sigurdsdottir, because they were the wrong sex.

"I'll go to the I.C.U. and examine him," Klein-Borgstedt replied.

Tekla saw her and Sigurdsdottir's eyes meet. Klein-Borgstedt gave a quick nod. So who would be taking on the case now? Nordensköld continued to report succinctly on three other patients he had admitted.

"Your turn, Tekla," Collinder went on.

She saw Moussawi's sarcastic smile and the telling way he looked up at the ceiling. To be fair, he did it discreetly, but he knew perfectly well that the junior doctors in the room lapped up the tiniest signal from the senior doctors. Like babies at their mothers' breast. Would he mention the injection of Propofol now?

"I didn't have time to cover this on Friday," Tekla said, swallowing hard. It felt as if one of Nordensköld's soft-boiled eggs had just been rammed down her throat. "But we had a 23-year-old man with knife injuries come in on Thursday night. He ended up in surgery. It was a bit of a drama."

Collinder leaned forward and looked at Tekla. She could picture how Carlsson had read him the riot act. But this was probably the right time for Tekla to come clean about her mistake. There was only one departmental meeting a week, and if she did not mention Thursday's goings-on, there was a risk that false rumours would spread about what had happened.

"Were you with the surgeon when he took care of it?" Collinder asked with a smirk.

Tekla looked down at her knees.

"No, I handled it myself."

Moussawi's head fell forward.

A murmur ran through the room.

She quickly added: "We had that very nice surgeon . . . Nawfal . . ."

"Nawfal al-Wadi," Klein-Borgstedt added.

". . . in the house, but we never had to call him. I inserted a thoracic drain before the police arrived."

177

"The police?" Klein-Borgstedt asked, having obviously not yet heard about the confrontation.

Tekla told them all about the S.W.A.T. team barging into A. & E., but left out the boy with the seizures.

"Jesus, Tekla," Sigurdsdottir said. "I'm impressed. My God, you did well."

The room split in two like the Red Sea. Half the doctors around the table nodded their approval, the other half shook their heads in dismay. Tekla felt a confusing blend of pride and fear.

"How's the stench thing going, by the way?" Nordensköld intervened. He probably wanted to shift the spotlight from Tekla. Everyone understood what was going on and turned to Collinder.

"I haven't had time to talk to the building management this morning, but from what I was told on Friday, their first attempt at identifying the cause was not successful."

Tekla felt relief that they had moved on from Thursday's drama.

"I also wanted to thank all those who volunteered to come in and help with the fire disaster on Thursday," Collinder went on. "There could easily have been many more casualties." He tapped very hard on the table with a crooked index finger. "We have three critically burned patients in the I.C.U. Tekla is the doctor in charge for the one with the worst injuries, a man whose identity is unknown."

Tekla felt Nordensköld's sharp look from the side.

"Is this anything to do with that van they're looking for?" Klein-Borgstedt wanted to know.

Collinder straightened up.

"I can't answer that."

"But I can," Moussawi said. "That's obviously what they suspect. Why else would they have policemen running in and out of the I.C.U.?"

Come to that, why had Moussawi himself been in the I.C.U., Tekla wondered and tried to see if Klein-Borgstedt and Moussawi were exchanging looks, but it was as if each of them was sitting in her or his own tent on opposite sides of a battlefield.

"O.K.," Collinder interrupted, raising a hand. "I'll let you read about that in the evening papers. As for the medical side, Tekla will be able to tell us more during the week." He finished the meeting with his usual: "Don't forget that we're better than the others."

They all knew who *the others* were. The new, privately owned hospital on the other side of the city: The NyX Smith & Klingmann Hospital, abbreviated to N.S.K. Like its predecessor, it was known simply as "the Solna side"; it had been since the '30s and still was today. And their mission was to fight that evil with all the means at their disposal. As if the hospital were the Death Star itself, far away at the other end of the galaxy.

There was a scraping of chairs as they got up. Several doctors patted Tekla on the shoulder as they filed out. Sigurdsdottir hugged her friend and hurried on. Some of the medical students stared at Tekla with large eyes while joining the procession heading for the exit.

"Tekla!"

Collinder came over, waving his outsized smartphone.

"I need to get going out there," she said in a vain attempt to delay the inevitable.

"Just briefly." Collinder lowered his voice. "I gather you saw Carlsson this morning. What did you talk about?"

Tekla could tell that this was a thinly disguised order. Collinder seemed to find it hard to look at her, his eyes were riveted to his mobile.

"She . . . just wanted to check that I was O.K. after the fire and everything."

"Everything?"

Tekla was reluctant to remind Collinder about all the drama in A. & E.

"Well . . . the fire, full stop."

"You don't have to lie."

"Lie?"

Collinder nodded and seemed to zoom out for a second. Tekla felt the scent of his sickly aftershave and took a careful step back.

"She and I were at medical school together. Can you imagine?"

"You know . . . I really have to get going with—"

"Watch out for her. Just my advice. She's . . ."

Tekla waited in suspense. Collinder fixed his eyes on her forehead.

". . . Monica Carlsson always has an agenda, whatever she does. Don't forget that."

"O.K. Thanks for the tip," Tekla said, happy to be able to end this awkward conversation.

Collinder nodded and finally looked away. He continued fiddling with his mobile. It seemed Carlsson had done a very good job of giving her lapdog a piece of her mind.

Tekla hurried after her colleagues as they headed for the coffee machines. She looked at her mobile and sent a text message: For God's sake Simon. Call me!

"How are you feeling?" Klein-Borgstedt asked, a mug of tea in her hand.

"O.K., thanks. You?" Tekla said, putting away her phone.

"I had the weekend off. Some sorely needed time with the family, just for a change."

"Do you have children?"

Anita smiled.

"Certainly do. Three of them, but they're grown up."

Tekla immediately regretted her question. She knew all too well that, for doctors, everything to do with family life is vitally important. Had she seen that in writing, she would never have forgotten. Other things that mattered to doctors: where you go on holiday. Which sports you do. Even which outdoor activities you engage in. And with male doctors over the age of fifty, you have to keep track of their latest sports car and ask about the year, make and horsepower.

Klein-Borgstedt waited for Moussawi and Nordensköld to go past. Just as Tekla was about to check her pager, which had bleeped, Moussawi came towards her. He leaned forward and whispered in her ear:

"Why don't you stick a needle in her arse so she nods off?"

Tekla looked up. Waited for him to continue. But Moussawi just patted her shoulder and hurried away to catch up with Nordensköld. Should she confront him and find out what he wanted in exchange for his silence? Or did he just want to unsettle her? Maybe he would not tell Collinder what had happened? It was almost a shame that he had not patted her on the backside, then she could have screamed and got him into trouble on the spot.

Klein-Borgstedt had not noticed anything and kept talking.

"You did an incredibly good job in Emergency the other day. From what we heard at the morning meeting, I mean."

"I'm not so sure . . ." Tekla saw that Moussawi was out of earshot. Her hands were shaking.

"You appear to have had it all under control. Now lap up the praise."

Klein-Borgstedt's sharp voice was like music to Tekla's ears.

"Not everybody seemed to agree," Tekla said.

"Just ignore Tariq and his . . . lackeys."

"But Hampus' drug overdose was an exciting case too."

Klein-Borgstedt dropped her teabag into the rubbish bin. "For sure," she nodded thoughtfully. "Definitely intriguing. It's got to be something else, something complicated that requires some expertise. Why don't we go to the I.C.U.?"

"Now?"

"I'm just going to read up on it a bit. But why postpone something so interesting?"

Tekla realised that this was all about power play.

"But wasn't Tariq going . . .?"

Klein-Borgstedt lowered her spectacles and looked at her mobile.

"I thought it sounded *very* challenging. Needs some *sharp* minds, don't you agree? Are you coming or not?"

Tekla was trying to weigh the pros and cons, but it all turned into one big, brown mush in her mind. In the end she went with gut reaction:

"Absolutely."

"Good."

After reading the file on the overdose patient, they left A. & E. and took the outside route to the I.C.U. As they strolled along the front of the hospital, Klein-Borgstedt stopped for a moment.

"You know that they had elephants at the inauguration, right where you're walking?"

"Seriously?" Tekla said. Her colleague did not seem to be joking. Tekla had never heard anything about any elephants. She knew very little in general about the Nobel Hospital's past. But the grand entrance and the old paintings in the corridors bore witness to an impressive history. Sometimes she would pause and marvel at all the portraits of men who had built their careers within these walls. Developed new surgical techniques. Saved patients and performed great deeds. Tekla recalled her job interview, how excited she had been at the idea of becoming part of this institution. A hospital with traditions. Now, a year after that June day when she had been given the job, she had come to understand that the Nobel Hospital's glory days were perhaps over. The research funds had run dry. Even if the hospital C.E.O. – and all the staff too for that matter – did everything possible to recreate a sense of greatness.

"It is actually true," Klein-Borgstedt said, with an odd smile which made Tekla nervous. There was something penetrating about her look, she seemed to be scanning what she was observing. "Right in front of the main entrance. The king was present. There are photographs outside the X-ray department."

There was a wonderful air of do-you-remember-how-much-more-snow-there-used-to-be-at-Christmas nostalgia about Klein-Borgstedt, with which Tekla could identify. Maybe they even shared some connection with Jämtland? If so, Klein-Borgstedt had worked hard at filing down her accent and replacing it with nasal "i" sounds and posh "ö"s.

Klein-Borgstedt got out a cigarette and lit up. It seemed a perfectly natural thing for her to do, but to puff away where a patient might see her, Tekla felt, was quite unacceptable. A doctor smoking outside a hospital.

They strolled along the poplars outside the entrance. Moussawi had clearly been keen to get to grips with the case in the I.C.U., but now Anita had stolen a march on him and got Tekla involved as well. Power politics had always been beyond her.

"When was that?" Tekla said. They stopped by the fountain and sat on a bench. There were two women smoking beside them, one with a bandaged head. Klein-Borgstedt looked to be thoroughly enjoying her "fresh air".

"1902. The first Nobel Prize had been awarded two years earlier. It was decided that the city's new hospital should be here, because a large number of the new rich were moving out to Saltsjöbaden. Besides which, there were already Roslagstull, Serafen and some other hospitals in the northern and central districts. It took just two years to build this."

Tekla looked up at the old brick facade, with its high vaulted windows and ornamentation. Then her eyes travelled a little higher. It was as if a large, dirty-grey shoebox had been placed on top of the fine old building.

"When were the additions made?"

"Not until the '30s. That large new bit was built in the middle of the '50s. It's all the grey stuff you can see."

"Looks like an old turtle which has been given a new shell."

Klein-Borgstedt inhaled deeply, coughed and nodded.

"That's one way of describing it."

She ran her fingers through her snow-white hair. She was unnaturally brown for the time of year, presumably thanks to some sunny spring holiday on the Costa del Sol. There was an aura of golf and cava about her. Tiny wrinkles fanned out from the corners of her eyes.

"How long have you actually worked here?" Tekla said.

"Not since 1902, if that's what you mean."

Tekla put her head to one side and smiled.

"I got here in . . . '88."

"Thirty years, in other words."

"But I'm not the longest-serving old trooper by far."

"Have you done a lot of research?"

Tekla was thinking about Klein-Borgstedt's pointed remark at the morning meeting.

184

"Of course," Klein-Borgstedt said, slightly offended. "You only become a good clinician if you combine practice with clinical research. But unfortunately the hospital management hasn't given that any priority these last years."

"But you've still got a group of researchers?"

"Yes, although we can't go on paying the poor doctoral candidates out of our own funds indefinitely. However passionate we may be about research."

The sun went behind a cloud and the temperature immediately fell. The June weather was as capricious as ever.

Klein-Borgstedt's gaze strayed for a while. Then she turned to Tekla.

"You need to stretch yourself."

Tekla straightened her back.

Klein-Borgstedt gave a strained smile.

"Not literally. In your very first week I saw what you were capable of."

Tekla felt her pulse quicken.

"You hold back the right answers. Don't you?"

Tekla did not want to lie. She kept quiet. Klein-Borgstedt looked away from her and up at the Nobel flags, which were swaying softly in the wind.

"Men don't have to try even half as hard to win the same recognition. But time will show us right. The bastion of male dinosaurs is slowly cracking up."

Only now did Tekla dare open her mouth.

"And what comes after that?"

"No more nepotism. And above all: a shift in how we communicate. Objectivity. Facts. Evidence-based care."

"So we're just talking about medical care?"

Klein-Borgstedt gave a fraction of a smile. They sat in silence for a minute or so. Tekla took the opportunity to check her mobile, but there were no answers from Simon. She changed the subject.

"What do you make of the drug overdose patient?"

Klein-Borgstedt got up and stubbed out her cigarette.

"He's still intubated."

"I saw that. He was positive for both cannabis and opiates."

"That doesn't tell us much. The first blood gas test was interesting. Have you thought about that?"

Tekla quickly ran through everything she had managed to read. The patient had been admitted to A. & E. with heroin overdoses three times in the past two years. He had been in the I.C.U. once before; the other times they had put him on an ordinary ward. He had hepatitis C but not H.I.V. He had even been to Kungsholmen Hospital for addiction treatment on a number of occasions. According to the latest notes on file, he stayed in different hostels around town, but in summer also with friends or sometimes outdoors. Tekla noted that at some point he had given Skanstull Bridge as his address. So in principle they were neighbours. Maybe she had walked past him as he lay there in his sleeping bag, perhaps greeted him. The ambulance report had not said anything more than that he was found unconscious in Björns Trädgård. They could not communicate with him on site, his pupils were small and he was breathing slowly. Accordingly, all the signs pointed to an opioid overdose. The ambulance crew had given him Naloxone, without much effect.

"His sugar levels were low and he had a fever," Tekla said. "Otherwise it was an absolutely straightforward heroin overdose: small pupils, low blood pressure, slow breathing. Couldn't be brought back to . . . he was Glasgow Coma Scale 4, I think. Potassium 3.9, creatinine 111 . . ."

Tekla realised what she was doing. Noticed that Klein-Borgstedt was staring at her. Once again she had attracted attention by rattling off numbers.

"You'll have to start sharing with the rest of us whatever is cooking inside that fantastic brain of yours," Klein-Borgstedt said gravely.

Tekla smiled to herself.

"I'll try."

Tekla and Klein-Borgstedt went in through the main entrance, proceeded to the west wing and took the lift up. A short corridor with offices led to the large, open-plan landscape of the I.C.U.

Klein-Borgstedt stopped in her tracks. Ran her chapped hands over her throat.

"But is it normal for heroin addicts to have a high temperature and low sugar levels?"

Tekla saw all the lab results before her.

"Temperature, no. There we would rather think infection. But they've tried every conceivable culture and found nothing."

"And the sugar?"

"If he's got a liver condition. Perhaps an alcoholic with poor glycogen storage," Tekla reasoned.

Klein-Borgstedt looked satisfied. So this is how it went, Tekla thought: a series of questions to check that one was on the right track. She thought of all the loose threads from the day before, but she tried to keep Simon's face away, to enjoy being around Klein-Borgstedt for a while. The mobile kept coming out on a regular basis, but it went on staring blankly back at her.

The intensive care unit of the Nobel Hospital had a long and rich history. The first ever ventilator prototype had been tested there on a man with peritonitis and shock. He died after three hours in the metal box, but the doctors still called it a "miracle". Eight years earlier, the premises had been totally renovated; walls were knocked down and an open-plan space was created, the size of a handball court. The patients in their enormous beds were plugged into the full range of modern equipment that one would expect to see at a med-tech fair in Frankfurt. The beds were separated by concertina partitions. Light flooded in through windows looking out in two directions. It was actually a waste to put the I.C.U. on the seventh floor. It would have been better to bury the department underground since the patients were all unconscious anyway, with plastic tubes down their throats. But of course, their relatives could look out over Årstaviken on one side of the building or the whole of southern Stockholm through the northern row of windows, while mulling the fact that their daughter, son, wife or husband had a fifty per cent chance of surviving. In Tekla's eyes, the best thing about the I.C.U. was the person in charge, Doctor Eva Elmqvist. She was now walking towards them, wearing a plastic apron and plastic gloves covered in blood, her arms raised in a pleading gesture.

"Can someone give me a sterile . . . one of those condom things for the ultrasound?"

A nurse understood what she meant and hurried away towards a well-concealed storeroom. They had truly managed to spirit away all cupboards and drawers in this ultra-modern creation, more like a space station than an intensive care department.

Tekla and Klein-Borgstedt followed Elmqvist, who was about to change their patient's central catheter. She started to run the ultrasound probe up and down his throat, searching for blood vessels.

"That sodding C.V.C. is blocked again."

"Bloody pain," Klein-Borgstedt said, leaning across the ultrasound apparatus. She was careful to keep her hands behind her back so as not to touch anything sterile.

Elmqvist tried to blow away a wisp of hair which had slipped down in front of her face. Tekla thought she looked funny trying to talk at the same time as she was blowing at her hair and making a mess on the patient's throat with the gel. In the end, Tekla stepped over and tucked the hair back.

"Great . . . thanks."

Elmqvist did not take her eyes off the catheter in her hand. It looked to be half a metre long and as thick as an index finger. In the end she inserted it and pulled out the guidewire.

"We'll have to see how that works. He's bleeding like a pig."

Klein-Borgstedt backed away, keeping a safe distance. Tekla was fascinated by the game that began as soon as these two older colleagues met. She realised that they must go a long way back, to judge from the rough but warm banter. Tekla took the opportunity to send another text message: Call me!!!

"Nothing to do with you, I'm sure," Klein-Borgstedt said in a friendly tone.

"His platelets have dropped below fifty twice now," Elmqvist sighed. "We've topped up with at least two bags. Maybe three . . . I can't remember."

"Is his glucose still going down?" Klein-Borgstedt said.

"Yes, and his kidneys are giving up the ghost."

"So what's the verdict?"

"Poor Miguel. Thirty-nine years old but looks like sixty. Probably hasn't been following the Eatwell diet. It's not clear what he's been taking. But very obvious that heroin wasn't the only thing on the breakfast menu."

Elmqvist pulled off her gloves and apron. "Shall we have a word?"

Tekla noted that Elmqvist had not greeted her, now that Klein-Borgstedt was with them. Tekla had been downgraded to plain air.

Elmqvist led them away to the central part of the handball court, about ten metres from the rows of beds. This was where the office was, without walls. Tekla had been told that there were sound-absorbing panels in the ceiling, so that the patients and relatives could not hear what was being said. They sat down in front of a large Mac. For some unfathomable reason, the I.C.U. was the only unit in the hospital which bought Apple products.

In silence, they read through the lab results. Behind them, two other I.C.U. doctors were sitting with some interns and nurses and discussing another patient's case.

Elmqvist turned to Klein-Borgstedt. "One thing first." She laid her hand on Klein-Borgstedt's thigh. Tekla did not know where to look, she suddenly felt as embarrassed as when she had walked in on her mother and father having sex in their bedroom when she was seven or eight years old.

"How's Walter?"

"Just fine, thanks," Klein-Borgstedt said, in such an intimate tone that for one second Tekla thought they had been transported to the drawing room of a manor house north of the city.

"That's good to hear."

Tekla could not resist looking at the friends, who then switched back to a different subject and tone.

"Acute kidney failure," Klein-Borgstedt said. "And that despite the fact that you've been topping him up with fluids, I imagine."

"Of course," Elmqvist sighed, removing her hand and looking worried again. "We've given a total of fourteen litres since he arrived yesterday."

"And still the creatinine is going up," Klein-Borgstedt noted.

"But no infection," Tekla said, realising immediately that she had been thinking out loud and had not asked permission to speak.

"I would have told you," Elmqvist replied, without taking her eyes off the screen. She shook her head in irritation.

"But nothing else in the drug tests?" Tekla persisted.

"Nope."

"And he's acidotic."

"Yes."

"Have you tried to bring him round?"

Elmqvist groaned and made no effort to hide her annoyance, as if Tekla were a reporter from some weekly magazine asking idiotic questions about celebrities.

"We can't. He's been having seizures, one every hour since yesterday evening. We X-rayed his brain. Nothing. But luckily, we repeated the E.C.G., which showed—"

"A wide Q.R.S.," Klein-Borgstedt interrupted, holding her reading glasses in a steady grip – as if they were forceps – while she studied the E.C.G.

"In that case, it must be multiple drug intake," Tekla said.

"No shit, Sherlock. That's as far as we run-of-the-mill intensive care types have got," Elmqvist remarked and got to her feet. She walked across to a large glass bowl filled with fruit, picked up a green apple and bit into it with a violent crunch.

"So we thought we'd ask for some help."

Hanging in the air was: "But all you've done is drag along some idiot of a junior doctor who blurts out inanities."

"A bit of expertise in internal medicine, in other words," Klein-Borgstedt said, smiling broadly as she shut her eyes. The effect was a little comical.

"I'll just examine our young man first."

Klein-Borgstedt went over to Miguel Vallejo. Tekla felt strangely grateful that her colleague had not sided with Elmqvist.

A nurse left them on their own to examine the patient, who was connected to E.C.G. electrodes and invasive blood pressure monitors. There were two large cannulas in the crooks of his arms, through which different medicines dripped with precision, thanks to the infusion pumps. The transparent plastic covering of the central line, which had just been placed in the patient's throat, was gleaming. A plastic tube ran from his mouth to the ventilator, controlling the breathing.

"Poor guy," Klein-Borgstedt whispered to herself. She raised the sheet and examined his belly, legs and arms, throat and face. Tekla was not sure what Klein-Borgstedt was looking for, but did not want to disturb her by asking; she presumed that everything she did was for a reason.

Klein-Borgstedt picked up her reflex hammer and tested all the nerves in the feet, arms and face. Then she put the sheet back, folded it neatly over Miguel's thorax and gently stroked his cheek. Tekla suddenly had the feeling that Klein-Borgstedt had been in this situation before, but as a relative, maybe sitting with a loved one. Had she perhaps had a child who had lain like this, intubated and waiting for death?

Klein-Borgstedt turned.

"Not much to examine. He's unconscious."

"No doubt about that," Tekla said.

"But that's what's so odd," Klein-Borgstedt went on.

"What?"

"That he's still unconscious after two days."

"Yes, but—"

"He shouldn't be. Not if it had been a normal overdose. Don't you agree?"

Tekla had not been following.

"I agree. But the tests may tell us more."

Klein-Borgstedt stopped, her eyes fixed on a point by Miguel's feet.

"It's all down to the medical history. That's where you find eighty per cent of the information. I think we're done here," Klein-Borgstedt said, lowering her voice. "And we should maybe take ourselves off somewhere else to *think*, so we don't disturb the *intensive care team*."

Tekla nodded her approval as Klein-Borgstedt opened her eyes wide, her lips taut. Now she was sure: they were a team. At least for today.

They left the I.C.U. and walked towards the lifts.

Tekla stretched herself and ran through the events of the past week in her mind: a young man admitted with knife wounds on Thursday evening while the little boy with sepsis was having seizures in A. & E. She had stabilised both patients, and they were still alive. And Collinder had raised no objections to her management of those cases. Check for that. An hour later she was by Söder Tower, trying to take care of patients with injuries from smoke and burns, the last one of whom was dead. But then turned out to be alive. The burns victim, whose life nearly came to an end when some maniac tried to suffocate him yesterday in the I.C.U. Tekla had prevented it.

Check, check. That left the baffling drug overdose in the I.C.U., which she could really get her teeth into. A case to crack right in front of Klein-Borgstedt's eyes, and, even better, Moussawi's. No check for that, for the time being. Then she thought again about Simon's text message and picked up her mobile: no answers. It was ten o'clock. An hour until her appointment with Rebecka Nilsén. It was going to be a long day. Tekla turned away from Klein-Borgstedt and got out the Lypsyl.

KARLAPLAN, STOCKHOLM
Monday, 10.vi

"Darling, I'm taking the big car today," Nina called out as she applied a final layer of lipstick.

"You don't have to shout," Jocke said. He came up behind her and held her in his arms. "And it's called an Escalade, your little toy."

Nina walked out of the bathroom and fetched a black jacket from her closet.

A doorbell rang in the background. Nina went out into the long corridor and shouted:

"Can someone open? It's Barbara."

"O.K.!" a child's voice replied.

"And get dressed. We're leaving in five minutes."

Joakim put his arms around Nina again. He was a head taller, and yet she was 174 centimetres.

"What's the matter, darling?"

Nina tried to struggle free, but Joakim held on and was insistent.

"You look stressed."

She dropped her shoulders. Stopped resisting.

"Lots of balls in the air at the moment."

"But you love that. You'd feel terrible if you didn't have a lot on. Do you remember last summer when we rented a house for the whole—"

"It's not that," Nina said, freeing herself. She straightened her jacket. "Can't have too many negative things on the agenda. For a start, I get furious with Carina always going on about everything at school. How come teachers are always the worst sort of parents?"

"Anything more?" Jocke said. "What else do you have on that negative checklist?"

"Nothing. I have to go now. And you've got lipstick on your cheek."

Nina's heels clattered against the parquet flooring as she went to give instructions to Barbara, their helper. But there was no Barbara in the hall.

"Pappa."

"Good morning," Umarov said, holding up a bag from Thelin's bakery.

"Cardamom. Your favourite."

Nina went up to her father and gave him a kiss on the cheek. He was wearing a black shirt, dark jacket and light shoes, and was throwing his car keys in the air and catching them.

"You're looking very smart," Nina said. "But what are you doing here so early?"

"Thought you might like a breakfast treat."

"That's sweet of you, Pappa, but we have to go. I've got loads to do today." Nina turned and shouted: "Kate! Emily! Hurry up now."

The twins came running and jumped up into their grandfather's embrace when they saw him.

Umarov got down on his knees and hugged the girls.

"Mmm. My little tigresses. Let me smell . . . open up. Have you brushed your teeth?"

Both girls opened their mouths as wide as they could and breathed on their grandfather.

Umarov steadied himself on his thighs to get up again. He patted the girls on the head.

"Shoes on. You heard Mamma."

The girls sat down on the floor and began to put on their sandals.

"Can we have a word?" Umarov said, lowering his voice.

Whenever he gave her that look, Nina felt undone. His sudden switch from joking and mischief to total focus. Then she knew that he had something important on his mind.

"Pappa, I've got . . ."

Umarov took hold of Nina's forearm.

"Just two minutes." He turned to the girls. "Are the monsters ready to be driven to prison?"

"Yaaaay!" the girls yelled as they jumped to their feet. They pulled on their rucksacks and opened the front door.

"Wait," Umarov said and he put the buns into Emily's bag. He winked at her and whispered: "Just in case the lions come."

They ran out into the stairwell.

Nina was shaking her head. "I wonder if those stories of yours are going to turn them into criminals."

"Surely not. They're being brought up by a totally uncriminal mother, after all."

Nina put on her coat and felt an uncomfortable lump in her stomach.

"I'm off now, darling," she called back into the apartment.

"O.K.!" Jocke's voice could be heard far away.

The twins took the stairs while Nina and Umarov waited for the lift.

"Is everything alright?" Umarov said.

Nina got out a lipstick so that she had something to focus on. She did not want to meet her father's X-ray eyes.

"Absolutely. Just an awful lot to do."

"You always have," Umarov said. "And I've stopped mentioning it."

"Was that why you came here at eight o'clock on a Monday morning?" Nina said, touching up her lips. "To see how I was feeling?"

They stepped into the hundred-year-old lift and closed the wrought-iron gate.

"I'd go all the way to Siberia to see how you were," Umarov said.

"I'm fine, I told you."

Umarov looked at himself in the mirror.

"Do you remember when we lived in London and Kristina was

your nanny and you were supposed to be baking a sponge cake? You swapped the sugar for salt. Kristina was livid. When Mamushka and I came home we sat down at the kitchen table and I asked Sardor and you to look me in the eyes. Do you remember?"

Nina remembered.

"Do you recall what I asked?"

"Who had switched the sugar," Nina said.

"And who was it?"

"Me."

The lift stopped.

"But you didn't have to say it, did you? I saw it in your eyes."

Nina started to get out of the lift. "Pappa, I don't really have time for your nostalgic stories right now."

They went out to the garage and Nina unlocked the car.

"In you get, girls."

They climbed into the back seat and Nina closed the doors. The garage fell silent.

Umarov went and stood near his daughter. She knew precisely what he was going to ask.

"Look at me, Nina."

"What?"

"Look me in the eyes and tell me that everything's O.K."

Nina steeled herself and stared into her father's face. Now she noticed that he was freshly shaved and even had some sort of pomade in his hair, which was combed back so that the curls were flattened into a shiny wave.

"You need a haircut," Nina said.

"I thought I'd get it done now as I'm in town."

Umarov held his daughter's gaze.

"And?" he said calmly.

"It's all good, Pappa," she said with a broad smile, but she could feel her cheeks straining. "For real."

She gave him a quick peck on the cheek and walked towards the car door.

"Enjoy your visit to the big smoke."

Nina drove off. She saw her father still standing there. He followed the car with his eyes as she drove up the ramp and out towards Karlavägen.

She accelerated away towards the English nursery school.

STRANDVÄGEN, ÖSTERMALM
Monday, 10.vi

After dropping off the girls, Nina drove to the offices of Seascape Properties.

Jeanette greeted her with a "Good morning" and placed a bundle of papers on the table in front of her. "Kaggholmen. All done, except for the last bit with the bank."

"Thank you," Nina said. The bank. Nina added another item to the day's to-do list. She had to agree the amount of their own loan on the house purchase in Rio. As usual, Joakim had no grip on it, relied on her for all the details, but he was perfectly happy showing his friends the brochure and the drone footage. They now owned eleven properties together. Four had been let out and three were in the process of being renovated. What was the point of having all these houses and apartments? She had no better answer than that they were always on the lookout for some new toy. Verbier was easy to justify: she and Jocke loved to ski. They usually managed three weeks a year. But the apartment in Palma, when was the last time they had been there? Nina could not remember. Kate and Emily had been in a pram. And how often would they manage to get to Rio in the next ten years?

At a quarter to eleven, she left the office and took the car to Kungsträdgården. Turned into the little street by the synagogue and parked. Knew that she would probably get a fine. But her thoughts were elsewhere. Umarov's little visit that morning had left her irritated and apprehensive. She had not heard anything back from the dental clinic, but she knew that the man from the F.S.B. was still in town. He had said that he would "stick around until all the loose ends have been tied up". She wondered which hotel he was staying at.

Piccolino's café was relatively quiet. Elena was sitting next to the wall, wearing a yellow fluffy sweater and drinking lemon juice.

Nina gave her stepmother a peck on the cheek and ordered a cappuccino.

"With soy milk, please."

"Everything O.K.?" Elena said.

Nina immediately felt a little wall come up. There was always a hidden agenda to Elena's meetings.

"Your father says he's worried about you."

"Really?" Nina said, feigning ignorance.

"That you're working too hard."

"He's a fine one to talk."

"These days, he's become pretty good at keeping himself at home."

"And looking after the pool."

"God, yes, that really gets to him."

Nina's cappuccino arrived. She tried not to be annoyed by the way Elena talked to her about her father. It was as if she felt a need to control what her stepdaughter knew about her father's life.

"I think you should spend some time together, just the two of you," Elena said.

"Yes, well, that would be nice," Nina said with an attempt at a smile.

"You never know with men. They can—"

"What? Keel over and die?"

Nina thought about her father's big belly and the fact that she had never seen him taking any serious exercise. She had never seen him run.

"He's no longer a spring chicken," Elena said.

"He needs to do more to look after his health," Nina said.

"And you and Sardor?"

"What about us?"

"Well, are you friends?"

"Why would we not be?"

"Just wondering."

Nina pretended to have just remembered something. Took out her mobile.

"Oops. I need to rush. But it was great to catch up."

She got to her feet.

"You see," Elena said.

"What?"

"You're stressing."

"It's Monday, dear. There's always loads to do on Mondays."

Nina drove to Humlegården. The dental clinic was two storeys up in the building, which dated from the late nineteenth century. Nina greeted Julianna in the reception.

After two minutes Julianna came and fetched her.

Nina walked to the end of the corridor and sat down in a consulting room, as usual. Waited. After a while the door opened and a man came in. He took the other chair in the room and rested his hands in his lap. Rocked forward a little, in his characteristic way.

Nina's pulse was racing. She tried to read from his lean face whether to expect good news or bad. He was neutral as always.

"It no work out," he said in his dreadful English.

"What didn't work out?"

"He still in hospital."

Nina closed her eyes. Took a deep breath.

"Weren't you going to send someone . . . professional?"

The man removed his thin-framed spectacles. For the first time, Nina noticed that he had green eyes.

"They increase security, so now harder get at him."

"But . . . surely you can—"

"Relax," the man said, holding up a hand covered in age spots. "I just tell you situation. He alive. We fail. Must think again."

He started to get up.

"Meaning what exactly?" Nina said. She went from being nervous and stressed to angry.

"We get back to you."

"When?"

"We get back to you."

"Shit," Nina said. "You're not going to be taking care of this over the coming week, are you?"

The man left the room.

Nina felt panic. This time, she could not rely on the F.S.B.

Her mobile buzzed. Tatiana wanted to meet up in Södermalm after lunch. Nina knew what would have to be done. She would have to fix it herself.

Skeppargatan 22 looked like any ordinary Östermalm address. Nina checked through the list of names in the doorway and found what she was looking for: Skeppargatan Activity Centre. A man with a nasal voice answered.

"Yes?"

"I'm looking for Jonna Fredén-Hansson."

There was a few seconds' silence.

"Are you a member?"

"No, but my colleague is."

"I'll let you in."

The door opened and Nina went in. She continued down into the cellar and, when she got to the room, she was blinded by white light. The wooden panels on the walls, the rubber floor, the reception counter, the clothes on the man who stood and waited for her, everything was white. The man was even wearing white spectacles. It put Nina in mind of a medical laboratory.

"What can we do for you?"

"I'm looking for Jonna Fredén-Hansson."

"I'll see if she is available."

Nina was shown to a white chair next to a minimal table. Soft music was playing in the background, it sounded like something oriental. There was a scent of eucalyptus. After a few minutes, Jonna walked in, wearing a white bathrobe and white slippers. Her face was red.

"Had a sauna?" Nina said.

"You ought to join me. I've just been doing some boxing with my trainer."

"Thanks, but I only fight with the kids. And sometimes Jocke."

Jonna wiped sweat from her face with a thick, snow-white terry towel. She tucked her wet hair behind her ears and turned to the receptionist. "Can I have one of those freshly pressed . . . things . . . with ginger and lemon?"

The man disappeared behind a curtain.

"How was New York?" Nina said.

"Fantastic. It inspires me just as much each time I go. It's tough coming home like this in the morning, though. I couldn't sleep on the plane."

"So shouldn't you be at home, having a kip? You can come to the office tomorrow."

"No worries. Now that I've had some treatment, I'm feeling better. How's it all going?"

Nina pressed her fingertips into her scalp, ruffling her short, dark hair. Then stretched her back.

"It didn't work."

"What?"

"My plan didn't work out."

Jonna leaned forward and lowered her voice.

"So the guy with the burns—"

"Is alive. With increased security. And now my contacts can't get at him."

"So what do we do?"

"Good question," Nina said. "What *do* we do?"

"Are you worried?" Jonna asked.

"Of course I'm worried. You should be too. If Pappa finds out what has happened, our real estate business will be closed down. And that will be the least of my problems."

"Why? It was you and I who set it up."

Nina smiled and shook her head. "You're so wonderfully naive. That's what I love about you. So Swedish."

"Leave off."

"There's so much you don't know," Nina said and she heard

someone switch on a food processor behind the curtains. "Where do you think we got our start-up capital from when we established Seascape?"

"You said you had some additional funds."

"Four million. It was Pappa's money."

"You never told me that."

"No. And there are other things you don't need to know either. But trust me. The police are going to investigate why the building burned like that. They'll analyse the blaze, find where the fire burned hardest, take a look at the cabling and conclude that it isn't standard, that it's one which is actually a lot more flammable than it should be."

"But in that case we—"

"No, it'll stop there," Nina said firmly. "It can't be traced back to us. Officially, it's the Latvian construction company that's responsible."

"I know, but Oleg—"

"Precisely," Nina said. "Oleg is the link to us. And that's why he mustn't talk to the police."

Jonna got her juice. She put it down on the table without tasting it.

"So . . . ?"

"I'm afraid I may have to ask my brother for help."

"Sardor?"

"Sadly, I have no other brother," Nina said and tasted the juice. "That's good."

"But what'll he do?"

"I don't know yet. The only thing I do know is that I have to talk to him. For a number of reasons."

"Do you think we'll manage to stay out of this?"

"The way I look at it, there's no question of 'think,'" Nina said. "I *know* we'll be fine."

"So why are you looking so stressed?" Jonna said.

Nina smiled. "That's to do with other things. The family."

Monday, 10.vi

Two guards were standing outside Room 1 in the I.C.U. Tekla felt like Frodo at the Gates of Mordor.

"Increased security," one of the guards said in a friendly tone. He took out a list. "And you are?"

"Tekla Berg."

He found her name.

"You can go in."

Tekla passed through the airlock on shaky legs. Suddenly it felt as if the clock had been turned back twenty-four hours. To before the message from Simon. She still had her doubts about the identity of the burns victim.

Nothing had changed inside the room. Nilsén was standing in a corner, talking into her mobile, but she hung up as soon as she saw Tekla.

"Hi. So glad you came."

"It feels a bit strange having guards here in the hospital," Tekla said.

"It's a whole different ball game after what happened yesterday," a voice behind her said. She spun around. She had not noticed the other person in the room, a thin man with a friendly face. He held out his hand.

"Marcus Safadi. Security Police."

"Security Police? Säpo?"

Nilsén was leaning against the bedhead.

"Thanks to your heroic effort yesterday, Tekla, he's still alive. You acted with such resolve. And thank heavens you did not come to any harm."

"Too true," Safadi said.

In her mind's eye, Tekla saw the limping man vanish down the service tunnel. The strange thing, which had also struck the policeman who questioned her, was that she had never seen the man's face. The hood of his windcheater was pulled up, granted, but he seemed to have nothing covering his face. He must have been turning away from her deliberately the whole time. And then the text message from Simon had arrived.

"The attack yesterday seems to have been carried out by a professional," the Säpo man said.

"A professional?" Tekla said.

"And we need Säpo to tell us that?" Nilsén said acerbically.

Safadi ignored his colleague's comment.

"We weren't sure . . . *are* still not sure . . . that there was a criminal act behind the fire."

"Give us a break," Nilsén said. She turned to Tekla. "This is how it is: Säpo has a theory about the garage where we've found some materials which could be used for making bombs. There's been a heightened security level in Stockholm for some time now and in particular a suspicion that there's a terror cell within the city centre. Or am I wrong?" She was waving a finger in irritation at her colleague from the Security Police. "The communication between us isn't always too good. We at N.O.D. are actually in charge of this and leading the investigation, while our dear colleagues at Säpo will be focusing on the terrorist aspects. Isn't that right?"

Safadi smiled. Tekla could not help feeling some sympathy for him. It must be tough to have Nilsén in the opposite corner.

Nilsén crossed her arms. She was wearing a long yellow dress and a black jacket. She even had some new glasses with a discreet blue frame.

"And so? You suspect that the burns victim here is a . . . terrorist?"

"We know nothing for certain," Safadi said calmly.

"Hence the efforts to identify the man," Nilsén added. "I probably don't need to say this, but we're relying on you not to spread this information any further."

"Absolutely," Tekla said and went to the intubated patient. The only visible change in his condition was a slight reduction in the swelling of his eye. Every now and then a tiny muscle near his eyeball twitched. Again she was full of doubt as to whether the text message could have come from Simon. She made an effort to stop her hand from shaking while at the same time pretending to examine the patient. She was still searching for identifying marks. The height was right, as far as she could judge. As for his build: Simon had always been slim, but sinewy and strong. The first description matched, for sure, but was Simon as muscular? Possibly not. Her eyes travelled to the hands: they were badly burned, but the thumb on the left hand looked relatively undamaged. Until now it had been bandaged. She ran her finger over the base. Just as with Simon, the joint was crooked, so the top of the thumb was angled inwards.

Her head spun and she was struggling to get air. She took a deep breath and stepped back. Pretended to cough and wiped some sweat from her upper lip. Then she braced herself and looked at Nilsén.

"Well, we'll have to see what comes of the D.N.A. test."

Nilsén had noticed something, that much was obvious, she had stopped messing about with her mobile. Tekla tried to deflect the penetrating gaze coming in from the side.

"Haven't you been able to trace that van by now?" she said.

"We've found a great many green Renault Transports, but not that precise one."

"So you have no idea who the van's passengers were?"

Nilsén hesitated. Then she gave a laugh.

"Why are you so curious?"

"I'm not," Tekla said, a little too quickly.

"But no, since you ask, we haven't found the men we're looking for. You've probably been following the reports in the media—"

"I don't read newspapers."

"No, you doctors only work."

Tekla did not bother to analyse the subtext to Nilsén's comment, but pretended instead to be in a sudden hurry.

"I have to get back to A. & E. now. We'll no doubt speak tomorrow."

"We will," Nilsén said, her eyes intrigued as they followed Tekla's back towards the door.

"See you," Safadi said.

Tekla paused by a drinking fountain to have some water. She felt exhausted. When would this shitty day ever end?

When she left the hospital, Tekla took a walk to Nytorget, the quarter of south-eastern Södermalm which was the gathering place for Stockholm's trendy middle class, for extreme hipsters, those with the longest beards, the most expensive retro prams and the most fashionable diets. Many of them came from small-town Sweden with dreams of making it in the big city. Suddenly, the thought struck her: was she one of them? But there was nothing trendy about her, and her reason for moving to the city was different from that of the bearded mafia. She lived there, in the same town, breathed the same air, trod the same tarmac, but she was not one of them.

Her stomach was empty, her sugar reserves depleted and she was shaking from all the bombs she had taken during the day. She dreaded going home to an empty apartment and just staring at her mobile. She must have sent thirty text messages to Simon's mobile during the day. Had the last two really come from him? She began to doubt it. At the same time, another part of her brain was assembling dark thoughts about the bad things that might have happened to him.

Nor in her heart of hearts had she altogether discarded the possibility that Simon was the burns victim in the I.C.U.

She sat on a wooden bench outside a falafel place waiting for her food to arrive. A woman of her own age settled down with her back to Tekla. Tekla glanced at her handbag. There was a book lying in it. A real, physical book. And, unlike all the other customers in the restaurant, the young woman was not playing with her telephone. Normally she would never have tried to strike up a conversation. It may, however, have been the bewildering events of the last few days that made Tekla take a small step beyond her usual boundaries. She could not help asking:

"What are you reading?"

The woman turned and gave a broad and friendly smile.

Tekla immediately regretted what she had done, but it was too late. "Your book," she said, pointing awkwardly at the woman's handbag.

"Oh, O.K." She picked it up. "Ferrante."

"Last year's best-seller, right? Is it good?" Tekla said.

The woman looked at it, turned it around, as if she were considering whether to give it away or not.

"So-so. A bit disappointing, I have to say. It feels . . . wordy. It's the first of a series of four about two girls who grow up in Naples, best friends, very different . . . how they develop throughout their lives. At the same time, I can't put it down. It's rather annoying."

Another infectious smile from the woman. This time Tekla felt a wave of warmth. There was something so natural about the way she described the book. It was unusual to feel personal contact with a stranger in this city. She was glad that she had come here and not gone straight home after work, she needed to meet some normal people. People who had a life. People who laughed and felt well. At least on the surface.

"Are you waiting for someone?" Tekla said. She saw how muscular the woman was – ripped was perhaps a better way of putting it, but in a natural way. She had the muscles one only gets from physical work, maybe as a firefighter or on a construction site. The woman was wearing a lime green dress and, over that, a black denim jacket. She had well-defined calf muscles and a back which would make the bouncers at the nightclubs on Stureplan think twice.

"My wonderful brother." She looked exasperated. "But he's late as usual. Come over and join me."

Tekla sat down opposite the woman. It felt spontaneous. At the same moment, the waitress brought her falafel. Then she reached out her hand.

"Tekla."

"Astrid. Good to meet you. Do you come here much?"

"I've never been before. Didn't know they served falafel. But it looks nice." She took a bite and was not disappointed. "That's really good, that is."

"My fave place in Söder. Unfortunately, I've moved to Vasastan since I got divorced. Nowhere near as nice. Do you live around here?"

"Gullmarsplan."

Astrid looked surprised.

"It's not as rough as you might think," Tekla said.

Astrid had frizzy hair which stood straight out, like a large lion's mane, but raven black.

"That's not what I meant. I just don't know much about the place."

Tekla kept on eating. Felt unusually hungry.

"When I was little, my dream was to work with books," Astrid went on.

"So what do you do instead?"

Astrid looked away for a second.

"Nothing interesting."

"But which books would you have wanted to publish?"

Astrid smiled and glanced at the Ferrante novel on the table.

"I'm embarrassed to say this, but probably fantasy."

"Why embarrassed?"

"It's not really seen as proper literature, is it? No Nobel prizes, for sure."

"But people read fantasy, don't they? Especially younger readers."

"And little me . . ." Astrid truly did have an infectious smile.

"It's hard to label you as little," Tekla said.

"I was born like this." She took off her short denim jacket and flexed her biceps. "No gym at all. Hate pumping iron. Even more, I loathe all those blokes who grunt and yell when they're doing their lunges or bench presses."

"Bloody hell," Tekla said, holding up a thin, pale arm.

Astrid felt it gingerly.

"Not too bad."

"You mean the way it looks, or what?" Tekla laughed.

Astrid smiled. "What do you do?"

"I'm a doctor at the Nobel Hospital."

"Nobel. Did you get many of the casualties after the fire?"

"No, it could have been worse."

"Are you saying there weren't that many burns victims?"

"No, there were, but it could have been far worse when you consider how fast the fire spread." She saw the unidentified man's one eye before her and a shiver ran through her body. "There's still one very badly burnt patient in Intensive Care."

"Will he make it?"

"Uncertain. He's got blood poisoning and . . ." Tekla's discretion was about to end up in the falafel.

"I get it," Astrid said after a long silence. "You're not allowed to tell me. But let's hope he pulls through."

"They're doing all they can," Tekla said.

"It's terrible to think it may have been done deliberately."

"I don't read the papers."

"All I've seen is that they've found explosives in a garage, and that they're looking for a green van."

They sat and watched the people strolling by in the sunshine.

Tekla changed the subject.

"Go on, tell me what you do."

Astrid laughed and clapped her hands together.

"Something as sad as P.R."

"But then I imagine you do a fair amount of writing."

"Don't know if you can call it writing. If you're thinking about my interest in books."

Tekla looked around. Ate her food and enjoyed having her mind on something other than her mobile for a while.

"You said that he's wonderful, your brother. In what way? Or were you being ironic?"

"He's my hero. I've had some tough years with an idiot of a husband who's also the father of my ten-year-old daughter. I wanted to stay on in our apartment, but he had the money . . . he's a successful music producer." Tekla noted the change of tone. "And an assistant in a P.R. business doesn't make a whole lot . . ."

"So your brother lent you some."

"He's always been frugal. But he had some savings which he let me 'borrow'. His word. I know I'll never be allowed to repay him. It's lucky for me that he works so hard. He hasn't been off sick for one single day in his entire life. He makes a point of it."

"Sounds like you're close. Was it always like that?"

"Yes, he's very much been a big brother to me. Ever since our mother died. I know he promised her he'd look after me."

Tekla remembered the promise she gave her own father on his deathbed, when there was just the two of them there. She thought about Iris, the little girl who had been nestling in her lap beside the bed where her brother was fighting for his life. Tekla tried unsuccessfully to bring back the scent of her hair.

Suddenly a man sat down at their table, he too an XXL.

"Late as always," Astrid said as she budged sideways. Tekla felt small compared to the two giants opposite. "This is Tekla. She's a doctor at the Nobel Hospital."

"Magnus," the man said, and held out a hand which enfolded the whole of hers. It felt warm and safe.

"Hi," Tekla said, retrieving her sweaty hand.

"We're talking books," Astrid said, "but not Mankell or Larsson. Sorry, Magnus."

The man smiled and gave his sister an affectionate dig in the side with his elbow.

"My mind could do with some broadening."

"Got it!" Tekla burst out, pointing at Lundgren.

"What?" Astrid said in surprise.

"You're a policeman, right?"

Lundgren looked at Astrid, his large torso squirming awkwardly.

"You were one of the policemen who came to A. & E. on Thursday, around midnight. Then you headed off to the fire."

Astrid smiled and gave Lundgren a nudge.

"Well, are you, or aren't you? A policeman . . . a member of the S.W.A.T. team along with all those other testosterone hulks. Or wait, I know that you're called the Reinforced Regional Task Force nowadays."

Lundgren looked uncomfortable and ran a large hand over his crew-cut hair.

"Let's talk about something else."

"I just thought I recognised your . . ." Tekla began before she faltered.

"His what?" Astrid demanded to know. She leaned forward and seemed to have picked up something she liked the sound of.

Bloody hell, Tekla thought. She'd done it again.

"His eyes, right? That's what you were going to say. You recognised him by his eyes. Because you cover your faces with those flame-proof balaclavas, don't you, Brorsan?"

". . . and you're a bit larger than average."

"Most policemen are," Astrid countered with a sly smile.

"Now I recognise you too," Lundgren said. "It's hard with you not wearing your blue scrubs."

"Aha!" Astrid said in triumph.

"O.K., can we talk about something else now?" Lundgren said.

Astrid gave a laugh.

"Sure, why don't we talk about the weather. Strong sunshine today. Best to cover up. You two should meet without me and discuss emergency services stuff," Astrid said as she gave her brother a teasing look.

"Sounds like a great idea," Lundgren said with a smile. "Why don't we have a drink one of these days? Text me when you're free."

Tekla would have liked to disappear into a hole in the ground, and she returned the invitation with a forced smile. But Astrid was right, the sun really was stronger than usual. Tekla picked up her black New York Yankees cap and ate a falafel ball. Then she remembered what she had been wanting to do in the I.C.U. the day before, when she surprised the man in the process of suffocating the burns victim: check if there was a birthmark on his ear. But now she was far too tired to go back to the hospital. That would have to await her morning meeting with Nilsén.

Sardor parked his car behind Bofills Båge by Södra Station. The area around Söder Tower was cordoned off. They had managed to extinguish the fire, and were now hard at work ensuring that the burnt-out skeleton of the building did not collapse. His mobile rang.

"Jarmo's going to make it," Eriksson said. "Minus a spleen, but who needs one anyway?"

"I've got a meeting," Sardor said. "Can we talk later?"

"Jensen's about to blow a gasket. He's set on seeing blood flow."

"What the fuck, it's been only three days," Sardor snapped. "He said a week."

"He's impatient," Eriksson said.

"Any word from the street?"

"Seems like the Northern Networks are lying low. I've got a tip-off that I'm going to follow up now."

"Spread the word that there's a 50k reward for info on the person who stabbed Jarmo at Kvarnen. Victor wants us to sort this out. Quick and smooth. Not step up the violence."

"Looks like there's also some trouble with the H," Eriksson said.

"What trouble?"

"Loads of overdoses this weekend."

"How do you know it's heroin?"

"The pushers have complained."

"What about? Our products?"

"I don't know, we're checking it out."

Sardor hung up and crossed Medborgarplatsen. He had to get on top of this. Felt the tension in his neck. What was that about a mass of overdoses? No way could that have anything to do with their stuff. Their business model had satisfied customers written all over it. And it would never do to mess with the quality, not under any circumstances. The best and purest heroin on the market. Not like the brown crap from the Northern Networks, which the junkies had to cut with ascorbic acid or citric acid before heating it up and injecting. It destroyed the vessels, was said to burn like barbed wire in the veins.

He walked into Burger King. Tatiana was sitting in the corner, well away from the windows. Shunning the light as usual. Opposite her Kaisa was drumming on the plastic tray with her long nails.

Sardor helped himself to an onion ring and sat down on a greasy aluminium chair next to Kaisa.

"Buy your own food." Tatiana slapped his hand.

"I know you're not going to finish it."

As Tatiana closed her eyes, her bright turquoise eyeshadow stood out. She was just as pretty today as she had been ten years earlier when Umarov recruited her to take care of the prostitutes. She was really rather like Nina, only more temperamental and foul-mouthed. She ought to have a family and children, Sardor thought, and channel that energy into something more worthwhile than running Russian and South American whores.

"Are you sure you're Uzbek?" Sardor said.

Tatiana sighed.

"You mean because I'm so much better-looking than you?"

Kaisa was slurping at a strawberry milkshake.

Sardor yanked up the zip on her pink hoodie.

"What the fuck are you doing?!" Kaisa cried.

"Don't forget who paid for those," Sardor said, nodding towards her silicone breasts. "And the strangle marks are still showing."

"Maybe you just don't want anyone else checking out the forbidden fruit?" Tatiana teased him.

Sardor did his best to ignore this jibe, but every comment from Tatiana got under his skin.

"Your sister's on her way," Tatiana said.

"Nina?"

"Do you have others?"

"How often do you two see each other, if I may ask?" Sardor said, sounding irritated.

Tatiana smiled.

"I talked to her yesterday and she had some delegation visiting from Karelia, some people who want to buy an underground shelter."

Tatiana looked up towards the entrance.

"Well, speak of the devil . . ."

Sardor turned and saw his sister's snow-white blouse flapping outside in Medborgarplatsen.

"Great, that's today ruined for me," Sardor said.

"You two should stop squabbling over your father's attention."

"What are you talking about?"

"You'll never change the fact that she's older than you."

"What's that got to do with . . ."

Sardor got a message on his mobile. From Eriksson. He read it rapidly.

"Well, well, if it isn't a family get-together," a cheerful voice rang out behind Sardor.

"I've got to go," Sardor said, ignoring his sister.

"Weren't you going to have something to eat?" Tatiana said with a smile.

Sardor seemed confused as he looked over at the queue.

"Come on, Sardo, stay," Nina said. "I'm having a salad. Hi," she continued, kissing Tatiana on the cheek. She sat down next to Sardor, who made a point of turning away.

"Right, so what have you done today?" Sardor said.

"Been to the dentist."

"Again?" Sardor turned towards his sister. "How often do you need to see that posh bloke?"

"My dentist?" Nina took off her jacket. "In fact, it's my hygienist, and I go there regularly."

219

Sardor looked sceptical. "Anyone would think you were having an affair."

"With Claes Neumann? Give me a break. He's hardly my type."

"I think she's lucky to have Joakim," Tatiana said. "He's bloody gorgeous."

"Thanks, sweetie," Nina said, and smiled.

"But it's a good thing you kept your maiden name," Tatiana said. "Nina Lundblad would have sounded like some second-rate pop star with silicone tits."

Kaisa was sitting there, putting on lip gloss.

"Talking of tits, I could do with some more filler for my lips . . ."

Sardor felt his head aching. He gripped Kaisa's slim wrist.

"Ouch!"

"Will you shut up about your fucking lips!"

"Can you take your hand off me, please."

Tatiana shook her head and gave Sardor a peremptory tap on the shoulder.

He let go of Kaisa's wrist.

"When will you stop doing a Victor?" Nina said, looking amused. "Don't you get that Pappa grew up in a tough climate? Do you think the Soviet Union in the '80s was some kind of children's playground?"

Sardor pushed his chair back from the table.

"No idea what you're talking about. I've got to go." Exasperated, he gave his sister one last, furious look. "You live inside a pink bubble and have everything served up on a silver platter. You ought to tag along some time and see what the real world is all about."

Nina shook her head and said: "You were brought up in the most luxurious parts of London. Can't you hear what you sound like? Pathetic. You just want to live up to something you'll never be."

Sardor got to his feet.

Tatiana also stood up, a fascinated smile on her face. "Where are you going?"

"The warehouse in Årsta."

"I'll come along and have a little look at that horrible real world."

"I was jok—"

"But why not?" Tatiana put on her leather jacket and picked up some onion rings. "Are you coming too?" she asked Nina.

"I didn't mean for you to join me," Sardor said, but they seemed to have made up their minds. He headed for the exit.

"A field trip," Tatiana teased him, and she waved at Nina who nodded and got up.

Kaisa stayed where she was, wielding her lip gloss.

Nina and Tatiana followed Sardor out. It was not what he had hoped for.

Tatiana caught up with Sardor on Medborgarplatsen and whispered in his ear:

"Maybe you should take a few more yoga classes to keep that famous temper of yours in check."

Sardor walked towards his car and tried to ignore the mocking laughter behind his back.

Monday, 10.vi

They passed Kakelfabriken, turned right and zigzagged their way over to the old vegetable warehouse. Tatiana got out and waited for Nina, who parked her car next to theirs.

"So this is where we do the packaging."

"Victor will go off his head if he finds out that you've been here."

Nina stroked her hot-headed brother's unshaven cheek.

"I promise, my sweet little brother. As quiet as a mouse. I was just curious to see what this place looks like. Besides which, you nicked my coffee companion."

Inside the warehouse they were joined by Eriksson and two others, Ben and Emre from the Red Bears. Sardor noted the testosterone in the air. He watched his bulky friend bring in his prey.

"And this is?"

"Lorik. Lorik Xhafas," Eriksson said, pushing forward a young man with a crew cut, black T-shirt, jeans, trainers and a swollen right eye. His whole being screamed, "You can all go to hell."

"Where did you dig him up?"

"Lorik's chick squealed when she heard about the reward. Seems she's with a guy from another gang now."

Ben and Emre kept their Uzis pointed at Xhafas' legs in case he decided to run for it.

Sardor considered the facts. A drunk girlfriend at Kvarnen late on a Thursday night. What if this was the wrong person? On the other hand: if they did nothing, what kind of a signal would that send? He had no choice.

His sister hung her black jacket over the back of a chair and Sardor wondered for a split second if they would be competing over who was going to deal with this Xhafas. Then he saw Nina go and sit next to Tatiana, who was rocking back and forth on her chair.

Sardor had made up his mind. He could sense Victor before him. Hear his words tearing through his brain like a chainsaw: *Sort out this mess before it's too late.*

He pulled out a knife and flicked open the curved blade. Silence weighed heavily over the warehouse. The ice-cold light from the fluorescent tubes in the ceiling flickered.

Suddenly, Sardor heard Nina's voice: "Let me know if you need any help, Brorsan."

Without turning, Sardor replied:

"You're not here."

Sardor took off his leather jacket and focused all his attention on Xhafas. Held up his knife. Xhafas opened his one functioning eye wide, steeled himself.

"So you're the one who knifed Jarmo at Kvarnen?"

Xhafas spat in Sardor's face, a gob of phlegm he had probably been collecting for several minutes. Sardor rammed the knife into Xhafas' thigh with all his might. It cut through the largest muscle in the body and penetrated half a centimetre into the thigh bone. Xhafas collapsed to his knees. With his free hand, Sardor grabbed one of Xhafas' ears and pulled him to his feet.

"Lorik, you seem to like knives. You'll have had your fill of them by the time I'm through with you."

Xhafas was whimpering through clenched teeth.

Sardor heard Nina's voice behind him, a little closer this time.

"Are you absolutely certain you've got the right person?"

It was all Sardor could do to refrain from sticking the knife into his sister instead.

"If you want to take over, be my guest. Perhaps you've got some manicure scissors in your pocket?"

"All I'm saying is that Pappa wants this handled nicely."

"Same way you do your business over in Östermalm, right?"

"Pappa has an eye on everything I do. Obviously. What did you think?"

Sardor turned. "If you're not going to help us here, I suggest you keep your trap shut." And then he said to Xhafas: "Why did you stab Jarmo?"

"I didn't," Xhafas managed to croak. "Fuck! I wasn't anywhere near that Swede-infested hole on Thursday."

"Oh you weren't, were you?" Sardor felt a sudden misgiving. "We have a witness who's identified you. And it's no secret that you guys in the Northern Networks are trying to get your hands on some of our turf."

"There's room for everyone," Xhafas said through gritted teeth.

Sardor burst into a contrived laugh.

"I do declare. A politician. There's room for everyone. Interesting." Xhafas nodded.

"Why didn't you stick to Gothenburg? Or Eskilstuna? Why have a go at a city like Stockholm, that's much too big? You know who the *vor* is in this town?"

"I'm not the one who makes the decisions."

"Sure. A rat in the street. But what were you and Jarmo fighting about?"

"I wasn't . . ." Xhafas panted, struggling not to faint. The knife in his thigh was shaking.

Sardor pulled it out and grabbed hold of one of Xhafas' hands. The backs of all his fingers were covered in tattoos. The palm was soaked in sweat.

"How do you like this then?" Sardor asked as he drove the tip of the blade under the nail of Xhafas' index finger, twisted it and ripped away the whole nail. Xhafas pulled back his hand and yelled again:

"Fucking hell!" He made a desperate attempt at staunching the flow of blood.

"What do you say, time to switch tactics?" Sardor said.

"Jesus! I'm telling you, I wasn't there," Xhafas stammered. He looked as if he were about to pass out.

Sardor was stuck. Now what? He couldn't afford to lose face. Mustn't show any cracks in the facade. He nodded towards Ben.

"The chair."

Ben pulled up a chair, which Xhafas slumped onto.

"Whisky, anyone?"

Eriksson said something, at which Emre walked into the back room, where they repackaged the drugs. He returned with a bottle of Jim Beam.

Sardor looked around. Tatiana sat there fiddling with her mobile, as if nothing had happened, while Nina was evidently interested in what was going on.

"Here," Sardor said.

Xhafas drank three large gulps out of the bottle and took a few deep breaths.

Sardor took the bottle from him.

"That's enough. Let's hear it now, otherwise I might as well . . ."

Sardor pulled his pistol out of his waistband and pointed the muzzle at Xhafas' temple.

"One last time now, let's hear it or—"

"But Sardo," Nina cut in.

He had not heard her come over.

"How do you expect him to remember anything if you pull out his fingernails and keep threatening him?"

Sardor turned to his sister. She gave a tender smile.

"I think it'd be best if you went and sat down," he said.

"Not at all. I think it would be best if I gave you a hand. This doesn't seem to be going so well."

"I see. Perhaps you'd like to pull out another nail?"

Sardor held out the bloodied knife.

Nina made a face.

"I don't like blood."

She turned to Xhafas and put her hand on his head.

"Could I have some water, please?" she said.

Eriksson fetched a glass of water while Nina went on patting the head of the wounded man.

"Here. Drink. In this atmosphere, you can easily get dehydrated. I'm sorry about my brother's behaviour. He hasn't been himself lately. Why don't you give us some more background on this unfortunate business at the restaurant?"

Slowly Xhafas raised his head. He was drawn to Nina's look. She stroked his cheek.

"All I've heard is that you've got problems with the heroin," Xhafas said in a low voice. "That it's not as pure as it used to be."

Sardor stiffened, felt an iron brace tighten across his chest.

"O.K.," Nina said. "Strange, because Sardor's always proudly claiming that we have the best goods in town. Carry on."

"The talk is . . ."

"That?" Nina said gently.

". . . something's happened. Our supplies are selling out faster than ever."

Nina turned to Sardor.

"Heard anything about this, Brorsan?"

Sardor shook his head and then looked at Eriksson.

"But what's that got to do with Kvarnen?" Nina went on.

"I've no idea. But you . . . should maybe ask . . . Jarmo. There were many others at Kvarnen that evening. But not . . . me. Not us."

"See, Sardor," Nina said. "Did you check Jarmo's story?"

Sardor ignored her.

Still turning to Xhafas, Nina asked: "And you know this because of what?"

"The grapevine."

"The grapevine, you say," Sardor repeated. "That seems to be about all you can tell us today."

Nina straightened up and turned to Sardor.

"It's the talk. Hear that, Brorsan? It's on the grapevine."

"Shut up," Sardor snapped, feeling that he was about to explode.

"Someone's cutting the stuff," Xhafas said.

"Cutting it?" Nina said.

"Someone's cutting your H with a whole lot of other shit," Xhafas said. "At least in some of your packages."

"We'll have to check that," Sardor said.

"Anything else?" Nina said brightly. "I need to get back to the office soon."

Sardor walked over to the sink to wash his hands.

Tatiana turned to Nina. "Guess we'll have to keep that coffee for another day."

"I'm going to stick around here a bit longer," Nina said.

"Can someone give me a lift into town?" Tatiana asked. Eriksson nodded and gave orders to Emre.

"Call if there's anything," Tatiana said and left the room with her driver.

Sardor tried to get his pulse down, but he realised that he had lost face and also the battle with Nina. He walked off into a corner of the building with Eriksson.

"That something you've heard?"

Eriksson shook his head. Pulled at his goatee.

"You haven't? But we've got to know what's going on out there."

"It would explain the overdoses," Eriksson said.

"Maybe so," Sardor said. "And we need to put some more pressure on Jarmo. Double-check his story. In the meantime, snuff this Albanian and dump the body in the sea. Make sure Jensen gets to see a hand or some fingers to keep him happy."

Eriksson nodded.

"By the way," Eriksson said. "I picked up one of those blokes that owe you money."

"What blokes?" Sardor said, sounding puzzled.

"The ones who were supposed to get hold of the money that disappeared from the Haninge warehouse. It's been more than a month now."

Sardor swallowed heavily. He felt queasy at the very thought of the conversation he had had when he forced Jonas and Simon to

227

find him the money that went missing during the raid on Haninge. They were meant to guard the warehouse but had been smoking pot and had fucked up, had not even noticed a S.W.A.T. team in the building. Three hundred thousand disappeared and they had been given a month to track the money down. But it was all his own fault in the end. His lack of leadership. He was the one who had set two pushers to keep watch that Walpurgis night. Two morons. And that information must never be allowed to filter out. Not to Nina. And especially not to Umarov.

"And when had you been planning to tell me?" Sardor said.

"Didn't get a chance because of that Albanian."

"Well, where are they?"

"One. I got hold of one of them."

"And where's *he* then?" Sardor asked.

"In the fridge."

"You mean here?"

Eriksson pointed towards the large cold-storage facility for bananas at the rear of the building.

Dahl could not help laughing when he saw what Lundgren was pulling over his head.

"That clothes swap evening must have been twenty years ago."

Lundgren smoothed the front of the washed-out, light grey T-shirt with the *Jurassic Park* logo on it. "Nothing wrong with this."

"And those are Rasmus' shoes, right?"

"Still work just fine," Lundgren said and pulled out his old badminton racquet from the end of the last millennium. "Let's see who wins."

"I'm going to beat the shit out of you," Dahl said.

"Talking about beatings," Lundgren said, drinking some water, "are you going to tell me what happened?"

"Nothing."

"Looks painful."

"It's not so bad," Dahl said and he pulled at his chin so that his jaw moved back and forth. "Nothing's broken."

"But you got a real going-over. Who did you manage to piss off? Some chick?"

Dahl smiled. "Don't know any chick who can hit that hard. Let's drop it."

They walked to the court. Dahl sat on a bench and crossed his legs. Lundgren swung his arms to get the circulation going.

"Amazing coincidence, by the way. I met that doctor I was telling you about. In Nytorget."

"Well now," Dahl said, juggling with his racquet. "What happened?"

"Nothing. She was having a meal with my sister."

"What, do they know each other?"

"Pure chance that they met. I hardly recognised her without her hospital gear, but she still looked great."

"So you asked her out?"

Two young couples who had just finished playing hugged each other. Lundgren glanced at the girlfriends' long, muscular legs and thought how long it was since he had last been on a date.

"Well . . ."

"Christ, you're such a loser," Dahl sighed.

They got to their feet. Lundgren started skipping. Dahl struck a shuttlecock high and watched it turn just under the rafters.

"Come on, let's start," Lundgren said, sounding impatient.

"Best of five," Dahl called and served.

Lundgren leaped up and delivered a straight smash. Just outside the short service line.

"One nil," Dahl said, switching to the other service court.

"Enjoy the only point you're going to get," Lundgren teased, and readied himself.

Dahl moved sideways like a pensioner with a hip replacement, but he had an incredible flick of the wrist. Lundgren had run a marathon only that summer and was in better physical shape, but struggled to reach Dahl's nasty drop shots right up by the net. He had to stretch, run all over the court and make a huge effort to keep pace with his former classmate.

He stood with his hands on his thighs to catch his breath.

"Jesus, you're on form today."

"It's all in the wrist," Dahl said.

"You've got the body of a walrus, but you play like a twenty-year-old Thai."

"Well, thank you," Dahl said, shaking his head. "A walrus, eh?"

Lundgren was using the high umpire's chair by the net to stretch his calf muscles, while Dahl sat on a chair spinning his racquet.

"What happened to the money?" Lundgren asked as he stopped stretching.

"What money?" Dahl said, looking genuinely surprised.

"Come on now. How long have we known each other?"

"You had a mullet and played ice hockey in the third division."

"You know what I'm talking about. The bag from the raid in Haninge that I gave to your investigator right there."

Dahl cast a lazy glance at some men who were playing two courts across from them.

"I figure that you took care of the money in some way," Lundgren insisted. "And not for the first time either."

"Not so loud," Dahl said, looking around.

"How much was it?"

"Three hundred. I had a few gaps I needed to fill. Are you happy now?"

In the sauna afterwards, they were alone. There was a hiss as Lundgren poured a scoop of water onto the heater. The steam rose, turned in the darkness above them and then fell like a scorching mist over their backs.

Dahl sucked in air between his teeth.

"Let's just hope Special Investigations don't take a look," Lundgren said.

"That would be seriously bad luck," Dahl said. "But you can relax. As I said, I've taken your name off that intervention. You weren't there. And the officer you gave the bag to would never shop you. We've known each other for ages. You can really stop worrying. We're square now. I won't ask you for any more favours."

Lundgren pulled off some dead skin with his nails and said:

"O.K., I'll let it go. Now tell me why you got yourself beaten up. Half your face is black and blue."

There was a moment of silence and they both sat staring at the heater that was clicking away with the temperature.

"Business," Dahl said eventually. "Just some business. Pour on some more water and then we can go for a beer. I'm dying of thirst."

"Glad I'm not involved in the same business as you," Lundgren said. "It seems dangerous." He took the scoop and poured on more water. The stones sizzled like a steak in hot oil.

WALDEMARSUDDE, DJURGÅRDEN
Monday evening, 10.vi

"At last some warm weather," Dabrowski said, removing his tie and undoing the top button of his shirt.

They passed the Italian embassy on their left and the small marina on their right. Carlsson noted that they were not the last to arrive; she saw some late guests a few hundred metres away strolling up the hill towards the museum.

"I had no idea you were such an art connoisseur," Dabrowski went on.

"What's wrong with developing new interests?" Carlsson said.

"But tell me again, why have a private view on a Monday night?"

"Maybe he's away at weekends? Doesn't he live in France a lot of the time?"

"You're the expert," Dabrowski said.

Carlsson kept her blazer buttoned up, even though she was beginning to feel sweaty. Her black trousers were a little too warm for the time of year.

"I like his art, not the man behind the works."

Dabrowski stopped but Carlsson pulled him on.

"That's something I've never been able to fathom," he said.

"What? That it's possible to walk and talk at the same time?" Carlsson said tartly.

"That you can separate a work of art from the person. They're so interwoven."

Carlsson smiled and patted her husband's bearded cheek.

"Is that what you learn when you secretly read family magazines at the hairdresser? How sweet."

Dabrowski ignored her comment and followed a couple of older guests through the swing doors of the museum at Waldemarsudde.

"The place is packed," Dabrowski whispered. "Strange that so many people have so little to do on a Monday."

"It's a question of priorities, darling."

They did not bother with the cloakroom and went straight ahead to the exhibition rooms. Carlsson showed the guards her invitation and followed the stream of visitors to the left. Many of Stockholm's cultural elite were there, dressed up for the occasion in sober summer dresses and light-coloured suits.

Carlsson greeted a former head of the Mediterranean Museum as well as the founder of one of the biggest architectural practices in town, and then briefly introduced Dabrowski to the managing director of the Film Institute. Carlsson was looking around for her old friend from university but could not see him anywhere.

"How do you two know each other?" Dabrowski whispered when they were handed a glass of cold rosé.

"We're on the same board."

"Which one?"

"Can't remember," she answered with a false smile on her lips. "Could it be Kulturhuset? No idea." She stopped in front of a painting.

"Isn't it fantastic?"

Dabrowski sipped at his wine.

"Too many animals. I prefer his abstract work."

"Bengt O. Hanzon doesn't do abstract."

"You know what I mean."

"No. Maybe you're talking about paintings like that one over there."

"Exactly. No animals."

"Well, say so then. Aren't you supposed to be the semantics expert? You have to be a bit more rigorous."

"Good word that."

"What?"

"Rigorous."

They followed the crowd towards the centre of the building.

"Talking of which . . ." Dabrowski tugged at Carlsson's elbow.

A few metres away they spotted Carl-Henrik Filipsson in a bright blue suit and matching azure spectacles, in loud conversation with the owner of Uppsala Auktionskammare, the auction house.

"He's not keeping a low profile," Carlsson whispered. "Aren't you going to say hello?"

"Cut it out," Dabrowski said, walking off in the opposite direction.

Carlsson kept searching, but in vain.

Bengt O. Hanzon's most important work was on display in the largest room. A solitary microphone stood by a high stool on a small stage. A reading or a pompous speech, Carlsson thought, and sighed.

At exactly five o'clock, two people climbed up onto the stage. One of them, Siri Karén, was the head of Waldemarsudde and she was wearing a dark cotton suit with a large scarf wrapped around her neck.

"She hasn't noticed that it's summer," Dabrowski muttered.

"She always wears a dark suit."

The other person was a woman of the same age, dressed in a pea-green suit and with blonde, somewhat tousled hair.

"Business leader?" Dabrowski asked.

"No. Åsa Malmborg, the County Council Commissioner for financial affairs."

"But isn't she the one who's—"

"Carl-Henrik's third wife. Twelve years younger. Meteoric political career."

Dabrowski turned and looked at his wife. Carlsson was concentrating on the speech and took no notice of him. She felt how Dabrowski let go of her elbow and demonstratively shoved his hands into his pockets.

". . . and could never have materialised –" with a stiff smile, Siri Karén turned to Åsa Malmborg, who was a head taller than her – "had it not been for the backing of our politicians. We in the world of culture have to face the fact that we cannot rely on funding from industry. We face murderous competition from the music sector, the gaming companies and social media. Our old institutions have to stand firm in staunch defence of the classical art forms, otherwise they risk dying out. And for that we *must . . .*" Karén paused for effect and looked out over the audience which was listening in polite silence, "have the support of our politicians."

Karén raised her glass in a toast and Malmborg took her place at the microphone.

"Thank you, Siri. You're absolutely right in saying that . . ."

"My God, the fawning," Dabrowski whispered.

"But she has a point," Carlsson answered.

"Which is?"

"That the public and private sectors have to work together."

Dabrowski smiled.

"And you're only thinking about the world of art?"

"Sure. What else?"

"You're a wolf in sheep's clothing."

"This is actually silk," Carlsson said, touching the lapel of her jacket.

Malmborg concluded her brief address and held her glass as high as the torch on the Statue of Liberty. The audience clapped and raised their glasses in a toast.

Now the evening's main attraction mounted the stage. Bengt O. Hanzon sat down on the high stool, his legs casually crossed. He lowered his voice, held a black copybook in front of him and began to read.

"Look around you. My job is to make others rich . . ."

Bengt O. Hanzon gave a long speech in praise of art and future generations of artists. Then he rolled up his black copybook and stuck it into his jacket pocket. The audience applauded at length.

"At last," Dabrowski said. "Can we go home now?"

"Shall we just have a look at the paintings?"

Carlsson said hello to the Dean of the Stockholm School of

Economics and chatted for a few minutes with a member of the board of one of the largest health care companies. She kept looking over towards the stage as she worked her way in a smooth arc down one of the long sides of the room. Moving imperceptibly towards the microphone. When Malmborg was left to herself for a second, and Dabrowski had finally found another publisher to talk to, Carlsson handed her glass to one of the waiters. The County Council Commissioner seemed to be looking for something on the stage.

Carlsson walked over.

"Good speech."

Malmborg turned.

"Monica Carlsson, C.E.O. of the Nobel Hospital."

Malmborg held out her hand.

"Yes, yes. Now I recognise you."

Rubbish, Carlsson thought, but she smiled back.

"My husband, Gregor Dabrowski, is a good friend – or rather, an old friend – of Carl-Henrik's."

Malmborg paused and gave Carlsson a puzzled look.

"You have lots of good ideas that I think could be applied to all sorts of activities in this city," Carlsson said. "Not only to art and its institutions."

Malmborg was waiting to hear more and seemed restless. It was obvious that she wanted to get away.

"There's something I'd like to discuss with you," Carlsson said. "It's about the future of the Nobel Hospital."

"Thank you," Malmborg said dismissively, "but I'm afraid you'll have to contact my office so we can make an—"

"I think we should meet just the two of us. Tomorrow for coffee."

Malmborg seemed startled.

"Do call my . . ."

Carlsson came closer so that no-one would hear.

"I would *really* like us to get together."

This stirred something in Malmborg. Carlsson recognised it: a primitive defensive reaction that the Commissioner could not hide, a flash of anger.

Malmborg seemed to be considering whether to snub the woman or not, but bit her tongue and looked resigned.

"Coffee tomorrow?" Carlsson said. "There's someone I want you to meet."

"O.K. But I've got to go now."

"Of course. I'll e-mail you the time and place."

While Malmborg could not retrieve her bag fast enough, Carlsson finally caught sight of her old friend from university. He was standing there contemplating a garish painting which showed a fox and two stags in a drawing room.

"Good of you to come," Carlsson said to Otto Nordin, C.E.O. of the Newman and Weisz consultancy.

"It's kind of intriguing when the head of Stockholm's second largest hospital calls up with an invitation to a private view. I noticed that you managed to talk to her."

Carlsson saw Malmborg's back disappear into the crowd.

"I guess you too are a busy man."

Nordin opened his jacket and drew his hand over his tie.

"I've got the best management consultants in town holding the fort."

Carlsson looked over at Dabrowski. He was still busy with his colleague.

"Only the best in town?"

Otto smiled.

"In the country."

"I'll get straight to the point."

"I was expecting nothing else," Nordin said.

"I want to get an extensive renovation of the Nobel Hospital done."

"I'd gathered that."

"And I need financing."

"I'm all ears."

"I'm fully aware that it won't be easy to raise private funding, after all the twists and turns with the N.S.K."

"No, that whole affair really wasn't handled at all well."

"But I know you're a discreet man."

Nordin nodded and a smile lit up his suntanned face.

"So would you be able to act . . . discreetly?"

"Of course. Do you have any particular construction company in mind?"

"Well, certainly not the one that N.S.K. used."

"But their main competitor?" Nordin said.

"Yes."

"You were the smartest of us all even when we were students."

"I didn't actually do an awful lot of studying."

"No, you were playing at being president of the student union."

"Playing at?"

"And you started your first business."

"When I wasn't studying medicine," Carlsson said.

"You weren't there an awful lot of the time."

"At the School of Economics?"

"Yes."

"Didn't seem necessary."

Nordin stretched out his hand.

"This is going to be fun."

Carlsson shook it.

"So you're on?"

"Do you think we would want to miss out on a chance like this?"

"I don't know how brave you are."

Nordin laughed out loud.

"Not as brave as you, you're the one who'll be front and centre if the shit hits the fan."

"But you'll have to call it something other than a P.P.P.," Carlsson said.

*

The sun was still shining when Carlsson and Dabrowski left Waldemarsudde. The sound of a ship's horn and the hubbub from Gröna Lund amusement park could be heard in the distance. They passed the entrance to Skansen on their right and strolled past Hasselbacken restaurant.

"You don't seem to be in a hurry," Dabrowski said.

"It's a lovely evening."

"When were you planning to tell me?"

"What?"

Dabrowski smiled.

"You are a wolf. Or rather a lion in tiger's clothing."

"I don't know what you're talking about," Carlsson said, relishing the June evening.

"You never leave anything to chance," Dabrowski said. "There's always a hidden agenda, isn't there?"

Carlsson took her husband's hand.

"Not always."

"Oh no? Just give me one example when you allow chance into your life?"

"When we play Yahtzee," Carlsson replied.

GULLMARSPLAN, STOCKHOLM
Tuesday morning, 11.vi

Tekla got out of bed and had an ice-cold shower. Simon's face had kept her awake all night again. After three balls of amphetamine to put some order into her memory, followed by four Stilnoct, she had dozed off, but it hardly qualified as a beauty sleep. She had not yet sorted out the images and the headache was still there.

For breakfast she had a "black twin bomb", coffee and amphetamine. The problem with this diet was the low energy intake. But she had no appetite. In the past month she had already had to go down one size in her work clothes. She was considering whether to start on dietary supplements. But that was so depressing. At five past six she got a text from Monica Carlsson: Coffee at 1 p.m., Wienerkonditoriet.

Tekla saw no alternative but to accept. The headache hit her again. She thought about the meeting with Astrid and her brother Magnus in Nytorget yesterday. Decided that they were both really nice.

She called Simon's mobile and sent him another text. No sign of life from his telephone for twenty-four hours.

Tekla walked briskly across Skanstull Bridge. Fluffed up her hair, since the Yankees hat had slicked down her short bob so that it looked like a bathing cap over her head. Sniffed at her fingers: they smelled of butter. Must wash my hair tonight, she thought. She wished she were one of those sporty types who spend their lunch break going to the gym and the sauna and then eat the lamb burgers and bulgur salad they have brought from home. A parallel dream life.

She thought more and more about her mother, who suffered from dementia and was living in a home in Nyhammar. She should go there and just sit with her. Hold her hand. Was this a premonition that something would soon happen to her mother? Or was it those articles she had been reading lately, about the results achieved by the London group? They were only at the stage of clinical trials, but the patients really had shown signs that it was possible to stop the rapid decline into dementia which is usually associated with Huntington's disease. The procedure did, however, require a stem cell transplant from first-degree relatives. She took her thoughts further: would she ever pluck up the courage to have herself tested? And tell Simon as well? Since he was unaware that their mother had Huntington's disease. And that there was a fifty per cent risk that he carried the gene. Just like Tekla. It all hung together. If she turned out to have the gene and he didn't, she would need stem cells from his bone marrow to survive. And vice versa.

The smell in the basement of the hospital was worse than before. It made Tekla feel ill at ease, it was as if something threatened the very existence of the institution. When she got up to the entrance to buy some chewing gum, she could feel the heat pouring in through the swing doors: the temperature had risen five degrees over the past twenty-four hours. According to the radio, it had been twenty-nine degrees the day before. No wonder you could hardly make your way along the crowded pavements: the pubs serving beer in Söder had doubled the size of their outdoor seating areas and were struggling to replace their empty barrels of Carlsberg fast enough.

Tekla sat down by one of the unit's computers to check what had become of the overdose patient in the I.C.U. His kidneys had now completely shut down. At midnight they had put him on dialysis since he had failed to produce any urine for more than twenty-four hours. On top of which, he showed signs of increasing acidosis, acid in the blood. They kept having to administer large amounts of bicarbonate as a buffer. But the cramps seemed to have abated.

Poor fellow, she thought. Only thirty-nine. According to a previous entry from A. & E., he had a son by a woman listed only as "the child's mother". What sort of existence had led to such a man being found outside Björns Trädgård with an overdose? And why was there so much acid in his blood? She saw that several overdoses had been admitted to the Nobel Hospital and other emergency rooms in the past twenty-four hours. Many of them had been difficult to wake up. Some had died, despite having been given an antidote. But she had not found any others whose blood was as acidic as that of the 39-year-old. Tekla flicked through the pages in her mind: *Harrison's*, 18th edition, page 1390. *Approach to the patient with metabolic acidosis.* There was nothing in the list that applied to her patient. She would have to search the net and some articles. One ray of hope: her brain still seemed to function as it should. After half an hour on the computer, Tekla had come up with some new ideas on the case. Her stomach was crying out for food and she longed for something other than hospital fare, but hurried off to the toilets instead and took the cap off her Lypsyl tube. After a further fifteen minutes of surfing, a thought began to take shape.

"Aren't you supposed to be at the morning meeting?"

Tekla looked up and saw Moussawi walk into the doctors' office. Her pulse shot up.

"Bloody hell." A glance at the clock told her that it was five minutes past eight.

"Right, I see that I'm not welcome here."

"I meant the meeting. Göran's already furious with me."

"One shouldn't worry too much about bosses."

Tekla debated trying to make it to the meeting, but she would attract more attention by arriving late than by not showing up. She could always blame it on a patient in the emergency ward.

"Everything O.K. otherwise?" Moussawi said and slumped into a chair. He swivelled back and forth as he casually entered his code on the keyboard.

His ingratiating tone made Tekla suspicious. Then a thought occurred to her:

"Are you supposed to be here today?"

"Standing in for Anita."

"I see."

Tekla's headache took on a different colour.

"There was something to do with her boat. Or apartment . . . can't remember. She's taken an extra day's compensation for overtime. Tell me about the I.C.U. case."

"The case?"

"The overdose," Moussawi said and tapped the keyboard with his index finger.

Tekla did not want to get caught between two rival colleagues.

"I don't know that much about it. You're better off asking Ani—"

"An unusual intoxication," Moussawi cut in and Tekla immediately got the impression that he knew more than he was letting on.

She summarised the patient's history and the more she told him the straighter Moussawi sat up in his chair. He was staring intently at the computer screen. Every so often he nodded to himself.

"Not an ordinary heroin overdose then?"

"They've not come up with anything else that fits," Tekla said.

"Does Anita have any thoughts on it?"

"I don't know."

"So what do *you* think?"

Although she suspected he was playing games, she told him briefly what she knew:

"He's got low blood sugar, kidney failure, E.C.G. all over the shop and cramps. Severe acidosis."

She went on reciting the lab results without looking at the screen. Her thoughts were straying to the articles she had been reading that morning.

"Incredible," Moussawi said.

"What is?"

"That you remember every single lab test."

"Well, I mean . . . I just checked."

Moussawi looked again at the screen.

"Even so."

Shit, Tekla thought. She must be more careful. But this case had captivated her. She remembered Carlsson telling her what her favourite drink was: gin and tonic. The English had started mixing gin into their tonic water to mask the bitter taste of the tonic which the Indians had been taking against malaria for centuries . . . She had to get over to the I.C.U.

"Quinine!"

"What are you talking about?" Eva Elmqvist asked as she straightened her black support stockings. She was the only person in the I.C.U. who wore a skirt.

"Sometimes they mix other things into the heroin: flour, baking powder, starch . . . and . . ."

"Quinine?" Elmqvist sounded sceptical.

"Quinine," Tekla said and located a 2008 textbook in her card index. "A basic alkaloid, thirty-two per cent of patients develop hypoglycaemia . . . other side effects include thrombocytopaenia, asthma, liver failure . . ."

She lost the thread. Elmqvist was gaping at her.

"Where are you reading all that?"

"Er . . . I had a quick look at quinine this morning."

"You're something else, Tekla Berg."

Tekla breathed out.

"But why quinine? That's a brand-new idea as far as I'm concerned," Elmqvist said, sounding intrigued.

Before coming to see Elmqvist, Tekla had read three case studies involving heroin and quinine.

"Because it gives the heroin a bit more of a kick."

"And his symptoms are consistent with quinine intoxication?"

"We'll find out once you've done some further testing," Tekla said boldly.

"That's going to be expensive. I'll need more convincing first."

Elmqvist sat down in front of a computer with Tekla standing beside her, reading over her shoulder. It was peaceful in the I.C.U. The only sound was the reassuring beep of the drip counter when a bag had to be changed.

Elmqvist began to search Pubmed, the article database, and found a review article about quinine overdoses. They read it together and both nodded in satisfaction. It all added up.

"I think you've cracked the case!" Elmqvist said enthusiastically. "We'll need to get more extensive tests done. They'll have to rush them through at Linköping, supposing that those lab rats know how to spell the word 'rush'."

Tekla straightened up. She looked at the clock on the wall; it was almost eleven.

"I'm afraid I have to leave. An update with the police."

"Any luck with the D.N.A?" Tekla asked, feeling like an expert on 'C.S.I.'

"Nothing at all, not in any database," Nilsén said. "But if you're a terrorist from the Middle East, you wouldn't necessarily feature in the Swedish P.K.U. register. Or in the police D.N.A. register for that matter. And we didn't have any fingerprints. There are severe burns on every finger."

"What's the next step?" Tekla said, frustrated. She wanted to move ahead, let go of her suspicions.

"The forensic odontologists get to show off with their dental analyses. Their *raison d'être*." Nilsén rolled her eyes. "It'll take time, though. We're in contact with a couple of dental practices in Södermalm, but we've no idea where he lived. I simply can't understand why we don't have a central database for all dental records, can you?"

Tekla was mystified by Nilsén's style of dress but enjoyed being with her.

"I think we can rule out the likelihood that he lived in the building," Nilsén concluded. "Unless it was a sublet or a sub-sublet, of course. All the occupants have been identified and accounted for."

During their conversation, Tekla approached the bed. She

pretended to be listening to Nilsén's explanations, but all her attention was focused on the patient's ear. The wounds and bandages made him look shapeless and bloated. The face, or what was left of it, was all but invisible. What with the dressings, Mepitel, sutures and tubes, it was quite impossible to see a human being underneath it all. But there was in fact an ear sticking out between bandages. She had to lean over the tracheal catheter to see the top of it.

But no. That area too was so red and infected that it was impossible to see if there was a birthmark there or not. Simon had a distinct birthmark on his ear, she knew that.

"Are you O.K?" Nilsén said.

"Absolutely, I'm sorry, I'm a bit tired and finding it hard to focus."

Tekla was thinking about the way her amphetamine consumption had gone up, but decided not to worry about it. She told herself that it fulfilled its function and that she would cut back as soon as everything around her had calmed down.

"It can easily happen when you only have yourself to look after."

Tekla jumped.

"How do you know that . . . ?"

"I assume that you pretty much live here at the hospital."

Tekla excused herself and left the I.C.U. On her way out she texted Simon one more time. And she sent off messages on Messenger, WhatsApp and Instagram. She had not opened an e-mail for ages, could not face having to deal with it. Better not to know.

Umarov rested his head against the rock-hard trolley and felt the rough paper stick to his back. The tiny, adhesive patches the nurse had put on his thorax seemed to weigh as much as ten-kilogramme dumb-bells. After his conversation with Nina that morning, he had had trouble breathing. It was as if an elephant were standing on his chest. From what she told him, Sardor's questioning of the man they suspected of stabbing Jarmo had turned into a regular torture session.

A woman doctor came into the room and held out her hand. Umarov sat up and felt the pressure across his ribcage subside.

"Ragna Sigurdsdottir. Emergency physician." Umarov thought that she did not look a day over twenty-five. Blonde, straight hair, neatly tied up in a ponytail.

Umarov was annoyed that Elena had driven him to A. & E. for his chest pain. It had, after all, eased once he was able to lie down on the sofa for a while. He was also irritated by his nicotine craving, which he never managed to satisfy. The only good thing about the morning so far was that Elena had an appointment with her hairdresser, and had not been able to stay with him. Sardor had joined him there.

"Victor Umarov. I'm sure you're a rising star, but I'm perfectly healthy. Just a slight cold."

Umarov began buttoning up his shirt and tried to remove the rubber cap on his finger.

"Just a moment," the doctor said. "I have to examine you first."

He let his arms drop. She looked determined.

"Am I right in understanding that you suddenly had difficulty breathing this morning and that the same thing happened again about an hour ago? But no chest pains?"

"That's correct," Sardor butted in. "He complained that he couldn't breathe."

Umarov was not going to mention the chest pains. They would probably think that he had had a heart attack. He was planning to save that for the day when he decided to die in his sleep.

"Has anything special happened?" the doctor said.

"I've been working quite hard lately to get my pool going," Umarov said.

Sigurdsdottir jotted that down on her spiral pad with a puzzled look.

Sardor's mobile rang. He picked up, but the firm look he got from the doctor told him that he had better leave the room.

Umarov tried to shut out the noise around him, but his stress increased whenever an alarm went off, a patient cried out or the door blinds rattled. He gave a start when the doctor placed an ice-cold stethoscope on his chest. You could hear the suction release every time she lifted the disc off his sweaty skin. Then a freezing, slightly clammy hand at the base of his spine and a light tapping. He winced.

"I'm only knocking a bit."

"Well, what do you think? A cold, it's only a virus, isn't it?"

"Have you had a cough or a fever these past few days?"

"No."

"And you say that you've been feeling tired in recent weeks?"

"Yes, but that's not so strange. There's a lot going on just now." He was thinking not so much of the Northern Networks, Tatiana's whores or the impending annual audit, but of the moss-green swimming pool.

The door blinds rattled again and a tall doctor walked in.

"Don't let me disturb you. Carry on," Tariq Moussawi said.

Sigurdsdottir understood right away.

"Victor Umarov, sixty-nine years old, presenting with acute onset dyspnoea without chest pain. Previous history of hypertonia and prostate problems. One litre of residual urine drained some weeks ago, but no indwelling catheter. I hear no breath sounds on the left side and—"

"It's only a cold," Umarov interrupted. "I have more important things to worry about."

"We've got to—" Sigurdsdottir began.

Moussawi put his large hand on Sigurdsdottir's shoulder. She seemed to shrink by about ten centimetres.

"My friend. Perhaps you do have a cold and we won't bother you any more than necessary. But you see, our Ragna here is a promising young doctor. She can't hear any breath sounds over one of your lungs." Moussawi managed to put on a really worried expression. "Of course, that may be because she has wax in her ears."

Moussawi walked up to the trolley.

Umarov had the impression that the light in the room was being dimmed.

Moussawi lowered his voice:

"And the fluid in your lung could mean anything from a cold to tuberculosis to heart failure to . . . other things."

Other things.

It was as if someone had struck a gong and the entire room was now vibrating from the deafening sound of the instrument. It rang in Umarov's ears.

Sigurdsdottir reclaimed the initiative.

"O.K. Shall we begin with a lung X-ray and take some samples?" It was not really a question. "We may still have to draw off a few millilitres to analyse the fluid and see what it is."

Umarov wanted to nod, but he was locked inside his own world. He could feel himself falling headlong down through a great darkness. Cliffs on either side. At the bottom there was a black pool, a waterfall. The air was warm and his eyes were shut. He tried to take deep breaths, but something was stopping him. Someone was standing on his chest. It was hot. Stifling. He tried to speak:

"Wa . . . water."

"You can have some water. We'll be right back," Moussawi said and left the room with Sigurdsdottir, just as Sardor came back.

For a while there was no sound from Umarov. He was waiting for the buzzing in his ears to go away. Then he said to Sardor:

"Have you talked to Jensen?"

"He seemed pleased that we'd found the bloke who knifed Jarmo. Eje just called, he's got rid of the body."

"Body?" Umarov sounded worried. "Don't tell me you've killed him?!"

Umarov closed his eyes. He tilted his head back and clenched his fists so hard that the knuckles whitened. He began to cough uncontrollably and had to get to his feet to be able to breathe. He paced up and down while Sardor looked on in trepidation.

"Do you remember that we talked about this? That I'm *vor*, not some kind of gangster boss who rubs people out in the street."

"He wasn't meant to die. I only—"

"Shut up!"

Sardor looked as if he wanted to sink through the floor.

Umarov kept circling around the small examination room. Like a caged lion.

"If only you'd gone to university and become . . . a doctor or something. Can't you see where this is leading us? Violence breeds violence. They'll want revenge for that brat." Umarov stopped.

"I can—" Sardor began.

Umarov cut him off. "Summon all the gangs in the Northern Networks. Have them come to some neutral location tomorrow evening. Tell them Umarov wants to speak to them before they do something stupid."

"Tekla, do you think you could check this E.C.G.?"

Tekla turned to see one of the younger doctors waving a piece of paper.

"A forty-year-old woman suffering from chest pains for the past three days. I've examined her and found nothing."

"Not even her heart?"

The intern gave her a puzzled look, but soon realised she was pulling his leg. He smiled.

"What I meant was that heart and lungs are norm—"

"I got that, sorry," she said, and resisted an impulse to put her hand on his shoulder. "So what do you think?"

"Not sure, because she's had this recent bundle branch block."

"Yes, I see that. Any previous history of heart disease?"

"None at all. Perfectly healthy."

"Strange. Let's take a look together. Where is she?"

"Cubicle 4."

Tekla went over to the cubicle. The woman lying on the bed was not well. That much was obvious. There was something about her breathing, the quick, laboured gasps. Tekla did not like what she saw as she stood beside the patient. The intern stole up beside her.

"Have you been coughing blood?" Tekla said, and congratulated herself on having swallowed a bomb just before. Her brain felt razor-sharp. She knew that it would not last, but right now her head was like a Pentagon computer.

"No."

The woman cast a worried look at Tekla, but before she had time to add anything, her face contorted and she clutched at her chest. A glance at the monitor showed her pulse at 130 per minute. Tachycardia.

"Are you O.K.?"

"Can't . . . breathe . . ."

"Get a nurse," Tekla managed to say before the woman lost consciousness. She felt her pulse: nothing.

"Sound the alarm. Cardiac arrest," she called to the intern, who was already heading for the secretariat.

Tekla started C.P.R. Since she was quite tall, she did not need to climb up onto the bed to reach the patient's chest. This woman was fairly slim and it was easy enough to press her sternum against her backbone, to compress the heart.

A nurse came running.

"Cardiac arrest. Probably lung embolism."

The nurse took over the resuscitation with a practised hand, leaving Tekla free to back away and run the rest of the operation from a distance. Soon they were joined by other medical staff. Tekla asked one nurse for adrenalin. And another to check the catheter, make sure it was working.

"Shall we move to the emergency room?" said one of the nurses, who was squatting down and examining the veins on the back of the woman's hand. "She'll need another catheter."

"No. We'll keep going here," Tekla said and pulled over the defibrillator. She applied three electrodes, could only register that there was electrical activity in the woman's heart but no pulse. Tekla's working diagnosis was still valid.

"Let's go for thrombolysis. I'll do a quick ultrasound to check if the right ventricle is enlarged . . . but it's got to be pulmonary embolism."

"Are you absolutely sure?" It sounded like a challenge. She saw Moussawi leaning against a pillar opposite the cubicle.

"What was that?" she said, pretending that she had not heard.

"Don't mind me. Carry on," he said calmly, although he probably had about twenty patients he had not yet seen over on his side.

She ignored him and kept working on the cardiac arrest.

"Where's the Actilyse?" Tekla shouted. She heard her voice crack-ing. She was shaking all over and there was a roaring in her ears, a high-frequency buzz that could have been due to all the noise in the emergency unit. Or all the chemical substances in her body.

"Here," said an experienced E.R. nurse. She was holding the drug that would dissolve the clots in the woman's lungs. "All of it?"

"Yes. Quickly," Tekla said, wiping the sweat from her eyes. They were crowded into the small cubicle. One of the assistant nurses was now kneeling on the bed doing cardiac compression. Behind her, two medical students were patiently waiting their turn. One of them, the young man, was paler than the wall he was pressed up against. The young woman next to him looked like a lioness, ready to pounce on her prey.

Moussawi stood there watching, his face immobile.

Tekla pulled back the ultrasound machine and made way for the nurse, who opened the three-way stopcock on the catheter and flushed it with Ringer-Acetate. Then she inserted the syringe and swiftly emptied the contents.

After a minute, Tekla said: "We'll take a break."

She felt the woman's groin.

"Pulse," she said and avoided Moussawi's look. But inside she shouted: *Yes!*

"She's breathing spontaneously," said the anaesthesia nurse, who was managing the airway. She continued:

"But she has an enlarged pupil."

Shit!

Tekla squeezed through to the patient's head, pulled out her torch, raised the eyelid and there it was: one pupil was dilated and not reacting to light. That could only mean one damn thing: intracerebral haemorrhage!

At that moment, Tekla's main concern was not the patient. Her focus was on her enemy *numero uno*, who was standing two metres behind her, still by the pillar. Now he could hammer the last nail into her coffin. She might as well go straight to Collinder and resign.

Fuck, fucking fuck-fuck!

Tekla steeled herself and turned her head towards Moussawi. He had left his sentry post and was now standing very close to her. She could smell the sharp scent of his aftershave. He leaned forward slightly and whispered so that only she could hear:

"You did everything right."

She must have misheard. Forced herself to meet his eyes. Instead of the usual sarcastic Moussawi smile, she saw a serious and honest look.

"I would have done exactly the same. She has pulmonary embolisms and thrombolysis is absolutely the way to go in those circumstances. Plucky and robust. Spot on."

Was he making fun of her? No, it didn't seem like it. Instead, he had given his blessing to the way she had managed the case.

"We'll have to send her off for a C.T. scan," Tekla said. "She's probably had a cerebral haemorrhage."

All eyes were on Tekla, but no-one said a word. The situation was tense but under control.

"You go and write the referral," Moussawi said. "I can stay here. And by the way . . . well done for the way you handled that idiot of a father in the E.R. last week."

Tekla couldn't believe her ears.

"I would have done exactly the same there too," Moussawi said.

"Thanks," is all she managed to say. She turned her eyes to the clock on the wall: 12.30. Half an hour before the coffee with Monica Carlsson.

BIBLIOTEKSGATAN, ÖSTERMALM
Tuesday, 11.vi, 1 p.m.

Tekla watched the hospital C.E.O. slip lightly out of the enormous, white Land Cruiser and carefully plant her high heels on the spotless pavement of Biblioteksgatan.

"Just wait till you try their cappuccino!" she called out over the noise of the traffic from Birger Jarlsgatan.

Tekla had rushed out of A. & E. and thrown herself into a taxi, where she had helped herself to two bombs out of the Lypsyl tube. The effect was beginning to kick in now. She muttered under her breath:

"I guess you can never have too much coffee."

Wienerkonditoriet was full of people finishing their lunch breaks. A waitress showed them to a table by a pillar. Carlsson stopped in her tracks.

"This won't do."

The waitress looked taken aback.

"We want a table by the window."

"I'll see what I can do."

"No, don't do that. Simply fix it. It was booked for four at one o'clock."

The bewildered waitress consulted her iPad, had a look around and found a solution.

"Just a minute, please."

"Not one second longer."

Carlsson looked at Tekla.

"Have you had time to recover? From the attack?"

255

"You mean . . . the one in the I.C.U.?"

"Have you had any others in the past twenty-four hours?"

"I'm fine."

"And what about the burns patient?"

"Oh, right. There's been no change, neither for the better nor for the worse. But he's extubated."

The waitress led them to a window table near the door.

As she walked there, Carlsson announced that she wanted a cappuccino.

"And the same for the young lady here, and two croissants. They'd better be fresh."

Once they had sat down, Carlsson put her mobile on the table and straightened the napkin.

"I see," she said. "So, no P.T.S.D., then? No. Doesn't look like it. You're from Norrland, made of good solid stuff. Or should I say Jämtland? What was it actually like, growing up in the country? I'm from Göteborg, myself. A childhood in the centre of town. Well, maybe that's obvious."

Tekla had a thousand questions but was unable to ask a single one. The coffee arrived and she took several gulps.

"Perhaps this isn't the right moment for a family history," Carlsson said, looking out at the street. "Let's do that another time. Tell me more about what happened instead."

"Tell you what?" Tekla had to hold the mug with both hands to stop the shaking when she raised it to her mouth. She had lost count of the number of bombs she had chucked inside her, on an empty stomach.

"The attack on Sunday."

"Oh yes." Tekla realised she had to assume that Carlsson knew about things before they had even happened. "It was really weird."

"Bloody morons," Carlsson said with a loud sigh.

Tekla could think of at least three people to whom the C.E.O. might be referring.

"I'm sure the intensive care doctors do their very best."

"The police."

"Right."

"How can they *not* catch someone who's got into my hospital and tries to kill one of our patients? I gather he was wounded, too. You stuck some . . . ?"

"Scissors."

". . . scissors into his leg. Well done you. But incredibly inept of the police to let him get away."

Tekla did not dare to disagree.

Carlsson looked thoughtful.

"The Nobel Hospital's falling apart. Have you noticed?"

"Can't say that I've paid much attention to it."

"You get changed down in the service tunnels."

"Yes."

"So you'll have seen the cracks in the foundations. And you can't have failed to notice the stench."

"Difficult to miss."

The hospital C.E.O. seemed to be preparing to say something important. All these bizarre meetings with Carlsson – Tekla assumed that there was an agenda. She had plenty of ideas as to what it might involve, but none that seemed more likely than any other. Perhaps she would find out now?

"Thank goodness you weren't injured."

"Maybe it was a bit reckless of me."

"Pity you didn't run faster."

"What do you mean?"

"You should have caught that bastard. Sneaking into my house and trying to murder an intubated patient. Bloody cheek!"

Tekla felt confused. Was she being criticised for not having been even more decisive?

"But you know that every cloud has a silver lining," Carlsson went on, with a knowing look in her eyes.

"Occasionally."

"No, it's a law of nature. But sometimes you have to make a real effort to see the light in all the darkness. That's what my old father used to tell his congregation."

"And you're good at that?"

Carlsson broke into a big smile.

"We got two patients more than the N.S.K."

"From the fire, you mean?"

Tekla was expecting her to elaborate, but nothing came. She was finding these sudden jumps from one topic to another hard to follow.

"I'm glad you could get away."

Tekla had had enough of waiting. She took a chance.

"What did you want to talk—"

"Have you heard anyone bad-mouthing Göran?"

"Göran?"

"Any criticism of him from among the doctors? If so, I want to hear it directly from you."

What was this all about? Was Tekla supposed to be some sort of spy for the C.E.O.?

"I don't believe I have."

"You don't believe?"

"I've not heard anyone say anything bad about Göran."

Carlsson undid a button on her silk blouse.

"I assume you do talk to your colleagues?"

"We discuss medical cases."

Carlsson smiled and looked around. Then at her watch.

"Five minutes."

"What's happening in five minutes?" Tekla asked with a worried look.

"You have a brother, don't you?"

"Yes."

"What does he do?"

Tekla assumed that Carlsson knew all about Simon. Was this all to do with him? She could feel her gut clenching.

"There," Carlsson exclaimed suddenly and stood up.

Tekla saw two people, a woman and a man, enter the café. They were both in their fifties and dressed in expensive suits.

"This is Tekla Berg, who I've told you about. A big hero at Söder Tower. Singlehandedly, she saved the lives of several people. A Nobel doctor if ever there was one."

The woman held out her hand in greeting and Tekla could have kicked herself for not having wiped the sweat off her palm.

"The city is grateful to you. Truly grateful."

The woman looked as if she meant every syllable.

Although the man was more hesitant, he shook her hand. He had an unnatural, almost orange, tan.

Carlsson summoned the waitress and gave the orders: a glass of fresh juice for the woman and a double espresso for the man. Tekla spotted a black B.M.W. parked in the pedestrian zone with a chauffeur leaning against the door, a mobile in his hand.

"As you know, Åsa is the Stockholm County Council Commissioner for financial affairs."

Tekla had never heard of the woman. Still less set eyes on her. She nodded carefully.

"Maybe you also recognise Otto?"

Tekla must have looked puzzled.

"No, you do keep a low profile, it's true. Otto is a management consultant, his clients include several players in the Confederation of Swedish Enterprise."

The man looked uncomfortable but went on listening.

"Tekla, have you heard of a P.P.P.?"

"Maybe . . ."

"A public–private partnership. A system for financing infrastructure. For some time now . . . I've been involved in discussions with Åsa and Otto here about the future of the Nobel Hospital."

As Tekla listened, she tried to make sense of it all. This day was becoming more and more peculiar. Åsa Malmborg looked tense. Uncomfortable with the situation. Tekla got the feeling that it was Carlsson who was pulling the strings and that Malmborg would much rather have been somewhere else. Malmborg stopped tapping on her mobile and looked straight at Tekla.

"What you did on Thursday was amazing. Amazing. Have you recovered?"

"From the fire, you mean?"

"It must have been dreadful," the Commissioner said.

"It's always tough when there are people suffering."

"But that's part of our job, isn't it?" Carlsson said.

Tekla glanced briefly at the man who was sipping his espresso. Suddenly, as if an alarm had sounded that only she had heard, Malmborg got to her feet and held out her hand to Tekla.

"It was really nice to meet you, Tekla." She nodded at Carlsson and Otto, then left the café.

"I need to get going too," Otto said and stood up. "We'll be in touch, Monica. Call me later."

Tekla remained seated.

"Have you thought about the way clothes make the man?" Carlsson said.

"His suit looked expensive."

"The shoes. It's the details that matter. They must have cost ten thousand and you can only get them in London."

"I didn't notice the shoes."

"But you do notice things at the hospital, don't you, Tekla?"

"I don't understand what you mean."

Carlsson ran her fingers through her hair, rearranging a few intruders that had got into her artful streak of white. As if she had a mirror in front of her.

"Unfortunately, there are others who see things too." Carlsson gave a little laugh. "And I'm not talking about that birdbrain Göran Collinder."

The C.E.O.'s eyes narrowed. Then a stiff smile appeared.

"We must get back to work now. Afraid I can't give you a lift."

"Doesn't matter. Thanks for the coffee."

Carlsson hailed the waitress and paid. Out in Biblioteksgatan, she suddenly stopped.

"Tekla, you've seen the underside, haven't you?"

Tekla glanced at the large car that was waiting for Carlsson. It looked new.

"The hospital's."

"Ah."

"It's falling to pieces. And the County Council doesn't have the muscle to renovate it. Something drastic has to be done before the place collapses. You know Anita Klein-Borgstedt, don't you?"

Tekla's head was spinning with all these twists and turns.

"We're colleagues."

"Anita's the union representative at the Nobel and would have to agree to any future renovation plans."

"Renovation?"

"With private funds from the business sector. Otherwise we might as well wait till the next century. And the union could put the kibosh on the whole thing. Anita Klein-Borgstedt basically *is* the trade union at the Nobel."

The penny dropped.

"Nod if you've understood what you need to do."

Before Tekla had even finished nodding, Carlsson had disappeared into her Land Cruiser. She felt her mobile buzz in her pocket and took it out. A sign of life, at last, a new text from Simon!

Meet me at Ringen, it said.

Where at Ringen were they supposed to meet? Simon had not picked up when she called him. Nor had he answered any of her texts. The shopping centre was not big, but it had two entrances. She was nervous, but angry too. She was going to give him so much grief for not getting in touch. For making her so worried. For being a total pain in the neck. Tekla thought she had better keep moving around, not stopping, that way she would find him. It was hardly the Mall of Scandinavia.

She was holding her mobile in case he called. The battery showed seven per cent. She took two Oxazepam and swallowed them dry. They stuck in her throat but eventually dissolved.

Tekla had just passed the Pressbyrån newsagent on the corner of Ringvägen and Götgatan when she spotted the backs of two men. One of them had dark hair and a black hoodie, the other was wearing a white outdoor jacket with a hood. All at once she felt as if she were walking on soft sand; one of her legs gave way, but she managed to stay upright. She regained her strength and began to move through the crowd of pedestrians, hoping to catch another glimpse of the men, who had vanished. She was all but certain that one of them, the one in the hoodie, was Simon.

Tekla was making her way around a pram when Simon turned to face her. They made eye contact. Her pulse shot up. A combination of nerves, anger and energy washed over her. His wolf-like grin. The way he screwed up his eyes. A hand raised in greeting.

At that moment, a dark van pulled up just past the entrance to the shopping centre. Simon gave a start. For several long seconds,

Tekla thought they must be waiting for someone who had now turned up. She walked on in their direction.

A man in a leather vest with a shaven head and his left arm in a cast jumped out and started moving rapidly towards Simon, who instinctively turned and darted in through the main entrance of Ringen. Tekla also broke into a run. At the same time, she saw Simon's mate lose his balance and another man in biker gear, with a long plaited goatee, easily catch him.

Tekla heard the crack as the friend's head hit the door of the van.

She ran in through the main entrance.

Simon was lying on the ground by the Cervera shop, the man with the cast leaning menacingly over him.

"Simon!" she shouted.

Simon looked up. There was a mixture of fear and surprise in his eyes.

The man turned and Tekla saw that he was older than she had at first thought.

"You stay out of this!" he shouted at her.

Tekla charged full tilt at her target.

But it was like running into a tree trunk.

The man simply pushed her away while he picked Simon up with his free hand and dragged him off. It looked as if he were carrying a block of Styrofoam.

The crowd of onlookers was backing away and Tekla saw many of them get out their mobiles. To film or call the police? She chased after the man, caught up with him and grabbed hold of his leather vest. Judging by the astonished look on his face when he turned around, he was clearly not expecting to see her again.

"Let go of him!" she yelled.

With his free arm, the man simply pushed her over. Tekla banged her hip as she fell, but the pain only registered as a shock through her body. She heard the people around them start to scream. Then she understood why: the man was standing right above her, pointing a

263

gun at her head. Simon was hanging like a limp rag underneath the arm with the plaster cast.

"So what's it to be?" the man spat.

Tekla did not move. She felt no fear, only utter, raging fury. And her overheated brain was busy processing different options.

"You'd better stay where you are so no-one gets hurt."

Behind him, Tekla could see people running away in a panic.

"Good girl," the man said and began to back away.

She lay there until she could see him moving out into the street. Then she leaped to her feet, looked around for a weapon and grabbed a large frying pan off a shelf.

"Be careful!" called a woman who was carrying a baby in a sling on her front. "The police are on their way."

Tekla ran out into the street and saw the van still standing there with the side door open. Simon's friend was lying on the floor holding his face, bleeding profusely.

The two gang members were shoving Simon into the van when Tekla smashed the frying pan into the back of the man with the plaster cast. She of all people knew exactly what sort of injuries she could cause by hitting him on the head; she only wanted to stop him in his tracks.

When the frying pan made contact with the leather vest, the wet, smacking sound of iron on leather echoed around the buildings in the street.

The man with the cast lurched, but that was all.

Then he turned to face Tekla, who froze. This was as far as her plan went. Before she had time to think, she saw a fist coming straight at her head. Instinctively, she turned her face away and the cast landed on her neck with a dull thud. It felt as if she had been hit by a falling tree. She was thrown to the pavement, but she managed to hold out her hands to break her fall. When a heavy boot hit her right in the stomach it winded her.

She heard someone laughing just above her head.

"You stubborn little bitch. Are you crazy?"

Tekla was struggling to breathe. She turned her face to the ground and curled into a ball to protect herself against any more kicks and blows. She heard him walk away. When she looked up, the man's black leather trousers were disappearing round the front of the vehicle, then the door was pulled shut with a bang.

Tekla dragged herself over to the van and swallowed the vomit that was on its way up. The engine revved. She was huddled against the back when the side door opened and Simon's mate was pushed out. He landed on his feet, looked around and picked something up off the pavement before running away. Tekla just managed to turn and note the registration number before the van disappeared. Then she sank into the gutter and really did throw up.

Somebody crouched down behind her.

"How are you doing?"

She wiped her mouth on her sweater and tried to sit up, but she was dizzy and her neck was throbbing.

"Come. We'll help you," a voice said and now Tekla saw three teenage girls squatting around her. They raised her to a sitting position, and steadied her.

"Thank you," she said.

Sirens were blaring. Tekla sat still and touched her neck. It hurt. But she was able to move both her hands and her feet. No numbness. No paralysis.

A woman bent down and began asking questions.

"Are you O.K.? I'm a nurse. Can I examine you?"

Tekla waved her away.

A police car stopped in the street nearby. In the background, more cars could be heard arriving.

A female police officer with her red hair in a plait put a hand on Tekla's shoulder.

"How are you?"

"You've got to get that van. The registration number is BOA 110."

"What happened?"

"Don't you hear me, you have to—"

"Many people have called in to report the same incident. We've got several patrol cars out there."

"But do you have the registration number?"

A male police officer crouched down at her side. He was holding a pen and notepad.

"Can you repeat that?"

"BOA 110."

"O.K. I'll pass it on," the man said and stood up. The policewoman stayed where she was.

"So what happened?"

"I was here to meet my brother, and when I saw him, a van with two men appeared and grabbed him and his mate."

"What's your brother's name?"

"Simon Berg."

"And yours?"

"Tekla."

"Berg?"

"Yes."

Tekla was feeling sick again and got up onto her knees.

"Are you going to vomit?"

"Maybe."

"The ambulance is on its way. Are you hurting anywhere?"

"He whacked my neck."

The policewoman pulled on some plastic gloves and ran her fingers over Tekla's head.

"No blood."

"He hit me on the neck."

"Perhaps you had better lie down."

"No."

Tekla could hear the ambulance arriving.

"You have to find that car. They took Simon."

"And his friend, right?"

"No, they let him go. He ran off in that direction."

Tekla pointed towards the Tunnelbana entrance at Ringvägen.

The male police officer returned with the ambulance crew, who were carrying a large, red bag.

"Could you have got that licence plate number wrong?" he asked.

Tekla visualised the registration number.

"No. Absolutely certain. Have you found it?"

"It wasn't a Volvo Duett, was it?"

"A black van, I tell you. It was a . . . I didn't see the make."

"So you may have made a mistake?"

"No."

"In that case the number plates may have been stolen ones," the female police officer explained. "Any idea why somebody would want to kidnap your brother?"

"No."

"What does he do for a living?"

Tekla thought.

"A bit of everything. He paints."

"Pictures?"

Tekla smiled.

"He's a painter. Among other things."

"Is he involved in any criminal activities?"

"Not that I know of."

"But he could be?"

Tekla was silent.

"Is he on drugs?"

"Don't know."

"But you wouldn't be surprised if he were?"

"You already seem to have made up your mind who my brother is."

"No. I'm just asking some questions."

"Find that van instead."

Tekla saw a police bus pull up. Several police officers got out. A paramedic asked Tekla to sit down on the trolley so she could be examined.

"Thanks, that won't be necessary," Tekla said.

Then she spotted a familiar face over by the police bus. Lundgren. Shit, Tekla thought. She really didn't feel like meeting him here.

"I've got to go."

"I think you'd better stay and let us—"

"Are you forcing me?"

"No, it's—"

"Good."

She started walking away from the police bus, stumbling over to the steps leading down to Skanstull Tunnelbana station. Her neck was still hurting, but she was beginning to feel less nauseous.

What the hell had happened? What had Simon got himself into? And who were those bikers? She tried to persuade herself that they were only some guys he'd been doing business with. Maybe he owed them money? Had he done some other stupid thing? It didn't necessarily mean that he was in real trouble.

Equally: they did carry weapons and had kidnapped someone in broad daylight, in a shopping centre in Södermalm. Who does that sort of thing?

Tekla took a bomb and two ten-milligramme tablets of Oxazepam out of her pocket. She didn't care if anyone saw her. She leaned her forehead against the cool tiles by the gates and shut her eyes. Tried not to think about anything, but all she saw was the shape of Simon being bundled into the van. His tousled hair. His pleading eyes. The anxiety. The fear. The panic.

IV

Twenty-four years earlier

Simon was going through the white drawer next to his father's bed. In the end, he found the Zippo lighter, put it in his pocket and shot Tekla a stern but apprehensive look. Waited, as if to see whether she would rat on him, but she was far too busy crying and holding their father's hand. Tekla looked around her. She had been in that room many times in the course of the year. Studying the matte yellow colour on the walls, which looked as if a thin film of water were running down from the ceiling. The corner cupboard stuffed full with his dirty clothes. The overbed table on rusty wheels that was covered in Simon's drawings.

Tekla could visualise every millimetre of the room. But she could not conjure up a single smell, and that frustrated her. Simon described a sharp stench, "like a mixture of sour diarrhoea and engine oil". Tekla was not able to detect any engine oil. Or any shit for that matter. It was as if she saw the orchestra in front of her but didn't hear a single note.

Liver function tests. Not that she ever saw his results, but she remembered her mother's look when she tore up the envelope from the hospital in Östersund. And then what she said:

"No. Not having any more disasters in this family. What shall we have for dinner, Tekla?"

Her father probably never saw the lab reports. He didn't want to. Why would he? He must have sensed which way the wind was blowing. And he was not going to waste his time worrying. After all, he had to finish the new shed. And soon it would be time for the highlight of the year: the elk hunt. What exactly made the hunt such a fantastic event? Tekla had gone out with the hunters many times, yet somehow she was still never really there. Not in the same way as Pappa and his friends. Their eyes lit up, with a joy she had seen only occasionally, when her father's forlorn look fell on their mother. She was everything to him. But she had a strange way of reciprocating that love. Only after his death did Tekla understand what her mother's existence had been like. A life with an alcoholic. A person who so doggedly destroyed his body from within, day after day, however much she begged and pleaded with him to stop. Now Tekla realised: her mother had known for years how the film would end.

Tekla skipped ahead a few days in her memory. Was it possible that he had just had a bowel movement? That they had given him strong laxatives in order to clear the system of toxins that his liver couldn't cope with? Maybe some medication that had made him more alert for a short while? Or was it merely a coincidence?

Tekla had been alone with her father, the room was still and quiet except for the ticking of a wall clock. The morphine pump on a stand by the bed worked away silently. The drip from the antibiotics bag was soundless. Even the high-tech mattress supporting his body made no noise, although it moved from time to time to prevent bedsores. Tekla had experienced the fascinating contraption herself, lying next to her father's motionless body and running her fingers through his greasy hair. It had turned grey in a matter of weeks.

But why worry about bedsores? Even Tekla had been thinking about how absurd it was. How unnecessary to provide an expensive mattress, surely a waste of resources. He was going to die anyway. The doctors had pretty much assured her of that. It was the only thing they could promise with any certainty.

And yet, a brief moment of lucidity, and an absolutely wonderful living presence.

"Hi, sweetie."

"Does it hurt?"

"The drain?" He smiled and stroked her cheek. "Not at all. I'm

272

getting mega-drugs." He pointed at the morphine pump. "Don't you worry. I'm not in any pain."

"Good."

"Look at you. How you've grown up. It feels as if I've been slumbering, like Sleeping Beauty . . . and then I wake up to find that my little girl . . . has turned into an adult overnight."

Tekla sat in silence. Had no idea how you talk to a dying person. Everything she had wanted to say in recent weeks, when he'd been out cold . . . if only she'd written it all down.

"Don't cry, darling. You've got Mamma and Simon."

"I don't want to be with Mamma. You know that."

"Don't say that. She loves you."

"She loves her cigarettes."

Her father laughed.

"You may be right there. She really ought to cut down. But you know, Mormor's eighty-eight now and she's been smoking a pack a day all her life."

"Not when she was a child."

"O.K., maybe she only started when she was eight."

Tekla smiled and dried her tears.

"Come here," her father said.

Tekla bent down over her father's large, bloated stomach, and hugged him. She tried not to breathe, thought he smelled disgusting. A cloying odour stuck to his skin and made her feel sick. Tekla remembered the nausea but could not conjure up the smell.

Her father held her and patted her short hair.

"But you have Simon. Always will have."

"All he does is tease me."

"Tease? But he's ten. Do you still tease at that age?"

"He'll never stop."

"You'll always have your brother. Remember that."

"Not always. One day, he'll die too."

"That's true. But so will you. I think that you ought to grow very, very old together."

"We'll try. I'm never going to start drinking alcohol."

She regretted it immediately. What was the point of twisting the knife now? A dying person who has inflicted this on himself. Consciously or unconsciously. Addicted or not. All those evenings, it was his own hand that raised the bottle to his mouth. His mouth that opened and swallowed all those thousands of litres of beer. It was his stick-like legs that had gone off to buy the bottles at Systembolaget. His brain that had decided to soldier on, to work at the factory, to toil away until his body could no longer take it. But equally: Tekla had never seen any letters from the Enforcement Authority. Never heard her parents having a row because there was not enough money at the end of the month. In some magical, tragic fashion they had managed to keep the wheels of his alcohol abuse spinning all these miles.

Tekla's father released her, and took her face in his cold hands. Looked into her eyes, red and swollen from weeping.

"If I could have rewound the tape, I'd have done things differently."

"Go on, do it."

"Rewind the tape?"

"Yes."

"Sadly, I don't have that kind of machine."

"Pity."

Her father stroked her hair.

"Promise me one thing."

"What?"

"That you'll look after him."

"Simon?"

"He's going to need your help."

"What do you mean?"

"You know what I mean. He's not as strong as you are. More likely to be influenced by what others tell him to do. You have to keep an eye on him. Not only now, later too, when you're adults."

"He doesn't need my help."

"You know he does. He always did."

"Maybe. But he'll soon have grown up."

Her father smiled.

"He'll never grow up."

"Maybe not."

"So promise."

"I promise."

"What do you promise?"

"To look after Simon. To protect him from evil. To—"

"That's good enough. That's my brave little knight."

She lay there against her father's chest for a long time. His breathing rattled more and more.

"Pappa?"

He breathed deeply. She panicked.

"Pappa?"

He looked up.

"I don't want you to die."

"Just do what you've always done," he said.

"What do you mean?"

"Be the person you are."

"But I can't manage without you. What about the boat? And the nets?"

"You can row by yourself."

"It's too heavy."

"You can do it with Simon's help."

Her eyes were stinging with all the tears.

"No."

"You'll be able to row far. Further than you think."

"But if the boat capsizes. I don't know how to swim."

"Don't worry."

"I do."

Tekla would never forget his last words:

"Next summer I'm going to teach you to swim."

Tekla fell asleep, curled up in the foetal position, just as the first rays of the sun were touching the roof of the Globen arena a few hundred metres from her apartment. When the alarm clock woke her, she switched on the T.V. and for a while her mind was taken up by something other than Simon: it had been established that the insulation on the electrical cabling and wiring used for the renovation of Söder Tower did not meet the specifications. An inquiry had been set up to identify those responsible for the supply of the non-compliant and possibly unlawful equipment. The hunt was also on for those who were to blame for the fire. As yet, no van had been found. "The police are following various leads ..."

Tekla switched off the T.V. and sank into her corner sofa. She rang Simon's number, but only got his voicemail. Did she seriously think that the bikers would have let him go after "having had a little chat with him"? In that case, why go to the trouble of kidnapping him? It didn't add up. Or maybe it had all just got out of hand because Tekla herself had been there and made a scene. Who was she trying to kid, other than herself? To hell with him.

She replayed the events in her head: Simon's back when he was being pushed into the van; the arm in the cast swinging at her head. The police officer she just spoke to had "nothing new to report". They were not about to deploy the national force to search for Simon, that much was obvious. The police had been matter-of-fact but pleasant. In their world, Simon was probably no more than a junkie who had only himself to blame. So how was she going to find him?

Once again, she reviewed her mental film of yesterday's happenings. Had a good look at the men. The one with the goatee was younger. He had a gold-coloured emblem on his jacket, but it was impossible to see what it represented. A hat? No, she couldn't be sure. The other man, the one with the plaster cast who had hit her, was older and seemed more worn out. His pale blue eyes were empty and cold. He was wearing a black leather vest and a belt with a large silver skull-and-crossbones buckle. His boots were rough, but she didn't recognise the style. If the registration number was wrong, how would she be able to identify them? Was there anything that stood out? She went through the clues she had. One: Simon's wayward past. To her knowledge, he had only been in trouble once, had had to pay a fine for a minor drug offence. He had been selling hash. But she had begun to suspect that he might himself be using harder and more expensive stuff than that. Did he owe money? Two: the man with the cast. If she were ever able to identify him, could she then find Simon? She was going to tackle that as soon as she got back to the hospital.

Checking her watch, she realised that she'd be late for work. Calling in sick was not an option. She'd go crazy wandering around her apartment waiting for the police to call. She jumped into some clothes and set off for the hospital.

The minute she came in through the eastern entrance, Tekla could tell that the stench had become even more noticeable, and down in the service tunnels it was worse still. Although her mind was on other things, she could not throw off a sense that the very existence of the hospital was under threat.

It was almost a relief to recognise the smell of E. coli diarrhoea coming from the toilets over by the isolation rooms in A. & E. They had also admitted a number of patients with chest pains. The poor old folks were not always able to drink enough in the heat, but they still took their pills for blood pressure and cardiac insufficiency, exactly as prescribed by their doctor. As a result, they became increasingly dehydrated, their kidney function deteriorated and they began to develop angina. And then the inevitable heart attack, as sure as night followed day. There were twenty-five patients waiting to be examined in A. & E. and Tekla knew that she needed a ball from her Lypsyl tube. Her body was aching and she was having trouble keeping her thoughts in check. Her eyelids were as heavy as lead. The high noise level around the patient reception area drilled into her ears and she could feel a dark migraine brewing. The toilets were busy, so she went into Emergency Room 2 and pulled down the blinds. Quickly, she poured herself a glass of water, unscrewed the bottom of the tube and shook out a small bomb that she washed down in one gulp. Since the bags were made of ordinary toilet paper with a twist so that the contents would not run out, she had always wondered whether the person who made them simply licked the paper before sealing off the end. She chose to believe that they used water.

She turned and noticed that you could see through the slats in the blind: she had not angled them. There was no-one out there, thank goodness. She left the emergency room.

The effect of the amphetamine was just as striking every time. After only a few minutes, she was not even bothered by the sight of Nordensköld with his slicked-back hair turning up for his handover report from the night. Tekla said hello and then casually beckoned over three medical students. She had apparently given them permission to spend the day in A. & E. with her. It came back to her that she needed to talk to Klein-Borgstedt about the financing business.

Tekla was aware that, in the course of the past week, she had upped the maximum dose per twenty-four hours from four bombs to five. She had to watch that. She kept thinking about Simon. The police did not seem to be taking his kidnapping seriously. So who could help her? She remembered Astrid's brother Magnus and his invitation to "have a drink one of these days". It went against the grain for her to take this kind of initiative, but she was curious to see him again. Was he really as nice as he had seemed when they met in

Nytorget? In any case, he was the only policeman she knew. And right now, she needed one. Tekla texted Astrid, asking for Lundgren's number.

For the time being, she was going to do some research into the man with the plaster cast. Tekla sat down at a computer and began to study the list of patients who had been admitted to A. & E. with traumatic injury to the left hand or arm in the past three weeks. Very few lesions required a cast for longer than that. She went through the register, one day at a time, looking at all the search criteria. She was conscious of the fact that she was not authorised to access patient files, but she also knew how unlikely it was that she would be found out. She could always claim that she had clicked on the wrong patient. She identified thirty-eight radial fractures that had been put in a cast, but all save three of the patients were over seventy. Of those three, two were women and the only male was a skateboarder in his twenties. None of them could have been the man outside Ringen. She had to broaden the scope of her search to other hospitals in town, but first she needed to check up on the overdose patient in the I.C.U.

In the long corridor behind the entrance lobby, Tekla passed people holding their hands in front of their noses, trailing children who were shouting, "Yuck!"

The I.C.U. was cooler and the smell less nauseating. Her mouth was dry since she had stopped breathing through her nose.

She sat down on a shiny, orange stool next to the intensive care physician.

"Are you coping?"

Elmqvist looked around.

"We keep getting these overdoses."

"What's the theory?"

"That the junkies have begun mixing in fentanyl."

"Which is difficult to disperse finely in the heroin," Tekla said. "Makes for brutal intoxication."

"Exactly."

"How's Miguel doing?"

Elmqvist pushed her reading glasses up into her bushy hair.

"I thought you knew."

"What?"

"He died during the night."

"What happened?"

"He started cramping again yesterday. The dialysis had gone well and we'd cleared the acidosis several days ago. So it wasn't that."

"And I heard that it *was*, in fact, quinine," Tekla said.

Elmqvist paused. She gave Tekla a knowing look from underneath her heavy fringe.

"And I know who solved the case. Yes, it was confirmed by Linköping. We had to enlist the support of our senior administrator to get them to test the samples so quickly. Normally it can take weeks. Sometimes months."

"Anything else?" Tekla said, pulling at her hospital pullover to get some air onto her sweaty chest.

"Fentanyl and diphenhydramine. Fentanyl is a hundred times more potent than morphine and acts in the same way as heroin."

"Just another opioid."

"That's right."

"But the other one, diphen . . ." Tekla pretended she didn't know the word. In fact, she could pick out in her head the only review article on the net dealing with diphenhydramine. She compared it with the information Elmqvist was giving her.

"Diphenhydramine, an antihistamine. Same story. A filler, so as to—"

"So as to be able to reduce the amount of heroin, which is the most expensive component," Tekla cut in. "And the antihistamine produces a pleasant drowsy-making effect." Tekla surveyed the room, every single cubicle was taken. Looking back at Elmqvist, she noticed the astonished look on her face, and realised her mistake.

"Precisely," Elmqvist said. "Then you knew . . ."

"No. Or rather, yes, I did know a bit about the antihistamine."

"You're a very unusual doctor, Tekla."

"I don't know about that. But what a mixture."

"Real jungle juice."

It was odd to hear Elmqvist – being the conservative, upstanding senior lecturer she was, a reliable source of learned articles – use the expression "jungle juice". Had she too pinched a slug or two out of her parents' drinks cabinet in her youth?

"What about the cramps?" Tekla said.

Elmqvist gave a resigned shrug.

"Could be a delayed effect of the diphenhydramine. Or permanent damage to the cardiac conduction system from all the crap he's been taking. Or a heart attack as a result of the strain on his organs. Not so important now that he's cooling out eight floors down in the morgue."

"Nine."

"What?"

"Nine floors down."

Tekla knew that, because she actually enjoyed calling in on Tweedledum and Tweedledee, the autopsy technicians down in the basement in Pathology.

Elmqvist got to her feet, revealing two dark patches of sweat under her large bosom. "Forgive me, but I'm afraid I have another nine overdoses to deal with. In spite of the fact that we sent three to the fancy hospital north of the city last night and one to Södertälje. But now they're all full. More than full. Damn junkies. Can't they keep an eye on what they take? And the ambulance service has run out of Naloxone."

She ran her fingers through her hair.

"I don't suppose you could help me out with a few I.C.U. beds?"

"Sorry, I can't," Tekla said and thought how much friendlier Elmqvist was towards her when Klein-Borgstedt was not around.

"Let's hope the police get hold of the idiots who're selling this poison."

"By the way, did you try physostigmine?" Tekla said.

Elmqvist eyed her younger colleague with suspicion. After all, A. & E. was a notch further down the food chain.

"Did I mention that he also had anticholergenic syndrome?"

"Er . . . no, but I thought . . ."

"Well actually we did, yesterday, after somebody called and tipped off one of our nurses about it. Without giving their name. And it worked."

Elmqvist shook her head and then with a shrug made it clear that she was not going to bother finding out how come Tekla knew everything.

"See you," Tekla said and left the I.C.U. She was thinking about all the cases of heroin intoxication. Terrified that one day she'd be standing in the emergency room when Simon's cold body was brought in. Dead of an overdose. Her mobile pinged before she made it back to A. & E. It was a text from Astrid.

Sending Magnus' number. Cool. Knew you'd be a good match! ☺

Reluctantly, Tekla sent off her question to Lundgren. And at once felt a knot in her stomach. When was the last time she had met a guy? She dismissed the thought. And went back to wondering about her meeting with Elmqvist instead. She had to get better at concealing her ideas and conclusions. Why was her brain not functioning as it should? In the past week, she had been unable to sort her images before going to bed. The cards in her filing system had got scrambled, and she saw flashes of light when she closed her eyes. But Tekla was not about to give up. For a few long seconds she considered what would happen if she were to be caught clicking her way through half the town's patients who had been seen in the past three weeks. Nordensköld would be ecstatic. If he found out, he would not hesitate to report it to Collinder. Or Moussawi. But had she won his approval now? She wasn't altogether sure. There was no doubt, however, that his attitude had changed after Tekla took care of the patient with the pulmonary embolism who developed a cerebral haemorrhage.

Only one more hour before the day's meeting with Nilsén.

Sigurdsdottir appeared to have the situation under control in A. & E., so Tekla went off to look for a computer, took a deep breath and clicked on "other healthcare providers". That pulled up all the hospitals in Stockholm, and she began to look through emergency admissions to surgical and orthopaedic units over the past three weeks. Then a thought struck her: since Carlsson kept such a close eye on everything she did, would she also see that she was accessing medical records? If so, it would doubtless come to light at her next meeting with the C.E.O. She was not going to worry about that just now, Tekla decided.

"How . . . are . . . things?" Tekla said, sounding as if she had just swum fifty metres freestyle and broken the world record.

"Perhaps you ought to breathe a little?" Nilsén suggested in a silky voice.

Tekla tried to bring her pulse down. She had interrupted Safadi and Nilsén in the middle of an intense discussion. Now that she knew for a fact that the critical patient with the burns was not Simon, the dread she felt when she went to the burns unit was gone.

"You do realise that you're not only bound by medical confidentiality rules?" Nilsén said as she removed her blazer. Her sinewy shoulders looked like oranges underneath the straps of her dress.

Tekla nodded. Breathed.

"Searching through dental records hasn't turned up anything. We've scoured several practices in Södermalm."

"So you still don't know who he is?" She saw that the patient was extubated. The plastic tube had been removed from his throat and he was breathing by himself. "Is he responding?"

"They're going to examine his head again this afternoon," Nilsén said. "To assess brain function."

"To see if he's a vegetable or not," Safadi added from his end of the room.

"By all means, put it like that if it makes you feel good," Tekla said without meeting his eyes. But Nilsén's smile did not go unnoticed. "You still haven't ruled out the terrorist angle?"

"Quite the opposite," Safadi said.

"What do you mean?"

Safadi seemed to be weighing up how much he could reveal.

"We have the results of the blood test from the man you chased down in the service tunnels."

"And?"

"No hits. But we got a lead from the C.C.T.V. cameras—"

Nilsén interrupted her colleague from Säpo. "Do you have to be so long-winded? He had tattoos on his hand that point to Russian connections, maybe the former F.S.B., and he acted like a pro when he saw that his plan to get out onto a fire escape had gone pear-shaped. What's more, he knew there was a way out to the staff car park via the tunnel."

"F.S.B.?" Tekla said.

"Russian security services."

"But what could be the link to the burns patient?"

Safadi behaved as if he were alone in the room with Tekla.

"We're working on that and on everything else too."

Nilsén seemed irritated that her colleague from Säpo was being so unforthcoming.

"They control a large part of the criminal activities in this town."

"Who, the F.S.B.?" Tekla said.

"Indirectly, yes. There's a so-called *vor* in Stockholm, or *vor v zakone*, a "thief-in-law" who runs it all like one big business operation. We have nothing on him, his behaviour is exemplary. He never goes anywhere near arms or drugs. Is scrupulous about his tax return." Nilsén smiled to herself. "Officially, I understand, he translates Russian literature. But in actual fact he controls the entire heroin market and most of the amphetamine deals through the loosely knit gangs which report to him."

"Where does the F.S.B. come in?"

"You could say that he works for them."

"Russian-organised crime accounts for one third of the whole European heroin market," Safadi said.

"Much of the arms and foreign currency smuggling, too," Nilsén added. "And human trafficking."

"Incredible," Tekla said, totally absorbed by this new information. "And the F.S.B....?"

"All this criminal activity is the F.S.B.'s number one source of income," Safadi said.

"Putin?" Tekla said, letting her thoughts wander.

"All sanctioned from on high," Nilsén answered with a smile.

"And none of this is secret," Safadi declared. "It's all there in documents available to the public."

"Which is what our man from Säpo feels duty-bound to say," Nilsén teased him.

Tekla looked at the man with the burns again.

"Let's hope he wakes up," she said, staring at the hole in the dressings under which a mouth was concealed.

Safadi lowered his voice again. The effect was striking.

"We would very much like to question him."

"When Marcus says *we*, he actually means N.O.D. Säpo are only here as observers."

After leaving Nilsén in the I.C.U., Tekla checked her mobile and saw that Lundgren had answered her text.

Love to! Come by for a drink tonight.

"Could you stay behind afterwards?" Collinder said. Tekla thought it sounded more like an order than a question. And he looked really annoyed. "It's been reported that you've been consulting patient records for which you have no authorisation."

"I—"

"Not now," Collinder cut her off and held up a hand. "After the meeting. But it's not looking good, Tekla. Not good at all."

Several doctors came ambling into the conference room and sat down. Many had brought their lunch. Tekla sank into a chair by the wall. This unusual behaviour was not lost on the medical students, who stared at the unoccupied chair at the big table.

"Hello everyone. Let's start with—"

"Please forgive me," said a familiar voice from the doorway.

Collinder looked up from his papers.

"Well, well, a distinguished lunchtime visitor," Collinder said stiffly. No-one could fail to notice that he had suddenly shrunk.

"Don't let me disturb you," Carlsson said and closed the door behind her. She went and stood by the wall and looked around the table. Tekla lowered her eyes.

"O.K., we can run through this pretty quickly," Collinder said. Never before had Tekla heard him outline the clinic's training programme in such a short space of time. He wound up the meeting and the doctors left the room.

Out of the corner of her eye, Tekla saw Carlsson go over and say something to Collinder, who nodded briefly, glared in her direction, then followed the others out. Tekla was puzzled.

"I happened to be in the vicinity," Carlsson said, and settled into the chair at the head of the table where Collinder had been sitting. She looked around with distaste. "Jesus, there's no air down here. How can you bear it?"

"Perhaps that's why staff meetings are so short," Tekla replied and took a seat at a safe distance, two chairs away. If there was one thing she had learned about Carlsson, it was that she never "happened" to be in the vicinity.

"Is he going to survive?"

"Who?" Tekla asked and immediately felt a cold shiver run down her spine.

"The burns patient in the I.C.U.," Carlsson said. She fished something out of her jacket pocket and put it in her mouth.

"Oh, I see."

"Who did you think I meant?" Carlsson said, giving Tekla a shrewd look.

"I see so many patients that—"

"Will he survive?"

"That's hard to say. It's his kidneys, mainly, that have taken a beating from the extensive dam—"

"Is the smell just as bad in the I.C.U.? I haven't visited our flagship for quite a while now."

In her mind, Tekla visualised the modern facilities of the I.C.U.

"It hasn't really struck me."

"But you have noticed the stench down here in the pressure cooker?"

Tekla couldn't help smiling.

"What?" Carlsson asked and now Tekla saw that the C.E.O. of the Nobel Hospital was eating salty liquorice dummies for lunch.

"You said 'the pressure cooker'."

"Isn't that what you call A. & E.?"

"It is, yes."

"But you're surprised that I know that."

"Sort of."

Tekla felt a sudden urge to ask Carlsson if she was eating liquorice because she had low blood pressure, maybe adrenal insufficiency, but she was afraid it was too personal a question.

Carlsson ran her fingers through her short fringe.

"That's why we need to arrange a good deal. Pronto."

"You mean the P.P.P.?"

"The building is rotting from within. Can't you feel that, as a doctor?"

"I focus mainly on people."

"I gather you're friendly with Moussawi."

"What do you mean?"

Carlsson fixed her with a stern look.

"Dr Berg. I'm still the one who asks the questions in our little relationship."

"All I'm saying is that I haven't given much thought to the reason for the bad smell," Tekla said. "I sort of assume that the hospital management has the situation under control."

Carlsson got up from her chair.

Here we go, Tekla thought. Now I've overstepped the mark.

Limping a little, Carlsson walked over to an oil painting of the former chief physician, Ralf Bergström, born 1902.

"All these men," Carlsson sighed.

"I do agree."

"So why are you hanging out with Moussawi?"

Tekla would have given a lot to find out where Carlsson got her information from, but knew it would be pointless to ask.

"He's kind of difficult to avoid."

"A bit like the stench in the building," Carlsson said to herself. "Nose plugs aren't enough."

Tekla smiled at the comparison.

"But I hear you haven't yet spoken to Klein-Borgstedt."

"Have I said so?"

Carlsson turned.

"No, that's the point."

Tekla felt a headache coming on.

"I'll get to it this week."

"It's more urgent than that."

"I'll talk to her today."

"Good," Carlsson said, straightening the blouse she was wearing under her jacket. Tekla assumed that she sweated just as much as everyone else in the heat.

"Tekla?"

"Yes?"

"Did you find what you were looking for this morning?"

"What do you mean?"

"In the medical records system of Kungsholmen Hospital. Which one is not allowed to access unless one needs to follow up on a specific patient."

Tekla froze. But she had no reason to lie.

"No, I couldn't get in."

"Is this the man you were looking for?"

Tekla took the Post-it note and read. There was a name and personal identity number. She wondered if Carlsson would ever cease to amaze her.

"And forget Collinder. There won't be any report."

Carlsson wiped some sweat off her forehead with the back of her hand and took another salty liquorice dummy out of her pocket.

"Do you want one?"

"No . . . No, thanks," Tekla stammered.

Carlsson popped the dummy into her mouth and walked towards the door.

"Call me when you've talked to Klein-Borgstedt."

Umarov picked up the black case with the pH tests and wandered out to confront the pool monster. His 94-year-old mother Marina was sitting on a chair underneath the awning by the pool, looking out at the water, which had turned a golden rusty brown. The sight filled Umarov with sadness. As if his mother were contemplating bygone times. From a distance, Umarov thought she might be asleep, but when he stood in front of her, he saw that she was wearing earphones and had vanished into another world. She opened her eyes and, when she saw him, untangled herself from the wires.

"Victor! My *malyish*. I want to talk to you about thing." She always insisted on speaking her imperfect Swedish.

He smiled. Kissed the top of her head. Shut his eyes. Her grey hair was brushed down over the collar of the knitted cardigan with its red and white pattern that reminded him of a Chinese dragon.

"Mamushka. What can I do?"

"The new Filipina maid, she not use the strong washing powder. Smell is chemical. Ruin sheets."

"I'll talk to Coco."

"Then me happy."

The old woman gave her only son a determined nod and put her earphones back on. Umarov guessed it was classical music. She had told him that she wanted to listen to audiobooks. But he had not been able to get hold of anything in Russian, let alone in Uzbek. Shostakovich would have to do for the time being.

"Victor! How is Nina?" the old lady shouted.

Umarov lifted off her earphones.

"Nina? Why do you ask, Mamushka?"

"I can see she not well."

Umarov looked across the pool. He was bound to agree. There was something wrong with Nina. She had not been herself lately.

"It's probably nothing, Mamushka. I think she's just very busy."

"Tell her must work less," Marina said.

Umarov fetched a pH strip and dipped it into the pool. He could see the robot cleaner – which had cost him a fortune – sweeping away right around the clock at the dirt on the bottom. The strip registered a pH of 7.9, which was three points too high. How come he could not manage something as straightforward as a swimming pool?

Sardor could be heard sounding his horn out in the street. Time to deal with the Northern Networks. No escalation of violence. No more dead Albanians.

"I bought Softcare, active oxygen," Umarov sighed. "I checked with one of Nina's contacts, who's said to have the cleanest pool in Djursholm. Whatever his name was told me to use Softcare, so I've stocked up on the stuff."

"You should be happy then," Sardor said.

"I am."

Sardor accelerated up onto Alviksvägen, towards Ålsten school.

Umarov saw two mothers come jogging along, each one with a sports buggy.

"Sardor."

"Yes."

"How's your sister?"

"No idea."

"But what do you think?"

"We don't talk, so how would I know? I expect she's busy flogging expensive houses in the archipelago and looking after that spoiled husband of hers. Not to mention all the properties they keep buying for themselves all over the world."

"Have they bought something new? Other than that house in Rio?"

"I don't know. But how many houses does anyone need?"

Sardor passed Äppelviken, had to brake every few minutes to allow prams and tired schoolchildren to use the pedestrian crossings.

"Whatever you say, she's the one who's taking over when I'm gone," Umarov said.

Sardor slowed down by Alléparken, drew up next to the pavement and turned to face his father.

"Why are you talking about dying?"

"No need to worry."

"I'm not worried."

"But it's important that you should hear this," Umarov said. "Nina is clean. She's never been involved in our activities, she's not in any registers and I want it to stay that way. She's the one who's going to make our business legitimate in the long term. All this crap has to end with me."

"Wonder how the Centre feels about that," Sardor said.

"You leave the Centre to me."

"It's nice for you that I don't have any kids then," Sardor said.

"What do you mean?"

"So my criminal genes don't get passed on."

"Now you're being unfair."

"But that's what you're saying."

"I'm not," Umarov said, looking quite dejected.

"But that's how it *feels*!" Sardor said.

Umarov put his hand on Sardor's arm.

"Sardor. Listen to me. Your shortcomings as a son are the result of my failure as a parent."

"It's in the genes."

"No," Umarov said. "I know that you always try to please me. And you've been incredibly dutiful. And I know that you have a really good grip on the heroin, the amphetamines, the whores and the weapons. But that's the whole point."

"What is?"

"That's all you're capable of. You barely know what 'escalate' means. How would you cope in the normal community? Never mind run a real business."

"So let me do what I'm best at," Sardor said.

"In another world," Umarov replied in exasperation. "In another world, my son. All this violence has to end. I don't want Kamila, Emily and Kate to have to keep looking over their shoulder when they're grown up. I've killed and injured far too many. I've made orphans of children. Allowed anarchy in the streets. Looking in the rear-view mirror as one grows older, one sees what one should have done differently. And you are my greatest failure, but it's not your fault."

Sardor stared straight ahead, an empty gaze. White knuckles on the steering wheel.

"You will, of course, get your share of the inheritance," Umarov said.

"But it's Nina who's going to take over?"

"Yes. And you have to learn to live with that."

They sat in silence for a while. Then Umarov said:

"And you know that I dream of having more grandchildren. It's never too late." Sardor revved the engine, threw the car back into the traffic and fell in dangerously close to a Volvo V90.

"That's not going to happen."

Sardor was now tailgating the Volvo.

"Men can have children late. You just have to find—"

"Cut it out!"

"Anyone would think you don't like women," Umarov said with a laugh.

Sardor nearly crashed head-on into a car coming the other way as he overtook the Volvo.

"Take it easy!" Umarov said.

"Nina's going to get it all!" Sardor shouted.

Umarov placed his calloused hand on the back of Sardor's.

"Of course not. And I want you to do as I say. I know that you're as good as your word."

Sardor knew that he had no choice. He braked at the red light by the Alvik roundabout. Breathed heavily.

"You will, won't you?" Umarov repeated. "Do as I say."

"I promise."

"What do you promise?"

"That we'll phase out the dope and the whores over time and let Nina take over with her legal business activities. Real estate and stuff. White as snow."

"You swear it?"

"I do."

"By?"

"Great-grandma's grave," Sardor said, crossing the Alvik roundabout and heading for the Ulvsunda industrial zone.

"That's what I like to hear," Umarov said.

BLUE OYSTER THAI, ULVSUNDA INDUSTRIAL ZONE
Wednesday, 12.vi

"Welcome!" Umarov said and held on to Zog Biba's hand for a few extra seconds. The leader of the Lions cast a scornful look at Sardor, who stood beside his father collecting everybody's weapons.

"So that you can mow us down with all the cameras switched off? No thanks."

Umarov let go of the hand and turned to welcome Tony Nordström from Jakan Crew instead, along with the two people accompanying him.

"If we wanted to kill you, you'd never have woken up this morning. See this as an ordinary Christmas dinner with the family. Surely you don't bring weapons with you when you go home to your mother?" Umarov said.

Nordström ostentatiously removed his leather jacket in front of Biba and pulled up his black T-shirt to show Sardor that he did not have any weapons stuck into his trousers.

"Come on, Biba," Nordström said, patting his tattooed stomach. "I'm as hungry as a lion."

Eventually the Albanian leader signalled to his men in black that they should hand in their weapons. They lifted up their jackets and let themselves be searched. Sardor lined up pistols, magazines, knives and mini Uzis in a neat row and led them in to Blue Oyster Thai's dining room. Sardor had hired the whole restaurant.

"We don't usually get much custom anyway so early in the evening," the owner had said the day before, accepting a bundle of banknotes. "Especially not during a heatwave when everyone wants to go for a beer in town."

The gangs turned up one after the other, with terse greetings and doubtful looks towards the interior of the restaurant.

By now there was no more room at the long table standing in the middle of the restaurant, with its drab decor. The atmosphere was tense and sweaty, and heavy with anticipation.

"Right," Umarov said and unbuttoned his jacket, smoothed down his white shirt and picked up a glass of cold red wine. "We'd also like to greet Jimmy Chu from No Way Out, Rickard Jakobsson from K-Men and Christian Jensen from Red Bears. Nice that you could get away at such short notice. I know that you're all busy men."

While Jensen and the vice-president of Red Bears, "The Count" Holmström, were drinking beer out of the bottle, Biba was sticking to water. The long table had been nicely set with napkins folded to look like swans, pink flowers between the plates and sauces served on small individual dishes. Jakobsson and his two companions from K-Men cast sceptical looks at Jakan Crew on the other side of the table, as they waited to see what would happen next.

"I suppose you've come straight from work," Umarov said, catching the eye of each one as he spoke, "so I suggest we eat first. The Treaty of Versailles was not negotiated on an empty stomach." Jakobsson scratched his red beard with a puzzled look and his eyelids drooped.

"We're treating you to a Thai buffet today," Umarov went on cheerfully. "There's beer and wine, all you have to do is ask the staff. Do the Lions want to go first?"

Biba stared threateningly at Umarov, but eventually the Albanian got to his feet and draped his jacket over the upholstered back of his chair. He walked slowly to the buffet, followed by two men in black shirts.

Umarov took a deep breath and slowly released the air through his nose. He went on nodding left and right around the table, where twelve of the leading lights in the Northern Networks were seated, together with the three representatives of Red Bears, the biker club from Skärholmen. Sardor was helping the staff to set out bottles of beer and wine.

One at a time, the gangs went up to the groaning buffet table. Nordström's men from Jakan Crew settled down with two heaped platefuls each and began to shovel in a mixture of spring rolls, green curry and bamboo shoots. Nordström nodded at Umarov from his end of the table, looking pleased. Raised his glass in a private toast.

"Not exactly a three-star restaurant," Chu said, sounding less happy as he walked by Umarov, adjusting his blue-tinted sunglasses. He was as tanned as ever, and his snow-white shirt was stretched taut over his sinewy muscles.

"We needed a place where we'd not be disturbed," Umarov said and gave the leader of No Way Out a pat on the shoulder. "The Grand Hotel was already booked for the annual meeting of the National Police Board."

Nordström gave a loud guffaw and even Jensen seemed to be perking up.

Umarov eventually sat down at the head of the table and asked Sardor to get him some food. Sardor looked around to see if anyone had noticed the patronising request.

"Let me begin by expressing my sincere condolences at the passing of Lorik," Umarov said in a sombre tone, looking at the far end of the table. Biba put down his fork and crossed his arms over his chest. He fixed his murderous gaze on a vase of flowers in the centre of the table.

"It was—"

"Bloody unnecessary," the Albanian leader cut in, grabbing the tabletop with both hands. For a split second Umarov wondered if he was going to overturn it.

Only Jakan Crew's men went on eating in silence. All the others were sitting still, waiting nervously to see what would happen next. Sardor set down a plate in front of Umarov, then backed up against the golden temples in the colourful wall painting.

"I totally agree with you," Umarov said and shook his head. "But it was only business. Nothing more than business. It's important to leave out emotions when—"

"Easy for you to say," Biba countered. "You haven't lost a family member."

"*Pusho ne paqe,*" Umarov said with his hand over his heart, and he saw Biba give a start. "May he rest in peace. It was entirely our fault. The responsibility is mine, and I'm sorry I didn't do a better job bringing up my son. He's a hothead, and that's always a bad thing to be. This time it really got out of hand."

The only person not looking at Sardor was Jakobsson, who had just found a chicken skewer that he was busy dipping in the peanut sauce.

Biba and his black-clad lions looked as if they were going to get to their feet any second. Biba spoke: "You killed the wrong guy. Lorik wasn't even at Kvarnen."

"You don't know that for sure . . ." Sardor began, but fell silent immediately when Umarov held up his hand.

"I'm very sorry," Umarov said and smiled across at Biba. "I see that you're better at keeping your sons in check. *Pune e mire,* well done."

"And what the fuck are you doing with your H?" Jakobsson from K-Men suddenly snarled. He broke a prawn cracker in two. "It's been cut with some crap. The junkies are dying like flies all over town."

"Glad you mentioned it," Umarov said, gesturing with his hand along one side of the table. "We're aware of the problem and looking for the culprits."

"Look harder," Jakobsson said, taking a bite of his chicken skewer.

"Absolutely," Umarov replied. "Eje and Sardor will be working round the clock these next few days to clean things up in town. And since you've raised this delicate matter, I'm assuming that you're all going to stop dumping your prices simply because we've had a temporary setback with our product."

Nordström leaned back and rolled his muscular shoulders. Then he said with a smile:

"Or is Jakobsson planning to grab some turf like he did when we ran out of coke last year?"

Two of Jakobsson's men got to their feet. They looked as if they wanted to settle the matter then and there, but the K-Men leader was not as steamed up as he appeared. He smirked and gestured to his companions to take it easy, so they sat down.

"We mustn't behave like a bunch of corrupt politicians," Umarov said. "All of us here are men who stand by their word. If you will all agree to stop dumping your prices then we, the Umarovs, promise not to extend our territories north of Järva restaurant."

"We're putting up the price of H. tonight," Jakobsson said, opening his brawny arms.

"Then we will too. Even though the food here sucks," Chu chimed in to scattered laughter.

Umarov looked over at Biba's end of the table. The Albanian had been following the conversation in grim silence. Slowly, Umarov got to his feet and walked around the table. He stopped a metre short of the Albanian gang leader.

"*Miku im,* my friend. I have three children I do everything for. Sometimes a little too much, maybe." Umarov turned to Sardor and shook his head. The silence weighed heavily in the dimly lit restaurant. All eyes were on Umarov's every movement. "So I know what family means. If anyone were to touch my children, I'd . . . Well, you get me. From the bottom of my Uzbek heart I beg you to forgive my son his mistake. We've all made mistakes; the important thing is to admit, apologise and then move on. I offer you a hundred per cent of the cocaine market in Stockholm by way of compensation if you'll let go of this and not step up the violence. None of us has anything to gain from more bloodshed."

The leader of the Lions, Biba, got to his feet, walked over to Umarov and put his arms around their Uzbek host.

The others sitting at the table clapped.

Umarov held up a hand to silence the assembled men. He looked at Sardor.

"And we're going to retrieve Lorik's body so he can be given a proper burial. Right?"

Sardor nodded.

"Sardor's going to fix it," Umarov said and shook Biba's hand.

Umarov went back to his seat, took his first bite of the meal and realised that he was very hungry indeed.

Once everybody had left the restaurant, Sardor and Umarov went out to the car park. It was a warm June evening. The sun had set, but it was still light.

"How does it feel?" Umarov asked.

"It's O.K."

"Sure?"

Sardor waved Umarov away.

"I had to give them something, so the violence doesn't go on. We've more important things to see to."

"Eje was going to talk to all the dealers," Sardor said and avoided Umarov's look.

"Good."

Umarov was breathing heavily. He was tired.

"How are you doing?" Sardor said.

"It's not too bad."

"I don't know, but it'd be better for you to have it checked."

"I will. And you know what?"

"What?"

"I'm going to contact the Centre and get them to send more weapons."

Sardor looked at Umarov in surprise.

"Why on earth?"

Umarov smiled.

"Do you seriously believe that Biba will settle for one bloated corpse and a little bit of cocaine?"

BJURHOLMSPLAN, SÖDERMALM
Wednesday evening, 12.vi

"This is really a hidden gem here in Söder," Lundgren said, looking out of the window towards Bjurholmsplan. "No-one knows about this park since there are no restaurants or bars in the area. Only families playing with their children and singles lying on a blanket reading a book. Do you want red wine or brandy? I didn't have time to go to Systembolaget, so that's all I have."

"Brandy," Tekla said. She had taken three extra Oxazepam and dug out a black blouse she hardly ever wore.

Lundgren filled half a water glass with the amber liquid for Tekla and poured himself a glass of red wine.

"I'm sorry I didn't tell you more when we saw each other in Nytorget. Silly of me. Sometimes I just want to forget that I'm a policeman."

Tekla smiled and shook her head.

"How come?"

"When we met with my sister the other day, I'd come from a couple of bloody awful shifts and I only wanted to be myself, not Magnus the police officer. Or Dolph, as I'm known in the team."

Tekla choked on her brandy and coughed hard. It was true, Lundgren bore more than a passing resemblance to the actor.

Lundgren burst out laughing and for a second the anxiety was gone from the pit of her stomach. After everything that had happened, it was a relief to hear a hearty laugh.

"Is it O.K. if I don't call you Dolph?"

"Sure. I hate it."

Tekla was already feeling tipsy and saw how the alcohol and the Sobril were ramping each other up.

"Are you from Stockholm?" Lundgren said.

"Definitely not."

"I know who *not* to ask for restaurant recommendations, then."

"I've been living here for a year, but I'd still be hard put to find my way around outside Södermalm," Tekla said.

"That's all you need to know."

"Is it that bad?"

"That good," Lundgren said and drank some of his wine. "There's everything you need in Söder. I've lived all over town, but Söder's the best."

"Where did you grow up?"

Lundgren seemed to hesitate.

"North of town."

"That I know even less well. As far as I'm concerned, north of Norrtull is Arlanda airport."

"But where do you come from?" Lundgren said.

"Jämtland. A place called Edsåsdalen."

"Then you can tell me all about shooting elk and eating fermented herring."

"You know what we call people who duck when an exhaust backfires?"

Lundgren shook his head.

"Stockholmers on an elk hunt."

Lundgren laughed out loud once more. "I would probably throw myself to the ground too."

Tekla went on talking. Told him about Edsåsdalen. About her father's job at the factory. About her mother who in theory was at home, yet was not present. That she had really wanted her mother to be working, so that she could be with her Pappa all the time. That she had loved to follow him up to the hillside huts in the pastures and cut the grass, get things ready for the elk shoot, repaint the boat by the lake, chop wood for the winter. Every little moment with her father was harmonious. His good humour, his funny stories and love of nature were catching. She never really saw that he drank too much. Only noticed it indirectly. Tekla described the way her mother used to nag her father, tell him off at breakfast and dinner. She moaned about the fact that they had no money, couldn't afford to go on holiday "like everybody else". Tekla could not understand her mother's yearning to travel and see the world. Surely, they had everything one needed: the lakes and the fishing, the forest with berries and mushrooms, the lawn to play football and tag on, trees to climb.

"It sounds as if you and your mother didn't have a great relationship."

Tekla smiled back. "No, we definitely did not."

"So you never went away?"

Thinking back, she could only remember one single trip. And her mother didn't come with them. Tekla took a sip of her brandy.

"We did once. We went to Portugal. Don't ask me where Pappa got the money from. Maybe he borrowed it. In any case, it was me, him and my little brother. Pappa had taken his guitar, and I remember that he spent most of the time by the side of the pool playing Cornelis' songs. 'How wonderful is this?' he would call out. We ate breakfast on the terrace under a pergola covered in vines. We had fresh-pressed orange juice and newly baked rolls that Pappa had gone to buy before we woke up. We could have eaten them just like that with nothing on, but he insisted that we have Nutella, even though we didn't want it. 'For heaven's sake, we're on holiday' he'd say, laughing, and I remember breathing in the smoke from the cigarette he had in the corner of his mouth. There was another more acrid smell, of sweat, but I tried to shut that out by breathing with my mouth open."

In actual fact, Tekla had no recollection whatsoever of these odours. This had always been a source of intense frustration to her, the images were crystal clear in her mind, but she could not remember the smells. It was why she was a notorious hoarder of scents. Her father's off-white shirt lay neatly folded in a shoebox in her cupboard. Together with hundreds of other items from her childhood. Just so as to preserve the smells of the important memories. And when she talked about things she had experienced, she would add specific olfactory memories which she thought would complete the picture.

She looked at Lundgren, who was listening intently. With a mischievous smile on his wine-stained lips.

"What?"

"Nothing. Carry on, you're such a good storyteller. What a memory."

Tekla looked out of the window and focused on the enormous tree right in the middle of Bjurholmsplan. She felt exposed and unmasked. Naked. But at the same time, it was surprisingly easy to talk to Lundgren about her childhood.

She drank her brandy thirstily.

"Pappa had mackerel fillets in tomato sauce on his sandwich. I got so badly sunburnt that I could pull long strips of skin off my back and shoulders and I drank Coca-Cola that Pappa bought. Normally, we were never allowed soft drinks when Mamma was with us, but now we could have as much as we wanted. It was like one long dream. At least until he got out the whisky bottle. I heard him unscrew it, heard the splash in the glass and then silence. His 'ah' put an end to the beautiful day. I always excused myself soon after dinner, saying that I was tired. Then I went to bed and put the pillow over my head. My fantasies could begin. I don't actually remember why Mamma didn't come with us."

"Maybe she was working?" Lundgren suggested.

"I don't think so."

"What about your brother, are you close?"

Tekla shut her eyes. Looked straight into Simon's face. He seemed a bit worried. His large eyes were wide open. A fag in his mouth. Stubble, and a silver skull earring. She felt her throat tightening.

"We've always been really close. Irish twins, isn't that what it's called when there's less than a year between siblings?"

"Maybe. Don't know."

Tekla did. She could see the home page in front of her eyes. The December 26, 2008 thread on the *Allt för Föräldrar* internet forum for parents.

"But we've been out of touch for a while. We had a row in the spring . . ."

"Family can be difficult. The closer you are, the rougher the arguments. And my God, the rows Astrid and I have. We're world champions when it comes to that." Lundgren laughed and shook his head. "But perhaps you manage to talk it through afterwards?"

Tekla wondered if the time was right to tell him about the kidnapping.

"But he's hopeless. He takes drugs."

"I'm sorry. Has he been doing it for long?"

"Since his teens."

"And we're not just talking the occasional joint?"

"I think it's worse than that now. I suspect heroin."

Tekla could feel Lundgren staring at her, as if wondering how much he could ask. Maybe he was more tactful than he had seemed at first. Being a police officer, he would know that many addicts are also dealers, to finance their own habit.

"I can tell from the way you look that something's happened," Lundgren said.

Tekla nodded. He didn't need to say anything, she could see what he was thinking. *Your brother's a pusher who's screwed up.*

"Do you want to tell me?"

Tekla felt sick. Drunk.

"Maybe some other time."

She did not want to spoil the pleasant evening by talking about the incident outside Ringen. The reason for wanting to see Lundgren in the first place had now been replaced by something different. And anyway, what could he do that the police weren't already doing?

"Is there someone you can talk to?" Lundgren asked. "A partner?"

Tekla was stuck in her thoughts.

Lundgren sounded apologetic: "Sorry, that was way too personal. Brain fade. Typical me. A real clodhopper. My problem has always been that—"

"It doesn't matter. But no, there's no-one. Not my thing."

"Your thing?"

"Relationships."

"Never?"

She could see how Lundgren was struggling not to say something clumsy.

"Partner. Actually makes me think of policemen sitting in the front seat of a car, sipping black coffee out of paper mugs while keeping an eye on an apartment in the pouring rain."

"You're right, it does sound like something from a film," Lundgren said with a smile.

"All I'm saying is that I haven't been in a relationship for a long time. Well, I mean . . . they come and they go."

"You're talking to an expert. At fucking up relationships," Lundgren said and let his shoulders hang a bit. "The only girl I get on with is my sister."

"She seems super nice."

Tekla felt their knees brush against each other.

"It's also hard to fit it in," Tekla said and sensed that she was coming closer to the truth. "Job, research, career."

"And trying to keep physical decline at bay." Lundgren pinched a fold of his own body fat.

"You don't look as if you have any trouble staying fit," Tekla countered.

"You haven't seen me naked."

Tekla eyed the tall man in surprise.

"Relax," Lundgren said, smiling. He seemed to regret what he had said. "I'm not going to eat you."

Tekla hesitated. "Is it O.K. if I do this?" She pulled out her scarf and dipped it in the remains of her brandy.

Lundgren laughed.

"Do you need some perfume?"

"Just a small souvenir."

His smile faded a little. He looked at Tekla, fascinated.

"You're seriously cool. As my old kickboxing coach would have said, 'you have personality in spades.'"

Tekla put the scarf into her pocket. It was going into a shoebox in her cupboard.

For a minute or so, they sat in silence. Tekla enjoyed the evening light falling through the window and making the walls of the apartment shimmer in beautiful tones of red and yellow. Lundgren fetched two glasses of water and a bowl of peanuts.

"Have you made up with your brother?" he said, breaking the silence. "You told me you'd fallen out."

"No," Tekla said and drank some of the water.

"What's his name?"

"Simon."

"Does he live in Stockholm?"

"Yes. Until he . . ."

Tekla hesitated.

"Until he what?" Lundgren asked.

She braced herself. Decided she had nothing to lose by telling him.

"He disappeared yesterday. Was taken away."

Lundgren put down his glass.

"What are you saying?"

"I really don't know. But I imagine he's involved in some shit. Maybe dealing."

"Has he . . . do you know if he's doing any hard stuff?"

"Not for sure. But there's a lot to suggest he is."

"Even if you haven't seen him for a while?"

"Precisely for that reason. Whenever I didn't hear from him, he'd be up to something he was ashamed of."

"Ashamed to tell big sister."

"Who can be quite strict, yes," Tekla said with a knot in her stomach.

"What are the police saying?"

"That they're looking for the van he disappeared in," Tekla said, and thought of the man with the plaster cast. She had not had time to find out anything about the man whose name Carlsson had given her: Johan Holmström.

"Kidnapping isn't really my department," Lundgren said, "but, nine times out of ten, a group is quickly set up to handle the case, although it depends a little on the circumstances. And you've not heard from him at all? No text messages?"

"Nothing." Tekla sighed. "But surely one can track a mobile?"

"It's not that easy. There are lots of rules when it comes to tracking. Those who do it are members of the Surveillance Unit."

Tekla was reluctant to go into any more detail.

"If you like, I can have a little look to see how it's going."

"Yes please."

"Then I need his details."

Tekla wrote down Simon's name and personal identity number on a paper napkin. She saw Lundgren react when he read Simon's name.

For a while they sat in silence, each lost in their respective world.

"We'll come up with something to find your brother," Lundgren said and stared resolutely ahead. "The police probably know that he's been using drugs, they're bound to have it on their files. So you believe that he's also a pusher?"

"Maybe," Tekla sighed.

"But you don't know if he's a member of some gang?"

"No."

"You've no idea?"

Tekla wondered if she should mention Johan Holmström.

"No."

"And now he's probably in trouble with some dealers."

"Dealers?"

"The second last link in the chain," Lundgren replied. "The guys who have like a kilo or a few hundred grammes and hand it out to

309

the street pushers. The actual distribution is often handled by gangs. There are others above them who pull the strings. At the top, there's an Uzbek family. The boss is called Victor Umarov, but no-one can get at him. Then the gangs have a whole lot of underlings, we call them dealers, who are individuals or small gangs and, in turn, dole out packages to the pushers who sell on the streets. Your brother could be a dealer or a pusher."

"And I expect the police reasoning is that he has only himself to blame."

"Maybe not quite so cynical, but yes. I'm going to check with my contact in the drug squad. But we can do some research of our own, I know where the pushers hang out." Lundgren emptied his glass and got to his feet.

"Where are you going?"

"We've got work to do."

"Now?!"

"No point in hanging around. Besides which, I need to pee."

When Tekla stood up her head started to spin. She would need a bomb to keep her going this evening.

"Are you always this impulsive?" she asked Lundgren when he came out of the toilet.

"Life is short," he said. "Let's take my car."

Tekla wondered how appropriate it was for a policeman to drive while under the influence, but decided not to ask. She followed him down to his car on Ringvägen and got in.

HÖGDALEN CENTRUM
Wednesday evening, 12.vi

It was ten o'clock by the time they parked in front of the hot dog stand in Högdalen. They had quizzed a junkie in Björns Trädgård opposite Medborgarplatsen who owed Lundgren a favour. After that they had come across two plain-clothes officers from the drug squad's street-market unit in the sunken plaza on Sergels Torg. They were having their dinner at a burger place in Vasagatan. They did not know anyone by the name of Simon Berg. But, as they said with a callous laugh: "It's not as if those guys use their real names." Tekla heaved a sigh of relief when they got back into Lundgren's B.M.W.

Once they got to the pedestrian zone of Högdalen Centrum, Lundgren looked around, searching for somebody.

"Do they know you here?"

Lundgren smiled.

"I'm not exactly someone who goes unnoticed, am I?" He fixed his eyes on something by the entrance to the Tunnelbana. "There."

After they passed the flower shop, Lundgren suddenly began to run.

Tekla chased after him. She soon realised they were pursuing a small man in a bomber jacket.

Lundgren caught up with him by the entrance to the Ica supermarket and shoved him in the back. The man fell forwards and landed on his side. Lundgren threw his large body over him and rammed his knee into his back, squashing him onto the pavement like a beetle, his arms and legs splayed.

"Take it easy, O.K.?" Lundgren said, as he made a reassuring gesture towards some people who had stopped at a safe distance to gawp at the action. "I'm a policeman."

Tekla nodded in confirmation, which seemed to have the desired effect, since the small crowd dispersed. It was not the first time they had seen violence in their pedestrian street.

"O.K., Bullseye. Do you want to talk or fight?"

The man seemed to have calmed down. He sat up when Lundgren took some of the pressure off him.

"Back off, you fucking—"

"Now, now," Lundgren said. "You know you're not supposed to use bad language." He beckoned to Tekla to come over.

The man was no more than twenty years old. With a shaved head and a beautiful face. Blue eyes giving her a cynical look. Gold ring in one ear. Tekla felt a mixture of fascination and pity.

"Bullseye here is a pusher for the Red Bears biker gang from Skärholmen. And he smokes quite a lot of hash himself. But he doesn't do anything harder. Do you?"

"What the hell do you want?"

"And since I've been cool with you in the past, I want you to tell us something."

"I don't owe you a bloody thing." The man brushed dust off his black jeans. He looked neither down at heel nor scarred. Tekla got the impression that he might even be a sporty type. Maybe he peddled drugs to top up the household budget and help his family. No harm in wishful thinking.

"Oh yes you do. Last time I let you keep a few small bags of white sweeties. Didn't I?"

Bullseye turned his head away. Revealed some tattoos that showed above his white T-shirt.

"Do you know a Simon Berg?"

Tekla shuddered to hear her brother's name like that out on the street.

"Come on, Bull. Simon? He may be a dealer, or perhaps a pusher."

"The dude with the big canines?" Bullseye said.

Tekla held her breath.

"He usually hangs out on the Farsta line."

"When did you last see him?"

The man shrugged. "Like, last week."

"Where?"

"Slussen. We were there to stock up."

"Meet your supplier?"

"I guess."

"What's the name of your dealer? Who's your dude? Give me a number."

Now the young man turned the other way and held his hand close to his body.

"Are you joking? You realise what—"

"I get that that's not how it's done. You leave a message on a mobile, someone calls you, yeah?"

For about a minute they sat there in silence. Then Bullseye whispered:

"From what I hear, he's fucked up."

"Simon?" Lundgren asked.

"Yes."

"How?"

Tekla crouched down. Her pulse was racing.

"He's fucked up, so they pulled him in yesterday at Ringen." Bullseye got to his feet. "I need to head off."

Lundgren let him go and watched him disappear quickly around the corner.

"Are you O.K.?" Lundgren said.

"A bit rattled."

"But not surprised?"

"Not really. I'm impressed by the way you got something out of him."

"I know how these guys work. You give and take. But they only give a little, so they can survive on the street."

Tekla thought about what she had seen and heard.

Fucked up.

Lundgren continued: "But now we know who he works for."

"The Uzbeks."

"It won't be the Uzbeks your brother sees, though," Lundgren said. "There are many levels of intermediaries. Like I said, we call them the dealers. Guys higher up in the hierarchy who handle the bigger packages. It's the Red Bears, a biker gang in Skärholmen, who do the dirty work. So he probably has a contact in the gang. If he really is a dealer. Or maybe only a pedlar of smaller quantities. We don't know yet."

Tekla wondered what she should do. Could she just go to Skärholmen and knock on their door?

"How do you know all this?"

"Well, it's our job. I know people on the drug squad. We talk."

"Are there many different gangs that push drugs in Stockholm?"

"They come in all shapes and sizes. From dudes peddling on their own, to gangs of more than twenty members. Often very young. Some get organised, others import directly from an uncle in Afghanistan or Colombia. There's constant competition for clients. Prices are dumped, maybe locally by some lone wolf in Rågsved; a rival gang sees that as their turf and now they have to mark their territory. So they threaten the lone wolf's sister at the hairdressing salon in Skärholmen and the lone wolf pays some Georgians to shoot one of the gang members in his car on the way to the gym. That's how the violence spreads through that particular drug chain. Very difficult to get a grip on everything, but the gangs in Hjulsta, Akalla, Tensta and those areas have got together and appear to be cooperating."

"Is that good or bad?"

"Depends on who you ask. It's not good for the Uzbeks. They think they control the whole city, but we've had information that a number of arms deals are under way."

"Do you expect that there'll be violence?"

Lundgren spread his hands in resignation.

"Who knows?"

"Assuming that he's dealing for the Uzbeks, who work with the Finns, why don't we call the police and tell them so they can go and check if he's with them? Carry out a raid or whatever it's called."

"I'll take care of it. But don't set your hopes too high," Lundgren said. "The chances that they're holding him at their premises are pretty slim. And he may already be back on the streets pushing the stuff. You did say that he's the kind who goes looking for trouble."

Tekla nodded.

"And is difficult to get hold of."

Tekla nodded again.

"I'll see if I can find anything," Lundgren went on. "But it's getting late, so perhaps we can continue tomorrow?"

"I'm grateful for all the help I can get," Tekla said. She knew that she had to get some sleep if she was to be able to work the next day. "I'll keep trying to call him."

"Are you O.K.?" Lundgren said.

"No."

"Of course not. Really sorry that . . ."

"I kind of suspected this."

"And now you know."

"Yes," Tekla said, resigned.

They began to walk, each busy with their own thoughts.

Fucked up.

Tekla shuddered.

Sardor was sweating in his leather jacket. To him, the Swedes around Stureplan were all but naked. Chicks in skin-tight white jeans and skimpy tops that did not hide a lot.

Nina pulled up in her Cadillac S.U.V.

"See you over in the park. I've just got to put the car somewhere."

Nina pulled down her sunglasses and drove off.

Brother and sister strolled aimlessly through Humlegården. Groups of people were picnicking all around them in the park. The residents of Östermalm were taking their poodles and dachshunds for a walk, the occasional jogger came running past with an outsized buggy in sport mode. Nina, in a suit, blouse and high-heeled shoes, blended in perfectly.

They passed the fountain and went on up, towards the playground.

Sardor saw that Nina had trouble deciding whether or not to leave her sunglasses on top of her head, in her short hair. Up or down. On or off.

"Should we be worrying about Pappa?" Nina said.

Sardor thought back to the way their father had dealt with the representatives of the Northern Networks in the Thai restaurant the previous day. The skill with which he had brought all that testosterone down to earth. And how he himself would have been incapable of doing something similar. But he could afford to relax a bit now. Victor no longer seemed angry with him and Eriksson for having snuffed that Albanian.

"He's not as young as he used to be."

"And whenever he moves, he starts to huff and puff."

"He went to the Nobel Hospital the other day. I think they ran some tests," Sardor said.

Nina was playing nervously with her mobile.

"Come on, let's hear it," Sardor said. "What do you really want to talk to me about?"

"I have a small confession. There's something I need to tell you . . ." She kept moving her sunglasses. "But it's got to stay between you and me."

"You'd better start talking now unless you want me to leave."

"Promise."

"Sure."

Nina hooked her sunglasses into the breast pocket of her jacket.

"There's a man with severe burns in Intensive Care at the Nobel Hospital."

"O.K."

"It's Oleg."

"Which bloody Oleg?"

"Oleg S . . . something. A Russian . . . one of the guys on the Söder Tower renovation job, who's worked for us on several projects in the archipelago. He's even been in the army for—"

"What renovation?"

"Söder Tower."

"Söder Tower? I don't know what you're talking about, Nina."

"He was found in the cellar. Burns all over his body."

"Nina!" Sardor was exasperated. "Take it from the top."

"Long story short, Jonna and I . . . when there was this possibility of getting in on the renovation works, we went all out for it. We were given the whole electrical cabling and wiring to supply and . . . well, never mind how it all happened, but you can imagine the sums we're talking about."

"So this is something Victor knows nothing about?" Sardor cut in, as the possible scale of the disaster began to sink in.

Nina avoided her brother's look.

"Jesus, Nina, what have you done?"

Nina straightened up with a jerk.

"You'd have taken the chance if it had come your way, but then you've got absolutely no idea how to make money."

"Don't go there," Sardor said grimly. "What the hell happened to that Oleg guy?"

"He was in charge of the whole thing and . . . when the fire began I immediately thought it could be the cabling . . . the stuff we'd supplied was . . . cheaper, but after a number of incidents it's no longer really used—"

"So here you supplied it under a different name?"

Nina nodded.

"Let's hear the whole story now! No bullshit."

"Chill," Nina said and fanned herself with her mobile. "Oleg knew all about it. He was the only one, apart from me and Jonna. So, there he was in the Nobel Hospital, and I realised that he could spill the beans. He's Russian, after all, not one of us. At any rate, there was too much of a risk that he might talk to the police. *If* he woke up. It simply couldn't be allowed to happen."

"My God, you sound like a full-on gangster," Sardor said, unable to hide his smile.

"Go on, twist the knife."

Sardor enjoyed seeing his sister suffer.

"So I tried to clean up. The F.S.B. were meant to take care of it, but—"

"The F.S.B.?" Sardor exploded. "For Christ's sake, Nina . . ."

"Can you keep your voice down? Yes, I reached out to them."

"But how the hell did you get in touch with . . . surely Victor's the only one who sees them?"

"Forget that," Nina said and looked away.

Sardor thought about what he had just heard. Considered various options.

"They obviously didn't succeed."

"The problem is still there," Nina sighed.

"Oleg's alive, then?"

"The police mustn't find out that it's him," Nina said.

"Come on, you're more scared of Victor than of the cops."

Nina squirmed and pulled down her sunglasses.

"It wouldn't be good if Pappa learned about this, most definitely not. And I think you'd agree with me."

Sardor began to laugh. It dawned on him that they finally had something in common: they had messed up, each in their way, and were terrified that their father would find out.

"So you want me to . . . what, kill him?"

"Of course not," Nina sniffed. "And even if I did ask you to, it would be impossible. The police have stepped up protection since the F.S.B. failed in their murder attempt. They believe that he's some sort of terrorist with Russian connections. But I thought you might have another idea. They've not been able to establish his identity. Can't we fix it so they think he's someone else? In any case, there seem to be doubts that he'll pull through. And if he does, he probably won't be talking. Would be best that way."

Sardor remembered something Eriksson had said. Something that guy Jonas in the banana cold-storage facility had told him. That he'd tried to get his friend Simon to borrow money from his sister who was a doctor at the Nobel Hospital. But that Simon had refused. Maybe she hadn't got any, Sardor thought. But she was, on the other hand, a doctor in the very hospital where Oleg was.

"And how come Pappa's girl can't fix it by herself?"

"I know you're good at these things, Sardo."

"What things?"

"Things that one . . . fixes."

"So what do I get?"

"What do you mean, get?"

"If I help you out. You haven't exactly been looking after my interests lately."

"Come on. Can't you see how humiliating it is for me to have to ask you for help?"

"And what makes that so terrible?"

"Go to hell."

"That's all I wanted. Some genuine expression of gratitude from your side."

"Will you help me, then?"

Sardor shook his head.

"You won't?" Nina exclaimed.

"It's not that," Sardor said. "It's just so typical. Victor wants us to phase out the drugs and the whores. Wants to turn us into a law-abiding family business under your direction. But now it suits you to come and ask your criminal little brother for help. When it's needed."

"Cut it out," Nina said. "Are you going to help me or not?"

Sardor nodded.

"Relax, Nina, anything for family."

KUNGSTRÄDGÅRDEN
Thursday morning, 13.vi

It was Tekla's first day off for more than two weeks. She and Lundgren were sitting in a café, surrounded by a crowd who were enjoying the morning sun in Kungsträdgården. The people of Stockholm had endured yet another long, drawn-out winter, with snow all the way into April. But now the city was looking its very best. Tekla moved her chair a step closer to Lundgren, into the shade. She thought back to what she had learned that morning. The police had no more information about the van, and Lundgren's investigations hadn't turned up anything either.

Tekla checked her mobile. Set it to flight mode and then back to normal, something had gone wrong, it kept switching itself off in her pocket and that stressed her. She sent herself a text. It worked. Then she had a look at her social media apps and was taken aback. The message she had posted on Messenger that morning had been delivered. Someone must have logged into Simon's account. She called Simon's number but got his voicemail again.

"Tekla, are you O.K.?" Lundgren said. She stopped fiddling with her mobile.

"When I woke up this morning, I had my pillow over my face," Tekla said. "I could hear pulsations in my ears. You know, when every heartbeat sounds like a thud. My hand was on my thigh and, there too, I could feel the throbbing. Suddenly I saw the entire vascular tree. Every single little branch leading from the aorta to the larger arteries in the leg, arm, throat, how they separate off and become smaller and smaller, thinner and thinner. I followed one all the way up into the forebrain. And, in my mind, I could see it bulging out.

321

A weakness in the vessel wall – an aneurism – protruded like a mushroom and looked as if it were about to rupture. Within the space of a minute or so, my brain would be filled with warm, swirling blood. I would be dead without the time for any reaction, other than a lightning headache."

"I was just about to ask if you were talking about your own blood vessels."

"I died. This morning I died right there in my uncomfortable Ikea bed."

Lundgren laughed.

"In that case, you have at least two lives. Or a neurosurgeon in the cupboard who saved your life."

Tekla shook her head.

"You don't get it."

"No."

"It felt as if, all of a sudden, I overcame death. As if I'd been given an extra life, as a bonus."

"That sounds wonderful. What kind of drug have you been testing?"

Tekla thought of the Lypsyl in her pocket.

"It brought home to me how fragile life is. And that Simon should have been dead long ago. He, if anyone, has had extra lives. At work, we're on our knees. There's not an I.C.U. bed to be had anywhere in the county. Those who suffer are the newly operated patients who have to go to ordinary wards. Every space in the I.C.U. is taken up by an overdose case."

"But why are they so many and so severe?"

"Because the dope is being mixed with other crap. Lots of organs are affected."

"Bloody hell."

"I suppose I should be asking you what the police are doing," Tekla said. "How come no-one catches the dealers?"

"I don't work in Narcotics, so I don't know the answer, but I do know that an enormous amount of extra resources have been deployed. We've been told not even to think about holidays this year."

"Literally?"

"Well, not literally. They'd have the union on their backs."

"In any case, he did get my message."

"Who did?"

"Simon."

"How do you know?" Lundgren said.

"Messenger. I saw that it arrived. Or someone's logged into his account. Probably on his mobile."

"Have you tried calling?"

"Of course. All I get is his voicemail."

"Why didn't you say something?"

Tekla tilted her head to one side.

"I'm telling you now."

"And no texts?"

"No."

"How's the morale?"

"Now you're doing it again."

"What?"

"Suddenly jumping in with a new thought," Tekla said. "You actually do that quite often."

Lundgren frowned.

"Does it bother you?"

"Not in the least. But what do you mean by . . . morale?"

Lundgren got out his mobile and a pen. He reached for a paper napkin and placed it in front of Tekla together with the pen. "You said that the mailbox responds and that your message on Messenger was delivered. Perhaps we have a window, if the mobile is switched on. Write down your brother's number."

Tekla did as Lundgren said.

"And you're O.K. to move fast if necessary?" Lundgren looked down. "You've certainly got better shoes than I do."

Tekla had no clue what he was talking about. But she felt safe with Lundgren, and would have jumped over the Niagara Falls if he had asked her to.

Lundgren picked up his mobile and dialled a number.

"Hi, it's me. Can you pick us up? In Kungsträdgården. Stop at –" Lundgren turned – ". . . we're in Karl XII's Torg . . . Great."

He made one more call and gave Simon's number. Tekla had no idea what was going on, but for once she relished the uncertainty.

"Your turn now. Call Simon."

"But he's not picking up."

"Never mind. Just call him. Let the voicemail kick in."

Tekla did as she was told. She could feel sweat breaking out along her hairline. Put down her mobile.

"Done."

"Right. Now we wait." Lundgren put on his black leather jacket. Five minutes later, Tekla saw a black car pull over by the bus stop fifty metres away.

Suddenly, Lundgren's mobile rang. "Årsta Torg. Good." He got up and set off towards the car. Tekla followed.

Two men in plain clothes were in the front seat.

"Årsta Torg," Lundgren said as he fastened his seat belt. "And let's have some flashing lights, please."

The driver pressed a button and accelerated. Tekla had not seen this coming and was thrown to the left as the car took a sharp right turn. A siren wailed and lights flashed through the windscreen.

"The guy who's driving is Jensa. The other one is Örjan."

Örjan turned around.

"Hi there."

"Hi," Tekla said.

In less than three minutes they had run every red light on the way to Årsta.

About a hundred metres from the square, Lundgren asked Örjan to switch off the blue lights.

"You can drop us." He pointed. "There, by Palmyra Kebab."

The car came to a stop on Årstavägen.

"Now we need you to find him," Lundgren said to Tekla.

She opened the door, and followed the other three, who were moving quickly towards the square.

As soon as they got to the end of a short passage in front of a hairdresser's, Tekla saw her brother's distinctive leather jacket with Darth Vader on the back. He was standing at the entrance to the Folket's Hus community centre.

"There!" She pointed, and before she had time to realise what was going on, Jensa and Örjan set off, with Lundgren in hot pursuit. Simon did not notice the plain-clothes policemen until they were thirty metres from him.

He turned, lost his footing on the gravel at first but quickly regained his balance and began to run from the square.

Tekla went after them. She had just reached Hjälmarsvägen when she saw Örjan and Jensa wrestle Simon to the ground. She crossed the road and got to the scuffle, which she knew her brother had lost before it even began. She remembered the unequal fights on the lawn. He had always been weak.

Lundgren pulled Simon to his feet and grasped him firmly from behind.

"Calm down," Tekla said.

The man stiffened.

"But . . ." Tekla said, "this isn't Simon. Who the hell are you and why have you got my brother's jacket and mobile?"

Now she recognised him. It was Simon's buddy from Ringen.

He stared at Tekla.

"What's your name?" she asked calmly.

"Jonas."

The man tried to tear himself away. Pulled and tugged, but he was held in a vice-like grip.

"Take it easy." Tekla pointed at Lundgren who was standing behind him. "This is my friend. He's also in the police, so chill. But you must tell us everything you know about Simon and what happened at Ringen."

"I don't suppose you want us to frisk you," Lundgren said in measured tones. "You wouldn't like us to find the stuff you have in your shoes or waistband, would you?"

Jonas stiffened. He looked as if he were thinking of protesting.

"O.K. I'm cool."

"Great," Lundgren said.

Tekla looked at the stained and worn black jeans. She noticed that he smelled of both urine and earth.

"They beat the shit out of me. Then they let me go, and the same day I was meeting Simon at Ringen. They must have followed me. We'd hardly said hello when they suddenly showed up."

"Why did they take Simon?"

"I don't know."

"Come on, Jonas. I was there."

Slowly he picked some gravel from his hand.

"What had you been up to? Taken some money off someone?"

"I'd messed up a bit. But it's all good now."

Gently, Tekla touched the ugly wounds on his temple. He was black and blue with one eye swollen shut and a busted lip.

"So they just had a go at you for the hell of it?"

Jonas tried to free himself, but Lundgren was too strong.

"We know that you and Simon work the street," Tekla said. "For the Uzbeks."

Jonas' nod was barely visible. She felt a lump in her stomach when she saw how emaciated he was. His cheeks were hollow. His stubbly beard was sparse, making him look even more like a down-and-out.

"Do you know where Simon is?"

"No."

"But where did they take you when they beat you up?" Lundgren said.

"I don't know. I had something over my head."

"What had you done to piss them off?" Tekla asked.

Jonas was silent.

"And why do you have Simon's telephone?" Tekla said.

He still said nothing.

"Was it you who texted me?"

Jonas avoided Tekla's look.

She saw the message down in the service tunnels: I need help!

"What kind of help did you need?"

Lundgren shook Jonas and said: "Come on!"

"We needed to borrow some money."

"And Simon didn't want to ask me, right?" Tekla said. She felt her throat tightening.

"I guess," Jonas whispered.

"So you nicked his mobile and texted me. Thinking you could perhaps persuade me if we met at Ringen."

Jonas nodded.

"But Simon didn't know about your plan?"

"No."

Tekla shook her head. She could see that Jonas was scared out of his wits.

"You're good friends, aren't you?"

She looked at Simon's old leather jacket. Only a close friend would be allowed to borrow that.

"Do you have any other number for Simon?"

"Yes."

He looked almost relieved to be able to help.

"I want it," Tekla said.

Jonas gave it to her and she keyed it into her mobile.

"Now I've got to get out of here," he said, sounding almost desperate. He tried to pull himself loose and Lundgren let go of one arm. Jonas turned and for the first time saw Lundgren's face.

Tekla registered the fear in Jonas' eyes. She also noticed how surprised Lundgren looked. Then Jonas freed his other arm with a jerk and ran away.

"Wait!" Tekla called and started running after him. Suddenly she felt Lundgren catch hold of her.

"Let go of me," she shouted. "We've got to get—"

"Let him run," Lundgren said sharply and held on to Tekla.

"Let go!" she screamed, but saw that Jonas had already reached the school. He disappeared into the streets of a residential area.

"What the fuck!" Tekla shouted and stared at Lundgren, whose face had turned white. "Why didn't you hang on to him?"

"He had no more information."

Tekla looked at Jensa and Örjan. Lundgren took Tekla to one side.

"Just calm down, will you?" he tried, but Tekla was shaking with frustration.

She looked at Lundgren.

"You recognised him, didn't you?"

"Who? Me? No."

Tekla brushed aside his hand and began walking towards the police car. She turned to Örjan and said, more an order than a request: "Can you drop me off at Gullmarsplan?"

Lundgren closed the car door. He could hear the heavy rhythm of the drums pumping out of the split-level house on the very tip of Stora Essingen. "Africa" by Toto. He hooked his sunglasses into the front of his short-sleeved shirt and walked past Dahl's 1000 cc bike, which was standing there in the drive, glittering in the sunlight. Lundgren stepped up to the door and tried the handle. Locked. The music was playing so loudly that the windows at the back of the house were vibrating. In some irritation he pressed the doorbell, but the sound was drowned out by Bobby Kimball's light voice. Had the house not been so isolated, surrounded by large trees and bushes, irate neighbours would have put a stop to it long ago.

Lundgren went past the garage and around the house. Teak outdoor furniture and the largest gas barbecue he had ever seen were set up along the short side. The last time he had been there, Dahl had given a sangria party for some thirty people and grilled a whole pig. Lundgren passed the flowering lilac bushes and climbed the steps to the large terrace that ran along the front of the house. One of the big sliding glass doors was open. Music came streaming out towards Mälaren, and could no doubt be heard all the way to Gröndal, he thought, as he entered the sitting room. It looked as if the green marble floor had just been cleaned, there were a few damp spots here and there.

"Hello! Håkan! Where the hell are you?"

No reply. And no sign of a cleaner either. The music switched to Earth, Wind & Fire's "Boogie Wonderland". Lundgren went into the kitchen, but there was no-one there. Only a bowl with some left-over yoghurt in the sink. He looked around, out over the long lawn, which stretched all the way down to a small boathouse by Dahl's jetty. There he was. Busy with his boat.

Lundgren went down to join him.

"Lucky you've got understanding neighbours."

"Magnus!" Dahl said, and looked up.

He was in the boat, working at something by the engine. "This is great, I could really use—"

"What exactly was that deal you and I had?" Lundgren cut in. He was standing with the morning sun at his back and Dahl had to pull down his cap to be able to see his friend's face.

"Just a moment. What are you talking about?"

"Haninge. I very much hope you haven't been lying."

Dahl had one hand on top of the large motor and was trying to attach something with the other.

"Can you help me?"

"You can do that later," Lundgren said, irritated.

Dahl looked up and smiled. He wiped off the sweat with his bare forearm. "Sure, but I'm in a bit of a fix. I've just mounted this 300 hp baby on the boat and can't get the last screw to go in. Could you just pull this here? Then I'm done."

Reluctantly, Lundgren jumped down next to Dahl and took hold of the motor above the casing.

"Christ, it's heavy," Lundgren said. "I suppose you had to buy the biggest one on the market."

"You can get larger ones," Dahl said, tightening the screw with both hands. "What did you want to talk about?"

Lundgren mopped his forehead and narrowed his eyes against the brilliant sunlight.

"My God, it's hot."

"So early in the morning too," Dahl said.

"Must be climate change," Lundgren said and looked at the motor. "How appropriate to buy a thing like that."

Dahl wiped the oil off his hands.

"What time do you start work?"

"Ten. And you?"

"Admin day," Dahl said.

The boat bobbed up and down in the wash of a passing motorboat.

"So, what was it you wanted?"

Lundgren felt a little calmer after the exertion with the motor.

"I hope for your sake that you don't have a whole lot of loose ends dangling after the Haninge raid."

"Jesus, you're in a state over that business," Dahl said and pretended to hit Lundgren's arm. "I hope you gave the money to the investigator like I told you?"

"Yes, there were no problems there. He came with the forensics, right after the patrol had taken care of the guys."

"So what's bothering you?"

"I bumped into one of the dealers yesterday," Lundgren said.

"What dealer?"

"One of the blokes who was there when I took the money in Haninge."

"I see," Dahl said tersely. "Where?"

"In Årsta. When I was trying to help Tekla find her brother. You know, the doctor."

Dahl picked up a fender and began tying it between the boat and the jetty.

"We've been hanging out for two days now. She's awesome," Lundgren said.

"Hanging out?" Dahl said, miming quotation marks in the air.

"We haven't had sex, if that's what you're getting at. But she was at my place yesterday. Nothing happened."

"What a waste of time," Dahl said. Then he gave a coarse laugh. "Just kidding. But good for you."

"It seems her brother is dealing for the Uzbeks, and now they've locked him up somewhere. We're trying to find out where he might be."

Dahl put his hands on his thighs and looked at his friend.

"The Uzbeks?"

"We believe so. Why? What are you thinking?"

"Nothing."

Lundgren could tell that Dahl's mood had switched.

"So, this guy in Haninge's called Jonas. He recognised me."

"What the hell are you talking about?" Dahl asked and got to his feet. He took out a tin of snus and made himself a big pinch.

"He recognised me from the raid in Haninge."

"Weren't you wearing a balaclava?"

"I'd pulled it down."

"Bloody hell, Magnus," Dahl said, shaking his head. "Are you serious?"

"Yes, unfortunately. What was I supposed to do? Put a bullet in their heads?"

Dahl fell silent. Left the question hanging there in the morning breeze. He was thinking. Stuffed the pinch of snus inside his lip and said:

"No worries."

"What do you mean, 'no worries'?"

"Take it easy," Dahl said. "I'll deal with this." He jumped up onto the jetty and pulled out a big chain with a block lock. He secured the boat at the bow.

"How?" Lundgren said. He climbed out of the boat and sat down on the bench by the boathouse. Fiddled with a fishing rod that was propped up against the dark red wall. Dahl joined him and the bench sagged under his weight.

"What did you say her name was? Your doctor babe."

"Tekla."

"What else?"

"Tekla Berg. Why?" Lundgren asked.

"And this guy Jonas is her brother?"

"No. The brother's friend."

"And what's the brother called?"

"Simon."

Dahl thought. "Do you have his number?"

"Absolutely," Lundgren said and produced two wallets from his trouser pocket. "I took their wallets as well during the raid. In case . . ."

Dahl burst out laughing and slapped Lundgren's thigh.

"Good work, Magnus. You're not as half-witted as you look."

Lundgren held out the wallets. "Yesterday Tekla got a new number for Simon. His friend had nicked his old mobile."

Dahl looked surprised. "Some friend."

"There's just one thing . . ." Lundgren hesitated.

"What?"

"Well, I really screwed up, I left my Sig Sauer behind in Haninge."

"You *what*?"

"Forgot my pistol."

Dahl jumped up and swayed frantically.

"I've changed my mind. You *are* a bloody moron, for Christ's sake."

"Give me a break," Lundgren said.

"I can't believe anyone can be so dumb."

"You think I did it on purpose?"

Dahl thought for a while. Pushed back the snus that had slipped down over his teeth.

"But—"

"I've reported it, yes," Lundgren said. "But I wrote that I lost the pistol on another raid."

Dahl heaved a sigh of relief. "Well, that's one good thing, at least."

"I have to get to work," Lundgren said and stood up. They set off towards the house. "Purple Rain" by Prince was pouring from the loudspeakers.

"Does this have anything to do with the bruises on your face?" Lundgren asked.

"What do you mean?"

"The money in Haninge. Did it belong to—"

"No, no," Dahl interrupted him. "You can relax. This was something to do with chicks." He put his hand to his cheek, which was still green and yellow. "For real. Chicks can be dangerous, sometimes."

The previous day's events had left Tekla shaken. Now she knew that Simon was dealing heroin for some criminal Uzbeks with connections to a biker gang from Skärholmen. She had also discovered that Simon's friend Jonas had stolen his mobile to try and trick her into lending them money. She had no idea how much, but probably a large sum. And then there was Lundgren's strange reaction when he saw Jonas' face. It was obvious that they knew each other. And Lundgren had let Jonas get away. Tekla had tried in vain to call Simon's new mobile, but it was switched off. She badly wanted to get hold of Jonas again.

It had been a tough morning in A. & E. Lundgren had texted her repeatedly, both the night before and that morning. He wanted them to meet again, wrote that he really wanted to help her find her brother. Tekla had not answered; she was seriously angry with him.

She went up to the I.C.U. for her daily meeting. The first thing that struck her was that there were no guards outside the burns unit. And Nilsén was waiting in an armchair in the corridor.

She stood up. "Hello, doctor. I just wanted to wind this up in a civilised way."

"Wind up?"

"The case. We've found the perpetrators."

"Now you've lost me." Tekla sat down.

"We managed to trace the van to a rental firm in Malmö. After that, it wasn't too difficult to identify the people who rented it: five football fans on their way to the Hammarby–Malmö game. They were in a garage preparing some Bengal lights and a few other pyrotechnic devices. But it all went wrong. Some rubbish started to burn and then some of the new electrical wiring being installed. They just hopped into the van and took off before it all blew up."

"You're joking?"

"Luckily not."

"Luckily?"

Nilsén picked up her leather jacket and draped it elegantly over her arm.

"This way we don't need to run around looking for terrorists."

"But what exactly exploded?"

"That's a bit unclear. Maybe the petrol tank of a car. They're still working on it."

"So it had nothing to do with the F.S.B.?"

Nilsén smiled.

"Nothing. You can forget all that."

Tekla gestured towards the room where the man with the burns was being treated.

"But what about him? Why would someone want to kill him?"

"You mean when he was attacked on Sunday?"

"Yes."

Tekla wondered what was so special about the injured man she had, for a long time, believed to be Simon. Who was he really?

"We don't know. And we're not planning to pursue that investigation either," Nilsén said.

"Why on earth not?"

"Oh, you haven't heard?"

"What?"

"He died. They're just—"

"What?"

"Sorry."

Nilsén put a hand on Tekla's arm.

"But who was he?"

"Who knows . . . Homeless. Junkie. Refugee in hiding . . . But who actually cares?"

"I do."

"Good. That way he had at least one person in this world who did." Nilsén picked up her bag and got ready to leave. "I just wanted to thank you personally for all your help."

Tekla stared vacantly along the corridor.

"All the best, Dr Berg. Perhaps we'll meet again."

Slowly, Tekla went back to A. & E., feeling both empty and angry. She tried to calm herself down. She did eventually manage to text her supplier that she needed topping up. The drawer at home in the kitchen was empty, and she had only about ten bombs left. Given the rate at which she was consuming them, that would scarcely see her through the next twenty-four hours.

She was about to ask for a new patient, when the lead nurse drew her attention to two men who were standing waiting a short distance from her.

"They're asking to see you. Shall I call the guards?"

"Me personally?"

"Tekla Berg. Said it was private."

Tekla looked at the men. One was quite short and in his forties, with black hair cut in a straight fringe, wearing a leather jacket and jeans. The other was at least a head taller, and also dressed in leathers.

"Go ahead and call the guards, I'll start talking to them."

Moussawi seemed also to have noticed the men. Tekla gave her recently acquired protector a reassuring signal.

"I'm Tekla Berg."

"Sardor Umarov," said the shorter of the two men. He held out his hand, but Tekla did not take it. She was taken aback by her ice-cold reaction.

"Hygiene regulations."

"Talking of which, I'd say you definitely have a problem with your drains." Sardor looked around. "Tell me, doctor, is there anywhere we can talk undisturbed?"

Tekla pointed at a door immediately behind him.

"The relatives' room."

They sat down on opposite sofas. Between them was a round pine table with a shallow glass bowl containing water and some flat stones. Next to it stood a glass candlestick with an unused candle in it. An enormous box of tissues. The walls were hung with large black and white photographs of tranquil scenes from nature: a deserted beach in autumn covered in reeds, a billowing field of corn with a tumbledown log cabin, a spring view of the mountains in Norrland when the snow is melting.

"You know Simon, don't you?" Sardor said.

Tekla felt her pulse shoot up.

"Where *is* Simon?"

"You're his sister?"

"Are you the ones who kidnapped him?"

Sardor looked Tekla up and down.

"I think you get the picture. Being the smart doctor that you are. You analyse and, what's it called . . . diagnose." He leaned forward. Studied her face. Tekla sat still.

"He's messed up big time. Owes us money."

"Where is he?" Tekla repeated. She felt herself shaking inside, but decided to stick it out for a few more minutes.

Sardor grinned and clapped his hands together with a bang that almost made Tekla lower her eyes.

"He's O.K. So far. But when you think what a little shit he is and the way he's fucked it all up for himself, then—"

"If you do anything to my brother . . ."

"Then what?" Sardor said calmly.

Tekla tried to control her breathing. Her head was spinning. She gritted her teeth.

"If you help us, we'll let Simon go."

"Help you?"

Over her dead body would she embark on a criminal career by committing some offence for this self-righteous gangster.

"Do you know of a man with severe burns in Intensive Care?"

"Why?"

"We want you to give him a new identity," Sardor said.

"What are you talking about?"

"He still hasn't been identified, has he?"

"I can't tell you."

Tekla had no intention of letting on that the burns patient had died.

"Well, I know he hasn't," Sardor said.

"Was . . . is he an Uzbek?" Tekla exclaimed in surprise.

Sardor seemed to be regretting what he had said. The doctor was gaining confidence.

"You haven't heard a thing."

"O.K., so he's an Uzbek," Tekla said triumphantly.

"We want him to get a new identity. By using the personal identity number of some . . . down-and-out or something."

Tekla nodded cautiously. Played along. She understood what they wanted of her.

"And what guarantee do I have that you'll leave me and my brother in peace afterwards?"

"I swear on my great-grandmother's grave. That's sacrosanct in our culture."

"And you'll let Simon go?"

Sardor nodded.

"I'll see what I can do," Tekla said.

"You have until Monday."

"I guess this is where I ask 'and if I don't?'"

"Come on, doctor. Now you disappoint me. You didn't protest when I said you were smart." He quickly drew a hand across his throat. Sardor smiled quietly and gave Tekla a slip of paper with a number on it.

"Here's where you can reach me. There won't be anything more. After that I promise we won't bother you again."

"Bother. Nice euphemism for blackmail."

338

"Call it what you like."

Tekla stared at Sardor's scarred face, then glanced up at his silent companion, who was standing behind him.

Sardor smiled.

"You're quick on the uptake. We'll let your brother go when you've fixed a new identity for the guy with the burns."

Tekla nodded briefly.

"And don't call the police, will you? Because if you do, you'll never see your brother alive again."

The two men left the room. Tekla remained seated, looking at the piece of paper, before crumpling it up and throwing it into a waste-paper bin. She knew there would never be an end to this. The nightmare would just go on and on. The minute she did something criminal, they'd use it against her. Ask her for more, maybe have her steal drugs. No, she would have nothing to do with these people. The man with the burns was dead now, anyway, as they would probably soon find out. At which point the "offer" would no longer stand. She had to think of some other way to get Simon released.

Tekla left the relatives' room and found Moussawi watching her.

"What was all that about?" he asked.

"A threat," Tekla said softly.

Moussawi glanced behind him, as if to make sure the men had indeed left.

"A threat?"

"Yes."

"Tell me."

Tekla was thinking. Sardor had said not to call the police, but nothing about telling anyone else.

"O.K., why not."

For some reason, her gut told her that she should talk to Moussawi. He, if anyone, would understand her dilemma, she thought. She described the meeting with Jonas in Årsta, the kidnapping of Simon, and told him what they wanted her to do.

"Did you say Umarov?"

"Why?"

"I'll help you," Moussawi said.

Tekla looked in surprise at the man who had given her such a hard time, whom she had disliked pretty much from her first day at the hospital. But something had happened in the last week. He had made an about-turn.

"I don't need any help."

"Yes, you do. Do you know why?"

"Tell me."

"You haven't got it in you."

Tekla hesitated briefly.

"I'll go to the police," she said.

"Go on, do it then. Get out your mobile." Moussawi saw her hesitation and continued. "But you won't do it. Because you know that then your brother might not come back alive."

Tekla lapsed into thought.

"My friend," Moussawi said, "have I told you what I did back home in Iraq? Do you know that I took part in the war against Iran in the '80s? That for five years I was a soldier in an elite unit whose job was to cross the border at night and conduct lightning raids on villages? Every night, in my dreams, the things we did there come back to haunt me. And will do until the day I go to sleep for good. Then I had had enough, and trained to be a doctor. I spent the rest of that war taking care of the wounded."

"No, I knew none of that."

"Do you have any idea the sort of things I've done?"

"I can't even begin to imagine."

Moussawi struck his chest with his fist. "I have a rock-solid ethic. My own. An excellent moral compass for what is right and wrong. But my right doesn't always tally with what the law says."

"Surely this would be an offence."

"You want to save your brother?"

"Yes, but—"

"Well, let's do it, then you can forget about those characters."

Tekla didn't know what to say. But she realised that she needed Moussawi if she were to give a false identity to the man with the burns.

"I could never kill anybody," Tekla said.

"Believe me, my friend, if the circumstances required it, you could."

"Never," Tekla said firmly. "I'm not condemning anything you've done. I can only speak for myself. Life takes precedence over everything."

Moussawi and Tekla walked side by side down the long corridor, away from the entrance lobby. To an outsider, they probably looked as if they were discussing a complicated medical case.

"Will you be alright with this?" Moussawi asked. "You don't look all that . . . good. How about going off sick for a day?"

"I'm O.K. I'll get some rest later on. In any case, I'm too busy to worry about how I feel."

"Anything for the family."

This jolted Tekla back into the past. She saw images of her mother in Nynäshamn, in the home where they cared for her dementia.

"Anything for the family. But how do you suggest we go about fixing a new identity for a dead patient?"

"We're not going to."

Tekla was confused. Moussawi pressed the lift button. He stood with his weight evenly distributed above his large feet and waited patiently for the elevator. Tekla felt anything but calm.

"Something tells me that they'll keep your brother anyway. You need to shift the balance of power."

"And do you have any idea how that's supposed to happen?"

"Maybe."

"Tell me."

"I need a computer."

Up on the ninth floor, Moussawi went into his office and pulled up a chair for Tekla. He logged on to the computer.

"Here," he said, pointing at the screen. "I was planning to call him in for an urgent appointment. This afternoon. I seem suddenly to have a free slot. You could be there too. And . . . chat to him a little. A bit of special treatment."

Tekla read the notes in the file. A man had come in on Tuesday for an emergency consultation because of breathing difficulties. Sigurdsdottir had removed some fluid from the pleura and they now had the results of the cytology test: adenosquamous cancer cells. A highly unusual form of lung cancer. The patient had to be summoned as soon as possible to be informed and discuss treatment.

When she saw who the patient was, Tekla shuddered.

She looked at the name one more time.

Victor Umarov.

V

Tekla crossed the car park at the back of the hospital. She was on her way to buy some lunch and also meet her dealer.

Suddenly she heard "Tekla!" She looked up and saw Carlsson standing there, car keys in hand. "How are things?"

"Hi. Well . . . it's . . . kind of tough."

Carlsson closed the car door.

"I heard about the burns patient in the I.C.U."

Tekla nodded.

"Tragic. I know how involved you were in the case. And talking of involvement," Carlsson continued, "the Health and Social Care Inspectorate will be here this afternoon, together with people from the public property administration. To inspect our premises."

As usual, Tekla found it difficult to keep up with Carlsson's zigzag train of thought.

"The Health and Social Care Inspectorate . . ."

"That's right." Carlsson sounded delighted. "And the stench is going to be especially bad."

"It is . . . ?"

"And it would be great if we could have some positive input from our colleague who represents the union."

Tekla's eyes moved nervously.

"Oh yes. I've talked to Klein-Borgstedt. And she has . . . a suggestion."

Carlsson looked intently at Tekla.

"Before you tell me. Is it her suggestion, or your suggestion to her that she thought was a good one?"

"The former."

"I appreciate your honesty."

Tekla braced herself. "Klein-Borgstedt is proposing that her research group get a grant of one million over the next two years. In this hospital, research hasn't been—"

"Yes," Carlsson interrupted her.

"Yes, what?"

"That'll be fine. You can tell her. I just have to fix the paperwork, it'll take a few days, but she has my word. She'll get her research grant."

"Just like that?"

Carlsson took a step forward, and for a split second Tekla thought that the C.E.O. was going to pat her cheek, as if she were a little girl. But Carlsson was only reaching out to shake her hand.

"It's not just like that. There are many of us who stand to benefit from a P.P.P."

"You mean financially?"

Carlsson smiled.

"You've got to learn when it's *not* the right time to ask every question that pops up inside that fantastic head of yours."

"Sorry."

"Not to worry. I should really be thanking you, Tekla," Carlsson said, unlocking her car door. "For letting me into your universe." The C.E.O. stopped and looked across at the skyline over Roslagstull. "Isn't this a great evening to have some fun? A visit to Dramaten theatre with Gregor . . . or maybe dinner at Wedholms Fisk? Haven't been for a long time."

"I don't know."

Partying was the last thing on Tekla's mind.

"I can already see the Inspectorate report in front of me," Carlsson went on, pretending to hold a sheet of paper in her hand.

"You mean . . ."

"They're bound to have something to say about the smell in particular."

346

"Most probably."

"Which means we'll be rapped across the knuckles. Which puts us under time pressure to renovate. And for a renovation you need . . . ?"

"Money."

"Of which there isn't any in the current budget of the County Commissioner for finance," Carlsson said with delight.

"So . . . ?"

Tekla thought she knew what the C.E.O. was getting at, but she had learned how these conversations went: wait and let Carlsson have the last word.

"When the public well runs dry, we have to turn to the private sector."

"P.P.P., in other words."

"Kallax did the job."

Tekla looked puzzled.

"The *surströmming* brand. You don't like it much, do you?" Carlsson said.

"No. Although I'm from Jämtland, I'm not a huge fan of rotten fish." But at least Tekla now understood.

"And I was raised on shrimps from the west coast, yet occasionally I really crave some *surströmming* on flatbread. Odd, isn't it, how one's taste can change later in life?"

Carlsson leaned into the car and brought out a bag of liquorice monkeys. She tore open the plastic. Put two sweets into her mouth. Offered some to Tekla who shook her head.

"Now we go into round two," Carlsson said.

"A P.P.P. can take a long time," Tekla said. "From the little I've read."

"So you *have* been reading up on P.P.P.s," Carlsson said, looking at Tekla through narrowed eyes.

"Only one—"

"Do you imagine that's what they thought when they built the Empire State Building?"

Carlsson surveyed the car park.

"What do you mean?"

"They saw time as their worst enemy. Three and a half thousand labourers worked their butts off. That skyscraper was inaugurated forty-five days ahead of schedule. It's all down to attitude."

Tekla stood silently, pondering what Carlsson had said. She could feel her body itching. She was going to be late for her dealer.

"So you're *not* planning to wait for the normal process to run its course?" Tekla said.

"Then there's our research, which needs a serious boost. And the I.C.U. We'll lick her into shape, you'll see."

"Her?"

"The ship."

Carlsson popped another liquorice monkey into her mouth and turned towards the hospital.

"It's lucky that we have people like you, Tekla, working with us. You've already been a big help. And I have a feeling that you'll continue to be so in the future."

"I'm happy to do what I can," Tekla said, without having the faintest idea what Carlsson had in mind.

"The normal process . . . does that sound like me?" Carlsson said.

"I don't know you all that well."

It did, however, strike Tekla that she'd had more discussions – and more serious discussions – with Carlsson than with any other person over the past year.

"But will it all work out in the end, do you think?" Carlsson said. "I mean with me pushing it, the way I am?"

"It looks like it."

Carlsson sniffed.

"You don't sound convinced." She took a deep breath. "I've made up my mind."

"What about?" Tekla said nervously.

"It's going to be a really good bottle of Chablis with Gregor at Wedholms Fisk tonight."

Carlsson opened her car door. Tekla was about to leave when she heard:

"Do also tell Klein-Borgstedt that the research council has had instructions to make savings over the next five years. Say you got it from Collinder, not from me."

Carlsson jumped into her car and was gone.

Tekla was walking down towards Tanto when it dawned on her what she'd done. Bloody hell. Lying to Carlsson was taking a big risk. Now she couldn't postpone it any longer. Since Klein-Borgstedt had taken a few days off, she'd have to call her. Ten minutes later, Tekla had managed to convince her to have the union back the hospital management's plans for a P.P.P. agreement. One million in research funds over two years was more than she could ever have dreamed of.

Umarov was unable to find a comfortable position on the hard leather sofa. For the third time now, he went over to the reception desk and tapped on the glass with his signet ring. He was not remotely bothered by the irritated looks of the other patients.

"Has the ventilation system in here packed up or something?"

"I think you'd better sit down so you don't faint. Dr Moussawi will be along very soon," the nurse told him.

"That's what you said a quarter of an hour ago."

"Outpatients is very busy today. The doctors are working as fast as they can, but, as you know, we've got—"

"Moussawi. Sounds like a Greek pie. He'd better be good at his job."

"Dr Moussawi is one of our absolute—"

"Yeah, yeah."

Umarov paced up and down in the waiting area. He wished that Elena could have accompanied him, but his visit had been arranged at too short notice. The appointment he had been given was "a cancellation", and they had recommended that he not turn it down.

When the nurse finally called his name, he dismissed his bodyguards with a wave of the hand.

"Sardor said—"

"To hell with Sardor. I don't want anyone else in the room when I get a finger shoved up my arse."

Umarov followed the nurse down a corridor with orange doors and was shown into Tariq Moussawi's office. The tall man whom

Umarov had seen the other day in A. & E. stood up and shook his hand.

"Welcome. Please take a seat."

Umarov settled onto a hard chair with a metal frame, ending up at least ten centimetres lower than the doctor on the other side of the desk.

"Umarov," Moussawi said. "Uzbekistan?"

"Glad someone could see me so quickly," Umarov said. "But too bad one has to wait so long once one gets here."

Moussawi rubbed his smooth cheek and looked at the patient opposite him.

"It's *palov*, isn't it? Very similar to many Iraqi dishes. In my battalion I had a Kurdish friend, whose mother I believe was from Uzbekistan. Or maybe his grandmother? Or sister . . ." Moussawi looked up at the ceiling dreamily. "In any case, it was delicious. Lamb and rice."

Umarov pulled at his shirt and strained to draw in as much breath as possible.

"You *are* from Uzbekistan, aren't you?"

"Originally, yes, but—"

"Is it called *palov*?"

"Have you got the results back from my tests?"

Moussawi was absent-mindedly tapping away at the computer beside him.

"I come from a family that was really serious about horses. My uncle back in Bardarash had horses. Not racehorses like the fantastic animals you have, they were mostly draught horses. But that feeling of a large, muscular, steaming beast in winter is something that stays in your blood. Don't you agree? You never forget that sensation."

Umarov looked around the sterile room. A washbasin and a mirror. An examination bed with a paper cover. Two windows with blinds that were pulled down. A rubbish bag on a white stand.

He craned his neck to read the name on the doctor's badge.

The only sound in the room came from the fan of the computer's hard drive.

"Listen . . . Tariq, I really don't care about horses, I'm not interested in animals. The only thing I care about is finding out if I have a dangerous disease and if you can remove this fluid in my lungs so I can host three hundred people at a small do tomorrow. Do you think you can fix that? Don't know where you got your training, but I'm sure it'll be good enough."

Moussawi stood up and unbuttoned his white coat. Unlike the other doctors there, he was always smartly dressed under his coat: a shirt and tie and dark trousers with turn-ups. He walked round the desk and looked up at the clock above the door.

"Royal College of Physicians."

Umarov looked confused.

"I'm a Member of the Royal College of Physicians in London, in case you were wondering."

"If you say so."

"I'm not saying anything. That's what it's called."

"Could we focus on—"

"The pleural cavity."

"What?" Umarov said, paying more attention now that it was beginning at last to sound as if they were talking about a medical condition.

"Fluid has accumulated between the visceral and the parietal pleura, the two membranes of the pleural cavity. It's a bit like two balloons that normally lie one against the other, but here, in your case, they've got fluid between them."

"O.K. Perfect. Can you magic away that fluid?"

Moussawi went over to the mirror by the washbasin, leaned forward and pulled out a thick, silver-grey hair from the middle of his wavy fringe. Then he ambled across to a shiny metal stool by the examination bed along the wall and sat down.

"Absolutely. We can do a bit of *magic*." Moussawi patted the examination bed. "Lie down here, please."

Umarov heaved himself out of the narrow chair and sat on the bed.

"I said lie," Moussawi told him in a matter-of-fact tone and pulled over a trolley. He removed a green cloth that had been draped over a number of medical instruments and drugs.

Umarov lay down on his back while eyeing the trolley nervously. Immediately, his breathing became more laboured.

"What's going on?"

Moussawi began systematically to pick his way through various flasks and packages.

"But we do have one thing in common: for centuries we've been squeezed between the large powers."

Umarov gazed up at the tall man's head. It was square, as if roughly hewn out of a large rock. His voice was low and rumbling, at the same time rasping and a little threatening.

"The Russians, the Mongols, the Chinese, the British . . . a curse to have so many borders to defend, don't you agree, my friend? But you Uzbeks have always been glorious warriors. You can take off your shirt so you don't get blood all over it."

Blood. Umarov struggled to remove his shirt. He was cold.

"We know how to fight, absolutely."

Moussawi's face brightened and he thumped his chest.

"Brute force rather than finesse, am I right?"

Umarov tried to smile until he saw a long needle, a syringe filled with liquid, come closer.

"First, something to calm you."

"It's not necessary—"

"Yes, it is. Lie still now."

Umarov felt a needle-prick in his arm. The muscle contracted a little.

Methodically, Moussawi began to disinfect the side of Umarov's thorax. The fluid felt like dry ice on the skin. The whole of his body started to shake.

"Do you have any problems with dental anaesthesia?" Moussawi said.

353

"What are you going to do to my teeth?"

Moussawi placed a large hand on Umarov's chest. It felt as if he were running out of air. His heart was racing.

"Have you ever had a bad reaction to an anaesthetic?"

"Er . . . no."

"Good. Here's the needle going in."

Umarov felt another jab; this one hurt more. He thought of Elena and his prick, and the solemn promise he had made that it would once again stand erect. He felt his heart beating harder and harder, as if it were caught inside a metal tin and wanted to get out.

Moussawi pulled on a fresh pair of gloves and placed a cloth over the sterile field.

"You're going to feel another prick."

Tears welled up in his eyes as the doctor inserted a sharp object into his side. He could feel the pain all the way to his spine. His heart nearly jumped out of his chest. He considered asking for more anaesthetic but decided to grit his teeth. His hands were ice cold and shaking, as if he had been chilled to twenty below zero.

"Done," Moussawi said. "It's trickling out. Now you have to lie absolutely still."

"Is it looking good?" Umarov managed to ask while shivering.

"Just as it should."

"And how come I've got that fluid there? Don't mince your words, how much longer have I got?"

Umarov felt his ears beginning to roar, he heard the doctor fiddling with something.

"Unilateral pleural effusion is rarely a good thing. If it's your prostate cancer that's metastasised, you have anywhere between six months to ten years left, depending on the treatment we give you. But it could be something different . . ."

Suddenly, Umarov had the elephant standing on his chest again. Six months. It couldn't be true. He felt as if he were about to faint from the pain. He barely noticed the doctor getting up and going over to a door, which he opened.

The rasping voice returned, more intense this time.

"We had been out on the front line for at least two months and were on the way home when it happened. I'm not going to blame my platoon commander, may his soul rest in peace, but he was an incompetent idiot who decided to take a shortcut through a mountain pass that day. I suppose he was just as tired and hungry as the rest of us, but for God's sake, you don't improvise in the field like that. I'm sure you know, I imagine you've seen a thing or two yourself . . ."

Umarov was feeling dizzy. His hands were alternately shaking and cramping. Was there someone else in the room?

Moussawi went on telling his tale. "It was in the afternoon, right before a rest break, there was a bang. Those bastards had followed us and waited for the right moment, just when we were at our most tired and vulnerable. They were firing with a mortar from the top of a ridge. I had gone off to relieve myself behind some rocks, so I and one other were the only survivors. I retreated, all I had were my pistol and a knife. I managed to make my way round the rise where they were lying and firing at us. They didn't see me creep up, there were only four of them. I got two of them, one died straight away and I finished off the other one later on, and the—"

Suddenly a female voice could be heard: "Hello, Victor."

Umarov looked up and saw a female doctor leaning over him.

"What—"

"Lie very still," Moussawi said softly, close to Umarov's face. "If you move, you'll bleed to death. I've inserted the drain right next to your aorta, unfortunately I *forgot* to pull out the sharp guidewire, so if it moves even a millimetre, the tip of the wire will puncture the blood vessel and you'll be dead within—"

"Like, a minute," Tekla piped up. She looked at the flasks on the trolley. "I see you gave him Ventolin instead of morphine. Any palpitations, Victor?"

Umarov looked terrified and tried to control his breathing.

"Clearly," Tekla said. "A side effect of a hefty dose of asthma medication. And saline solution instead of anaesthetic. Naughty boy, Tariq."

"What the hell are you—"

"There, there, Victor," Tekla said and sat down on the examination table by his feet. "Think of that needle next to the aorta."

Umarov took a deep breath and wished he had not told the bodyguards to stay outside.

Moussawi continued his story: "The guy with the mortar was lying on the ground, but the last man was on his feet so he managed to turn and fire off a few shots. I got one in the thigh, but I only noticed it later on. I'd run out of ammunition, but pulled out my knife, threw myself onto the guy with the pistol and stabbed him in the throat. He lay there, bleeding, while the man with the mortar and I rolled around in the mud. He got in a couple of punches, but I saw red, I just wanted him to die, you know that numbing feeling when you don't care what happens to you, all that matters is getting rid of the bloke, and I was going to do the job with my own hands. He passed out when I banged his head on a rock. Then I tied him up and took off his jacket. After that, all I remember is the calm and methodical way in which my hand hacked and hacked at his entire body until I buried the knife in his chest, sort of twisted it around until it came spilling out, that warm, beautiful, pulsating—"

"Bloody lunatics, do you know who I am?" Umarov hissed.

"Shall we twist that drain a little?" Moussawi said.

Umarov felt a new, more explosive pain radiate through the whole of his thorax as his ribs were pulled apart. Just as he opened his mouth to let out an almighty roar, the pain suddenly disappeared.

"You know," Moussawi said, "there are two types of people in this world: the ones holding the weapon and the ones who have it pressed against their temple. It struck me, once that guy's blood had pumped dry, that during those minutes I had completely stopped thinking about my dead friends down in the ravine."

Umarov shut his eyes. He heard the voice of the woman doctor again:

"Now I'm going to examine you properly."

Tekla asked Moussawi to help her roll Umarov onto his side. She pulled down his trousers.

"This may be a little uncomfortable, but it shouldn't hurt."

Umarov could feel something going on near his anus. As if a light breeze were blowing on it. Then it got a whole lot worse. The doctor was digging around with her bony little finger, it was as if a rope full of knots was going up and down his rectum like an elevator.

A few seconds later, he heard her triumphant voice:

"Aha!"

"What?"

She pulled out her finger and removed the gloves with a smacking sound.

Moussawi turned the patient over onto his back again.

"My name is Tekla Berg. Do you hear me? Your people have taken my brother Simon, but you're going to let him go and then you're never going to touch him again."

Umarov managed a derisive smile.

"Very funny."

"It's not funny at all. Not when you think about the disease you have."

"What's wrong with me?" Umarov asked breathlessly.

"Free my brother and I'll treat you."

"I don't know any Simon," Umarov said.

"Well, I can tell you that your son Sardor and his bikers have kidnapped my brother and slapped him around. You have a chat with your son and tell him to let Simon go."

Umarov was silent.

"What's to stop me just calling for my bodyguards? They'll wipe you out and all the other idiots in this surgery in the blink of an eye."

Tekla took a chance.

"The fact that I'm the only one who knows what's wrong with you. What makes you think you'll find someone else who can work it out?"

"There are hundreds of doctors who can do the prostate."

"That's not your main problem. Your prostate cancer is of the type that progresses slowly," Tekla said, "but it's not going to kill you. The fluid in your lung is caused by something else."

"What's that?"

Moussawi bent over him.

"I've no idea what she's thinking of either. But I do know one thing: this doctor who's just examined you has a brain like no-one else in this town. And if she's put two and two together, I'd listen very carefully to what she has to say."

"There are other doctors," Umarov said, less confident now.

"But not one of them knows what the test of the fluid in your lung showed up," Tekla went on. "I've removed it from your file. And I've also checked to see what unusual treatment could save you."

Umarov was breathing heavily.

"Ring Sardor," Tekla said. "Tell him to let Simon go. We'll wait here until I get a call from Simon to say he's free."

Umarov smiled.

"Don't you have other patients to attend to?"

Moussawi gave an even broader smile.

"We've cancelled all our consultations."

"You have a duty to treat me as your patient. You're not allowed to withhold treatment if you know of one."

"Do you have any proof?" Tekla said. "You didn't put anything in the file, did you Tariq?"

"No."

"Do you realise what you're doing?" Umarov tried to shout. "Are you guys tired of living?"

Umarov closed his eyes.

"You're dicing with death."

Tekla whispered something in Moussawi's ear.

"The devil's strength is that he pops up when you least expect him. Do I look as if I care about your threats? The only thing that matters to me is that I get to see my brother alive."

Umarov looked Tekla in the eyes. They were completely without expression. It was as if he were staring through transparent lenses into a vast darkness. He nodded.

Umarov looked grim as he was handed his mobile. First, he rang Sardor, and when he got no answer he called Eriksson and instructed him to let Simon go.

"I don't give a shit what Sardor has said, or that he owes us money. Just let him go." Eriksson tried to object, but Umarov didn't want to know. "Because I say so! Just do as I tell you this once and don't talk back."

Then he hung up on him.

"Can we stop playing this game now?"

Moussawi pulled out the guidewire and left the drain where it was.

"It will take another hour or so before all the fluid is drained. That'll give us time to wait for confirmation that Tekla's brother is free. Do you want some morphine?"

With a great deal of effort and swearing profusely, Umarov managed to extract himself from the S.U.V. When Sardor had picked him up outside the entrance to the Nobel Hospital, he had looked a complete wreck. But he did not want to talk about his visit to Outpatients. If the end of Umarov's life was drawing near, what would the future look like for Sardor and Nina?

Sardor held a large golf umbrella over Umarov and walked him past the two heavily armed hulks by the barrier fence. A third one reversed the black Humvee and let the two of them pass on their way in to the Red Bears' clubhouse.

"You realise that you're not supposed to be here?" Sardor said.

"Well, now I am."

"As *vor*, you risk—"

"Shut up," Umarov cut in. "It's too late for regrets now."

"The guys at the Centre aren't going to be pleased."

Jensen was sitting at the large wooden table, puffing and blowing through his red beard. The vice-president was slumped by his side, his arm in a cast.

"How's your hand?" Sardor asked The Count in an unconvincing show of sympathy, before taking a seat.

Next to Eriksson was Jarmo, who had been discharged from hospital after treatment for his knife wound. He nodded stiffly at the Uzbek guests.

"Thanks for coming," Jensen said, directing all his charm at Umarov.

"I understood that this was something I couldn't miss."

Sardor felt the air thicken.

Eriksson signalled to Jarmo that he should start talking.

It looked as if every muscle in the young man's body had wasted away during his stay in hospital. His white T-shirt hung loosely over his skinny shoulders, and the tattoos seemed to be in the wrong place. His bare head suggested chemotherapy rather than membership of a criminal gang.

Sardor noted the injuries on the right side of Jarmo's face, and saw that they were recent. At first he thought that he had got them in the assault at Kvarnen, but, if so, they would have healed by now. Someone at the club must have had "a serious word" with him.

"He lied to us because he was scared," Eriksson said. "Didn't he?"

"He threatened to kill me—"

"Who?" Umarov asked, confused.

"Simon Berg," Eriksson replied. "The pusher who . . ."

Umarov did not move a muscle. He stared at the young man with all the bruises. Jarmo had been keeping this information to himself for far too long.

Jarmo took a deep breath, looked around nervously, and said: "He nicked a packet of your H to sell on the side. Then he ordered carfentanyl on the net . . . from China, chemical morphine, like ten thousand times stronger than morphine, and began mixing it with the horse to stretch it out. That's when all these overdoses started across town. It's impossible to disperse that synthetic dynamite enough and it only takes a few grains to floor a rhinoceros . . ."

As if all those at the table had immediately asked the same question, Jarmo went on:

". . . which I didn't know, the bit about mixing and diluting with carfentanyl, that is. I swear. Jonas told me everything last night. He wanted to unburden his heart, so he said. But that's bullshit, he just wanted to make sure that everything pointed to Simon . . . At the same time, Simon began to sell the stuff on the side and put the money into his own pocket. He uses as well, of course . . ."

"The bastard . . ."

Jensen's face had turned Coca-Cola red.

Jarmo sounded less nervous, as if he sensed that all the anger was now directed at Simon.

". . . and I caught him flogging it at Kvarnen. Purely by chance, I was there with some mates when I saw him dealing in the toilets. That's my bar, my turf, so I confronted him but we were both pretty pissed . . . Then I didn't see him for like an hour, but when we were getting ready to leave he was suddenly standing behind me. He started threatening me, said he'd kill me if I told anyone I'd seen him dealing there, at Kvarnen. I lost it and hit him. When I turned to go, he came from behind and stuck a knife in my side. He bent over me as I lay there on the floor and whispered in my ear that I'd better keep my trap shut and say that I'd been stabbed by some Albanian from the Northern Networks. If I squealed, he'd kill me next time. The guy's stark raving mad."

"Hang on a minute, are you saying that everything that's happened . . . the little knifing drama at Kvarnen, the overdoses, Lorik's death and the conflict with the Northern Networks –" Umarov surveyed them all, one grim-looking face after the other – ". . . all of it is the fault of this . . . Simon? We're in this big mess because of a tall story told by a cowardly junkie?"

Looking down at the table, Umarov laughed softly. Then he turned to Jensen.

"How long have you known?"

"For two hours. I swear. Eje rang me."

"Jesus. This is almost comical," Umarov said to himself. Then he looked up at Sardor. "Damage control. We've got to get hold of the Northern Networks." He rose quickly.

"Calm down," Sardor said. "You've got to chill and let me—"

"Never," Umarov shouted. "I've run out of patience now."

"Think of the Centre," Sardor said. "Think what it—"

"I don't give a shit about the consequences," Umarov said and looked around.

Jarmo seemed to be expecting a bullet in the head. Eriksson had put a large hand on his shoulder, in case he tried to run away.

Jensen smiled his piggy smile.

"Simon Berg doesn't have many more hours left of his miserable life. The only question is, which one of us is going to have the honour."

Sardor changed his grip on the Glock. He turned to Eriksson.

"Is he still in the old slaughterhouse area?"

Eriksson looked at Sardor, then at Umarov and back again.

"But . . . Victor called this afternoon and told us to let him go. I thought you knew . . ."

Sardor looked at his father in surprise while Umarov stood absolutely still, staring into space.

Tekla had just put back a dislocated shoulder, inserted an ascites drain and done battle with a case of malignant hypertonia when Klein-Borgstedt rang.

"Monica told me about the research funds! You were right."

"How nice," Tekla said, and scanned the room to see how many patients were waiting. It looked like a normal Friday afternoon. And the cherry on the cake was the absence of any stench in A. & E. But she could not bring herself to rejoice over research money or clean air. She was still in a complete state after the meeting with Umarov. Simon had called after half an hour, on his way to somewhere in a taxi. They had let him go and he promised to be in touch. "When I get there." Tekla had rung him half an hour later but got no reply. She wanted to find him and see how he was. Only one hour to go before the end of her shift, but it felt like an eternity.

"Isn't it fantastic?" Klein-Borgstedt trilled. "One million. Did you hear that, Tekla, I've been given one million per year for five years. Never in my wildest dreams could I have hoped for that. In spite of the demands on Collinder to make savings. Wonderful!"

"Per year . . . for five years," Tekla said in surprise, remembering the shrewd look on Carlsson's face. Was the bit about savings even true? She would never know.

"Congratulations," she stammered. She was beginning to understand how Carlsson's brain worked. First build up expectations. Then top them.

"Time now to support the hospital's funding plans," Klein-Borgstedt said, in a somewhat lower key. Perhaps she realised that she had, in some way, sold her soul to Mammon. But it was, after all, in the interests of research.

Klein-Borgstedt hung up, and Tekla saw Collinder appear, blazer and all.

"Now that's better," he said. He filled his lungs and closed his eyes. "Like my rose garden in Österlen." He was beaming with pleasure as he looked at his colleagues. "At last we can breathe again."

One of the nurses asked: "But where did that stench come from?"

"We don't know," Collinder said, throwing his arms wide. He looked as if he meant it too.

Was it conceivable that they had no idea? Now they were back to normal: the usual dank hospital smell.

Tekla struggled to get through the day. Around four o'clock, she was unenthusiastically studying some lab results in the doctors' private office when she heard a familiar voice by her side.

"Hi, Syrran."

She looked up and stopped breathing. Before her stood her barely-one-year-younger brother. He had always been slim, but she had never known him this skinny or pale. His tousled hair stood out in all directions, he stooped like an old man and half his face was covered in bruises, some older, some more recent.

"Simon . . ." Tekla tried not to show how horrified she was.

Simon looked around, stressed and nervous. Tekla wanted to leap up and hug him, but restrained herself. She pointed to an empty relatives' room. They stood in the doorway for a second, as if unsure who should go in first. Tekla felt the same way she had the first time she encountered a patient with Aids. An unwarranted fear of bodily contact. In the end she went and sat down on a sofa. Gestured to a chair opposite her.

Simon's eyes fluttered like a butterfly Tekla couldn't catch. She looked down at the floor. Nike trainers that were too big, had no laces and looked as if they'd been fished out of a rubbish bin. He smelled of smoke and something else, something sweet and musty that she wasn't able to identify.

"Do you want anything?" she said.

"Thanks, I'm alright," Simon whispered.

Tekla had already transferred three thousand kronor to his account. She had even called her uncle in Edsåsdalen to see if he would let Simon use his apartment in Spain for a few weeks. Said that Simon was burnt out and needed to get away from town. It hadn't been a problem, their uncle didn't even ask why.

"How are you feeling?" she said. "What have they done to you? If you needed money, surely you could have come and asked me?"

Simon was looking at the window onto the inner courtyard that the staff used. The blinds had been pulled down.

"I'm O.K. It'll all work out."

Work out. It never worked out for Simon. Nothing ever worked out. It went in the same direction all the time. And what hurt most was that he was the only one in the whole world who did not see it. Or maybe he just accepted it. The incurable optimist. Tekla remembered every smile, every laugh, from the age of seven onwards.

She had to deal with this. And at the same time be careful not to lose him again. Proceed with the utmost caution. She knew how easily he could be scared.

"Simon . . ."

"Yes?"

"Remember what I said . . . what happened at Hellasgården this spring . . ."

"Oh, forget it. I don't even remember what we were talking about."

Simon grinned, showing his wolfish teeth. There were grey streaks in his sparse beard, which used to be jet-black. But dark eyebrows and eyelashes still framed his large, blue eyes.

"I guess I'm not allowed to smoke in here."

She tried to smile.

He produced a pack of Marlboros from his trouser pocket, pulled out a bent cigarette and played with it for a while. He also got out a Zippo, which he fingered nervously. Tekla recognised their father's lighter.

She really ought just to drop it. She knew he didn't like to talk about feelings. But her thoughts had gone back so many times to that fateful day last spring at Hellasgården. When she had spoken her mind about his addiction and his chaotic life and the way she kept having to tidy up after her useless brother. She remembered his exact words: "Well, don't do it then. You never need to see me again. I'll stay away." Then he had left. Tekla had stayed. Too tired to run after him. Dejected and empty, with no idea how to make him happy again. She gave up then and there. Felt that she no longer had the strength.

A week went by. She began dialling again. Missed him so much her body ached. But he kept ignoring her calls. Made plain that he wanted to be left alone. Manage by himself. At least try.

"But I only want to tell you that I didn't mean what I said. Of course I want to see you. You're my brother. The only person I have except for Mamma, and she's completely out of it. Do you understand?"

"All good. Forget it," Simon said.

Tekla thought about the burns patient in the I.C.U., the way she had spent days worrying that it was Simon. And how stupid that felt now. Her eyes registered something she had not noticed at first: how he was scratching his arms. His body was twitching. He was jumpy.

"Don't you think you should have those wounds in your face seen to?"

Simon glanced at Tekla.

"Well, you're a doctor."

"I know that you won't let me examine you."

"That's true."

"So can I get a colleague to have a look?"

"It's only some bruises."

He lit the Zippo a few times, then put the cigarette into his shirt pocket.

They sat in silence for a minute. Listening to the voices out in A. & E. Friday afternoon. Tekla knew there would be a rush of patients after work.

"You do realise that you've got to get out of town, don't you?" she said.

Simon was in his own world. Scratching hard at his elbow.

"Do you still see any of the old gang? Micke? Rakel? Paul?"

Simon studied the rough backs of his hands and picked at a scab.

"They aren't my friends any longer."

"But surely you see someone?"

Simon nodded.

"I have an old schoolmate who moved here last year because he'd got some girl pregnant. She's kicked him out, but he inherited a bit of money so he bought a summer house outside town. We've gone fishing there a few times."

Tekla saw Simon brighten up. Fishing had always been his great passion.

"And what have you been doing for those Uzbeks?"

Simon fell silent. Squirmed a bit. Tekla had the feeling he might get up and leave. *Be careful. Don't scare him.*

"They were here this morning," she said quietly.

"What's that?" Simon said, and looked nervously at his sister.

"That guy Sardor and some other beefcake came here to talk to me this morning."

"What did they want?" Simon said.

"Doesn't matter."

"Yes it does. Tell me!"

Tekla thought back to when they were in their teens and Simon tried to prise some secret out of her. His undisguised curiosity.

"They asked me for something I wasn't prepared to give them."

"Christ, Tekla. I didn't know they would—"

"It doesn't matter, Simon. I'll never see them again. They've let you go, and that's all that matters."

"It was crazy. All of a sudden, they just let me leave. No explanations."

Tekla thought about Sardor's claim that Simon owed them money. He still did. Sooner or later they'd demand that he give it to them.

"So what have you been doing for them?" Tekla said.

"I help them with a bit of this and that."

"What sort of things?"

"This and that. I'm their . . . like, consultant."

"Consultant?" Tekla suppressed a laugh. "Sounds fancy. Do they pay you?"

"Sure. They pay on time. Per job."

"So, depending on what you do, they pay you?"

"Correct."

"Simon, tell me," Tekla said, cautious not to push him too hard, even though she felt like banging him on the head and drowning out his lies with her shouts, "what exactly is it that you do?"

Simon looked taken aback.

"It's all above board. Come on, Tekla, why do you look so suspicious? Why do you always have to be like that?"

"Like what?"

"Older-sisterish. Always believing the worst of me."

"No, I don't."

"Cut the crap, for God's sake. You were like that by the time we went to school."

Tekla fell silent. She was not going to walk into that trap. All too often it had ended with doors slammed in her face. She knew he didn't mean it. Knew they had had a close relationship. She had always been there for him. Knew several of his friends, some were hers too. They confided in her, trusted her, told her that they worried about Simon. And she looked after him. Took care of his problems. Picked up the broken things he strewed around him. Mended them and put them back while he was asleep. Washed Simon's clothes when her mother no longer could. Folded them and put them into his drawers. Got up in the middle of the night when his friends knocked on the window and asked her to help them bring him home. Propped up his stinking body so he could get to the car. Showered him down with the garden hose behind the garage, gave him a headache pill and helped him into bed.

"Simon, I'm not stupid. I know that it's to do with drugs. And that you've done something to annoy them. That's why they picked

369

you up outside Ringen. And that's why they've been beating you up. You owe them money. I've already transferred a little bit extra so you'll be O.K. for a few days. And I can start making a regular monthly payment again."

Simon looked at his older sister through cyan-blue eyes, and lovingly tapped her forehead with three fingers.

"How's that jam-packed head of yours doing? How are *you* feeling, Syrran?"

Tekla looked down at the pine tabletop.

"It's giving me more grief than usual."

She was reminded of the stem cell treatment in London that had occupied her thoughts. Perhaps she ought to tell him about their mother's dementia, about Huntington's. That he should get himself tested. That they could do it together. And *if* one of them turned out to have the gene, they could give the other one stem cells from their bone marrow. Maybe. Provided the London researchers continued to obtain positive results.

"You need help," Simon said.

"There's no help I can get, you know that. I just need time to sort out all the images."

"Time you don't have."

"Or don't give myself."

"And I assume you don't tell any friends or the people at work about your . . . condition?"

Tekla shook her head slowly.

"It doesn't sound good, Twiglet."

That was a long time ago. When Tekla was a child, she was no more than skin and bones, and Simon and his friends used to call her Twiglet. Back then it had been an insult; now it gave her a nostalgic memory of something she shared only with her brother.

"Next time you need money, tell me before you do something stupid."

He shook his head.

"It'll sort itself out."

He smiled his big grin, so wide that his silver skull earrings jiggled. He had two of them now.

"I've got several things going. It'll be fine."

"You can't stay in Stockholm, Simon. Don't you get that?" She had a lump in her throat. "Please, you've got to look after yourself better. You have to eat."

He laughed.

"Need to go now."

Tekla raised her voice. "No."

"What do you mean, no?" Simon said.

"I hope you're joking. After everything you've been through. You've got to leave town."

Simon laughed, but Tekla could see how painful the bruises on his face were.

"That's not possible."

"Because they own you or what?"

"What do you mean, they?"

"Cut it out, Simon. I've met both Sardor and Victor Umarov."

Simon looked as if Tekla had spoken of the devil himself.

"Victor Umarov is terrifying," Tekla said.

"They're not that dangerous," Simon said, but Tekla saw him shudder.

"Have you had a look in the mirror? Hey? Have you seen yourself? Does it look as if they only *chatted* to you? I'm not stupid, you know."

Simon got up. Tekla followed him. She must have crossed some line. Simon was heading for the door. Tekla took hold of his skinny arm, but he pulled himself loose and kept walking.

Smoke and old clothes. Now she recognised the third smell: pseudomonas. He had an infection on the skin, maybe an abscess full of evil, antibiotic-resistant bacteria.

"Simon!"

He turned around. For the first time during his brief visit, she saw a glimpse of her brother of old. The closeness. A spark of life in those gorgeous eyes. The curiosity.

."We've got to get you away from this town. I'll buy you a ticket to Spain. You can borrow Uncle Mikael's house. Only for a short while, until things have calmed down."

"I can't, Syrran."

"I can take a few days off and come with you."

"No."

Tekla could feel the panic rising in her. She wanted to force him not to leave. Every cell in her body was screaming to her to make him stay.

She pushed past Simon, stood with her back to the door. Should she tell him about the Huntington's now? No, it would only frighten him, he'd run away and put his head in the sand.

"Get out of my way," he said.

"Simon, listen to me. They let you go because I . . . did something."

Simon started.

"It wasn't anything extraordinary," Tekla said. "But you've seen what they're capable of. You've got to get away from them. Cut the ties."

Simon smiled.

"I don't have anything else."

"Of course you do!" she said. "There are masses of jobs. And I promise, I'll help you."

Just then Simon's mobile rang. He got it out, looked at it, froze. Tekla could feel the fear in the small room.

"What?" she asked.

Simon rejected the call.

"Nothing."

He looked panic-stricken.

"Come on, what? Tell me."

"I have to go . . ."

"No, no, no, Simon. You're not going anywhere."

He swayed, overcome by dizziness.

"Shit. Shit."

As if he had had a stroke and could not keep his balance. He went back to the chair and sat down.

Tekla breathed a sigh of relief.

There was a knock at the door and a nurse looked in.

"There are two people out here who want to talk to you, Tekla."

"Patients?"

"No. Private."

"Can you ask them to wait?"

"I don't think so," the nurse said, casting a frightened glance at Simon. She beckoned to Tekla to come closer.

"It's the same guys as this morning," she whispered.

Tekla's heart stopped. She turned to Simon, who was pressing the buttons on his mobile.

"Shall I ask them to leave?"

"No. Is the staff pantry next door free?" Tekla said. Her heart was spinning like a centrifuge.

"I think so."

"O.K., tell them I'll be out in a minute," Tekla said, and saw the nurse nod. "And please . . . can you do me a huge favour and not let anybody come in here with my . . . brother. It'll only take a few minutes."

"Of course. You know that everyone here is happy to help you."

"Not everyone," Tekla said.

"Well, almost," the nurse said and disappeared.

Tekla took a deep breath, tried to look relaxed. Under no circumstances must she let the panic show. She turned to Simon.

"I'll be right back."

Simon was lost in his own world.

"Simon?"

"Yes," he said, looking up.

"Stay here. Promise."

"Sure."

Tekla went out and shut the door. Tried to stop her hands from shaking.

373

ACCIDENT & EMERGENCY, NOBEL HOSPITAL
Friday afternoon, 14.vi

Sardor and Eriksson passed the pharmacy of the Nobel Hospital on their way to A. & E. Since Jarmo's confession at Skärholmen, it was all out in the open. Sardor's lousy leadership, the raid in Haninge. You could say that he was to blame for it all. If he had not set those two junkies to guard the money, if he had not put the screws on them afterwards . . . Umarov had blanked him when they left the bikers' clubhouse. All he said was: "You clean this up now. Make sure you find that pusher and put an end to all this."

At the desk in the patient reception area, Sardor told a nurse they wanted to see Tekla Berg. A few minutes later, the doctor emerged from a relatives' room. Her eyes narrowed when she saw Sardor.

"What are you doing here?"

"We need to talk," Sardor said.

"We're done talking," Tekla said.

"Not quite."

"What the hell do you want?"

"Not here," Sardor said calmly.

Tekla thought for a moment. Then she said:

"Follow me."

She led Sardor and Eriksson to the staff pantry next to the relatives' room. She closed the door and leaned against a kitchen table. A leather corner sofa, a low pine table, two kitchen tables and a dozen heavy pine chairs had somehow been squeezed into a space of some twenty square metres. A narrow glass door gave onto a small inner courtyard where the staff went to smoke and, in summer, to sit on the dirty plastic furniture to eat their packed lunches. The pantry was empty: no-one was heating up food in any of the three micro-wave ovens on the wall above the tiny sink. A sign on the refrigerator said "STAFF ONLY", and someone had stuck a note on the dish-washer: "YOUR MUM DOESN'T WORK HERE".

Sardor sat down on one of the chairs. Eriksson placed himself in front of the door, in case someone wanted to come in. Or go out.

Tekla went over to the coffee machine and pressed the button for a double espresso.

"Just one quick question," Sardor said. "Where's your brother now? If you tell us, I promise we won't mess with you anymore."

Tekla sniffed.

"Not here, at any rate," she said and picked up her cup with both hands.

"We already know that." Sardor could see Tekla's barriers coming up in zero time. He relaxed his shoulders and tried to smile. "We only want to have a last little chat with him. Clear up a few question marks."

"You can shove those question marks right up—"

Eriksson chuckled.

"Wow."

Sardor was not so impressed. In a second, he had leaped up and grabbed Tekla by the throat, pushing her so that she fell backwards onto the leather sofa. The coffee cup bounced on the linoleum floor and the contents splashed up against the wall. Sardor held Tekla's head down, and put a knife to her throat. Pressing his lips to her ear, he said:

"Now you listen, you fucking maniac. You don't seem to be all that afraid for your own life."

Tekla caught his look and gripped the sofa.

"I'm all ears."

"You and your brother are close, right?"

Tekla clenched her teeth.

Sardor pressed the knife hard against her throat. "Aren't you?"

"I'd do anything for him."

Sardor turned to Eriksson and nodded.

"In that case, where is Simon?"

"No idea."

"Don't play games with me."

Sardor pressed the steel so hard against her skin, she began to bleed.

"Where?"

"You can cut as much as you like. I haven't a clue where he is. I've tried to call several times, but he's not picking up. Give it a try yourself."

Sardor removed the knife and stood up.

Tekla slowly raised herself and leaned back on the leather sofa. She reached for a paper napkin and wiped the blood off her throat. There were only a few drops. A mere scratch.

"Didn't your father arrange for Simon to be released?" she said.

Sardor stared at the doctor.

"I don't know what the fuck you did to him to force him to make such an idiotic decision."

"It's confidential," Tekla said.

"But since then, some more shit has come to light about your brother," Sardor said. He noted that the doctor was listening carefully.

"I think you would be wise to stick to what your father wanted," Tekla said.

"Fuck!" Sardor yelled and drove the knife into the wooden table-top. "Don't you hear what I'm saying? Whatever you managed to get Victor to do, that's over now. Your brother's messed up big time."

Tekla did not move a muscle.

"So you want to 'have a chat' with him."

"There's a chance for you to save his useless life," Sardor sneered. "Tell me where he is and I might not cut his throat."

"Are you done?" Tekla asked in a calm voice.

Sardor did not reply.

Tekla got up and walked to the door. She stood in front of the man in the leather gear, who gave her an impassive look and did not budge.

"Would you mind letting me out?"

"Let her go," Sardor said. Eriksson moved aside.

There were two Securitas guards outside. Eriksson heard them ask Tekla what had happened.

"We've got to get out of here," he said to Sardor, who nodded slowly, coming back down to earth.

Tekla breathed a sigh of relief when she saw Sardor and the giant walk off towards the exit. A. & E. was overflowing with waiting patients. The nurses were hurrying back and forth trying to get a grip on the situation. Tekla went back to the relatives' room where Simon was waiting.

She opened the door. The room was empty. No Simon. She ran out and looked around, but he was gone. She called his mobile, but got only the mailbox.

The nurse who was supposed to keep an eye on Simon came up to Tekla.

"I'm sorry: he ran away. I told him to wait for you, but he pushed past me and raced off. He looked terrified."

"Shit!" Tekla yelled out in frustration across the crowded clinic.

She realised that the deal Moussawi and she had struck with Umarov no longer held. It was null and void. Something had happened. Whatever it was, the Uzbeks must not be allowed to find him under any circumstances. And she was the only one who could save Simon.

Friday evening, 14.vi

The air in the apartment stood still. Tekla opened the window and the door to the balcony, but it was hard to tell which was worse: the heat that had wiped out the evidence of the afternoon downpour or the noise of traffic on Gullmarsplan. She took a cold shower, drank two glasses of grapefruit juice and ate three pieces of oatmeal crispbread with raspberry jam. She was neither hungry nor full. There was only a relentless hollow feeling gnawing at her stomach and a roar building in her ears. She closed the window and the balcony door, pulled down the blinds and lay on her unmade bed. She spent twenty minutes there, sweating and trying to wind down, but the images of the day came flashing by faster and faster until she was overcome by nausea and had to sit up. In the bathroom, she got out a packet of Oxazepam. She swallowed eighty milligrammes. She had never taken more than fifty before. She went back to bed to lie down, but she might as well have sucked some throat lozenges. No effect whatsoever.

She got up at about nine, had another shower, hot this time, and pulled on a pair of thin linen trousers and trainers. Although the outdoor temperature must have been in the high twenties, she wore a thin hoodie underneath her lilac velvet jacket and left her hair loose. After much hesitation, she had decided that there was only one person who could help her. She got out her mobile.

HAVE TO SEE YOU! BABYLON NEAR BJÖRNS TRÄDGÅRD IN 30?

She downed three bombs and put another five into the Lypsyl tube. Although she fancied some red wine, she knew that she might pass out if she mixed alcohol with all the Oxazepam she had been taking. A little amphetamine was what she needed.

She slammed the door and jogged down the stairs and out into the summer evening. Twenty minutes later she was standing at the bar counter, rubbing shoulders with a crowd of Söder hipsters in party mood. Ten minutes later, Lundgren appeared.

"Guessed you'd want a beer," Tekla said.

"You got it right," Lundgren said, taking off his leather jacket. He downed half the bottle in one go.

"I'm happy you got in touch," he said. "I was worried you'd deleted me from your contacts."

"I only know one policeman," Tekla said curtly.

"So that's why I'm here?" Lundgren said, and drew a hand over his unshaven cheek.

Tekla met his look.

"You lied to me. You did recognise Jonas when we were in Årsta."

"I can expl—"

"Don't bother," Tekla said. "I've seen Simon."

She didn't want to hear any lies. Only one thing mattered to her: to save Simon.

"That's great," Lundgren exclaimed with a look of relief. He finished off his beer.

"No, it's not great. He looked like a walking corpse."

"What have they done?"

"Beaten the shit out of him."

Tekla shuddered at the thought of Simon's battered face. She took a large sip of the cold red wine and felt Lundgren's hand on hers.

"What's happened?" he said. "You're shaking."

"Sardor Umarov and another gorilla came back to see me at A. & E., wanting to get hold of Simon. Despite Victor Umarov's promise that they'd leave him alone."

"Victor Umarov?" Lundgren exclaimed. "The *vor* himself. The person who controls the entire narcotics market. But I don't get it. Have you been talking to Victor Umarov?"

Tekla swallowed some more wine. She remembered how the gangster boss had trembled when she drove her finger up his rectum.

"I can't say any more. But he promised to leave Simon be."

Lundgren was still staring at her. "You're dicing with death, Tekla."

"So what do I do?" Tekla said, finishing off her wine.

"You—"

"Hang on," she said, and went over to the bar to order another round. Minutes later she was back with a beer and a glass of wine. She felt dizzy and was beginning to see double.

"So what do you want me to do?"

"Nothing." Lundgren sighed. "Just sit tight without rocking the boat and let the police—"

"No way," Tekla interrupted him. "There's no time for that. They're going to kill Simon. I have to find him and send him abroad."

"You still haven't understood who you're up against."

"I don't give a shit."

Lundgren smiled, his hand on hers again.

"But I do. Let me handle this. It's my job."

Tekla felt her pulse slowing a bit. She sipped her wine and left Lundgren's hand where it was. She could feel a migraine coming on, and her hallucinations were getting worse. It was like a line across the lens of the eye whenever she looked at a lamp.

There was still daylight outside, but the temperature had fallen. The staff were handing out white fleece blankets to the customers.

Lundgren cast a worried look at Tekla.

"Have you had anything to eat?"

"Nothing much."

"Shall I order something?"

"I'm not hungry."

"You're the doctor, remember. Who's going to take care of you if you faint?"

Tekla smiled.

"Maybe some fresh air."

"Absolutely."

380

Tekla took some deep breaths. But the lights from the bar were still hounding her. She knew what was going on, but she could do nothing about it. She hadn't brought her Oxazepam.

"Let's go over to the steps," Lundgren suggested. He led her a few metres away and they sat down. "Why won't you let me tell you about the thing with Jonas? I can explain."

"Forget it," Tekla said. She was much too tired. Besides, he'd only dish up some half-truths which she'd see straight through. Right now, she was just happy to be with him again.

"I want to—" Lundgren started, before Tekla's mobile interrupted him. She got it out and looked at the display.

"It's Simon."

"Well, what are you waiting for? Answer it!"

Tekla picked up.

"Hello."

Tekla put it on speaker, so that Lundgren could hear.

"Hi, Tekla."

"Where are you?" There was traffic noise in the background.

"Hanging with Jonas."

"Why did you leave the hospital?"

Silence.

"Simon?"

"Uh. Nothing special . . ."

"But we weren't done."

Again, no sound from Simon.

"Why don't we meet?" Tekla said carefully. She knew how easily he took fright. That he could simply cut off their conversation and vanish, the way he had done so many times before.

Her hand was shaking. Lundgren held it in his warm clasp.

"Simon?" she said again.

"Listen, Tekla, don't freak out now but . . . there's a price on my head."

Tekla had to change her position so as not to drop the mobile.

"What . . .?"

381

"But," Simon went on calmly, "I've got a plan. It'll be O.K."

Tekla could feel Lundgren's hand on her shoulder.

"What are you talking about, Simon? You've never had a plan!"

Simon laughed.

"But this time I do." He still sounded calm and happy.

"Well, what exactly is it?"

"For heaven's sake, just relax," Simon said.

Tekla felt her temples throbbing.

"Jesus, Simon, I get these maniacs coming to me at the hospital, asking where you are. You've got yourself into trouble, that much I've gathered, and you can't fix it by yourself. Just as you've never in your life fixed anything by yourself. But *I* am going to work out a plan for you."

Simon laughed. "I've got to hang up now, so—"

"Don't hang up. We have to—"

"I'm sorry, Tekla. Sorry."

"What are you talking about? Why—"

"I love you. I'm so sorry."

The line went dead.

"Simon! Simon!"

Tekla called back, but got his voicemail.

She shut her eyes and saw his wolfish smile.

STORA ESSINGEN, STOCKHOLM
Friday evening, 14.vi

Dahl was turning up the gas on his barbecue when he heard a voice behind him:

"Isn't gas cheating?"

He considered reaching for the knife he always had strapped to his ankle, but there was something familiar about the voice. He turned to see Sardor Umarov, a taunting smile on his face.

"Jesus, don't you know what a doorbell looks like?"

Sardor looked out across the bay. Two sailing boats with their sails lowered came chugging past. The water was as smooth as a mirror, the air stood still, and several bright yellow hot-air balloons with advertising slogans contrasted with the pink evening sky.

"How the hell can you afford all this? Surely a cop doesn't make this much money?" Sardor said.

Dahl peeled the vacuum wrapping from an entrecôte and wiped off the juices with some kitchen paper.

"This is a garden shed compared to Victor's place in Bromma."

Sardor came out onto the terrace and leaned against the fence.

"The world's largest garden shed, in that case."

Dahl mixed soy sauce, garlic salt, pepper and a few drops of Worcestershire sauce in a bowl. Put the meat in the marinade. Then fetched an ice-cold Brooklyn Lager from the kitchen.

"Have you come without a bodyguard?"

"Don't need one when I visit harmless people," Sardor said. "And what about you, no girlfriend tonight?"

"She's been having nightmares ever since some dodgy types showed up last Saturday."

"I see," Sardor said. "She doesn't like night-time visitors, then?"

"Not when they knock her boyfriend about in the sitting room."

Sardor went over and smelled the marinade.

"What are you serving it with?"

"Chips and Béarnaise. Is there anything else?" Dahl said. Where had he left his pistol? He realised that it was in the bathroom cupboard and that he wouldn't make it there in time. "And gas works perfectly well. Charcoal's a bloody bore."

Sardor removed his leather jacket and wriggled out of his shoulder holster, tucking his pistol into the waistband of his trousers.

"Great weather."

"It's going to rain tonight," Dahl said.

Sardor looked up at the sky and laughed. "Nope."

"Want to bet?"

"I never gamble," Sardor said. "It can go terribly wrong. If anyone knows that, you do."

There was a hiss as Dahl put the meat on the hot grill. He went into the kitchen to have a look in the oven, and saw that the chips were almost done. He popped celebrity chef Lallerstedt's ready-made Béarnaise sauce into the microwave, and undid one button on his short-sleeved shirt. The back was soaked with sweat.

"Do you have a glass of that delicious whisky you gave us the other night?" Sardor said.

"Gave you . . ." Dahl snorted.

"Are you pissed off?"

"Me? Pissed off?" Dahl asked. "It was only business, like you said."

"Absolutely."

"And this is just a social call, right?"

"Absolutely," Sardor said. "The whisky?"

Dahl poured some whisky into a tall crystal glass and handed it to Sardor. Then he went back to turn the meat.

"If I'd known you were coming, I'd have made more food."

"Thanks, but I won't stay long."

"That's good," Dahl said as he set down a plate of chips and

Béarnaise sauce, removed the meat from the grill and turned off the gas. He switched on his Sonos sound system and started playing "One More Night" by Phil Collins.

They went through the sliding doors into the sitting room. It was warmer inside than out. The sun had been beating down all afternoon. Dahl ate with his plate on his knees.

"There's this dude I need to find," Sardor said. "You're good at that sort of thing, aren't you?"

"What sort of thing?" Dahl took a large bite of the red meat.

"One of our pushers. Simon Berg," Sardor said.

Dahl grinned and drank out of the bottle.

"What's so funny about that?" Sardor asked.

"Why would I help you?"

"Do I have to remind you that you raped one of our girls last weekend?"

"Can't have been the first time," Dahl said.

"That you raped one of our girls?"

"That she got raped."

Sardor squeezed the armrests of the easy chair he was sitting in and looked down towards the jetty.

"Violence is rarely good for business."

"But it was last weekend, when you beat me up in my own home," Dahl said, chewing noisily.

Sardor lowered his voice theatrically. "A wise man once told me about this guy he wanted to get hold of. He looked for him in the village where the man lived, but no-one had seen him. At least that's what they said. But he knew that they were scared of him because of everything he'd done before. So he decided to give the villagers a warning. He got up in the middle of the night and took a sheep from one of the neighbours. He cut its throat and slit open its belly. Then he strung it up in the middle of the village where everyone would see it the next morning. By lunchtime, some of the men had found the guy and handed him over to the wise man, who thanked them for their help."

Dahl finished his beer and got up to fetch another one.

"And?" he called from the kitchen.

"Nothing."

Dahl came back and sat down. Suddenly he burst out laughing.

"You don't remember how the story ends! Your father told it to you, didn't he?"

Sardor took a sip of whisky. Cracked his neck to both sides. Eventually he said:

"You're going to help us with this guy, Simon."

Dahl stood up and Sardor reached towards his pistol.

"Where are you going?"

"Chill," Dahl said. "I'm getting something from the hall."

Sardor stood up and followed him. Dahl picked up two wallets. He pulled out a driving licence.

"Is this your Simon?"

Sardor leaned forward.

"Perfect. How—"

"If I give him to you, I want you to get rid of this one too."

Dahl held out the other driving licence.

"Jonas," Sardor said. "His mate?"

Dahl nodded.

"Why?" Sardor asked.

"Do you ever dream?"

"Dream?"

"Well, do you dream?" Dahl repeated.

"What kind of stupid question is that?"

"I always dream at weekends. No idea why, but I never dream during the week. At weekends, I often wake up in the morning and I remember my dreams. But today is Friday. And when I had a nap this afternoon and woke up, I'd been dreaming about that dude."

"Jonas?"

"So it wasn't at a weekend."

"What are you getting at?"

386

"I dreamed that I put a bullet in his head."

"Well, do it then. I'm not going to stop you," Sardor said and shook his head. He drained his whisky. "Actually, I'll tell you what. I think you ought to get rid of both of them yourself."

"Me?" Dahl said, setting down his plate, which had only the strip of fat left on it. "Didn't you just say that you wanted this Simon? So, while you're at it, I suggest you take care of both of them."

Sardor smiled.

"I don't think so. Now that I think about it, Tatiana wasn't best pleased that you only got three whacks. She would have liked to see your finger in a box, or, better still, your prick. She lost it when she realised that I hadn't put a bullet in your fucking head."

"Tell her from me she's spent too much time watching 'The Godfather'."

"No," Sardor said firmly. "You're going to do this, and then we'll say you're all square with Tatiana."

"Why the fuck do you care what Tatiana thinks?"

Sardor stared out of the window.

Dahl leaned forward. "You don't really go for chicks, Sardor, do you?" he whispered.

Sardor shut his eyes and cracked his neck again.

The music switched to "Just the Way You Are" by Billy Joel.

Dahl got himself another beer and opened it against the counter-top in the kitchen.

"You Uzbeks, you have an interesting logic."

"You think so?" Sardor said, fingering his pistol.

"All that stuff about balance of power."

Dahl sat down.

"Balance of power?" Sardor asked.

"Yes, between you and me. You think I owe you. I believe the opposite. I wasn't going to mention it, but I happen to have some information about you and your dad that I didn't think I'd need to use, except in an emergency. A phone tap of a conversation between you and Victor's accountant, Boris . . . is that his name? I'm the only one who has it. Things about your accounts that would throw open a Pandora's box if handed to the right prosecutor. Want to see if I'm bluffing?"

Sardor was about to say something, but changed his mind.

"I thought so," Dahl said. "And I'm not one to bear a grudge. What happened last weekend was stupid. I won't do it again."

"Don't think there'll be a whole lot more girls for you."

"Oh yes there will. I'm sure of it," Dahl said. "But, as I said, it was stupid. And you got even. So we're quits. And now you come along and talk about rubbing out some poor pusher who screwed up. And sure, I can help you. But then you take care of his mate. Balance of power . . ." he continued, drinking straight from his bottle of Brooklyn lager. The Pointer Sisters' "I'm So Excited" could be heard from the loudspeakers.

Sardor looked at the driving licences in front of him.

Dahl cleared his throat.

"And another thing . . . there are two recordings. One with you and another with your father."

Sardor looked up.

"Victor and Christian Jensen discussing where best to dump the bodies of the guys you snuff. Not that I care. You're welcome to clear the town of those dregs. But some prosecutors might construe it as murder. They'd both be looking at a really long stretch in the slammer."

Sardor was still staring at the driving licences when he said:

"You can do what you like with the last recording."

Dahl put down his bottle.

"Really? Is that so?"

"He's losing his grip," Sardor muttered. "Thinks my sister should be taking over."

"The estate agent?" Dahl said.

"He's got this idea that we're going to wind up all our activities on the streets. That we're going to go legit."

"My goodness," Dahl said, sounding almost sad. "Do I take this

388

to mean that you wouldn't mind seeing your father . . . descend from the throne?"

"Maybe. I'll be in touch."

They sat in silence while Sting belted out "Roxanne", and the rain started to fall on the terrace. A cool breeze blew into the sitting room.

"So we have a deal," Dahl said.

Sardor nodded.

"I was right," Dahl said.

"About what?"

"It's raining."

BJÖRNS TRÄDGÅRD, SÖDERMALM
Friday evening, 14.vi

"You're a wreck," Lundgren observed. "And it's not only the alcohol, right?"

Tekla shook her head slowly, but she kept her eyes shut. She wanted to hang on to the images of Simon on the beach. A football. Some of Simon's friends. A warm summer day.

"You need to get help."

"You mean with . . .?"

"The cocaine, the amphetamines . . . whatever it is you're doing."

It came as a relief to hear him give a clear diagnosis. Until now, he had been tactful, hadn't mentioned anything. But he was a policeman after all, saw plenty of addicts. And if Lundgren had noticed, how many others around her had too?

"But first we've got to find Simon," Lundgren went on. "May I try and call him again?"

Tekla felt her body sinking to the ground. She felt the warmth of Lundgren's thigh against her cheek. It smelled of detergent, but of something else too. The distinct odour of sex soothed her. It had been so long . . . She saw images in her mind, Lundgren undressed under the covers, long, sinewy muscles. She wanted to stay here. In this position.

She gave Lundgren her mobile.

Lundgren tried the number, but it went through to voicemail.

"It's switched off."

Tekla opened her eyes and straightened up.

"We have to get hold of him before the Uzbeks do."

"I know," Lundgren said. "We can begin by sending out a missing persons alert to all our patrol cars."

"That won't be enough. He's good at hiding."

"Maybe. But you think he's still in town, don't you?"

"He hasn't had time to go anywhere yet. Besides which, he's too out of it to realise that he needs to get as far away as possible."

Tekla thought about her conversation with Simon. Something was not quite right.

Lundgren had his big arm around her. She persuaded herself that it was a friendly gesture. Putting one's arm around someone didn't necessarily mean anything.

They sat looking out at Björns Trädgård and the sausage grill to the right, lit up by red neon signs.

"Is it possible to track his mobile?" Tekla said. "Like you did with Jonas'?"

"In theory you need permission but . . . I've got contacts."

"Who?"

"A colleague in Special Investigations. Although it's really the Reconnaissance Team that tracks mobiles."

"You must be close friends."

Lundgren drew a line in the gravel with his heel.

"Well, he used to work in Reconnaissance and still has a few contacts there."

Lundgren got to his feet.

"Can you manage to stand up?"

"But why would your colleague help us? Surely there's a risk that he'll get caught?"

Lundgren avoided Tekla's look.

"We have history."

Tekla got up with difficulty and began to walk. With Lundgren supporting her, they went towards Medborgarplatsen. It started to rain. She was aware that her brain kept coming back to something in her conversation with Simon. Something that didn't add up.

"I'll check to see if my colleague can help us. I'll be in touch as soon as I know anything," Lundgren said. He caught the eye of a taxi driver who signalled that he was available. "But you must sleep."

She fixed Lundgren with a look.

"What's the matter?" he said. "Did I say something wrong?"

"Simon was much too chilled. Didn't that strike you?"

"No."

"Didn't you hear? He sounded totally cool – happy, even. Instead of panic-stricken, which he should have been, knowing that there was a price on his head."

"You think . . . ?"

"I thought he was apologising for having been so hopeless and not getting in touch."

"Well?"

"Don't you get it?"

"No."

Tekla was struggling to breathe. Tried to calm down, but her body had begun to react, the adrenalin was pumping at full tilt.

"Don't you see why he was so relaxed and happy?"

"Tell me," Lundgren said.

"He'd made up his mind."

"About what?"

Tekla felt as if she were about to faint. She slid down onto the pavement.

"He's going to shoulder the whole lot. Take the blame for everything that's happened. He has no intention of running away. On the contrary: he's going to let them kill him!"

Lundgren crouched down and took hold of Tekla's arm.

"You don't know that."

"I know my brother."

Lundgren pulled Tekla back onto her feet.

"I hate to say this, but you look—"

"Bloody awful."

"Go home and sleep now," Lundgren said. "Recharge those batteries and we'll carry on tomorrow."

He helped Tekla into the taxi and told the driver where to go. Tekla didn't have the strength to protest. Realised that she was on the verge of a breakdown. She had to hold herself together for Simon's sake.

A dark sky hung over the Umarov family villa, but at least the rain had stopped. Sardor was following a lorry that was crawling along Grönviksvägen, trying to avoid scraping against the large, shiny S.U.V.s that were parked there. Sadly, he did not have Simon Berg's scalp lying on the seat beside him. A couple of hundred metres away, in front of the house, there was frantic activity, so Sardor parked in front of one of the neighbour's three garage entrances.

A marquee with long tables was being erected by the pool. Two Filipina maids were busy decorating the stone wall with floral arrangements, which had probably cost as much as Elena's Golf. A beautiful streak of evening light from Lake Mälaren shone through a crack in the clouds and lit up the flowers in a burning array of colours.

"Sardor!" Elena called from the sitting room. "I'll be right there. Just need to help Coco with the china for tomorrow."

Sardor waved to his stepmother and went on trying to find the patriarch himself amongst the bevy of servants. He tracked him down by the pool house. Sardor was just about to say hello when, to his surprise, he saw his sister Nina on her knees, busy pouring some grey liquid into a tube. He considered going away and coming back later, but Umarov had already caught sight of him.

"Fantastic," Umarov exclaimed, looking happier than he had for a long time.

"What?" Sardor asked. He was surprised. He had been expecting a dressing-down.

Umarov stood up and wiped his hands on his trousers. His

striped shirt was soaked in sweat and stuck to his large stomach. His hair was impeccable.

"Nina's a magician. I don't know how she does it. Apparently, a friend of hers has a similar problem, and she went all the way to Rönninge to get the liquid. And just look . . ." Umarov gestured at the pool. Sardor had to agree that it was beginning to take on a colour that was a lot closer to blue than when he had last seen it. It was not altogether clear yet, but there was a distinct improvement.

Umarov looked up at the sky, where the clouds were being pushed aside by the bright light. The wind was rattling the three flagpoles by the steps to the house. "All we need now is some sun tomorrow." He took hold of Sardor's ear and pulled it annoyingly hard. "Amazing, isn't it? That you have such a smart sister."

"Amazing," Sardor said grimly and met Nina's cocky look.

Umarov patted Nina's hair. "If only you'd been born a man. Then you would have been perfect."

Sardor snorted. How the hell could Umarov stand here looking so unperturbed? Talking about his perfect daughter. As if all the crap with Simon Berg, the money, the adulterated heroin and the Northern Networks was no more than a hiccup.

"How's it going? Is he still alive?" Umarov said, turning to Sardor. His tone had changed, as if someone had suddenly flipped the sub-woofer switch.

"We'll find him any minute now."

"So you don't have a clue where he is," Nina said.

"We're searching everywhere," Sardor protested. It required a huge effort not to slap his sister across the face. The balance of power had shifted.

"Just take it easy, you two," Umarov said. "I'm sure you'll find him. And then I want his head on a platter, nothing less."

Sardor didn't know what to say.

"You have to admit that it's pretty fascinating, the damage that guy has managed to do," Nina went on.

Sardor detected the sarcasm in her voice, but he wasn't sure that

Umarov did. He seemed much too excited by his victory over the pool and the preparations for the party.

"It's not my fault . . ." Sardor began.

Nina's eyes were flashing underneath the dark purple make-up.

"I'm only saying . . . if one of the girls at the office had messed up, I'd have noticed it sooner."

Sardor's hand flew up and was halfway to his sister's face when Umarov caught it. He squeezed Sardor's wrist so hard that it cracked.

"Never hit a woman, do you hear me?"

Sardor could not help seeing his father's face change colour.

Umarov released his grip. "You stick to real estate," Sardor said and glared at Nina.

"Don't you dare be condescending about Nina's business. It's a cornerstone of our activities and our lawful future. And I want us to start pulling out of the heroin right away."

Sardor nearly lost his balance.

"Are you serious?"

"Just as serious as my agony about the pool was, but you didn't seem to care too much about that."

Sardor swallowed and tried to regain his composure. He had been unprepared for this. And he knew that what he said here and now would be of crucial importance for his future. He had expected the battle to be a little more drawn out. Had assumed that all the talk about phasing out was still a long way off.

"I see."

"Do you?" Umarov said.

"But why this sudden hurry, if I may ask? I thought—"

"I'm sick, Sardor. Don't you see that?"

Sardor thought that Umarov looked the same as always. His greying hair. The stubble on his bloated face. The large belly.

"You look in good shape to me."

"You're lying," Umarov said. "Just as you've been lying to me lately about this carfentanyl scandal we're saddled with."

"I haven't lied—"

"In my world, withholding the truth is the same as lying," Umarov said sternly. Elena was calling Umarov from the house, but he dismissed her with a wave and continued:

"It's time Nina stepped in and I took my place on the sidelines."

Sardor tried to avoid looking at Nina, to stop himself from exploding. He chose his words carefully.

"I think that sounds good."

The moment he said those words, he made up his mind about two things. One of them he would take up with Umarov straight away. There wouldn't ever be a better opportunity.

"Fine," Umarov said, in a more neutral tone. He began walking towards the large covered area under the awning. Sardor followed him.

"There's one thing I need to tell you," Sardor said in a low voice. "It's to do with the fire at Söder Tower."

Umarov stopped in his tracks.

Sardor saw that Nina was at a safe distance and that Elena was busy by the long tables, with Coco and the rest of the staff.

They were on their own. Father and son. He had Umarov's undivided attention.

He took the plunge.

"Nina's behind it."

The warm evening sun just above the horizon cast a red light over Umarov's face.

"What do you mean?"

There was a lump in Sardor's throat, but he swallowed and went on. "Nina and her colleague bought sub-standard electrical wiring and cabling and sold it on for the renovation of Söder Tower."

Umarov shook his head and shot a quick glance in the direction of his daughter.

"No."

"Yes, I'm sorry to say," Sardor said, moving closer to Umarov. "The equipment was rubbish. That's the reason why the fire took hold and spread so quickly. Why so many were injured by the smoke and flames. The police are going to—"

"That's enough," Umarov cut in. He stared down at the pool. "It's . . . enough. Another day. Let's talk about this another day. I don't want anything to spoil Elena's party. Nothing."

"I'm sorry that—"

"Stop." Umarov studied the tense look on Sardor's face. "You're not sorry. I know exactly what you're feeling."

He turned and walked over to Elena.

Sardor was left standing there. He got out his mobile to act on the second decision he had taken. He texted Dahl:

Go ahead with that other thing we talked about.

Saturday morning, 15.vi

It took seven rings before Tekla realised it was the doorbell. She got up and had to steady herself against the wall in order not to faint. She pulled on some jogging pants and a sweatshirt and went to open up. It was Lundgren.

"What's the time?"

"Nine," Lundgren said, and stepped in. "Sorry if I woke you."

"I haven't slept until nine for months."

"We're close to locating Simon's mobile."

"Where is he?"

"I don't know, but my colleague told me he'd be calling shortly."

Tekla needed some bombs and lots of caffeine to wake her up.

"Sorry about the mess," she said and started making coffee in the kitchen.

Lundgren went into the sitting room. "Nice apartment. Easy to keep clean."

Tekla came out from the kitchen. "Because I don't have that much stuff?"

"Less trouble keeping it tidy."

She sat down by the coffee table. The window overlooked the entrance to the Söderled tunnel.

"I've got this feeling that Simon is dead."

Lundgren sat down opposite her.

"We can't possibly know."

Lundgren's mobile rang.

"Yes. Yes? Where? O.K."

Lundgren covered the telephone with his hand.

"It's Håkan, my colleague. He's tracked Simon's mobile."

"Where is he?" Tekla was wide awake now. The coffee pot could be heard gurgling in the kitchen as she ran into her bedroom to change.

"Muskö."

"Muskö?"

"Yes. Do you know anyone there?"

Tekla saw images in her mind's eye. Tried to decipher the messages from her subconscious. She had spent the past twenty-four hours trying to think of places where Simon might be hiding. Where he'd feel safe. Where would she go if she had a death sentence hanging over her? To Edsåsdalen? To Dalarna? Maybe. But they'd go looking there. And Simon had been so confident yesterday. Tekla was convinced that he was just sitting somewhere waiting for his tormentors. And the person he wanted to keep away was Tekla. He knew that she would try to save him.

"What are you thinking about?" Lundgren said, and went to the kitchen to pour the coffee. He came back with two large cups.

"I'm looking for something."

"You're standing there with your eyes shut," Lundgren said and held out a cup. "It'll be difficult to find—"

"Just give me a minute," Tekla said, opening her eyes and taking the coffee. She paced back and forth in the small apartment. Kept searching. Closed her eyes and let the images come. She was feeling dizzy, but somehow knew that there was a picture she was looking for. Something she'd been trying to find in the last twenty-four hours, but without success. It was as if her brain was offended that she hadn't heeded it before. She tried to get her pulse down. Concentrated on her breathing. Something began to take shape. It was spinning around on the left edge of her field of vision and kept coming back, as if in a loop. A name. A class photograph.

She opened her eyes.

"Go to Search."

Lundgren got out his mobile.

"But Håkan has given me the co-ordinates. All we need is—"

"Please do as I say."

"Sure. Tell me?"

"Google Daniel Sundström."

"Who's that?"

"Simon mentioned that an old classmate had moved here. Bought a small house outside town. He'd gone there to fish. I wonder if it could be one of his old school friends from Edsåsdalen . . ." Tekla checked herself, but then carried on. "I . . . had a look at Simon's sixth grade class photograph."

"What do you mean, you had a look at?" Lundgren scanned the room, as if hoping to see some old school yearbook.

Tekla pointed a finger at her head.

"In here."

Lundgren looked perplexed. "Are you saying that you remember all the guys who were in sixth grade with your brother?"

"It's not that I remember. They're *here*."

She put her hand to her temple.

"You scare me, Tekla. What on earth are you saying?"

"If I shut my eyes, I see the class photograph. There were only four of them in that year."

Lundgren shook his head nervously.

"That really is—"

"We can talk about it later. Please go to Search."

Reluctantly, Lundgren took his eyes off Tekla's face and keyed in "Daniel Sundström".

"There are none in Stockholm. One in Nacka."

"Try Svante Lindberg."

Lundgren kept searching.

"There are quite a few. But none that seems right."

"Tobias Almén."

A few seconds later, Lundgren lit up.

"Yes. Bingo. Muskö."

"It has to be there!" Tekla said and moved towards the door.

Lundgren followed her out to the street. They got into his rusty

B.M.W., and set off across the Gullmar roundabout and down Nynäsvägen. Lundgren raced past the Globe Arena, took the left-hand lane through Enskede and on towards Farsta.

Tekla kept her eyes fixed on the road, trying not to feel sick. Realised that she had forgotten to take any bombs with her coffee.

"Please let him be there," she said, her body tense with anxiety.

When they passed Länna, the speedometer was pushing 160.

They sat in silence. Tekla could feel the tension.

Dahl rang, Lundgren took the call on hands-free.

"Are you on your way?"

"Yes. Passing Haninge."

"O.K.," Dahl said. "I'm ten minutes behind you."

"See you there, then," Lundgren said, meeting Tekla's worried look. "I just hope we get there first."

"What do you mean?" Dahl said.

"The Umarovs are looking for him."

There was a brief silence.

"Magnus," Dahl said.

"Yes?"

"Do you want something that'll get Victor Umarov put away for good?"

Lundgren turned to Tekla, who was looking pale.

"What do you mean?"

"Do you?"

"What the hell are you talking about?" Lundgren said. Tekla could not help noticing how aggressive he sounded.

"If you want the S.W.A.T. team to be on their way within half an hour, then . . . I promise, they'll lock him up and throw away the key."

Lundgren turned to Tekla. She nodded and leaned back in her seat. She knew what she needed to be able to get through this day.

"Go for it," Lundgren said to Dahl, ending the conversation.

Umarov tiptoed across the fitted carpet as carefully as if he were holding a newborn baby against his hairy chest and trying not to drop it. He stopped in front of the bed where Elena was lying. Made sure that he had her attention. Then he slipped off his dressing gown. His erect penis stood straight out, like a flagpole at the royal palace.

Elena lifted the duvet and began to unbutton her lilac nightgown.

"Quick," Umarov said and crawled onto the bed on all fours. "Before it slackens."

"And before the guests arrive," Elena said. There were only a few hours to go and they still had plenty to do.

He stepped out of his slippers and began to kiss Elena's breasts. She grabbed him by the hair and firmly pulled back his head.

"Whoa, my little stallion."

Umarov paused.

"Little?"

Elena turned him onto his back and slipped nimbly out of her knickers. Then she mounted her husband. Began riding him, rhythmically back and forth, her nails digging deep into his chest muscles.

Umarov was enjoying it. Elena had her eyes closed and Umarov glanced over to the side. When he saw their reflection in the mirror, now replaced, he thought that life could not be better.

After taking a shower and putting on his linen suit, Umarov stood admiring his bright blue pool, sparkling in the sunlight. Only a single solitary cloud came gliding towards them from a bustling Västerbro Bridge on the horizon. He had enjoyed his morning fuck, but could not decide what had given him the most happiness. The clear water in his swimming pool probably came across as the greater miracle. He wasn't going to let the shambles over that dealer or the children's betrayals and intrigues ruin this day. All that would have to wait.

"What did I say?" Elena rested her head on her husband's shoulder. She made sure that she didn't flatten her perfect blow-dry or leave a smudge of her make-up on his white suit.

They were standing on the stone ledge above the pool, in front of the rose-covered wall that separated them from the neighbours. The Russian guard was hovering nearby, smoking and casually checking his mobile. In a while, their three hundred or so guests would be arriving, most of them from Bromma.

Umarov and Elena watched Coco and the other waiters and waitresses set out champagne bottles in straight lines and place the crystal glasses next to silver dishes of oysters, fresh shrimps and langoustines before heaping Russian caviar into large crystal bowls. Elena had tried to dissuade him from the fish roe, but Umarov was determined "not to skimp on anything, not today of all days". Elena gave his hand a loving squeeze.

"How do you feel?"

"My chest doesn't hurt as much as it did yesterday."

Elena waved to Kamila, who had finally emerged from her room after three hours of changing her clothes and doing her make-up. She was with her best friend Filippa, who had come for a sleepover.

"God, she's beautiful."

Umarov thought that his daughter's get-up made her look like one of Tatiana's whores, but since this was a special day he was not going to make a scene. The apple of his eye was the most beautiful of all, regardless of what she wore.

Kamila looked up at her parents and, to Umarov's delight, broke into that captivating smile where she cocked her head a little to one side. She was happy, he could see that. He leaned forward towards Elena, whispered in her ear:

"What I'm about to say now, I want you to keep in your heart forever."

"What? What's happened, darling?"

"Don't say anything. Just save this moment, for my sake. For us. For the future."

"Something *has* happened?"

"It's happening here and now. The happiest moment of my life. Do you see how beautiful she is, both inside and out?"

"I just said so."

"Nothing will ever happen to you all. I promise. Look at me."

"What?"

"I promise to protect each one of you with my life."

Umarov took Elena's hand.

She looked at her daughter and dried a tear.

"You scare me."

Umarov let go of her hand and put his arm around her shoulders. He gave a laugh.

"That wasn't my intention. I just wanted to savour the moment, suspend time for a bit."

Kamila and Filippa came wobbling up the stone steps in their far-too-high heels and stood next to Umarov and Elena.

"You look gorgeous, darling," Elena said and kissed Kamila.

"Mind my make-up," her daughter said tetchily and pulled at her clothes. She was in a pale green dress that stopped halfway down her thighs, longer than usual.

Filippa greeted Umarov with a quick curtsy. She was wearing a short white dress that left nothing to the imagination. Her hair looked as if it had been flattened in a printing press. The gold earrings hung all the way down to her prominent collarbones.

"When are the guests arriving?" Kamila sounded impatient.

"The invitation says from one o'clock."

A faint, high-pitched sound could be heard from the street.

"Who's that?" Elena asked, surprised. A green military jeep with a white star on the bonnet came up the drive.

"Who do you think?" Umarov gave a small wheezy chuckle. "Joakim's Second World War toy."

"A real one?" Filippa asked, looking impressed.

"Genuine American rust."

"Wow! Can we go for a ride in it?"

"Ask him."

The group walked down the stone steps and met Nina and Joakim by the pool. Joakim was dressed in a riot of red, white and pink, sunglasses perched in his shock of glossy fair hair. Nina looked similarly summery, if a little less flamboyant, in a white suit.

Filippa and Kamila went over to the jeep and struck some poses for their Instagram updates.

"You look terrific, Pappa!" Nina exclaimed, and hugged Umarov. He met his eldest with a glass of champagne.

"You're a terrible liar. But today we're going to forget all our problems."

"What problems?" Nina downed the glass as if it had been water, and summoned a waiter, who filled it again. "And just look at the weather you've laid on! You've staged it to perfection." She looked up at the virtually cloudless sky and then over at the wall. Nina lowered her voice.

"Have you hired extra people?"

"What does it look like?"

"A well-guarded presidential palace. In worst Escobar style."

"Treasures need to be kept very safe."

Soon afterwards, the guests began to arrive. In honour of the occasion, they had all put on their summer best. Many came on foot but, within an hour, the street was packed with big, expensive cars. Mostly German makes, predominantly black and grey.

Umarov and Elena were busy hugging, back-slapping and complimenting the guests as they made their way into the garden. There were many neighbours and other acquaintances from Bromma.

About ten people from Nina's real estate agency had been invited, as well as a few wealthy Russian contacts. There was no sign of anyone from the Red Bears in Skärholmen. Sardor had not even asked if they could come.

When the terrace, the pool-side area and the lawn by the open glass doors to the sitting room were full of guests and the sound level had reached a peak, Nina approached Umarov.

"When's Sardo arriving?"

"I told him to come, but they're chasing that junkie. He said they wouldn't give up until they'd found him and finished—"

"Shall I call and tell him to join us? If it means a lot to you . . ."

"Don't bother. He wouldn't enjoy it anyway. Let him do what he's good at. That's what he likes best of all."

Nina lit up when she spotted an estate agent from a rival firm in Östermalm.

"Äppelviken. What a great party. 'Not a cloud . . . as far as the eye can see . . .'"

Nina raised her eyes only to see some large, dark clouds on the horizon.

"Here comes Sardor," she said.

Umarov noted that Sardor was wearing his leather jacket as usual.

"Doesn't he own a blazer?"

"Maybe a leather one," Nina said with sarcasm, vanishing into the house.

Umarov helped himself to some salmon and was just about to pick up a bottle of mineral water when he heard the sound. At the same time, he saw Sardor quicken his pace. None of the guests appeared to have reacted to the police sirens in the background.

"Are they coming here?" Umarov asked and let go of Elena.

"Afraid so," Sardor said.

"What the fuck's going on?" Umarov roared. "Quick."

Sardor looked up at the sky. Kicked himself for not having left it until after the party.

"Håkan Dahl?"

Umarov stiffened. He could hear more sirens, and they were coming closer.

"When were you in contact with him?"

"Yesterday," Sardor lied.

Umarov looked at his son. "What the hell have you done?"

"Nothing," Sardor said. "I asked him for a favour, to find Simon Berg. He'd really blown it with one of Tatiana's girls, so he owed me—"

"O.K.," Umarov cut in.

"What's going on?" Elena said in a worried voice. The police cars had managed to make their way through Grönviksvägen and were stopping in the street below the house.

"They're coming to lock me up," Umarov said without looking at his wife.

"What are you talking about . . .?"

"Listen to me," Umarov said. "Take Kamila with you and go inside. Just stay calm. Call Boris and tell him they've arrested me. He'll know what to do."

"But . . ."

Umarov took Elena by the arm. "Please do as I say."

Elena went to find Kamila by the pool. The guests were still standing around with glasses in hand. Voices could be heard down in the street.

Umarov turned to Sardor and Nina. "You two should be ashamed of yourselves. You know there's only one thing that's important in this world. What?"

Sardor shrugged.

"What?" Umarov repeated patiently.

"The family?" Sardor said tentatively.

"Your word," Umarov said, raising his index finger.

"Get that, Sardor. Your word. You like that, don't you?" Nina said.

"You two-faced bloody snake!" Sardor growled.

"Wonder who's the two-faced one here." Nina's voice mingled

with the shouts of the policemen on the far side of the property. "You've totally failed to keep control over your business, and what about that bloody dope pedlar?"

"And *just maybe*, Nina, you've been leading us a merry dance all this time," Umarov continued. "Don't think I haven't noticed that you've been trying to out-manoeuvre your brother. I may be sick, but I'm not blind."

"I—"

"Enough!" Umarov shouted and then lowered his voice. "You've been doing things behind your boss' back. Mine! Your father. How dumb can one be? Selling dodgy construction material on the sly like that? Which then causes a catastrophic bloody fire. Do you realise what you've done? And what in God's name did you need more money for? All you had to do was ask me. You were supposed to stay away from criminal activities. That's the one thing I've been saying, over and over again. Our entire future was built up around you and your lawful career in real estate. I'm deeply disappointed."

Umarov saw members of the S.W.A.T. team fanning out around the pool.

"Listen to me now. What I'm saying is important. The doctors have given me eighteen months to live."

Nina and Sardor came closer.

"What do you mean?" Nina cried out in dismay.

"You heard."

"But . . . how long have you known?"

"You've both messed up. In different ways and to varying degrees. But the worst thing is, you haven't been honest with me. Your father. Still, you're my children. My flesh and blood. You're all I have."

"On the ground!" the leader of the police team shouted from a few metres away. Now they were surrounded.

Umarov carried on as if they were standing in the sitting room on a Sunday evening after a long and pleasant family dinner.

"So I'm giving you one chance, and one only, to fix this."

"Down! Or we shoot!" the team leader shouted.

Umarov did not flinch.

"I'm giving you six months to sort out this disaster. First, the two of you have to patch things up. Then I want you to build up our business, *legally.*"

"What do you mean, the two of us?" Nina said.

"You both," Umarov said. "Sardor's got to be given a chance. He never really had one. You were born with a silver spoon in your mouth. Sardor with a loaded pistol."

"It's going be tough to do all this from Kumla prison," Sardor snorted.

"I'm the only one going in. My lawyer will see to that," Umarov said with a smile. "There's a plan for this kind of situation. Always has been. And in any case," he added with a wink at his children, "it'll give me plenty of time for my translations."

Calmly, Umarov continued. "You have six months to regain my trust and show that you're capable of working together."

"How can you be so sure that you'll get out?" Sardor said. He remembered that Umarov had once said he would put a bullet in his head if he ever went to jail again. He obviously hadn't meant that literally. Maybe a good lawyer was all you needed.

"Down!" the policeman shouted again.

Umarov smiled.

"Trust me. But I'll be keeping an eye on you from there. And the first thing I want you to do is make up and apologise both to me and to each other."

Some shots rang out from an automatic pistol. The leader of the team had fired into the ground, right next to where they were standing by the pool. Several guests threw themselves down, yelling in panic.

"But keep my illness to yourselves. If I hear anyone outside our circle so much as mention the fact that Victor Umarov is sick, I'll know you've talked and then I'll give the lot to Kamila. Or Eje. Or whoever. Coco . . ."

Slowly Umarov put up his hands. He smiled. Turned to Sardor and Nina.

"Now I'm going to be a good boy and go off with this nice police officer and you'll see that everything will be just fine."

Sardor and Nina watched as their father put his hands behind his head and was then handcuffed by two massive officers. The first raindrops fell on the bright blue swimming pool.

MUSKÖ, STOCKHOLM ARCHIPELAGO
Saturday, 15.vi

Tekla stepped out of the car and took some deep breaths. She opened the Lypsyl tube, but found that she had forgotten to fill it up. She faltered and leaned against the car. Large raindrops had begun to fall from the thickening cloud cover. She could hear Lundgren talking in the background, but it sounded as if he were calling through a tunnel.

Tekla looked up at Tobias Almén's red weekend cottage, set back in the sparse vegetation of the pine forest. There was no-one to be seen. Simon's class photograph flashed past in her mind and there were Tobbe, Simon and all the other faces on the black and white print. Then the pages in the album began to turn. Class after class. All the teachers, the headmaster standing in the middle. The kitchen staff with light-coloured caps and aprons. Images from childhood took shape in her head, the school bus and the driver with his red nose and gruff appearance, the kitchen at home where she and Simon tore open the plastic bag with the loaf of bread and made themselves O'Boy chocolate drinks in tall glasses.

Tekla shook off the images and walked up to the house. Her legs felt as heavy as if she had done a brutal workout at the gym the day before. More memories and pictures were crowding in on her. Golgotha, where Jesus struggled with the cross. Her forehead was burning and she felt a searing pain inside the frontal lobe. A big shot of morphine was what she needed. On her way up the slope to the cottage, she passed two smaller huts, maybe for guests. Or were they tool sheds? Suddenly she had the impression that the house was hundreds of metres away. She tried to stop the images from flying around before her eyes, but it was as if the skies had opened and the whole card index of memories were cascading down on her in between the raindrops. She slapped her face, tried to release some adrenalin to clear her brain. Took deep, deep breaths to keep the nausea at bay.

The steps up to the cottage were slippery, she steadied herself against the red wall of the house and inhaled the odour of paint and summer rain. Something she had not smelled since she was in primary school, playing by the garage at home in the village. She tried the door handle. The door was open. She walked in and immediately identified the next smell: resin from the wooden walls and a distinct scent of leather from the chunky sofas. She was torn between the fascination of remembering long-forgotten smells on the one hand and the terrifying experience of what was going on in her brain on the other. Could she be heading into a psychosis?

"Hello!" she called out, but it sounded as though someone were holding a hand over her mouth. The cottage seemed to be empty. What could she take instead of amphetamine? Her brain was about to explode with so many past images. They were assaulting her from all sides. In a corner she spotted a fireplace that reminded her of the Hitchcock scene in which the birds invaded the room. Tekla could smell the ashes underneath the grid. Then other pictures from her childhood surfaced: the cottage by the spit of land, Pappa on his haunches cleaning out the hearth with a long iron rake.

She staggered on into the kitchen. Dirty plates, a sickening smell of ketchup and roast onions. Tekla yanked open a cupboard and quickly found a bag of instant coffee. The aroma came wafting out, as if from a magic lamp. She poured some of the bitter powder into her mouth. Filled a saucepan with lukewarm water and washed it down. The coffee had an intense smell of chocolate and acid. The taste of starch from pasta in the saucepan. She bolted down several mouthfuls of the powder, chased it with large amounts of water and managed to suppress the retching over and over again. She was not going to vomit. It simply must not happen. For a while, the storm of

413

images abated and settled like a cloud above her head. Ready to descend on her again.

Tekla groped around in the semi-darkness of the cottage, fascinated by all the odours she picked up: the damp smell of a linoleum floor in the bathroom, the fragrance of some invisible lavender bags in the bedroom and the hand-carved cork handle of a knife hanging on a hook in the hall.

She walked out onto the terrace. It was raining harder now and far down the hill she saw Lundgren moving about erratically. She wiped the sweat from her eyes, but everything was still a blur. Tekla picked her way carefully down the steps and walked in the direction of the car. She heard Lundgren's voice from the gravel path. It sounded as if he were shouting through a pillow.

"Is there anyone up there?"

"The mobile's on the table and the door's unlocked," she said. The words stuck in her dry mouth.

"Then he's somewhere nearby."

Tekla felt almost paralysed by panic. The Umarovs were bound to be only a few minutes away. They'd get there before them. And this time they'd finish her brother off.

"Simon!" she yelled, then coughed and felt her chest tighten. She pulled at her T-shirt, which was glued to her skin.

She saw Lundgren searching a hut, a privy and a woodshed.

"Nothing," he said and checked the mobile. "Håkan's on his way."

"He must be nearby," Tekla heard herself say. There was a note of desperation in her voice that she didn't like.

Tekla looked up at the sky. The rain kept coming and going, now it was getting heavier. Twenty metres above her head, the wind whistling through the swaying treetops told her that the last of spring was fighting back, gripping the island in an attempt to stave off summer. Tekla was shaking from the caffeine shock, from cold and fear. She was still being assailed by images. Scenes from the hospital: Elmqvist from the I.C.U. waving an ultrasound over an intubated patient, Moussawi charging into the emergency room, Collinder's mouth just centimetres away from her face, but she couldn't hear him, only knew that he was trying to shout something at her.

"How are you doing?" Lundgren said. He was only about a metre away, but his voice made a rushing sound.

"Simon . . ." Tekla panted. She asked herself if nicotine, maybe snus, would give her an amphetamine-like rush, but she knew there was a risk that she would vomit. Must keep those images at bay. Must be strong. Must save Simon.

Lundgren went to get something from the car. Tekla tasted blood in her mouth. Saw Lundgren's back everywhere. In several places at once. As if her eye registered but her brain did not have time to take it in. A glitch in the mechanism.

"He's not here," Lundgren said.

"He is," Tekla gasped. "I just know he is."

Suddenly she was on the beach by the lake. It was raining harder. Her mother was calling out in the background, but Tekla could not hear what she was saying. She was standing on the jogging trail outside the hospital in Umeå. Snow was falling. Lundgren was there, she spotted his back in between the trees. Then he was gone. Her father chopping wood. Simon falling in the grass.

"I'm sure he's . . . Of course! He's down by the water. They're fishing," she mumbled.

"Let's check," she heard Lundgren say, as if through a filter.

Out of the corner of her eye, she saw him begin to move towards the forest track. In fast-forward mode. Or else her brain was shutting down. She felt no fear. Too focused on keeping her body upright and getting it to move.

They were running along a path. Smells threw themselves at her: rain-soaked ferns, rotting banana skins in a wastebin, the saltiness of the sea that was coming closer, blueberry bushes and everywhere bark from fir and pine trees. But her vision was deteriorating by the second. She was seeing double. The colours faded and turned to greyscale. Once again, Tekla wiped the sweat from her eyes.

They passed two houses with the corner posts painted in white and an old rust-brown shed. Ahead of her, Lundgren's back pitched from side to side. She caught a glimpse of the sea. As they drew closer to the shore, the forest grew increasingly sparse and gave way to stones and gravel.

Tekla looked down towards the water, there was a jetty and a boathouse to the left. On the right, the shoreline was clear, with only a few dark boats turned upside down. Lundgren went off to the right, Tekla in the opposite direction. Suddenly she saw a man emerge from the boathouse. Her body reacted instinctively, she knew it was Simon, but she couldn't make out his face from so far away. She called his name. Heard Lundgren's muffled voice shout to her to wait for him.

Tekla felt she was about to lose her balance, her shoes sank into the wet sand. It was further away than she had thought. Desperately, she yelled Simon's name, but there was no reaction from the man. Her voice had forsaken her. She felt panic strike, a wall of memories crashed onto her and she slapped herself in the face. Then the colours came back.

A car could be heard in the background. The rumbling sound of someone accelerating, maybe to get up a hill. Tekla turned, saw Lundgren's big shadow approaching, and behind him, way up by the edge of the forest, a car. She turned back again, determined not to lose her balance, and had only one aim: to get to Simon before anyone else did. Just as she reached the jetty, Simon turned to face her. He looked surprised. She had time to think that she would black out at any moment. That the clouds would envelop her. But she managed to stay upright and keep her balance, even as her trainers hit the slippery wooden deck of the jetty.

"It's Håkan," she heard Lundgren calling and saw a tall man come running past the boathouse.

Tekla threw her arms around Simon, but shrank back when she felt his bony shoulders and ribs beneath the jacket. He was stooped and his straggling hair stuck out in all directions.

"Simon. Listen to me, just this once. You've got to get out of here."

Simon gazed back at her. He was deathly pale, but his look was clear and he seemed perfectly calm. A hurricane of smells swept over her: tobacco, gastric acid mixed with cheap beer, greasy sweat, unwashed hair.

"We have to go, but not the way we came. They're following us," Tekla said. It was a huge effort to get the words out.

Simon looked at her and smiled.

"No, Tekla. I'm not going anywhere."

"Simon!" Tekla shouted. Her words were ringing in her ears. She wasn't hearing herself properly. "Simon. Please. We've got to get out of here. Now."

"No."

She hugged him. Whispered in his ear:

"I'm sorry. Sorry for having been a lousy sister. I'll never, ever lose you again."

Simon looked her straight in the eyes. For a second it seemed as if something had woken up inside him, as if he were being taken back in time. She had almost got through to him, she could tell, but still it was not enough.

"It's too late," Simon said.

She could hear voices in the background. Those of Lundgren and another man, but she did not look around.

"No, it's not," Tekla cried. "I know what you're doing. You're going to take the blame for it all. But that's not how it works. It's not your fault that you've got caught up in all this."

Simon smiled so that his wolf teeth showed.

"Whose fault is it, then?"

"Never mind that. We just have to get away from here," Tekla said, looking around. "That boat there. Whose is it?"

"Tobbe's."

"Where is he?"

"In town."

The rain was falling harder. It had soaked through Tekla's clothes, and she felt it running over her skin. She couldn't tell if it was burning hot or ice cold.

"Could you get it started?"

Simon nodded.

Tekla almost pushed her brother into the boat and tugged at the painter. The end of the rope was tied fast. Eventually she managed to undo it and she jumped on board. Her fingertips were sore.

Suddenly she heard Simon yell and point towards Lundgren.

"What's he doing here?"

"What do you mean?" she said.

"It was him! It's all his fault. He's the guy who took the money at Haninge. He threatened me, put a gun to my head."

Tekla saw a wave coming and gripped the rubber railing of the boat. She looked up at Lundgren, narrowed her eyes to correct her double vision. Called to him through the heavy rain. Waves rocked the boat so that she lost her bearings.

Lundgren was shaking his head, but Tekla could tell that it was true. He tried to grab hold of the prow. Tekla picked up an oar that was lying in the bottom of the boat and pushed off so that Lundgren could not get in. She wanted to scream at him, hit him, but she needed all the strength she had to paddle away from the jetty. Simon was busy connecting the petrol tube to the engine.

Tekla looked up at the jetty again and saw that Lundgren had taken his eyes off her and fixed them on something diagonally behind her instead. She turned to see Dahl standing with a pistol pointed at Simon's head. He had run along a metal boom protruding from the jetty and jumped into the boat while it was still alongside it.

"Keep pushing the boat out," Dahl shouted through the hammering rain. "Then you and I change places. You start up the engine."

Tekla did as she was told. She heard Lundgren's voice, but she could not make out the words. She glanced at Simon, who was sitting with his hands between his knees. He showed no sign of fear. It was as if he had already given up.

MUSKÖ, STOCKHOLM ARCHIPELAGO
Saturday, 15.vi

The wind had grown stronger across Mysingen. Further out in the bay, the waves were building up. There were only a few boats about, but a solitary coastal destroyer could be seen on the horizon, making its way towards the Älvsnabben monument.

Lundgren held his pistol in one hand; with the other he was trying to shield his eyes from the rain. He strained to see what was happening in the small boat that was pitching in the waves some twenty metres away. He could hear the low rumble of the naval vessel far out at sea, but his mind was busy going over what had just happened. Simon had recognised him from Haninge and, from where he was on the jetty, there was no way he could have explained the situation to Tekla. Any small amount of trust he had been able to establish was now destroyed.

There was nothing to be seen. No other boats by the jetty. Not another soul in sight. He tried to think clearly. Analyse quickly and take action. But why on earth did Dahl want to kill Simon? Why had he jumped into the boat and put a gun to his head? Lundgren raised his pistol and took aim, but the boat was being tossed back and forth. He could not shoot at Dahl without the risk of hitting the others.

His whole body was screaming: "Do something! Act! Save Tekla! And Simon!" In a way, it was all his fault. He had agreed to take the money at Haninge, and after that everything had gone horribly wrong.

Lundgren took a step back, jumped off the jetty and waded a little way out into the cold water. As the waves lapped at his thighs, he knew that there was not enough time for him to swim out. It would take too long and it would be easy for Dahl to shoot him when he came closer. Fucking Dahl! He must be in serious trouble. Must have sold his soul, maybe he'd already done that a long time ago. Was he in cahoots with the Uzbeks? Or the Red Bears? Lundgren realised that Dahl had been using him all along, perhaps ever since they were at police college. He felt naive and cheated.

He waded back to the shore and looked around. There was a surfboard propped up against a tree, but would it work in those waves? He also spotted a small rowing boat lying upside down, but the wood looked pretty rotten. A little further away: a kayak. Lundgren pulled it down to the water and turned it the right way up. Shit, no paddle. The boathouse. Maybe he'd find one there. Was it worth taking the time to run over? Should he just use his hands?

A shot rang out from the boat.

Instinctively, Lundgren threw himself to the ground, tried to see what was happening, but by now the boat was fifty metres away and the rain was pelting down. The waves washed up against the kayak when Lundgren pushed it out. He lay face down on it and paddled with his hands, having tucked the pistol into the back of his jeans. The safety catch was off. How many shots? A full magazine, he'd checked that while they were running down to the jetty. It was second nature to him, but this time he had a personal stake. Because he had been on so many S.W.A.T. operations and had the physical and mental training, he was able to switch off, zone out and go onto autopilot. Dahl should not be a problem for him. In terms of physical strength, he was no match. He only had to get himself into the boat without being shot.

The kayak soon began to fill up with water. It would be difficult for Dahl to hit him, lying down as he was in a pitching boat. But whatever lay ahead, he had made up his mind: he would sacrifice himself to save Tekla. She must not be allowed to die because of his one wrong choice.

When he was halfway there, he saw two upright silhouettes in the boat. He heard repeated attempts to start the ignition, but the engine refused to catch. It seemed to be taking him forever to reach them. Water splashed onto his face, it tasted of salt. He paddled faster. What kind of pistol did Dahl have? A Sig Sauer, the same as he had. Like the one he'd lost in the raid at Haninge. Did Dahl have any other weapons? Not that he knew of.

Lundgren was only about ten metres from the boat. Two people were on their feet out there, shoving each other. One was Dahl, but he couldn't see who the other was. He heard voices and identified Tekla's. So who had been shot? Simon?

Just as he got to the boat, he heard the sound of a body being thrown into the water on the far side. Or someone having jumped in. Then another one. The boat was rocking violently, but Lundgren managed to hold on. He steadied the kayak against the boat but felt it slipping away, it was full of water and about to capsize. With a huge effort he managed to heave himself up over the gunwale.

He saw someone lying in the bottom of the boat, in the stern. It was Simon. Lundgren crawled over to him and saw that he had been shot in the arm. He was in shock, and looked terrified.

"You . . . !"

"Don't worry," Lundgren said. "I'm here to help you."

He peeled off his shirt and twisted it to make a pressure bandage for Simon's arm, all the while searching the water for Tekla and Dahl.

"Tekla," Simon shouted in between gasps of pain. "She can't swim."

Lundgren let go of Simon's wounded arm and stood up. He saw Dahl swimming towards Tekla. She was desperately waving her arms and kept sinking out of sight.

Lundgren pulled out his pistol and tried to take aim, but the boat was rocking and the visibility poor because of the rain. Before he was able to find a good firing position, Dahl had reached Tekla and pushed her below the surface.

Lundgren dived in and began to swim. The cold water made

him gasp, and his clothes felt like lead. He summoned all his strength and, swimming under water, headed straight for the spot where he thought Dahl and Tekla were. He couldn't see a thing in the dark water, but got hold of a leg that he knew right away was Dahl's.

He tried to drag him under, but Dahl kicked out. Lundgren struggled to the surface, and managed just one gulp of air before Dahl's hand on his head pushed him down again, holding him underwater. He tried to force Dahl away, but he was tiring now and unsure which way was up. He was aware of Dahl reaching for something, his hand by his foot. Did Dahl have a knife?

Lundgren got a grip on Dahl's jacket and pulled himself up towards the surface, centimetre by centimetre, fighting for his life. Dahl wrestled with him but had been longer in the water, and his movements were losing their force.

Summoning all his strength, Lundgren put his hands around Dahl's throat, squeezed hard and felt the life ebbing out of him. Together they sank below the water.

After what seemed an age, Dahl gave up. His body went limp. At that, Lundgren had second thoughts, relaxed his grip on Dahl, sending his body to the surface. Heard the roar of the waves. Dahl was struggling to breathe. Trying to swim away.

"How can you be so dumb? Giving up everything for two loser junkies," Dahl gasped between breaths.

Lundgren looked at his old friend. Caught that sneering smirk he had seen so many times. Felt an explosion of anger as it dawned on him just how shallow their friendship had always been. How deep the treachery.

Dahl reached down to his foot for the knife he had been trying to pull out earlier. Lundgren caught Dahl's hand just as the knife was driven into his midriff. He felt the tip cut into his skin, then go further and further through the strata of his abdomen. Splitting the muscle fibres in two, penetrating the tough layer of connective tissue, painfully piercing the sensitive surface of the peritoneum. Although

422

the water was freezing, the knife felt even icier, a searing pain through to his spine.

Dahl drew out the knife to stab him again. Lundgren tried with all his might to push the knife away, he was beginning to sink, could hardly move his legs. One last desperate attempt: he stopped swimming with his other arm and, using both hands, seized the fist holding the knife and gave it a twist. Bit by bit, Dahl's grasp on the weapon loosened, their faces mere centimetres apart.

Then Lundgren stabbed him. In the heart.

Dahl's body shuddered.

Lundgren froze. He shouted, "I'm sorry!" but Dahl's life was fading. His brain had registered what had happened and, for a few excruciating seconds, his heart was dead but not his brain.

Lundgren looked away and pushed Dahl's body from him.

He turned to look at the boat and there was Simon, standing up and pointing with his unhurt arm. But Tekla was nowhere to be seen. She was gone.

He took a deep breath and dived. Felt a sharp pain in his abdomen. Lundgren could see almost nothing. He surfaced again, breathing frantically. His body was rigid with cold and exhaustion. Down he went once more, but he could not stay under for long. When he came back up for oxygen, the waves washed over his tired head. He took one last breath and plunged a third time, swimming a few extra strokes down towards the seabed and, just as he was about to turn, he felt an arm. He mustered all his strength and dragged the body to the surface. Tekla was lifeless. Holding her against his chest with one arm, Lundgren swam towards the boat. The pain in his abdomen grew worse. When he finally got to the boat, Simon helped him lift Tekla in. He shouted out her name as Simon started to give his sister the kiss of life. Lundgren heaved himself into the boat and collapsed beside Tekla.

"Tekla!" he cried out again, sitting up on his haunches and pressing down on her thorax. Blood was flowing from his stomach. He realised that he would have been dead by now had Dahl managed to hit an artery. Seconds later, Tekla began moving her arms. Lundgren stopped the compressions. Simon stopped blowing into her lungs.

She began to cough, bringing up water from her lungs. Slowly she rolled onto her side. She coughed. She shook. She was alive.

EPILOGUE

THE CREMATORIUM, LIDINGÖ CHURCHYARD
Friday, 28.vi

The coffin was made of pale wood. Simple, Tekla thought, but still lovely. She was observing the calm, methodical work of Jan Sjöberg, the crematorium technician. He was moving the coffin on a trolley from the cold room to the furnace. Although the room was cool, Tekla could feel the warmth from the flames in the oven. Sjöberg checked a gauge and adjusted something. He had been surprisingly accommodating when she had asked if she could attend. As his "referring physician", she had said.

There was a roar from the furnace. Like a waterfall. Sjöberg told her how many cubic metres of fuel were burned during each cremation. There was a red fire extinguisher hanging on the yellow tile wall. And a metal bucket filled with old prostheses on the floor.

Tekla was standing on the red stairs leading down to the crematorium. She leaned against the tiled wall. Shivered a bit and longed to get out into the beautiful summer day.

Sjöberg raised the coffin to the height of the oven. It slid slowly into the flames.

Tekla thought about Simon. Wondered if he'd ever live long enough to need a new knee or hip. The chances were minimal. But for the time being she could relax. She had eventually managed to persuade him to borrow their uncle's apartment in Malaga. For a change of scenery. To get away from everything. And so that Tekla could breathe easy. He had signed up for a rehab programme. Had even sounded quite cheerful when he rang a couple of days earlier. How long would the respite last? Weeks? Months? Tekla did not want to think that far ahead. At least she was getting a well-deserved break. She was going to try to live in the present.

The coffin was inside the furnace. Sjöberg pressed a button. A shiny steel door came down.

Suddenly Tekla heard a rustling behind her and a familiar voice.

"Would you like one?"

Carlsson's image was reflected in the closed door of the oven. Tekla turned. Saw the bag of liquorice monkeys.

"What are you doing here?" Tekla said, astonished.

"Have one," Carlsson insisted, shaking the bag.

"Thanks but . . . Well, why not?" Tekla helped herself.

"Good of you to come," Carlsson said.

Tekla had never seen the hospital C.E.O. in such casual clothes: white slacks, black blouse, canvas shoes.

"How long does it take?" Carlsson called out to Sjöberg.

"We're up to a thousand degrees now," Sjöberg replied through the roaring.

"No, how much *time* does it take?"

Sjöberg came towards them. "Oh, I see. About an hour and a half."

"Shall we get some coffee?" Carlsson said.

"Sure."

They walked up the stairs and left the crematorium.

"I know a place," Carlsson said.

They headed down towards the water, to an old red cottage which turned out to be a café.

"Have you been here before?" Tekla said, as she ordered a coffee with a mazarin almond pastry.

"Wrong question. You ought to be asking why he's being cremated here, of all places."

"That was going to be my next question."

"I think it's a nice location," Carlsson said. "By the water." She ordered a Zingo orange drink and a napoleon pastry. "Besides, our family grave is out here. So I know the pastor well."

"That's at least a partial explanation."

They sat down by the window. Carlsson squeezed in behind the old table.

"How are you?" she said.

"Fine."

"You're not a good liar."

Tekla gave it some thought.

"Everything's relative."

"True," Carlsson said and used her spoon to cut through the pink icing of the pastry.

After they had been to collect the urn and sign some papers, Carlsson said:

"So, where's he going to be buried?"

As she stood there, holding the sand-coloured urn, Tekla considered her answer.

"I have an idea. But I'm not sure that my boss should see what I'm about to do."

"Do I strike you as someone who always follows the rules?"

Tekla smiled.

"Come," Carlsson said, as she led the way into the warm June sunshine. She glanced up. "Summer's here to stay."

Tekla set out across the gravel to the car park.

"Do you want to come?"

Carlsson nodded.

They went down to the water. Past the café and on to the headland a few hundred metres away. The lilac was flowering. A lawnmower could be heard droning away in the distance. Boats were passing slowly in the strait before they were allowed to accelerate out into the open sea. Tekla felt small next to the imposing C.E.O. But her presence was reassuring. It felt good not to have to do this alone.

Seagulls swooped down on the path.

Carlsson said: "When you pass through the waters, I will be with you. And through the rivers, they shall not overflow you. When you walk through the fire, you shall not be burned, nor shall the flame scorch you." Carlsson looked out across the water. "Matthew 14, verse 22."

"More like Isaiah 43, verse 2," Tekla replied.

Carlsson stopped, turned to Tekla and smiled.

"I didn't think you read the Bible."

"I don't," Tekla said without thinking.

"But you have *seen* those pages some time?"

Tekla realised that she had fallen into a trap. Carlsson knew about her photographic memory.

At first Tekla felt exposed. Naked. But it quickly passed. With everything that had happened, they had established a balance between them. Tekla knew just as much about Carlsson as she did about her. "Through hell and high water, right?" Tekla said.

They kept walking towards the promontory. Left the road and continued down a path through the birch trees and out onto some rocks. They had the bay before them. Some houses along the shore on the opposite side. But no people anywhere near.

The two of them stood in silence, contemplating the waves. A breeze was blowing out to sea.

Tekla took the lid off the urn.

"But who was he?" she said.

"Nobody," Carlsson replied.

"Well, he was to me. Was he Russian? Uzbek? Did he have a family? A name?"

"Oleg Simarov."

Tekla turned to Carlsson.

"How . . . ?"

She now understood why she had thought that the injured Oleg was asking her if she knew how to swim. His family name, *Simarov . . .*

"Go on, spread his ashes," Carlsson said. "Get rid of some of that disquiet. So we can move on. There's a policeman you need to go and visit in hospital, isn't there?"

Tekla took a few steps out onto the wet rocks and threw the ashes over the water.

CHRISTIAN UNGE works as a senior doctor at Danderyd Hospital in Stockholm. He spent the early part of his career working for Médecins Sans Frontières in Congo (DRC) and Burundi, later publishing a memoir about his experiences. *Hell and High Water* is the first in a series of thrillers starring ER doctor, Tekla Berg. Film/TV rights have been sold to FLX, producers of the Netflix series *Quicksand*.

GEORGE GOULDING's translations from the Swedish include *The Girl in the Spider's Web*, *The Girl Who Takes an Eye for an Eye*, *The Girl Who Lived Twice* and *Fall of Man in Wilmslow*, all by David Lagercrantz, *The Carrier* by Mattias Berg and *The Rock Blaster* by Henning Mankell.

SARAH DE SENARCLENS was born in Sweden and educated in Sweden, Austria, England and Switzerland. After a career as a simultaneous conference interpreter based in Geneva, she now works as a translator of fiction.